MERCY was in Hart's room, mixing him his evening draft. "I'm making it a little stronger tonight," she told him. "I think we're going to need all our wits about us tomorrow."

"As bad as that?"

"Quite as bad. Hart, whatever happens, promise you'll never stop loving me."

"How could I? You're part of me, Mercy. It would be to stop loving myself."

A cold finger touched her spine, and she made herself very busy with his medicine. "Never do that."

"I shall like myself better when I have had my turn against the British," he said. "Remember, Mercy, if they should take the town tomorrow, you're going to load my musket for me and then hide in the cellar with the others."

"Let's take tomorrow as it comes, my dear." She handed him the glass into which she had poured all the laudanum Dr. Flinn had given her. "For tonight, drink this, sleep well, and remember I love you with all my heart."

He raised the glass in a silent toast. "Mercy, if we survive tomorrow, marry me the next day?"

Fawcett Crest Books
by Jane Aiken Hodge:

WATCH THE WALL, MY DARLING

THE WINDING STAIR

GREEK WEDDING

MARRY IN HASTE

SAVANNAH PURCHASE

STRANGERS IN COMPANY

SHADOW OF A LADY

ONE WAY TO VENICE

RUNAWAY BRIDE

REBEL HEIRESS

JUDAS FLOWERING

JUDAS FLOWERING

A NOVEL BY

Jane Aiken Hodge

A FAWCETT CREST BOOK

Fawcett Publications, Inc., Greenwich, Connecticut

JUDAS FLOWERING

THIS BOOK CONTAINS THE COMPLETE TEXT OF THE
ORIGINAL HARDCOVER EDITION.

A Fawcett Crest Book reprinted by arrangement with
Coward, McCann and Geoghegan, Inc.

ISBN 0-449-23221-2

Alternate Selection of the Doubleday Book Club, March 1977

Printed in the United States of America

10   9   8   7   6   5   4   3   2   1

1

Hart Purchis was late, took what he hoped was a short cut, and found himself, at dusk, on the wrong side of one of the many inlets in the swamp between the Savannah and Wilmington rivers. His mother might not worry, but his aunt would. Seventeen is too old to be worried over. His horse refused the crossing, and he turned angrily back the way he had come, only to pause at a side turning and the sound of shouting.

The mob must be out again. No affair of his. That was what his mother and aunt both said. "Keep away," they kept telling him. "Nothing to do with us," they meant. Things were better ordered on the plantation of Winchelsea. So well ordered, indeed, that he was unarmed. This did not prevent him from turning towards the sound of shouting. Because what happened here, in the Winchelsea district, was his affair. Whatever his mother, or Aunt Anne, or even Cousin Francis said, he was the owner. He was responsible.

Was that a girl's scream? He kicked his horse to a dangerous gallop and rounded a corner of the canebrake to see a small wooden shack with too much smoke pouring from it. Down at the rough landing stage, a girl was filling a bucket, every line of her thin body spelling out the urgency of disaster. The sound of the mob came from farther off—behind the house somewhere—in full cry. "Down with George the tyrant!" "No taxation without representation!" "Three cheers for Boston; and to hell with tea and taxes!" And even, "1774: British no more!" Did they know what any of it meant? He doubted it.

Now, more ominous still, the cries suddenly ceased. The girl picked up her full bucket, saw him, and froze, white-faced, gazing.

"Don't be afraid! I'm not one of them!" He pulled his horse, Thunder, to a halt beside her, jumped down, looped the reins to a post by the landing stage, and turned back to where she still stood, staring, her eyes huge and dark in the thin, pointed face, her shabby stuff dress drenched with the water she had been hastily drawing.

"Give me the bucket." He reached for it. "Have you another one?"

"No! The house doesn't matter!" She dropped the bucket and held out both urgent hands to him. "Please! They've got Father! They're . . . I'm afraid. . . . Make them stop. He won't tell them where he hid the press . . . of *course* he won't. They'll . . . they'll hurt him!"

"Press? Cyder? But, why?"

"Printing, idiot!" Her deep voice vibrated with rage. "You're rich!" A scornful glance flicked towards Thunder. "You're doubtless a Loyalist. Of a kind. Who do you think takes the risks? Prints the Loyalist broadsheets in Savannah? Father did. He was Johnston's right-hand man. I suppose you've heard of Johnston the printer!"

"Of course. *The Georgia Gazette.* But . . ."

"There's no *time*. Father printed the things Johnston didn't dare to. Secretly. Only—they got onto us. Someone must have talked. We came out here to hide. No one knew where we were. There's a traitor. There has to be." She stopped, aghast, as a sudden roar rose from the far side of the little house: no words now, just the half-human cry of the pack out for blood. "Quick! Please . . . before it's quite dark. Stop them! He'll never tell."

"I'll do my best." He knew what she meant. Mobs, merely mischievous in the daylight, became deadly after dark, when face was hidden from face. "You try to save the house."

"No use. Look!" A great burst of flame as the roof fell in gave them their first clear sight of each other. His great height and square shoulders had misled her. "You're only a boy." Disappointment was acid in her tone as she saw his curly fair hair and the ruddy cheeks that had never been shaved. "I'm sorry. I shouldn't have asked."

"I'm Purchis of Winchelsea." He untied the horse and swung himself into the saddle. "Of course I'll try. Some of them may know me." Silhouetted huge and black against the fire, he sounded older, more confident than he had looked. "If I don't come back, hide in the woods. Promise? And go to my mother at Winchelsea in the morning. It's not far." Another burst of shouting drowned her protest. "Promise to *hide!*" He kicked Thunder into action, forced him past the

6

flaming house and along the river bank in the direction of that bestial noise. Once past the house, he could see the light of another fire, driftwood-built, no doubt, on the edge of the river. How long had they been at it? He should have asked that distracted girl. But—too long? There was something, at one side of the fire—tied to a stake, perhaps? Something that screamed, once, and then, dreadfully, was silent.

It silenced the crowd for a moment. Then, "Fools," came a shout from the far side of the fire. "You've killed him. Now, how do we find his press?"

"The girl!" This was another voice, and the others chimed in from all sides of the fire. "Yes, she's bound to know." "Should have brought her in the first place." "She'll be hiding in the woods now. Spread out, you lot, and search."

Hart did not wait for more, but turned and rode, fast and unseen, back the way he had come. Behind him, it was taking the mob a little while to recover from the shock of what they had done. He had time—a very little. And there, thank God, she was, still standing where he had left her, gazing at the flaming wreck of the house.

"Did they listen?" She came towards him eagerly. "I thought they stopped. But where is he?"

"I'm sorry." He leaned down to reach for her hand. "I was too late."

"Too late?" She would not understand him.

"I'm sorry," he said again. She must understand, and fast. "He's dead."

"I don't believe it! You're lying, because you are afraid. They couldn't have—"

"They did." He had her hand in a grip that hurt, and was meant to. "Now they're angry because he wouldn't tell them where the press is. They're coming for you. I'm not asking you whether you know. It makes no difference to what will happen to you. Besides, when they come to themselves, they won't want witnesses to this night's work. So, quick, up in front of me."

"No!" She tried to pull away from him. "I don't believe you. You didn't even try. Coward!"

No time for this. He and Francis had done it often enough to Cousin Abigail, in play. Could he now, in earnest? He leaned over, let go her hand, and while she was still furiously protesting, had her round the waist and so onto the saddle in front of him. Lucky for them both, he thought grimly, that she was a featherweight and that his mother had defied Aunt Anne and given him Thunder—a horse more than up to his weight—for his seventeenth birthday.

Her free hand had raked his face in the struggle, and he felt the blood flow as she tried to bite the hand that held her. "I've told you the truth." His voice broke on the words and added to his fury. "If you want to get us both killed, this is the way." The sound behind the house had changed. It was calmer now, organised. The mob were beginning to beat their way forward through the woods.

She heard it too and was still against his arm. "He's really dead?"

"Yes. I'm sorry." What else was there to say? He urged Thunder forward into the sheltering darkness and felt her begin to cry, silently, against his shoulder. "Had they horses?" he asked.

He felt her make the effort to pull herself together and admired her for it. "No, they came by boat, I think. We didn't hear them till they were all round the house. He hadn't a chance . . . he made them think he was taking them to where the press was hidden. That's why they left me behind."

"You should have run for it."

"And left him?" Scorn crackled in her voice. "As you did!"

"Believe me, there was nothing I could do."

"Nothing you dared do." She was struggling again. "Let me down, I tell you. There's a back way. Through the woods. I've got to make sure."

"I *am* sure. Must I tell you?"

"Yes."

Reluctantly, as he turned Thunder down the familiar path towards Winchelsea, he began to describe the scene: the fire, the stake. "I think they were trying an Indian torture." After all, why should he spare this virago whose nails had sent the hot blood streaming down his face to soak into the ruffle at his neck. "And put the stake too near the fire. Perhaps you should think he was lucky. Because, honestly, Miss—"

"Phillips." The response was numb, automatic. "Mercy Phillips."

"I think they were beyond reason," he went on. "Even if I'd been in time, I don't think I could have saved him. If they'd been locals, some of them might have known me, but riff-raff from Savannah . . . I'm sorry."

"You could have tried."

"And got you killed too?" There, at last, was the familiar turning for Winchelsea and, looming black against the thickening dusk, the avenue of young live oaks his father had planted the year before he was killed. The shells that made the drive crunched at Thunder's hoofs.

She was struggling again. "Where are you taking me? This isn't the Savannah road!"

"Of course it's not." He was tired now, and the arm that held her was hard with anger. "Have some sense, girl. Savannah's where they'll look for you. I'm taking you home to my mother. To Winchelsea."

" 'Purchis of Winchelsea.' " Her voice mocked him. "Lot of good that was."

"At least it means you've somewhere to hide. They'll not think of coming after you here."

"I should rather think not." Her accent seemed to broaden as she spoke. "A slum wench like me. What will my Lady Purchis say when she sees what you've brought home?"

He had been wondering that very thing, but her use of the local nickname for his mother irritated him into a quick answer. "She'll bid you welcome. Like a lady."

"Not like me, you mean." She was crying again. "Father said it was our only chance. America. To get out of the London gutter. He sold himself for the passage. After Mother died. He said, 'In America, all men were equal.' "

"So they are." His voice lacked conviction, and he knew it.

"You and me? Just you wait till my Lady Purchis sets eyes on me and you'll know just how equal we are." And then, on a note of pure amazement, "Coo—that's never your house?"

Lights in the windows made it seem even larger than it was, looming there against the darkening sky. And, to one side, in the servants' quarters, there were lights too and the sound of cheerful voices.

"Slaves." She struck a new note of contempt. "Father said slavery was the abomination of desolation."

"Oddly enough"—he made his voice cool—"my father agreed with yours. He came over, with Grandfather, on the *Anne* with Oglethorpe. Slaves weren't allowed then. We've never had them on Winchelsea."

"So who are these?"

He had turned away from the front of the house to ride

quickly into the stable yard, and they were instantly surrounded by a smiling, questioning crowd, black faces agleam in the light of torches.

"Servants," he said shortly, jumped from the saddle, and gave the reins to an eager pair of outstretched hands. "Jem, see Thunder gets a good rubdown, would you? We've had a hard ride of it." He lifted the girl gently to the ground. "And you, Amy, tell Madam Purchis I've brought a guest. A neighbour—in trouble."

"Madam Purchis is here." The clear voice drew all eyes around to a newly opened side door. "What's made you so late, Hart? Sister and I have waited supper this hour."

"I'm sorry, ma'am. It's trouble, as I said, the mob's out. Poor Miss Phillips here has just lost her father." He had her firmly by the arm and led her towards the open doorway.

"Lost?" And then, "Phillips? I don't seem to recall the name."

"You wouldn't." Mercy Phillips withdrew her arm from Hart's and moved forward into the light from the doorway, a thin, almost childlike figure, who nevertheless held herself with a kind of tense dignity despite damply clinging skirts and tear-marks down her smoke-blackened face. She looked for a moment at Martha Purchis, plump and prosperous in her evening velvet, then, surprisingly, swept a handsome curtsey. "Forgive the intrusion, madam. Your son would bring me. If you'll give me a corner for the night, I'll go back to my father in the morning."

"I don't understand." Martha Purchis turned irritably to her son. "Anything."

No more did he. What was this girl with the face of a starved boy and the voice that was sometimes a guttersnipe's, sometimes a duchess'? "I'm afraid the mob have killed Miss Phillip's father," he began, saw that she was swaying on her feet, and took her arm, gently this time, to help her indoors.

"The Whig rebels?" Martha Purchis was angry now. "And you've led them here! Idiot boy. We'll all be burned in our beds, most like."

"Nothing of the kind." Unwonted anger rose in him to match hers. "We got clean away, thanks to Thunder. They'd come by boat. They're doubtless still looking for Miss Phillips in the woods, if they haven't slunk home, ashamed of what they have done." But it reminded him of something. He turned to raise a hand and silence the tumult in the servants' yard. "Listen, all of you. Nothing's happened out of the way tonight. We've got no guest. Understood?" And then, recognising that few did, he turned to his own servant, Jem. "You, Jem, make them understand?"

"Yes, sir, Mr. Hart. We don't want none of those rebs stravaging round here tonight. Or any night. I'll get it through their thick heads, don't worry."

"Thanks, Jem." He turned and led the girl into the lighted doorway, only to be stopped by a shriek from his mother.

"Hart! You're wounded!"

He felt the girl stiffen beside him. "It's nothing, Mother." He put up a hand to the dried blood on his face. "Just a tree branch as we rode back." A small, grateful squeeze of his arm made him look down and take in the full extent of his protégée's dishevelment and despair. "Mother, Miss Phillips has had all she can stand. Do you think Abigail—"

"Abigail!" Mrs Purchis bridled. "Old Amy shall look out for her." She had still not spoken a word directly to her unexpected guest.

"No, Mother." For the second, extraordinary time he found himself contradicting her. "Abigail would be better." And turned with a quick breath of relief at the sound of a voice from halfway up the stairs.

"What would Abigail be better for, Cousin Hart?" Abigail Purchis came round the corner of the stair, ready dressed for supper, golden ringlets glowing against the white shoulders exposed by her low-cut dress. Then, seeing Mercy Phillips, "Oh, the poor thing!" She picked up blue silk skirts and came hurrying down to join them. "What happened? No, don't tell me. Not now." She held out both hands to the girl. "Come with me, dear. Tomorrow will be time enough to talk. Hart, send me Sally with some hot milk and a dash of rum. And tell them to start heating the water for a bath. Or"—with Mercy Phillips' arm in hers, she recognised her exhaustion—" "perhaps you had better help us upstairs first.

"No need." The girl's neat chin went up. "If you don't mind touching me, I can manage."

"Mind? Nonsense!" Hart had never been so near to loving his cousin. "Come, dear. Aunt Martha, will you excuse me from supper?"

"Well!" Mrs Purchis watched angrily as the two girls climbed the stairs slowly, arm supporting arm, one a Dresden lady, the other a figure to scare crows. "I hope you know what you are doing, Hart!"

"Indeed I do. I'm going to tell Sally about the rum and milk, and that hot bath. And will you excuse me from supper too? I will be sadly late, I'm afraid, by the time I've made myself fit to be seen."

"No matter for that, child. It's a poor world if Winchelsea can't wait for Purchis. I'll explain to your Aunt Anne."

"Do, Mamma." He was at once grateful and aware that something basic had changed between them. She might call him "child" as she had always done, but she was treating him, now, as the man he felt himself. "And Francis?"

"Dines out. I quite forget where. I know your aunt was not best pleased. Low company, she said."

"Oh? Francis gaming again?"

"If that's the worst of it. Which we must hope. Dear Hart, what a comfort you are to me."

"No credit to me that cards bore me to death. Now, do you make my peace with Aunt Anne, while I do Cousin Abigail's commissions and make myself presentable. Ten minutes?"

"As many as you need, dear boy." Something had indeed changed between them.

In the servants' quarters, Hart found that Abigail's orders were already being obeyed, milk and water both heating on the great outdoor range. It was a reminder, as if any were needed, of how complete was their lack of privacy in a house full of servants. Lucky they are our friends, he thought, hurrying upstairs to his own room, where Jem awaited him with his evening dress laid out on the bed and hot water in the basin.

"Must I?" He looked with distaste at black knee breeches and silk stockings.

"You know you must, Mr Hart." Jem and Hart had grown up together and he spoke with the ease of long friendship. "Missus Mayfield, she's in a pretty tearer already, long of Master Frank's being off again. You'll never turn her up sweet in day clothes. She's wearing her black tonight." He pulled an expressive face.

"Oh, is she?" Hart sighed and laughed, and let Jem help him out of coat and bloodstained shirt. Everybody in the house knew that when Aunt Anne Mayfield put on her mourning black, there was trouble coming. Everybody in the

12

house knew everything, he thought, dabbing carefully at dried blood.

"That was some branch you ran into," said Jem, confirming this. "Basilicum powder, I think, and a plaster to hide the worst. And I'll tell Sally to cut the young lady's nails for her."

"Thanks!" Impossible not to laugh, but then, on a grimmer note, "Her father had just been killed, Jem. The less anyone knows . . ."

"No one knows nothing. 'Cept we got a guest, and you're going to be late for dinner, and the poor madam's having a bad time with her sister. Talk of Charleston again, I do hear." He helped pull on the fine silk stockings Cousin Frank had brought back from England, and handed over the detested knee breeches.

"Damn Charleston," said Hart. "Savannah customs are good enough for me."

"And us," said Jem succinctly. "Home ain't been precisely home since the Mayfields came to stay."

"That's enough, Jem." Hart adjusted the ruffles at his wrists with a quick, angry flick. "Yes, my face looks much better. Thanks. Tell them to dish up in ten minutes, will you? And the French champagne."

"But madam said—"

"French champagne, Jem." He left the man gazing after him with a mixture of surprise and delight.

"Well, I'll be darned." Jem gathered up the bloodstained shirt. "If it ain't old Master Hyde come to life again, and that I never did hope to see."

In the elegant drawing room, with its gilt-backed, uncomfortable chairs, expensively imported from France, the Hart sisters were making a similar discovery. Given his mother's maiden name at his christening, Hart Purchis had lost both his father and his younger Uncle Purchis in the last year of the French and Indian War. Inevitably, it had meant petticoat government for a boy left fatherless at five years old. His mother, one of the two rich Misses Hart of Charleston, South Carolina, had run the Winchelsea estates to a marvel, everybody said, and when her ailing sister-in-law died of grief, had merely added Abigail Purchis, two years Hart's senior, to her family, Hart had been delighted when the debts his cousin Francis had run up in Europe had forced

Aunt Anne Mayfield to let her Charleston house and bring him to stay in what she found the barbarous solitudes of Winchelsea. Cousin Francis was a great gun, if ever there was one, with his stories of Oxford capers and his brief experience of Europe. But Aunt Anne was something else again.

Tonight she was in a very bad temper indeed. Used to being the centre of attention in Charleston, she had never quite settled down to her position in her younger sister's house. An illness that Martha Purchis had recently suffered had been the last straw. Mrs Purchis' heart trouble, brought on by overwork, had been the signal for serious spasms of nerves on her sister's part. Any breach of household routine would be the signal for one of these, and Hart was not surprised to find her fanning herself angrily and talking of her "poor nerves."

"Madeira, Aunt?" He saw that her glass was full, gave his mother her favourite cordial, and poured himself a brimming glass. Then, aware of a bristling silence, "I trust my mother has made my apologies to you, Aunt."

"It is an explanation that I want," said Mrs Mayfield in her most quelling tones. "What's this about some guttersnipe you've brought home—and set your Cousin Abigail to wait on? Miss Purchis! And turning the house upside down with demands for this and demands for that, so that, no doubt, we are to wait all night for our supper. And you know what that does to my nerves."

Hart looked at his father's big gold watch, the only ornament he wore. "In fact," he said, "I told them to serve up in five minutes. I am sorry if you've been inconvenienced, Aunt, but we do not turn away those in distress from Winchelsea."

It went closer to the bone than he had intended. Seeing his aunt go first white, then red with rage around the rouge she used so freely, he had the answer to a question that had only recently occurred to him. Clearly, Anne Mayfield was not paying anything towards her lodging at Winchelsea, or her expensive son's. No affair of his. It was his mother who had made Winchelsea rich, first with her fortune and then with her good management. It was not for him to question what she did with her own. Besides, he loved having Francis, and his mother seemed to enjoy her sister's company. But he rose with relief at sight of the majordomo beaming at the door to announce dinner. "Let me give you my arm, Aunt."

She had made a quick recovery and smiled up at him with an attempt at archness. "So gallant, dear boy. And so elegant! We owe a great debt to Francis, do we not, Sister? What a hobbledehoy it was when we first came, remember?"

"I was thirteen." Hart gritted his teeth and felt the blood start under the plaster on his face.

"And such a big boy, too. All bones, and muscle, and exercise. I wonder you have not joined the army. Dear Francis would have given anything for a commission—in England, of course—could he but have afforded it. And you have such a tradition in your family, dear boy."

"Don't speak of it!" Martha Purchis did not often use such a tone to her older sister. "How can you?" she went on now. "After two such losses as I have suffered! A husband—such a husband—and a brother-in-law, all in one year. No, no, Sister, my dear Hart is going to stay at home, take the burden of the estate off my shoulders, and be a comfort to his mamma, are you not, my dear?

"Well." He found himself, suddenly, at an expected hurdle, and took it fast. "Not precisely, Mother. I have been meaning for some time to tell you that I rather think of going to Harvard College in the fall."

"To Harvard!" said his mother.

"To New England!" His aunt was appalled. "Where all the trouble started!"

"Ridiculous," said his mother.

"They won't take you," said his aunt.

"As a matter of fact"—he smiled at them both—"they have. Ah, here's our champagne at last. Will you drink to my success as a scholar, ladies?"

"Champagne?" said Aunt Anne.

"I ordered it. You'll forgive me, Mother? I thought we might need it."

"We do." Suddenly, with tears in her eyes, she smiled at him. "Dear Hart. I drink to your great success."

2

Mercy Phillips woke to broad daylight and an extraordinary mixture of sensations. Memory first. Horrible. Her father, that howling mob, the boy who had been so sure her father was dead. How should he know death, a sheltered child like him? She had watched her mother die, in the garret behind Drury Lane, and many others, too, on the crowded, stinking ship that brought them to America. But always there had been Father, with his wonderful confidence in the future. "In America all men are equal."

Equal! She was lying on a bed of unbelievable comfort, in the most luxurious room she had ever even dreamed of. She was wearing a nightgown of material softer and finer than the shirts she and her mother used to stitch, hour after hour, to eke out the meagre livelihood her father made by his writing. And she was clean. Really clean for the first time, it seemed to her, since the three of them had left their Sussex home and gone to London, following that will-o'-the-wisp hope of her father's. If the great Dr Johnson could make a fortune with his unaided pen, could not others? Could not a grammar-school scholar who had carried every prize of his day?

He had been wrong, of course, disastrously wrong. It would have been better for all of them if he had gone on running the little country school that had made such a successful start, but he had felt he had something to say to the world, and a duty to say it. And when Father got an idea of that kind fixed in his head, there was nothing to be done. Mother had cried all the time, while they were packing up, and Father had been gentle, loving—and obdurate. Well, he had been like that. It had been the same over here. Tears began to trickle slowly down her face. Father would never learn . . . Father would never have the chance to learn. . . .

"You awake, ma'am?" A smiling black woman in a scarlet turban moved into her line of vision. "No, don' you stir. Miss

Abigail told me you was to lie quiet, while I fetched her to you. *And* your breakfast. I reckon you'll be ready for that."

Shameful to be hungry, after yesterday. She looked up, speechless, her eyes filling with tears.

"Don' you cry, missy. What's done's done. Just you thank the good Lord you've fallen among friends." And then, divining the question Mercy did not dare to ask. "Mr Hart, he rode out at first light. He ain't back yet. He took Jem with him. *And* his father's pistols. I'll go call Miss Abigail."

"Thank you." Alone, she wiped streaming eyes with the soft, frilled cuff of her nightgown. It was the advice her father would have given. "Praise God for all His blessings, and serve Him with all your heart." And this was his reward. *I'll be revenged*, she thought. And then, *Idiot. Revenged on whom? On God?*

A gentle scratching on the door heralded last night's angel of mercy, Miss Abigail, who had insisted on helping to bathe her, had washed her hair, and helped her into one of her own nightgowns. At the time she had been too weak and shocked to resist, but now the memory sent hot colour flooding her face.

"Good morning." In demure day-time grey, Abigail Purchis was prettier than ever. "I do hope you slept well, and feel better."

"Yes, ma'am. I don't know how to thank you."

"Don't try, dear. It was only what any neighbour would do. Now, you're to stay in bed and eat the breakfast Sally's bringing and get your strength back. My cousin Hart has ridden out. Presently, he will be back with news."

"Bad news," said Mercy.

"I'm very much afraid so. They're horrible, these mobs. They seem to whip each other up until they don't know what they are doing. Oh, we've not had them here." Proudly. "My grandfather came over with General Oglethorpe. Everyone knows how much he did for the colony. Why, the very design of Savannah was his idea . . . modelled on Winchelsea, the English village he came from. He worked like a Trojan —Oglethorpe's right-hand man, everyone called him. And lived like all the others, first in a tent and then in a kind of log cabin. . . . It was my Uncle Hyde that built this place," she explained. "Or"—with a smile—"you could almost say my Aunt Martha. She's from Charleston and didn't much fancy living in a log cabin, even if it was on Oglethorpe

Square. Poor thing, she was widowed before this house was finished. Her husband and my father both died gloriously, fighting for their country."

"Which country?" asked Mercy Phillips.

Abigail flashed her a startled look. "Hush! We're all Loyalists here. And so, surely, was your father, or the mob wouldn't have—"

"Yes. I just wonder, sometimes . . ." The tears were starting again.

"I know, dear." Abigail moved forward to give her a quick hug. "So do we all. But we never, never admit it. And now"—with relief—" here's your breakfast, and I'm going to see you eat every bite of it."

Hot chocolate, rolls, and the best Johnny cake Mercy had ever tasted. She looked up at Abigail. "It's dreadful to be hungry."

"I know." Abigail had seated herself, very upright in a straight-backed chair. "I remember when my father was killed. He was scalped by the Indians." She said it almost matter-of-factly. "You get used to it in the end. I promise you do. But—I remember—Mother couldn't eat a thing, and I was hungry all the time."

"Your mother?"

"Died. Swamp fever, they called it. She was never happy here at Winchelsea. Not the way I am. She came from New England, you see, a place called Lexington. It's quite different there, seems like. They have schools for girls. Or let them study with their brothers. My cousins learn Latin."

"I know some Latin." Mercy could not help the boast.

"Do you so? You're a proper puzzle, Miss Phillips, that's one thing certain."

"Do call me Mercy."

"That's a pretty name."

"My father chose it. He said it was a mercy I was a girl, because if I'd been a boy, I'd have been cannon fodder, one way or another."

"Oh."

"Yes." She ate one more delicious bite of Johnny cake. "Why am I a puzzle, Miss Purchis?"

"Abigail, dear. Because . . . " She coloured. "It's the way you speak. The ways you speak . . . and then, Aunt Martha said, you swept her a curtsey . . . like . . . like a duchess."

For the first time, Mercy Phillips laughed, the thin face

coming alive with pleasure. "Like a play actress, more like."
She lapsed into broad cockney. "We lived in a garret behind
Drury Lane." Now it was the King's English, with just a
hint of Southern drawl. "I used to run errands for the actors,
and when the house wasn't full, they'd let me in. Papering it,
they call it. You know—better a free audience than none."
She pushed the tray aside and sat up straighter in bed.
"Please, may I get up now? When . . . when the news comes,
I want to be ready."

"Yes, dear, of course." Abigail picked up the tray. "I'll
send Sally to you. With some things of mine. You won't
mind?" She smiled ruefully. "There are two or three I can't
get into anymore, since I took up riding with my cousins,
and you're thin as a rail."

"I could let them out for you," said Mercy eagerly. "I'm
a devil with my needle. If you'll promise to let me do that,
I'll borrow something gladly for now. Father always said
false pride was one of the worst sins, because it made everybody uncomfortable. Father—"

"Don't, dear," said Abigail. "I'll send you Sally."

Mercy was ashamed all over again of the pleasure it gave
her to wash in the hot water Sally brought, and let the kind,
talkative woman help her into plain calico underwear and
a grey stuff dress very like the one Abigail had worn, with
the same almost Quakerish white collar. "Miss Abigail, she
like to dress plain," said Sally, almost in apology. "Evenings,
she puts on something bright, for her aunts' sake, but this
is what she likes. Lawks"—she was fastening neat buttons
down the back—"ain't you just tiny. I'll find you a sash of
Miss Abigail's or you'll look like a pint in a quart pot."

"Do you think you could find me a black one, Sally? A
ribbon, anything . . ."

It was Abigail who returned with the black ribbon and the
news that Cousin Hart was riding up the drive. "No need to
hurry. We've still got to decide what's best to do with your
hair. He won't be here for half an hour," she explained.

"Then how do you know?"

"That he's coming? The servants have a system. Learned
from the Indians. There's always someone working on the
rice fields where our drive turns off. If they see anyone
coming our way they send a signal. Like this." She put her
hands to her mouth and produced a high, musical "cooee."
"One for danger, two for family, three for friends. This was

19

two. It has to be Hart. Unless"—she coloured—"I hadn't thought. It might be Cousin Francis, home from Savannah, but I wouldn't think so, not so early!"

"Who's Cousin Francis?" Mercy was running a borrowed comb through short, lifeless hair.

"Aunt Anne Mayfield's son. He's not my cousin really, but we've known each other forever." She made rather a business of tying the broad, black sash. "Of course, you've not met Aunt Anne either. She's Aunt Martha Purchis' sister. She's—" She paused.

Mercy smiled at her in the big glass before which they were standing. "I'll find out soon enough. Father said you should never talk about people behind their backs."

"He was quite right," said Abigail energetically. "I can tell you, entirely too much of it goes on here at Winchelsea." And then, "There I go, doing it myself." She took the comb from Mercy's hand. "What in the world happened to your hair, dear?"

"Awful, ain't it?" Mercy lapsed into cockney and grinned infectiously. "Father cut it for me on the boat coming over. There were lice, of course. And the places we've been staying since . . ." She turned impulsively to Abigail. "I can't tell you what it's like to be clean again. I'm only ashamed."

"Don't be," said Abigail, persuading a hint of curl into the limp dark hair. "There. Now you'll do to face the aunts." She smiled like a naughty child. "Won't they just be surprised!"

"Oh?"

Abigail's fair skin coloured easily. "Well . . ." She hesitated. "I don't think Aunt Martha rightly understood, last night. Goodness knows what they're expecting. You won't mind, will you?"

"Why should I?"

"Good. Then let's go down and get the first surprise over before Hart gets back. They'll be in the morning room, ready for visitors. Not that we get many these days. People stay home, mostly." She opened the door and led the way across a wide hall and down a shallowly sloping flight of stairs. The whole house shone with polish and smelled of beeswax. The bare, gleaming wooden floors would be cool in summer, Mercy thought, but now, in February, they struck cold through the satin slippers Abigail had lent her, and she was glad of the woollen stuff of her gown.

Abigail must have read her thoughts. "Aunt Martha says Winchelsea will never be warm in winter because it's a widow's house. But there will be a fire in the morning room, you'll see." She crossed a downstairs hall that must run under the upper one and pushed open a door to reveal two formidable ladies sitting over a blazing wood fire. Both wore black. Both had been beauties in their day, and one was still trying. The other rose at once at sight of the two girls. "Why, Abigail, my dear! Surely . . . can this be?"

"Miss Mercy Phillips," said Abigail formally. And then, to Mercy as she sank once more into that stately curtsey, "My aunt, Mrs Purchis, whom you met last night, and my other aunt, by kindness, Mrs Mayfield."

This lady had risen more slowly and merely gave a languid nod in acknowledgement of Mercy's second curtsey. "Quite a transformation, from what I hear." She spoke across the two girls to her sister. And then, "Dear Abigail, what a miracle worker you are."

"Is she not?" said Mercy warmly. "I cannot begin to thank her. Or you, ma'am," to Mrs Purchis, "for your wonderful kindness." To Abigail's relief, she was using her purest accent, and the two older ladies exchanged surprised glances before embarking on what struck both girls as a pre-arranged set of questions.

"You are Miss Phillips?" asked Mrs Purchis, unnecessarily, but more kindly than she had intended.

"Yes, ma'am. Mercy Juliet Phillips. The Juliet was for my mother. She died . . . back in London . . . two years ago . . . when I was fourteen."

"And your father?" Mrs Mayfield broke ruthlessly through the little sympathetic silence.

"Is a printer." She used the present tense defiantly. "And a writer. He said the two went together. Only—in London—nothing went right. So, after Mother died, he sold everything, except his press, to pay for our passage. He had to work as an indentured man, to pay for shipping the press."

"Indentured!" Mrs Mayfield was shocked. "Why, he might as well have been a slave. Sold at auction, like so much beef on the hoof!"

"Yes." The girl's lips folded hard on the word. "Some of your customs over here struck us, Father and me, as quite strange, ma'am. It was not precisely the welcome to a land of liberty that we had hoped for. But Father was lucky. Mr.

Johnston, the editor of *The Georgia Gazette*, was in Charleston that day. He bought Father." She used the word "bought" defiantly.

"I'll warrant he did," said Mrs. Mayfield. "Once he knew about the press! He wouldn't have wanted Mr. Phillips setting up in competition. He's making a nice thing of that paper of his, by all accounts."

"I remember now." Mrs Purchis intervened before Mercy could speak. "Someone told me. One of James Johnston's brothers, of course. It must have been Lewis because it was after one of the council meetings. About a stroke of luck his younger brother had had. An assistant from England who wrote like an angel. Would that be your father, dear?"

"Yes." The unexpected kindness had the girl near tears. "Mr Johnston let Father write some of the letters—you know, that correspondence about the Townshend and Stamp acts. Father was Phil Anglius." She spoke with pride.

"Very good letters," said Abigail. "I remember them But . . . dangerous."

"Yes." It brought Mercy back to the present, and her thin face blanched. "It was to be a secret, of course, but it got out somehow." Her hands clenched at her sides. "Such a secret! If I could only find out who—"

"Don't, dear," said Abigail.

"They were such a group of friends. If it was one of them . . ." And then, with an effort, "But Father always said that vengeance was in the hand of God." This time she had used the past tense. Her head went up, listening. "Someone's coming."

"Hart." Abigail was at the window. "And Francis with him."

"Well, I declare." Mrs Mayfield had moved over to join her. "Still in his evening dress, the wicked boy." She threw open the window and leaned out. "Come right up here, Francis Mayfield, and explain yourself, before I have one of my spasms." And then, "Well, Hart, what is it? Why the long face?" And, in answer to an inaudible question, "Yes, she's here. Come on up, boy, and stop making mysteries. It's bad for my nerves."

Abigail moved quickly over to take both Mercy's hands. "I've never seen Hart look like that. You'll be brave, won't you? For his sake? He's only a boy, really."

But Hart, when he walked into the room a few minutes

22

later, was, visibly, a man. His square jaw was set rigid; the
blue eyes that went with fair hair were sombre. He towered
over his darkly elegant cousin, who was pale with lack of
sleep, but every inch the European beau in black evening
dress and ruffled shirt.

A quick bow for his mother and aunt, a smile for Abigail,
and Hart went straight to Mercy. "I'm sorry, Miss Phillips,
it's bad news."

"He's dead?"

"Yes. He . . . they . . ." He looked round the silent little
group as if for help.

"You'd better tell her." Francis Mayfield's smile for Mercy
was full of sympathy. "If you don't, someone else will."

"Tell me what?" asked Mercy. And then, "Please, if
there's worse, I'd rather have it now. All at once."

"Yes. Miss Phillips, you must believe me. The fire killed
him. He was dead, for certain, when you and I got away.
Only, later, sometime in the night, someone must have come
back and"—he swallowed hard—"scalped him."

"Indians!" screamed Mrs Mayfield. "And you've left a
trail straight here."

"I've done more than that, Aunt." He looked at her
squarely. "I've sent some of the men out to bring the body in
for burial." A firm hand stopped a further tide of protest,
and his mother and cousin looked at him with surprised
respect. "Will you mind, Miss Phillips, if we bury him here,
in our family plot? Less noise, that way. And if, as I hope,
you are going to stay with us . . ."

"*Is* she going to stay here?" Anne Mayfield was gobbling
like an infuriated turkey hen.

"I hope so," said Hart again. "With your permission,
Mother?" And then, to Mercy, "I'm afraid, whoever came
back, they finished the job on your house. There's nothing,
today. Nothing." He looked, suddenly, less than his seventeen
years. "I'm sorry. I should have sent a guard out last night.
Done something. It's my fault."

"Oh—the house." She dismissed it. "But, Mr Purchis,
you're sure. About Father? That he was dead?"

"Dead as a doornail." It was suddenly apparent to all of
them that not only was Francis Mayfield still elegant in
evening dress; he was also still afloat on his evening's wine.
"Believe me, Miss Phillips—" And then, awkwardly, "Haven't
been presented, your pardon. Deepest condolences, but, word

23

of honour, I know what I'm talking about. The fire killed him. Nothing could hurt him after that. Dr Flinn will say the same."

"Doctor?" She was holding herself as stiff, almost, as the corpse they were discussing.

"We've sent for him," explained Hart. "I thought . . . thought you'd want it. And"—he hesitated, colouring—"the Reverend Zubly. You won't mind?"

"Damned rebel," said Francis. "Told you you should have asked her first."

"No," said Mercy with her quiet little dignity. "I'm—grateful, Mr Purchis. Father said—" She swallowed a sob and went steadily on. "Father would have liked . . ." She stared around at them blindly. "Oh, please . . ."

"Come, dear," said Abigail. "You've had enough."

"But you'll tell me? When they bring him?" The appeal was directly to Hart.

"I'll tell you." He opened the door for the two girls, then closed it behind them. "Thanks, Francis. You were quite right; it was best to tell her."

"But I don't understand," said Francis' mother plaintively. "Where do you come in, Francis?"

Francis laughed and yawned. "Terrible late night at the St George's Society. No, no, Mamma, no need to look so shocked. Not cards, just drink and talk. On my way home in the blissful dawn I met Cousin Hart here, looking like death, on his way out. So, good cousin that I am, I went too. And a deuced unpleasant scene it was. I hope to God you're right, Hart, and it wasn't Indians."

"Horrible enough either way," said Hart. "That a white man would do such a thing."

"Yes," said his mother. "You're sure, Hart? That the poor man was dead?"

"Kindest to say so," said Francis. "And probably true. My advice, at all events. You'd better make sure Dr Flinn bears me out for that poor girl's sake. Plain little thing, ain't she? What do you reckon to do with her, Hart?"

"Care for her," said Hart. "If she'll let us. You won't mind, Mother?"

"Of course not, dear." They were all aware that the balance of power in the household had somehow, imperceptibly, shifted overnight, and that his request was now merely a matter of courtesy. "She'll be company for Abigail. They seem to have taken a fancy to each other."

"Time you got that girl married off," said Mrs Mayfield. "How old is she now? Nineteen if she's a day and not a prospect in sight. Pretty enough, too, if you like them blond. Pity your uncle left no money, Hart. If he had, perhaps that New England missishness of hers wouldn't matter so much."

"Don't fret, Mamma." Her son had taken her point and smiled at her lazily. "She may be pretty as a pink, but I'd as soon pay my addresses to that little shrimp of a Miss Phillips."

"In that case"—his Aunt Purchis rounded on him—"I'll thank you to stop looking April and May at Abigail, and breathing sweet nothings into her ear. It ain't fair, Francis Mayfield, and if your mother hadn't spoken out, I would have. Frankly, I thought it was bonnet over the moon with you, and I'm afraid it is with her, poor child. If you're hanging out for a rich wife, I suggest you go and do it in Charleston."

"Nothing I'd like better," said her nephew promptly. "What do you say, Mamma?"

"That we can't afford it, of course, stupid boy. Not till your debts are paid, and God knows when that will be."

"Oh, those debts! Shall I never hear the end of them." His handsome, saturnine face modulated into the sulks, then brightened. "Never mind, if it really comes to war with England, there'll be no more question of sending money across the Atlantic. To pay debts or anything else."

"War with England?" said his mother. "You can't be serious, Frank."

"Of course I'm not. Just some talk I heard last night at the club set my teeth on edge a bit. There are a lot of hotheads down in St. John's Parish who think they could run our affairs better than the King, God bless him. And now, if you ladies will excuse me, I'm for my bed." He yawned elaborately. "I'm too tired to make sense. But wake me in time for the funeral, Hart, there's a good little cousin. Must pay my respects to the poor printer, for Miss Phillips' sake. I suppose it will be today?"

"Better so," said Hart. "This evening, I hope. As quietly as possible. What worries me," he spoke to them all, "is the matter of Mr Phillips' press. Someone had been searching, last night, after I left . . . someone who may, we must face it, have found poor Phillips alive, questioned and killed him. No way of telling whether they found the press or not. They

25

certainly searched hard enough. But if they haven't found it —well, we all know what a printing press is worth, with the country the way it is. Right now, Mr. Johnston has the only one here in Georgia, and though he keeps things pretty even in the paper, everyone knows he's a Loyalist at heart. The Liberty Boys would give their eye teeth—and any life that stood in their way—to get hold of a press of their own."

"I wonder if Miss Phillips knows where her father hid it," said Mrs Purchis.

"She said not," her son told her.

"I hope she spoke the truth."

3

Hart's wish for a quiet funeral was to be frustrated. Inevitably, news of the killing reached Savannah in the course of the morning, and before either the doctor or the minister had arrived, people started coming out from town in twos and threes, some by boat and some, the longer land way, on horseback or in the light carriages that were used for traffic between town and country houses.

By now, the body lay in a cool ground-floor room in one of the plain coffins the estate carpenter kept always ready. Hart had wanted the lid nailed down over that savaged head, but had felt in honour bound to consult Mercy Phillips first and had been surprised by her fierce refusal. "I must see him," she said, "and if you'll give me my way, so shall anyone else who wishes. Who knows? There may be truth in that story in the play that blood flows again at sight of the murderer."

"But surely the murderer would never come," said Hart.

"How do we know?" They were talking in a small, seldom-used downstairs parlour from whose window they could see the sweep of the drive with, already, a little group of people, quietly, respectfully waiting. "People always loved Father," she went on. "There might, perhaps, be someone who did not dare be seen not to come. And now, please, Mr. Purchis, may I see him?"

"If you are sure. But, first, while we are alone—Miss Phillips, I'm anxious about you. You said last night that you did not know where your father had hidden his press. The more I see of you, the harder I find that to believe. Other people may well feel the same. Mind you, the press may have been found already. There was a search made last night."

"At the time of the scalping?"

"Probably." He was treating her as if she was another man. "Impossible to tell whether it was found or not. But, if not, you must see—"

"That I am in danger? Yes. They tortured once. They would again. Well"—she smiled up at him—"for what it's worth, Mr Purchis, you have my word that I do not know where Father hid his press."

"And what is it worth? Your word?" Francis Mayfield had come quietly into the room, soberly dressed now for the funeral.

"As much as yours, I daresay." She turned from him to Hart. "May I see Father now, please?"

Hart and Francis exchanged glances, then, "If you're certain," said Hart, and "I'll fetch Abigail," said Francis.

On Hart's orders, the body, in its plain coffin, had been covered with February-fresh leaves so that only the face was visible. Mercy stood there, silent, for a long moment, gazing, then, "May I be alone with him?"

Abigail, joining her five minutes later at Hart's request, found her kneeling by the coffin, tears running quietly down her cheeks. "Mr Johnston is here." Abigail held out a hand. "He and his friends ask if they may come in, to see . . ."

"Oh . . . thank you . . . yes. . . ." Mercy took the hand and rose to her feet. "If they wish it. Only, I don't want—" She bent, kissed the cold cheek, then turned away, blindly, still holding Abigail's hand. "Of course they should see him," she said. "Some of them were probably part of the mob last night. Let them see what they have done." Her grasp on Abigail's hand tightened. "I'd meant to watch them, but I can't."

"Of course not. It would not be proper anyway. But Hart said to tell you that he and Francis will. They are coming now." She urged Mercy gently out into the hall and up the stairs towards her own room, which was at the back of the house, as far away as possible from the crowds, who

27

now began to move quietly forward through the open front door and into the little room where Hart and Francis stood, silent, at the head of the coffin.

Upstairs, Mercy turned almost desperately to Abigail. "Give me something to do," she said. "I can't—I don't think I can bear it."

"To do?" Abigail looked shocked. "But, dear—"

"Oh, I know," impatiently. "I ought to be reading the Bible. That comes later. When Mother died, I cleaned the house. What there was of it." A wry glance took in the shining upstairs hall of Winchelsea. "I can see that would hardly do here. It's so big, it frightens me. And all those servants."

"I'll show you round," said Abigail, relieved to have thought of so unexceptionable an occupation. "If we keep to the back we won't see anyone. The air will do you good."

A narrow back stair, used mainly, Abigail said, by the servants, took them down to a little door that led out onto the back porch.

"We could sit here." Abigail was wondering about the propriety of going farther.

"No, please! Let's walk. It helps me. What's down there?"

"Oh!" Abigail joined her to look through a screen of ilexes and other evergreens towards a low wall. "It's the graveyard. I'm sorry. I should have thought."

"Don't be. Could we go there? Now? Without anyone seeing?"

"I suppose so." Abigail still sounded doubtful. "There's nothing beyond but the river."

It was a mild spring morning and the grass under the trees was embroidered with jonquils, huge violets, and a blue flower Mercy had never seen before. "It's peaceful here," she said as they entered the little graveyard. "It's good of Mr Purchis." She stopped by the miniature Greek temple Martha Purchis had built in memory of her husband. "Only, not here —in a corner somewhere? Father liked to be alone. Oh! Look!" She moved away from Abigail to the corner of the lot farthest from the house, where a Judas tree stood, its leafless branches bejewelled with purple blossom. "Here," she said. "Would you ask Mr Purchis, please? You can't see the house. He'd be quiet here."

That day seemed endless to all of them, but the Reverend Zubly and Dr Flinn had been out of town and did not arrive until evening. By then, the unexpected crowd of mourners had returned to Savannah. Dusk was falling and Hart had ordered tall wax candles lit by the coffin. Dr Flinn put a tentative hand among the withering leaves, then turned to look very straight at Hart. "Do we really want to know how he died?"

"Miss Phillips does."

"It would mean delaying the funeral until tomorrow. And even then, I shall very likely not be sure. It won't bring him back to life, poor man, and may well lead to trouble."

"I have a wedding tomorrow," said the Reverend Zubly. "I must leave at first light."

Hart looked from one to the other and recognised defeat. "Very well," he said. "I will explain to Miss Phillips."

"Why tell her?" asked the doctor. "What she don't know won't trouble her."

"Because she will ask," said Hart. "And I'll not lie to her. Well, I'm sorry to have got you here on a wild-goose chase, Doctor. You'll spend the night, of course. And you, Mr Zubly."

"Delighted." Zubly looked rather ostentatiously at his watch. "If we are to bury him tonight . . ."

"Yes. I'll just explain to Miss Phillips."

"Tell her afterwards," said Dr Flinn.

"No."

Left alone, the two men looked at each other across the coffin. "Whew," said the doctor.

"He's grown up," said Zubly. "I hope the girl don't fuss."

Upstairs, Mercy was looking at Hart with a kind of white calm. "What they are saying is that they don't want to find out how he died?"

"I'm afraid so. You must see, Miss Phillips, that it would only mean more trouble. Many of the people who came out today were true friends of your father's. Francis and I were watching, we could tell. But some of them were notorious Liberty Boys, come to see how the land lay."

"And the body did not bleed."

"No, Miss Phillips. Nor did anyone blench at the sight of it. If we had not known, Francis and I, which the Liberty Boys were—"

"Many of them?"

"Enough."

"So." She was working it out painfully. "If I refuse to let him be buried tonight, insist that the doctor examine him in

29

the morning, it may mean trouble for you here?"

"I'm afraid it's simpler even than that." He did not like having to tell her. "In effect, the minister and the doctor have settled the question already. The doctor won't do it, no matter what you say . . . or I do."

"I thought you were Purchis of Winchelsea."

He blushed painfully. "So did I."

"I'm sorry." She held out a hand to him. "You've done so much for me. I'm a brute. Well." She lifted her chin in a gesture he was beginning to recognise. "So I'll never know." And then, "What's that?"

He had recognised the noise at once. "They have begun to nail down the coffin. I told them to wait until I had spoken to you. So much for Purchis of Winchelsea."

To his relief, she did not insist on attending the funeral. Indeed, she went further. "I would much rather not meet these two dictatorial gentlemen," she said. "Will you tell them that I am in strong hysterics, or whatever else you like, and give them my thanks for their kindness."

"Not strong hysterics," he suggested, liking her better than ever. "The doctor might feel it his duty to pay you a professional visit."

"And what he won't do for Father, he shan't do for me. Thank you, Mr Purchis. Tell them I am prostrated with grief. In fact." She looked up at him through tears. "I am."

Only Hart and Francis attended the funeral, and when they returned to the house with the doctor and minister, it was to find Mrs Purchis and Mrs Mayfield alone in the big drawing room. Abigail, explained Mrs Purchis, greeting her guests warmly, was staying with poor Miss Phillips. She pulled the bell rope that hung close to her chair. "We will sup at once. You two gentlemen must be exhausted."

Winchelsea was famous for its informal suppers, and over turtle soup, deviled oysters, canvas-backed ducks, and a variety of other delicacies, washed down by the claret Hart's father had imported from France, everyone relaxed a little. "A bad business," said the Reverend Zubly to no one in particular.

"Yes," said the doctor. "What do you propose doing about the girl, Mrs Purchis?"

"We shall keep her here," said Martha Purchis. "Hart decided that."

"I drink your health, Mr Purchis." The Reverend Zubly

used the formal mode of address for the first time.

"Thank you." But soon after his mother and aunt left them to their port, Hart, too, made an excuse to retire. "I couldn't face them," he told Francis, who visited him, much later, in his room. "Couple of canting hypocrites."

"Don't know about that," said Francis. "Could call them practical men. Be grateful, even." He pulled forward an upright chair, back to front, and sat down astride it, his arms on the back, facing his cousin. "Meant to warn you anyway. Joseph Habersham said a word to me at the club last night. Oh, friendly enough, but a warning just the same."

"Oh?" Hart's face was uncompromising. "What did Mr Habersham have to say?"

"Nothing much. Something about going back to my den of Tories. A joke, if you like, but a warning, too. Frankly, I am going to have another try at persuading my mamma that she would be happier in Charleston. Winchelsea is a delicious place, dear boy, and I'm more grateful than I can say for all your hospitality, but the way things are right now, I'd feel a deal happier in town—with neighbours. The Liberty Boys burned Mr Phillips' house last night. What's to stop them coming to Winchelsea tomorrow? Specially now you've got that plain little bit of a daughter here. Take my advice. Get rid of that girl just as fast as you can. If she don't spell trouble, my name's not Francis Mayfield."

"I can't, Frank. I gave her my word."

"Then take it back again, for God's sake. Or"—he leaned forward, pointing a graceful finger at his cousin—"better still, persuade her to hand over that press of her father's to the Liberty Boys."

"Never! Anyway, she says she doesn't know where it is."

"Believe that, Hart Purchis, you'll believe anything. Oh, maybe her father didn't actually tell her; I can understand that, but I bet she knows just the same. I know her kind. They can't keep their noses out of anything. So, for her sake, if you like, get her to tell you."

"And hand it over to the Liberty Boys? I think not, Francis. Things are bad enough as it is without them being able to print inflammatory handbills. You know how much Johnston has done by keeping things cool and level in *The Georgia Gazette*, and at what risk to himself. Sir James Wright was saying just the other day how lucky we are here in Savannah. I'll do nothing to spoil it, and if I were you, Frank, I wouldn't think of going back to Charleston. By all reports the mob's pretty rough there too, and you know your mother."

"No worse than yours, little cousin. The truth of it is, they egg each other on. That's why I think they would be better separated." He sighed. "Oh, for a shower of gold, a win in the lottery, or a rich heiress."

Hart rose to his feet and moved about the room, fidgeting first with silver-backed hair brushes and then with the set of his cravat. "You haven't considered, perhaps"—his tone was diffident—"going to work?"

"Work, dear boy? What, pray, do you mean by that?"

"Well, I'd been thinking, there are fortunes to be made. If I spoke to Saul Gordon . . ." He ground to a halt at Francis' explosion of laughter.

"You'd apprentice me to your man of business! My dear little cousin, that passes everything. And I'm to sit on a stool with a quill behind my ear and say, 'Yes, sir' and 'No, sir' and 'That will be ten pounds the bushel, sir.' Are you out of your mind, Hart?"

"No. Just anxious about you." He took off his cravat and laid it tidily on the back of a chair. "And now, if you'll excuse me, cousin, I'm for bed. It's been a long day."

Francis shrugged and rose gracefully to his feet. What had happened to the young cousin for whom his word had been law? He yawned. "A long two days for me. Sleep well, and let's hope the mob stay home."

"Amen to that."

Hart was up early next morning to say good-bye to the doctor and minister and thank them, rather stiffly, for coming. They were both mounted and ready to leave when the Reverend Zubly leaned down for a last word. "And, Hart, if the girl says anything about that press, send for me at once.

"For you?"

"Yes. I have, if I do not flatter myself, some influence with the wilder elements in Savannah. I think I could undertake that the press would be collected without trouble and put to the best possible use."

"I see." Hart smiled up at him. "The trouble, is Miss Phillips doesn't know where it is. Very likely the mob has it already. And, if so, you'd be doing me a great kindness, sir, if you would send me word."

"You'll know soon enough if they have," said the doctor. "It won't lie idle—that's one thing certain."

But to Hart's surprise and relief, though there was no sudden spate of revolutionary handbills, neither did the mob visit Winchelsea. Francis, returning from one of his frequent visits to town, explained this. "Fact is, they believe the girl," he told Hart. "Well—a woman—a chit—makes sense. Kind of."

"It's not what you thought yourself."

"No ordinary girl. That's what they don't understand. But —lucky for us. And lucky too that Winchelsea has such a good name. Besides"—he laughed, throwing down whip and riding gloves on a settle in the corner of the room—"had you thought how your Harvard plans look to the Liberty Boys?"

"Frankly, no. How should they look?"

"Like paying a visit to the rebel camp. Betting's two to one at Tondee's Tavern that you'll come back a confirmed revolutionist. In the meantime, they'll wait and see. Surprising how well you're liked."

"Tondee's Tavern? You're keeping pretty radical company yourself, aren't you?"

"Peter Tondee has the best house, the best Madeira, and the best talk in town. I hope we haven't reached such a pass, yet, that one must be careful even in one's choice of a tavern."

"So do I," said Hart. There had been no more talk on the Mayfields' part of a return to Charleston, and he assumed that the financial argument had proved overwhelming. Or was there something else? It seemed extraordinary to him, but his dashing cousin was actually paying marked attentions to Mercy Phillips. Remembering Francis' description of her as a "plain little bit," he found it at once a puzzle and worry. Mercy was his protégée and he meant to protect her, but he had not expected to have to protect her from Francis and did not rightly know how to set about it. He had always been in awe of his splendid older cousin and had enjoyed listening to his tales of European conquests. They had been far away, unreal. Now, watching Abigail turn silent and Mercy's eyes begin to sparkle when Francis appeared, he did not find he enjoyed himself. Mercy was such a gallant little figure, with her cropped hair just beginning to curl, her swift, neat movements, and those huge eyes that always had a special, grateful welcome for him. She must not be hurt.

As for Mercy, she was still too numb from the shock of her father's death to be anything but grateful for every small bit of kindness. She was ashamed of it, but the huge house frightened her, and so did the hordes of black servants, whose faces she only slowly began to be able to tell apart. And then there were Mrs Purchis and Mrs Mayfield. She was almost sure there had been a bitter quarrel between the two sisters as to how she should be treated. Inevitably, Mrs Purchis, or rather Hart, had won, and Mercy ate her meals with the family, aware all the time of Mrs Mayfield's dislike and Mrs Purchis' doubt, and equally afraid of disgracing herself before these formidable critics and before the servants. It was all very well to be able to put on the manner of a duchess at will, but what use was that when faced with a battery of forks and spoons and no clue as to where to begin?

But, quietly, Hart and Francis and Abigail helped her all the time, and so, she began to think, did the servants. One fork would be pushed a little out from the others. Glasses would whisk themselves into position. Or Jem, standing as always behind Hart's chair, would flash her a quick glance of warning. And if she retired to her favourite refuge, the sewing room, Abigail would join her with a volume of Richardson's *Clarissa Harlowe* and read aloud to her. Abigail hated to sew and loved to read, and it was soon an understood thing between them that she would entertain Mercy while Mercy set her torn flounces to rights. And when the two girls went out, there was Francis, always ready to escort them on walks down by the tidewater or, having discovered that Mercy had never sat a horse, to begin teaching her to ride on a sober old pony outgrown by Hart.

Hart himself, very busy overseeing the spring planting, had little time to spare, but often met the three of them as Mercy grew bolder and their rides took them farther and farther afield. He was down by the river one morning, inspecting the sluices that would flood the fields when the women had finished sowing the rice, and was covered, as a result, in black river mud, when the sound of galloping hoofs brought him up to the level of the path in a hurry. Horses ridden at speed might mean anything, and he and his overseer, Sam, exchanged a quick, anxious glance before relaxing at the sound of a characteristic halloo from Francis. He was in the lead, with Abigail just behind him and Mercy bringing up the rear, flushed, laughing and triumphant. She looked a different creature, Hart thought. Still small and plain, she glowed, now, with what he supposed must be happiness.

Abigail, on the other hand, though, like Mercy, she had acquired an unladylike tan for which the older ladies chided them both, looked tired and strained beneath it, as if she had not been sleeping. As always, she sat her horse gracefully, but there was just the hint of a droop about her shoulders, and the dark shadows under her blue eyes told their own tale.

"Oh, Mr Purchis." Mercy leaned forward in her side-saddle to pat her sweating pony. "You are to congratulate me on my first gallop. And I am to thank you for the loan of your Caesar. I had no idea it would be so exciting."

"More exciting than wise." Aware of dirt and dishevelment, Hart knew it sounded grudging as he spoke. "Surely, Francis, you have not forgotten how pitted this river bank is with alligator holes?"

"Count on you and your myrmidons to have taken care of them, cousin." Francis shrugged elegant shoulders in the London-cut riding coat and smiled benignly down on his flushed and sweating kinsman. "What a sort of toil you are, Hart, and what lilies of the field you make us seem. Should we all get down and play mud pies too?"

"These mud pies of mine are our bread and butter," said Hart shortly. "Forgive me, ladies, if I am not exactly dressed to receive you. And forgive me, too, if I leave you now. I have six more sluices to check before dinnertime." He turned away, regretting the ungracious speech as he spoke it, then back again, "And no more galloping on the river bank. Please."

"Oh, cousin." Francis pantomimed dismay. "Might we spoil your dikes?"

"You might break one of the ladies' necks, which, oddly enough, I should mind more."

"Good God, a gallant speech! Well, for that, we will proceed back as demurely as a funeral procession." And then, quickly, a hand held out to Mercy. "Forgive me, Miss Phillips, I quite forgot."

Hart watched them go with an anxious frown and surprised Sam by leaving him to inspect the last two sluices. "After all, Sam"—they were the oldest of friends—"you will have to take over when I go north."

"I wish you wouldn't go, Mr Hart." It was an old argument and Hart did not let it delay him. He wanted a word with his mother in the privacy of her room before the party assembled for dinner.

She was reassuring. "Yes, of course I've noticed. Most marked attentions to Miss Phillips and poor Abigail a very unhappy girl. But, truly, Hart, it's for Miss Phillips that I am anxious. I'm glad that Abigail should have her eyes opened about Frank. In fact, if I'm not wide of the mark, this is all the result of a word I spoke to him and to his mother."

"You?"

"You think, since I was ill, I am content to sit here, see nothing and do less, don't you, dear boy? Well, you may have taken over the estate, but I still run the family, and I don't intend to have my niece's heart broken if I can help it. If you remember, I warned Francis once about his dallying with Abigail. When that had no effect, naturally I spoke to my sister. Granted the choice between behaving himself and going to starve in Charleston, Francis seems to have seen the error of his ways. But I'm sorry he should have chosen such a brutal way of making the position clear. And anxious for little Miss Phillips, too, who seems in a fair way to have her head turned. What a strange creature she is, though. There's no understanding her. Do you remember how broad she spoke that first night she came, and now there's not a pin to choose between her accent and Abigail's. I expect, all in all, she's quite capable of taking care of herself."

"I certainly hope so," said Hart.

"I'm sure she is." Mrs Purchis had convinced herself. "She's certainly made a place for herself here at Winchelsea. But whether that's a good thing—We have to think of the future, Hart, hers as well as ours. I wish you would let me look out for a situation for her."

"A situation? What do you mean?" His tone surprised her.

"Well, as a governess." She gave him a quick, almost apologetic glance. "Or a housekeeper? She'd be worth her weight in gold to a widower with a houseful of children. Or there's Saul Gordon. You know how his poor wife ails. He said a word to me just the other day."

"No," said Hart Purchis. "I invited her here, and here she stays."

"Oh, very well." His mother shrugged it off and picked up her embroidery. "I won't say she doesn't make herself useful.

36

I just hope Francis doesn't break her heart for her. Sometimes I almost wish he'd go back to Charleston."

"So do I," said Hart, and surprised himself.

4

The spring planting was finished, the fields had been flooded for the second time to kill the weeds, and the young rice stood four inches high, when an unexpected guest drove up the long ilex avenue to Winchelsea. One look at the emblazoned panels of the light carriage and Mrs Purchis sent a servant hurrying across the fields for her son, while she cast a quick, approving glance over the dark silk dress Mercy Phillips had made for her, and hurried down to greet her visitor.

"Sir James, how good of you!" She held out a warm hand in greeting. Regardless of politics, everyone in Savannah liked Sir James Wright, who had been royal Governor of Georgia for ten years and had done much to keep the peace there.

"I have sent for my son," Mrs Purchis said when the first greetings were over. "He will be here directly. I hope."

"He works hard, I hear." Sir James seated her courteously and then took an upright chair himself.

"Too hard, I think. With the plantation in the daytime, and his studies at night." She coloured. "You have heard, perhaps, about his plans?"

"For Harvard College and the dangerous north? Yes, ma'am, I must tell you that that is, in part, my business with him. But we will save it until he comes, if you please."

"Yes." She sighed. "If only I could have let him go to England as he wished. But how could I, Sir James? My only son, and I left as I was. Winchelsea needs Purchis."

"Then I hope we can persuade Purchis to stay at Winchelsea." He turned as Hart entered the room, his fair hair sleeked damply down from a rapid combing, his cravat showing unmistakable signs of hasty tying.

"Forgive me, sir." He took Sir James' hand in his firm

grasp. "I was out at the sluices when I heard you were come."

"You were quick," Sir James approved.

Hart laughed. "We have a system," he explained. "It's useful. It's a bad day, and trouble for everyone, if it takes more than ten minutes for me to know who is coming to Winchelsea, friend or foe. I am happy to greet so good a friend, sir."

"I am happy to be so greeted. And I congratulate you on your precautions. These are bad times; and, I hear, you have taken in a particular hostage to fortune."

"Miss Phillips, of the mythical press? Yes, sir, and it is true that I increased our precautions when she came to live here. You will stay to dinner, I hope, and meet her."

"I'd like to, but I am making a tour of your district. I am just come from Thunderbolt and have Wormsloe, Bonaventure, and New Hope still to visit. But, forgive me, Mr Purchis, you said 'mythical press'?"

"Well," said Hart. "If it existed, would you not think it would be in evidence by now? I can only imagine that it must have been destroyed when poor Mr Phillips' house was burned."

"I devoutly hope so," said Sir James. "But to the point, if you will forgive me for being discourteously brief. I am come on two errands. First, to urge you to come into Savannah for the celebrations of the King's birthday on the fourth of June. This year, of all years, I wish to make a particular point of the festivities, and I would like to see Purchis of Winchelsea, and his family"—a bow for Mrs Purchis—"established in their town house for the occasion."

"Oh." Hart suddenly looked younger than his seventeen years. "I had meant, of course, that we should come into town for the celebration, but to stay—" He looked, with appeal, to his mother, then took a deep breath and continued. "To tell the truth, Sir James, I am hard pressed just now to get things on the plantation in proper train before I leave for the north."

"Yes," said Sir James. "That brings me to the other half of my message. Hart"—he used the Christian name with emphasis—"we are old friends, you and I. Can I not persuade you that this is no moment to be going to the North?"

"It is not to the North that I am going, sir, but to school."

"To Harvard College. Which means Cambridge, in Massachusetts, with those Boston hotheads just downriver. I wish you would think again, my dear boy."

"Oh, so do I!" Martha Purchis leaned forward eagerly, mittened hands clasped in her lap. "Dear Hart, I haven't liked to interfere, but, truly, when you think of last winter, when those crazy Bostonians dressed up as Indians and threw all that good tea into the harbour, I cannot make myself like your going there."

"They still have some of that same consignment of tea locked up at Charleston, Mother, and refuse to let it be sold."

"Yes, but at least we don't behave like barbarians down here in the South."

"No?" he looked at her from under thick, level brows. "What of Mr Phillips, Mother?" And then, turning back to Sir James Wright. "Forgive us, Sir James, but you will see that this is a subject we have thought much about. And I have made up my mind. Ever since my cousin came home from England I've been aware of how much I lack, of education, of knowledge of the world, of everything. I wish with all my heart that I could go to England, but that's not possible. Harvard College is. President Langdon has accepted me—I mean to go. Surely," he appealed to Sir James, his tone an apology for the blunt statements, "things are easier now? Have they not understood, in England, that we must be treated no worse and no better than their own voters? After all, they did repeal both the Townshend and the Stamp acts when they understood how ill they were taken over here." And then, flushing to the roots of his newly combed hair, "Forgive me, sir. I don't know what I am thinking of to be reading you, of all people, a lecture in politics."

"I shall be only too happy if you are proved right." Sir James rose to his feet. "But my mind misgives me as to what action may be taken at home as a result of that Boston tea business last December. If only the mails were not so slow. But in winter . . ."

"It's the one reason why I prefer Harvard College to England for my studies. At least, there I shall be in close touch with home by way of the Charleston packet."

"Yes." There was still a note of doubt in Sir James' voice, and he hurried to turn the subject. "At least I can count on your family, Hart, for the fourth of June?"

"Let us all go, Hart," said his mother. "I will see to the arrangements for opening the town house, and, indeed, it is time it was aired and used. We have been shocking country mice since I was ill, and it will be a high treat for the girls."

"For Miss Phillips?" asked Hart doubtfully. "After her last experience of Savannah?"

"All the more reason why she should come back, and if I may say so, publicly, under your and my protection, Hart." Sir James was drawing on his gloves. "You will all dine with me, I hope, after the celebration, and watch the illuminations from the Council House with me. I am inviting the Habershams and the Joneses, among many others."

"Both fathers and sons?" asked Hart. Everyone knew that both the Joneses of Wormsloe and the wealthy Habershams were divided politically, fathers in each case adhering faithfully to King George III, while their sons, if not actually Liberty Boys, were certainly confirmed radicals and frequenters of Tondee's Tavern.

"But, of course," said Sir James. "We all love our King, here in Georgia. There has never been the slightest question of that. His birthday seems to me the ideal opportunity for an easing of the strife that has divided father from son, and brother from brother in these unhappy colonies."

"Yes." Now it was Hart's turn to sound doubtful. "If only it works out."

"At least"—Sir James bent gracefully over Mrs Purchis' outstretched hand—"I am to congratulate you on a united household here. Though young Mayfield, I believe, keeps every kind of company when he's in town."

It was almost a question, and Martha Purchis chose to answer it. "I'm afraid my nephew cares more for a hand of cards and a bet on it than for politics," she said. "He's a sad anxiety to my sister, Sir James. I only wish some office could be found for him."

"Oh, shame, Mother," protested Hart. "To be begging of Sir James, and without even Frank's permission. Besides," shrewdly, "if he were offered a place, I doubt he would take it."

"And this is no time for the giving of places." They were all thinking of the mob violence that had threatened people who were even suspected of being appointed collectors of the unpopular Stamp Tax nine years before.

As Hart escorted Sir James out to his carriage, the governor gave him a keen look. "Just the same," he said, "your cousin does keep odd company. You think him sound?"

"Completely. He was saying only the other day how much

he wished he'd been able to take a commission in His Majesty's forces when he was in England. He's just"—Hart reddened—"lazy, I am afraid, and a little spoiled. I'd hoped he would look after the plantation for me when I go north, but it's no use. He thinks such work degrading."

"I wish you wouldn't go, my boy."

"Sir James, I'm so ignorant! Why, even Miss Phillips can put me down in an argument. She was talking about Locke and Montesquieu the other day, and I didn't even know what they had written. Surely you must see that if we are to come through our present troubles we need educated men in positions like mine. What use am I to you as a mere farmer?"

"A great deal. You're making a fine thing of Winchelsea, I can see, and a profitable one, I imagine. But"—he smiled the smile that had made him so many friends—"I'll leave sermonizing, Hart, and give you my blessing."

"Thank you, sir. And we will be happy to be your guests on the fourth."

He expected, and encountered, opposition from Mercy Phillips. "I know you're still mourning your father"—he anticipated the heart of her objection—"but so does Sir James, and he made a particular point of your coming. I hope you will do so—to oblige me, if for no better reason."

She looked mutinous for a moment, then smiled. "Purchis of Winchelsea? Well, it would be a rude return for all your hospitality if I were to refuse you so small a favour. And, besides, it should be an interesting occasion, if all the embattled families Sir James is inviting really come."

"Embattled?"

Francis laughed and joined the conversation. "She's quoting me, cousin. I visited the Habershams the other day and there weren't any pleasant words between father and son there, I can tell you. And as for Giles Habersham, if he and his cousin aren't at each other's throats before the fourth of June, I'll be amazed. He's only been back from England a few weeks and already they are at daggers drawn."

"Giles," said Abigail thoughtfully. "I remember him. He used to come to parties and be sick."

"Better not remind him of that now," said Francis. "He's very much the Bond Street beau. And so loyal to George the Third I reckon he'd take off his hat and bow to his effigy on a silver coin. If there were such things anymore." He laughed.

"I always pay my gambling debts in paper. It comes much less expensive."

After some discussion, Mrs Purchis took Abigail into town with her at the end of May to make sure that the Purchis house in Oglethorpe Square was ready for occupation. "You know what the town servants are like," she reminded Hart. "They will have let all go to sixes and sevens in our absence."

"Most likely. You'd best take a few stalwarts from here. You must not over-exert yourself, Mamma."

"Thank you, dear boy. You can rely on me to take good care of myself. All shall be ready when you come in on the third."

"And Francis goes with you?" Hart had thought Francis' acquiescence somewhat doubtful, and wished to be reassured on this point. "I do not want you and Abigail to be left alone in town."

"I should think not. No knowing what the mob may not get up to by way of celebrating the King's birthday. I shall be glad when you get to town, Hart."

"I'll try and get there by the second. The worst of it is, I don't think Miss Phillips should be there too long."

It earned him a sharp look. "Mercy Phillips is very well able to take care of herself, as I have had reason to tell you before. If you ask me, she has positively bewitched the servants, and there's Abigail dotes on her, and as for Francis . . . if I were your Aunt Anne, I believe I would encourage him to go back to Charleston, whatever it cost."

"Oh?" He blushed suddenly.

"Yes, indeed. I'd never have believed it, but I really begin to think it's a case with Francis. Quite unsuitable, of course. Hopeless. And poor Abigail . . . though, mind you, it's a blessing in a way. No money there either. But I wish I knew what Francis sees in that plain little Mercy Phillips."

Plain? He asked himself the question. He had more sense than to put it to his mother.

"I do hope it is all for the best." Mrs Mayfield had joined Hart and Mercy on Winchelsea's Corinthian portico to watch the carriage out of sight and receive a last wave from Francis, who rode beside it. "Were it not for my poor nerves, I would almost have been tempted to go too."

"Yes." It was what Hart had wished. "If you will excuse me, Aunt, I will get back to work. The sooner we can join them, the happier I shall be."

"Work," she sniffed. "Do you think of nothing else, Hart?"

"Not much, right now. There's so much to do, if I am to get away as I wish, at the end of the month."

"So soon?"

"Well, yes. You know it is the quiet time here on the plantation, and it will give me a chance to get myself established at Harvard, and, I hope, do a little preparatory reading before things begin in earnest in the fall. I'm afraid I'm going to find myself a sad dunce among all those bright boys."

"And so much older, too," said his aunt with malice. "You'll be Gulliver among the pygmies with a vengeance." And then, turning her irritation on Mercy, "Well, Miss Phillips, in a dream again? Had we not best try on that dress of mine, if it is to be ready for the birthday?"

Mercy, who had indeed been dreamily watching the end of the avenue, where the carriage and its attendant horseman had finally disappeared, pulled herself together with a start, gave Hart a smile of muted sympathy, and followed the older woman into the house.

"I'm glad to have a chance to talk to you," said Anne Mayfield as Mercy fastened the buttons of the refurbished silk down her plump back. "I've been meaning to this age, but there's never a chance, somehow, with the house so full."

"Yes?" Mercy had her mouth full of pins and spoke round them, with difficulty and some constraint.

"I feel it my duty," began Mrs Mayfield. "Ouch! Be careful where you put those pins, child."

"I'm sorry, ma'am." Put ruthlessly into the position of servant, Mercy found herself equally understanding and resenting it. But why should she? Besides . . .

"It's about my son, Francis," went on Anne Mayfield, and felt Mercy's hands stop for a minute, then go on, more busily than ever, with their pinning. "I told him some time ago that he must leave paying such obvious attention to poor little Abigail. It was just at the time you came, as a matter of fact. He saw my point, of course. Poor Francis. He must marry money."

"Because he has spent so much?" Mercy had pinned the last dart in the heavy silk and stood back to consider the result.

"Because he needs so much, poor boy," said his mother.

"Such refined tastes! Only, when I told him that it was hardly fair to raise false hopes in Abigail's silly head, I had not thought how he would set about making the position clear to her."

"You mean"—Mercy could not resist the tiniest hint of cockney—"by setting his cap at me."

"That's just what I mean. I am only relieved you recognised it for what it is."

"Ah, but do I?" asked Mercy. "And for the matter of that, do you?"

"My poor child, if you are deluding yourself that he is in the least serious, I am more glad than I can say that I have nerved myself to this extremely painful conversation." She was enjoying every minute of it. "My poor Frank has been an incorrigible lady killer since he was first breeched."

"What a pity, in that case, that Mr Mayfield hasn't bagged a fortune yet," said Mercy drily. And then, firmly changing the subject. "What do you think, ma'am? Will it do?"

"Why, yes." Grudgingly. "I really believe it will. No doubt about it, child, you're a marvel with your needle. Where in the world did you learn?"

"Behind the scenes at Covent Garden Theatre." Mercy began unbuttoning the dress with hands she would not let tremble. "We were constantly remaking costumes there. This is nothing to it." She did not let herself add that this particular job reminded her vividly of letting out dresses for elderly actresses who would insist on staging yet one more "final appearance." Things were quite bad enough between her and Frank's mother as it was.

She missed him more than she liked to admit to herself, and made a succession of good resolutions after that painful talk with his mother, but it was still impossible not to look forward to the birthday celebrations. Her own dress, inevitably left to the last, was of a fine muslin with black dots that she had found lying, still in its bolt, yellow with age, in one of the seldom-visited attics of the house, Mrs Purchis on being shown it, had exclaimed and remembered. It had arrived from England the year the French and Indian War broke out, and in her distraction, she had put it away and forgotten all about it. Of course Mercy might have it. "But no black ribbons, child." She had anticipated Mercy's plan. "Hart says there must be no hint of mourning. Are you sure you can make it fit to wear?"

"Oh, yes." As always, Mercy was amazed at the prodigality of life at Winchelsea. Mrs Purchis would undoubtedly have given the shabby-looking bolt of material to one of the maids. Mercy descended to the wash-house and washed and aired and bleached and starched until the material came up as good as new, if a little shrunk. But there was plenty of it, and not much of her. She made it up as simply as possible, by a pattern she remembered using, once, for a last-moment Ophelia at Covent Garden, and was delighted with the result. It was just the thing, neither mourning nor otherwise, neither in style nor out of it. "He loves me"—she was sewing buttons down the back—"he loves me not." They came out even and a superstitious tear fell on the last one. And serve her right, she thought, for thinking so much of Frank Mayfield, with her father only three months in his grave. What would Father have thought of Frank?

She found herself boggling at this question and was grateful to be disturbed by Hart, who had sought her out with the news that he would be ready to leave next day. "I promised my mother I would try and get us there by the second, and I think we can do it. You'll be ready?" He looked down at the billowing material in her lap.

"Oh, yes. Mr. Purchis?"

"Yes?"

"Could I wear just one bit of black ribbon? For Father?"

"What did my mother say?"

"She said no."

"Well then." But the disappointment in her small, pointed face hurt him. "Wait a minute." He left her, hurried up to his room, created chaos in a cedarwood chest, and returned triumphantly with an ebony locket on a fine, gold chain. "Wear this." He handed it to her. "No one can mind that. We all had them when my aunt died—Abigail's mother," he explained.

"Oh, thank you. I would dearly love to borrow it." She was playing with the catch of the glass-fronted locket and it opened, revealing the fine curl of hair that had slipped invisibly to one side. "Oh!"

"I'm sorry. It's my aunt's." They looked at each other in silence, remembering her father's scalped head.

"I'll pretend it's his." She pushed the pale curl gently back into the centre of the locket. "Just for the day."

"No, no. You must keep the locket." He smiled at her,

45

but with embarrassment. "You can see it's not much use to me. And"—he hesitated for a moment—"no need to pretend. I thought you might want— I cut off . . . from the back of his head . . . I wondered whether to tell you. . . ." In moments of acute discomfort, like this one, he still blushed a schoolboy's blush.

"You mean! My father . . . and you never told me. Oh." She jumped up and let the muslin fall where it would. "I *do* thank you!"

William, the coachman, had brought the phaeton back from Savannah, and early next morning had it ready on the carriage sweep. One of the light waggons Hart used on the farm had been loaded up with Mrs Mayfield's big box, Mercy's tiny one, and Hart's carpet-bag. Mercy and Hart were waiting in the morning room. Of Mrs Mayfield there was no sign. Hart sighed, took a turn about the room, and looked for the twentieth time at his watch. "We'll be late for dinner," he said. "Mother is counting on us. Mercy, would you very much mind—"

She did mind, but there was no help for it. "Of course not. Very likely it's some problem of her dress. I'll go directly."

She found Mrs Mayfield apparently ready, but standing at her window, gazing out, a letter crumpled in her hand. "Oh, it's you!" She greeted Mercy without ceremony. "Tell Hart I want to see him."

"Here?" Mercy cast a quick glance round the big, untidy room, so unlike any other at Winchelsea. Where Martha Purchis relied on home-made soap and toilet water for her complexion, her sister's dressing table held a shabby battery of the tools of beauty's trade. Even now, with, presumably, the most vital potions packed, the room reeked of orris root, powder, and other unidentifiable odours.

"No. Tell him I'll be with him this instant." She was treating Mercy like a servant, and they both knew it. "Oh, and first, hand me my fan, there's a good girl. And my vinaigrette. I've had bad news."

Her skin, mottled under the rouge, confirmed this, and Mercy, sorry for her, did as she was bid and hurried down to warn Hart. "Something's wrong, I'm afraid. She's had a letter."

"I know. From Charleston." He turned as Mrs Mayfield

entered the room. "I'm sorry, Aunt. Mercy tells me you have had bad news."

"Mercy, is it?" Mercy had never seen anyone but an actress bridle before, and she made one of her quick notes on human behaviour while Mrs Mayfield sank into a chair, angrily fanning herself. "Would you believe it, Hart, my tenants have quit my Charleston house, without warning, and without paying what they owe me! It's the most monstrous thing you ever heard of! I'll have the law on them if it's the last thing I do. Why, without what they pay I don't know how I shall contrive. I shall have one of my spasms, I know I will!"

"They are English, are they not, Aunt?" Hart spoke into her furious silence.

"Yes. I thought the English were such models of good behaviour! To hear Frank speak, they are all perfect paragons. Well, let's just wait to hear what he says about this. And to make bad worse, they have sailed already. They say they don't feel safe in Charleston. Not safe! In Charleston! I ask you." She uncrumpled the letter she was still holding, and looked at it again. "Yes, sailing the day they wrote. Of all the unprincipled . . ."

"Yes," said Hart. "I do hope it doesn't mean they know something we don't. We must tell Governor Wright about this, and the sooner the better. Are you ready to go, Aunt? You will wish to discuss your course of action both with Sir James and with Francis, will you not? But, I'm afraid, if they have actually sailed for England, you have not much hope of redress."

"No." She was getting angrier by the minute. "They were friends of Frank's, too. He put them in touch with me. I'll have a word to say to that boy."

"Privately, I do beg. We must not do anything to spoil the birthday celebrations."

5

Like Winchelsea, the Purchis house in Oglethorpe Square had been built with Martha Purchis' money and to her specifications. Still homesick, she had had it planned like a Charleston single house, with an end fronting the street and high, screened porches along the shady garden side. Her husband's one stipulation had been that the simple one-storey frame house in which his own father had lived during the early days of Savannah must be preserved, so there it was, small and shabby beside the gleaming white paint of the new house.

"Goodness!" Mercy had never been in this part of the town and was amazed at the size and style of the house. "It's grander than the Governor's Residence!"

"Not really." Hart was always mildly embarrassed by the house. "It looks bigger than it is."

"It's that absurd little shack beside it makes it look so strange," said Mrs Mayfield. "It's a perfectly good Charleston house otherwise."

"Yes." Hart held up a courteous hand to help her alight from the carriage. "Only this is Savannah." He held up his hand in turn to Mercy, who jumped lightly down onto the loose sand of the street. "The 'little shack' next door is the one I promised to show you," he told her. "It's the original house my grandfather lived in. It must have been a great day for those first settlers when Oglethorpe finally consented to move out of the tent he had lived in since they landed. Imagine what it must have been like for men used to a life of luxury back home in England to rough it here in tents on the sand. That shack must have seemed the height of comfort."

"Yes." Mercy's soft slippers were full of sand already. "It's lucky the forest around the town keeps the worst of the wind off, or there would be no enduring it."

"There's no enduring it now," said Mrs Mayfield. "To be standing here chattering in the street like a parcel of peasants."

"I am a peasant," said Mercy, but luckily neither Hart nor Mrs Mayfield heard her, since he was opening the wrought-iron gate to usher his aunt into the garden, from which the house was entered by way of its long screened porch. In the first enthusiasm of building, Martha Purchis had planned a formal garden in the Italian style for her town house, and there were still evergreen trees and hedges and a tumbledown summerhouse as evidence of her ambition, but years of neglect had let the garden sink back to a jungle of sweet-smelling jasmine through which a path had been recently cut to the porch door.

Mrs Purchis herself was there to welcome them and ask, with a quick, anxious glance for her sister's raddled face, "What's the matter?"

"Matter enough." Mrs Mayfield subsided on a rocking chair in the cool of the porch. "My tenants have quit without a word of apology or a penny paid."

"Come." Hart took Mercy's arm to lead her across the porch and into the big, cool room behind it. "Aunt Anne will feel better for telling my mother." He explained his retreat. "And you will be glad to go to your room. Ah, here's Abigail. How are you, cousin?"

"Well, thank you." Abigail's looks belied the words. "It's good to see you both. My aunt's been fretting."

"Oh?" Hart had been moving towards an inconspicuous door in the corner of the room. "What's the matter?"

"Frank. We've hardly seen him since he brought us here." *Abigail had been fretting too*, Mercy thought. "Oh, he sleeps here, I collect, but that's the end of it. Aunt's been in terror of the mob."

"Poor mother. How are things in town? It seemed quiet enough as we drove in."

"Almost too quiet," said Abigail. "As if everyone was waiting . . . but what for?"

"The birthday celebrations, let's hope. I'm sorry, Abigail." The genuine sympathy in his voice was for more than her temporary trouble. He saw her eyes suddenly aswim with unshed tears and hurried on, "Mercy's tired. Be an angel and take her to her room. I have no doubt the servants are all at sixes and sevens still."

"Twelves and fourteens." Abigail managed a watery smile. "And you're off to your office, I take it?"

"Just so. I asked Saul Gordon to meet me here. I've a

world of business to get through with him. If all goes well, I hope this will be my last visit to Savannah before I leave for the North."

"I wish you weren't going, Hart."

"Oh, Abigail, not you too! Ah, Gordon!" He turned with relief as the door in the corner of the room opened to reveal a black-clad, sallow, smiling man.

"Mr Purchis!" He advanced, seized Hart's hand and pumped it up and down. "This is a sight for sad eyes. And— can it be?—Miss Phillips, of whose praises I have heard so much from Madam Purchis. Do, I beg of you, present me."

"Yes, of course." Hart did not sound best pleased. "Mercy, let me present my right-hand man, Mr. Gordon."

"Miss Phillips!" His hand was damp. "Mrs Purchis has led me to hope that you would do me the great kindness of calling on my dear, afflicted wife. She pines for company, my poor Rachel, she quite pines for company."

"I shall be delighted." Mercy was afraid she did not sound it, but she did not much like this hint of an arrangement behind her back.

"And I'll come too," said Abigail. "Why did you not tell me Mrs Gordon was lonely, Mr Gordon?"

"Always so kind, so condescending, Miss Purchis, but I could hardly presume . . . a member of the family . . . my poor Rachel would be overwhelmed."

"Business first." Hart cut him short with a firmness that surprised Mercy. "Visits later. Excuse us, ladies? I'll be in the study, Abigail, if my mother should want me."

"His study?" asked Mercy, as Gordon bowed low to them both and followed Hart through the little door.

"He uses the old house next door. He had the doorway cut through. Aunt Martha doesn't much like it, but it suits Hart very well. And nobody seems to mind the mixing of work and ordinary living here in Savannah."

"Why should they?" Mercy lapsed into cockney. "Work's 'ow they live, ain't it?"

"Heavens!" Abigail glanced quickly out to the porch, where the two sisters were deep in agitated talk. "Don't let my aunts hear you speak like that or they will think you as bad as the revolutionaries."

Mercy laughed. "My accent, love, or what I say?" And then, modulating from cockney to the pure English she normally spoke, "Forgive me! I'm afraid all this luxury brings out the worst in me. I can't seem to get over how different things are here from the other side of town where Father and I lived. And the shameful thing is, I still can't help enjoying the comfort."

"Why shouldn't you?" Abigail led her upstairs to the bedroom floor, where the rooms also looked out onto the screened porch, and left her to rest.

Francis did not appear until late in the evening, when his mother was just crossly preparing to go to bed. "A million apologies, Mamma." His face was becomingly flushed as he bent to kiss her hand. "I meant to be here to greet you, but have had business I didn't much like to detain me."

"Business?" asked Hart.

"Yes." Francis turned to him with an odd, sideways smile. "Even I am capable of some kinds of business, little cousin. I have been doing my utmost to persuade the hotheads at Tondee's Tavern that the King's birthday is no time for a revolutionary demonstration."

"I hope you have been successful," said Hart.

"I rather think I have."

"Tondee's Tavern," said his mother. "Pah, Frank! No wonder you stink of spirits."

"My dear mother, you must look on it as a sacrifice made in the cause of peace." He turned to Mercy. "Miss Phillips! It grieved me particularly not to be here to greet you on your return to Savannah."

"I am glad to think you were so much more profitably occupied, sir."

"Now." He turned his flashing smile on Abigail. "Am I to look on that as a compliment or a setdown, I wonder?"

"Choose for yourself," said Mercy, and was relieved when Mrs Mayfield plunged into a catalogue of grievances over her absconding tenants. Francis looked grave over this, very much as Hart had done, and when she finished her tirade with a triumphant "So what else can I do but go there and see that they have at least left things in order," he looked graver still. "You'll come, of course, my dear boy?" She was sure of him.

"Ma'am, I wish I could, but, do you know, my conscience tells me that I ought to stay in Savannah just now. I begin to think I can serve a useful purpose here, as friend to both Whigs and Tories."

"A dangerous position," said Hart drily.

"Indeed, yes. But these are dangerous times." He turned to Hart with one of his flamboyant gestures. "These last two days here in Savannah have taught me a great deal. Little cousin, I am about to approach you, cap in hand, and ask if you would still consider letting me have the management of Winchelsea when you go north."

"Manage Winchelsea. You? You really mean it, Frank?"

"I really mean it. Unless, of course, I can persuade you not to go. You must realise, cousin, that there are many people here in town who think your going to Harvard merely a disguise for secret revolutionary sentiments."

"Then they think a lot of nonsense," said Hart.

"That's not the point. Of course, you and I know that Purchis and loyalty are the same word, but you can't expect the mob to understand that. So all the more reason, if Purchis is absent, for a confirmed Loyalist, and however humble a member of the family, to continue in charge at Winchelsea."

"And you'll really do it?" asked Hart.

"If you'll trust me. I'm afraid I am the most absolute tyro, but with Saul Gordon here, and Sam at Winchelsea, I will do my best to learn."

"And what about me," wailed his mother. "How am I to get to Charleston? You know I am not well enough to travel alone!"

"I'd been thinking about that," said her son. "Why not let Hart escort you? If I promise to see that all goes smoothly at Winchelsea, Hart, will you see my poor mother through the worst of her arrival at Charleston?"

"I shall be only too happy. This is *good* news, Francis. I shall rest much more easy at the North for knowing that you are looking after things down here. And protecting my mother and the girls at Winchelsea."

"Yes," said Mrs Mayfield. "And who, pray, is going to protect me at Charleston when you have left, Hart?"

"Why, if you'll be ruled by me, Aunt, you'll let me help you find a new tenant, and come back to Winchelsea as soon as you can. I don't much like the idea of you on your own in Charleston. That house of yours is too near the water for safety if the mob were to come out. I don't want you exposed to any Charleston tea parties."

"Surely you don't expect such a thing?"

"Ma'am, as long as that tea is stored at Charleston harbour,

52

anything can happen at any time. I wouldn't wish you to be a witness to a tarring and feathering."

"Ugh!" said Mrs Mayfield. "Barbarous."

Whether through Governor Wright's peace-making tactics or, as he himself suggested, through Francis Mayfield's active intervention, both at Tondee's Tavern and elsewhere, the fourth of June celebrations went off peacefully enough. As they did every year, Sir James and his council marched ceremoniously to Fort Halifax through the dust to drink the King's health, while cannon boomed along the bluff and the Savannah Rangers joined in the salute with a rattle of small-arms fire. Back at the Council House, the ladies joined the party for the ceremonial dinner in honour of George III's thirty-sixth birthday, which was to be followed by a ball and illuminations.

Mercy had not wanted to come, pleading her recent bereavement, but Hart had overruled her, on Governor Wright's direct orders, backed by some pressing from Francis. "Besides," said Frank, "I want the promise of the first dance, and the pleasure of escorting you to the illuminations. Spectacular, I can tell you, when you see them from the bluff, reflected in the river below."

"A terrible waste of powder," said Hart. "And I wish Fort Halifax was in better trim. I was surprised to see how it had been let go to rack and ruin. And the other fortifications too."

Mercy, accepting Frank's invitation for the first dance, found herself wondering, a little anxiously, what would be Abigail's fate, but when Francis joined them after dinner, he brought a stranger with him, a tall, dark man with the unmistakable air of elegance that meant, to Mercy, a visit to Europe.

Abigail, standing beside her, gave a little gasp as the two men approached. "Giles!" she said. "It's never you after all these years!"

Giles Habersham laughed and bent to kiss her hand. "Shall I dare remind you that the last time we met I was sick all over your best party taffeta and you boxed my ears for me?"

"I couldn't reach to do it now!" Mercy had seldom seen Abigail so animated.

"Nor, I hope, will you try and teach me the figure when

53

I take you out to dance. Do you remember how angry I used to get?"

"Yes, but you never did know it. I take it they have taught you to dance in Europe?"

"That, among other things, but nothing so happy as this return." He turned reluctantly away as Francis made to present him to Mercy. "Your servant, ma'am." Then, back to Abigail, "But, come, the fiddlers are striking up."

"You have not yet asked me to dance." Her tone was teasing.

"I am presuming," he said gravely, taking her hand, "on our old acquaintance."

Following them, "You will have to console me as best you may," said Francis to Mercy. And then, with a laugh, "So much for my mother's fretting. I knew all along it was but for Giles to return and my luck would be quite out."

"And your heart, of course, is breaking, you squire of dames."

"Your squire, I hope. You must know—" But the dance was beginning.

Later, when the signal was given for the illuminations, he found her shawl for her and led her out into the warm darkness to watch. The crowd spread out loosely along the bluff, with faces suddenly illuminated as a firework soared up, then lost again in the deeper darkness that followed. "Come this way." His arm was warm under hers. "You are so tiny, you will never see unless we get a little out of the crowd. Your hand is like a child's." His fingers were tracing its outline in the darkness.

"Stronger." Mercy tried in vain to withdraw it.

"Mercy, I want to talk to you."

"Miss Phillips to you, sir."

"Oh," impatiently, "I'll call you whatever you wish, child, so long as you will listen to me. I'm anxious about you— for you, Miss Phillips."

"Too kind." She gasped, as a new burst of light showed the crowd, surely, she thought, somewhat dwindled. "Where has everyone gone?"

"Best not ask. Drunk the King's health—now, another toast, a less public one. Sir James has more sense than to take note of the absentees, and, for the time being, I think we shall shuffle along well enough here under his able guidance. But I am still anxious about you and won't be put off.

Trouble about you"—his fingers were warm in the palm of her hand—"too intelligent for your own good."

"I beg your pardon?

"Dear Mercy, no one but a fool would believe for a moment that you did not know where that press of your father's is hidden. And the Liberty Boys here in Savannah are many things, but not fools. So, for your own safety, I beg you will tell me so that we can dispose of it for the best."

"The best? Whose best?"

"Yours, of course. For what else do I care?"

"For our sovereign lord, King George, perhaps?"

"Oh, that's of course. But, Mercy, it is about you that we are talking. You—and me."

"Yes?" A cloud of sparks had left it suddenly dark again, and she saw him give a quick glance round to make sure there was no one within earshot.

"Must know how I feel about you. Difficult, until now, because—ashamed to have to say this—because of Abigail. That was a madness, cured the day you and I met. Must have seen that since then I have had eyes for no one but you."

"Eyes?" She thought about it. "Yes, perhaps. Frankly, it has puzzled me."

"Modest little Mercy. No one ever told you that you were beautiful?"

"No. And if they did, I wouldn't believe it. I have a looking-glass, Mr Mayfield, and two good eyes of my own."

"Ah, but your sparkle, your charm, your many voices, wise little serpent that you are—you are not in a position to recognise them. I tell you, they have enslaved me."

"Against your will? Oh, poor Mr Mayfield."

"I wish you would call me Francis."

"And I wish you would not call me Mercy. You seem to have forgotten the immense gap that exists between us. I am nobody, Mr Mayfield, the merest dependent. Your eyes would be better employed elsewhere."

"Just what I told them." He took the wind out of her sails by agreeing with her. "No use. Quite right, of course," he went on with a kind of rueful frankness. "If my mother cut up rough over Abigail, what would she have to say about you? That is why, dearest Mercy, I have chosen this private chance to speak to you."

"I don't much care for private chances." Once again she tried to pull away from him, but he still had her hand fast.

"You're right, as always, but these are no ordinary times. Must understand, Mercy, changing my whole life for your sake. When I am master at Winchelsea, I shall be in a position to speak to you. Until then, let me be your secret slave, I'll find all my happiness in working for you."

"Master at Winchelsea? That has an odd sound, surely?"

"You insist on misunderstanding me, my precious girl. Hart will be away for three years at the least of it. By the time he returns, I will be an experienced plantation manager, and —for he will be generous, if I know Hart—will have more than enough put by to start a plantation of my own—dare I say our own? It may mean moving west for a land grant, but who cares about that, so long as we are together?"

"You would really do that? Leave your life of luxury and take up new land in the West?"

"For you. Yes. With you—anything. Dearest Mercy, I'll move mountains for your sake."

"You may find running Winchelsea a less exciting task." She had not intended it for capitulation, but he took it as such, pulling her suddenly into his arms. "Mercy!" He kissed her, gently at first, then hard, demandingly, his lips bruising hers. "Oh, Mercy!" Reluctantly, he let her go just before a new burst of fireworks illuminated them.

She looked up at him. "I've never been kissed before." Her voice was shaking. "How can I tell?"

"Told me already. Those lips of yours. Did you not feel them say, 'I love you, Francis Mayfield?'"

"I . . . don't . . . know." And then, moving a little away from him, towards the diminished crowd. "Mr Mayfield, please, no more tonight."

"My dearest, your will is my law." He tucked her arm under his and began to lead her back towards the crowd. "We will talk again when I have proved myself at Winchelsea. What shall we call our own plantation, dear? Where did your father come from in England?"

"Mr Mayfield, you go too fast for me." But he could feel that the reference to her father had moved her. "Singleton," she said at last.

"Singleton." He rolled it over on his tongue. "I like it. Shall we be master and mistress of Singleton Hall, you and I? But"—he stopped for a moment, holding her back—"speaking of your father reminds me. My dear, I do not like to harp on it, but I am truly anxious about you . . . the

Liberty Boys. To be able to print their own pamphlets: great thing for them. For all our sakes, I think you should tell me where your father hid that press of his. You would not wish to see Winchelsea treated as your home was."

She was shivering now—with cold, with fear? "God knows I would not. But, Mr Mayfield, how are we to persuade the Liberty Boys that I truly do not know what my father did with his press?"

"My dear, God knows. God knows too that I will do my best." Something in his tone made her wonder if he quite believed her, but at this moment they rejoined the diminished crowd. "We'll talk again." The pressure of his arm was a promise. "It's high time we found the others. Poor Hart will be dead bored with gallanting his mother and mine."

But the two older ladies had refused to risk the dangerous evening air, and Hart, coming out onto the bluff to look for the others, had been just in time to witness that one, long passionate embrace. Turning quickly away, he found himself grinding his teeth, as he used to do once as a boy, that bad time after his father was killed. Making himself stop, he turned his thoughts resolutely to Harvard and another life. He had let himself dream a dream about Mercy. It was over and must be forgotten.

6

The mob did not come out on the fourth of June, but it was out with a vengeance a few days later. An exhausted messenger had ridden into town with the news of the Boston Port Bill, the repressive British answer to the Boston Tea Party.

"Madness." Francis Mayfield had hurried to Oglethorpe Square with the news and a warning that the ladies should stay home. "Can't imagine what they're thinking of back in London. It can only make matters infinitely worse here. The messenger says there have been spontaneous demonstrations of sympathy with Boston all through the colonies as the news has broken."

"But what exactly does it mean?" asked Mercy.

"Total ban on Boston as a port. No goods to be landed or discharged except for military purposes. Salem to be used instead . . . could be the ruin of Boston. And some ways worse, talk of an increased garrison, a military governor."

"It's bad." Hart had joined them from his office next door, followed by Saul Gordon. "And you say the other colonies are siding with Boston? It would be a golden chance for New York and Philadelphia to take over much of their trade. Not to mention Salem."

"A chance they do not mean to take, little cousin. Instead, they talk of sending provisions to Boston, helping in every way, demonstrating. They are planning one, this minute, at Tondee's Tavern. There must be no going out for you ladies today."

"Alas." There was something at once timid and sly about Saul Gordon's tone as he eased his way into the conversation. "And my poor wife was so looking forward to another of your charming visits, young ladies. She says you quite cheer her up, Miss Phillips."

"But not today," said Mrs Purchis. "And, Hart, you must see that this quite changes your plans. You cannot possibly consider going to Harvard College now, when you cannot even land in Boston."

Hart's firm jaw set hard. "Mother, it is settled. And after all, what difference can Boston's affairs make to Harvard College back inland at Cambridge? Oh, there may be a trifle of unpleasantness, I suppose, and I shall have to go up to Salem and then back down by land, but that will merely serve to make my journey more interesting."

"Too interesting by a half, if you ask me," said Francis. "Be ruled by your mother in this! Go to William and Mary College at Williamsburg after all. Always said it would be best."

"Yes, Frank, and I have always said I didn't want to be sneered at by those haughty young Virginians, as well you know. Besides, think how stirring it will be to be so much at the heart of events. Perhaps I may even have some chance of serving the Tory cause up there as usefully as you do here in Savannah."

"Why, thank you for that, cousin. Just the same, can't help feeling you would be more usefully employed here, where you are Purchis of Winchelsea and carry some weight, than up north, a stranger. Do, pray, think again of this."

"Oh, do, Hart," cried his mother, lace-trimmed handkerchief to her eyes. "I hate to think of you going so far away at a time of such danger."

"I'm sorry, Mother, but it's settled," he said again, reminding her more and more of his father.

"Better give in gracefully, ma'am," Francis advised with a laugh. "You know there's no budging Hart when he sets his chin like that. And after all, he's to spend the rest of his life as a worthy plantation owner here in Savannah. Should be allowed this breath of freedom before he settles to the yoke. Everyone says the teaching at Harvard College is remarkable these days."

"Yes," put in Abigail, who had so far been a silent spectator. "And, Hart, you did promise you would visit my mother's family at Lexington and write me news of them. So at least you will not be without connection there, whereas at Williamsburg we have no friends at all." She turned to Mrs Purchis. "Think, ma'am, even if there should be trouble in Boston, and it should spread as far as Cambridge, which seems unlikely, Hart has only to go and visit my aunt in Lexington and be quite out of harm's way. You know she has already written urging that he spend all his vacations with them. Oh, how I wish I could come with you, Cousin Hart."

"Are you sure?" asked Francis teasingly.

"Well." She laughed and blushed. "Of course, I know it's impossible." She broke off as a servant appeared to announce Mr Giles Habersham.

He had come, he said, greeting them all, to urge that none of the ladies leave the house that day. "I came down Broughton Street on my way here and passed the Liberty Pole outside Tondee's Tavern, and I can tell you, I don't much like the look of things there."

"Are they out in the street yet?" Francis picked up his hat and cane.

"Yes. They're all the way down Whitaker Street from Broughton to the Bay. Presently they will start marching along the bluff, and then Lord knows what they may not do."

"Please God they don't come this way," said Mrs Purchis. And then, "You're never going out, Francis!"

"Duty calls, Aunt. I have, I flatter myself, some influence with those radical hotheads. If all else fails, I will do my best

59

to remind them that this is a house full of loyal Savannahians."

"Loyal is an unlucky word to use today," said Giles Habersham. "Sir James and his council have been in session all day. I just hope the mob does not choose to pay them a visit. I am afraid my cousin Joseph and his father are at daggers drawn over the Boston news already. If Joseph and his radical friends make trouble for Sir James, I don't like to think what will happen between him and his father."

"A bad time," said Francis. "Well, Giles, shall we go and see if we can talk some sense to these madmen?"

"But what about us?" wailed his mother.

"My cousin Hart will take care of you, ma'am."

Hart looked mutinous for a moment, then shrugged his shoulders. "I imagine I'll be as usefully—or uselessly—employed here as you there. But it's true, I've a million things to do, if Aunt Mayfield and I are to leave as soon as she wishes." And then, to his aunt, "I am afraid we have the explanation now, ma'am, of that cavalier behaviour of your tenants. They must have been warned that trouble was coming and decided to go while the going was good. You had best try to find yourself a reliable American tenant."

"American?" asked his aunt. "What are you intending, boy?"

"Why, nothing in the world, Aunt." He beat a hasty retreat to his study.

"American, indeed!" said Francis Mayfield with a light laugh. "You'd best keep an eye on your son, Aunt Purchis, or you may find him turning rebel on your hands."

"Nonsense," said Martha Purchis robustly. "And you know it. I'd as soon think of you as a rebel. Or you, Giles."

"Thank you, ma'am." Francis made her one of his elegant bows, managed a private smile for Mercy, and took his leave.

Inevitably, this new crisis made Mrs Mayfield more eager than ever to get to Charleston. With the mob prowling the streets of Savannah, harmless so far, but always menacing, it was certain the same thing must be going on in Charleston. "And an empty house," she wailed. "Anything could happen."

Hart was glad enough to fall in with her demand that they leave as soon as possible. Now that Francis had agreed to take over responsibility for Winchelsea, he was eager to be off, away from his mother's reproachful looks and stifled sighs, and from the pressure Sir James Wright was still quietly putting on him to change his plans. But he had a stronger reason still for longing to be gone. Memory of that passionate embrace he had witnessed between Francis and Mercy haunted him, and so did the question of what, if anything, he should do about it. More than anything in the world, he wanted to be away, clear away from the anguish and the problem of Mercy. He should have warned her about Francis, earlier, when he first thought of it. Now, how could he—and yet, how could he not?

His mother was pressing her to accept Saul Gordon's invitation to go and help nurse his sick wife. Did Mrs Purchis, too, perhaps suspect that something serious was afoot between Mercy and Francis? Hart could not, himself, much like the idea of Mercy in Saul Gordon's lonely little house on the edge of the Common. And yet it would get her away from Francis. In the end, urged both by his mother and by Saul Gordon, he spoke to Mercy about it the day before they went back to Winchelsea.

"You want to get rid of me!" She flared up at him.

"No, no . . ." Furiously, he felt himself blush. "Nothing of the kind. I sometimes think my mother is more ailing than she will admit and would be only too happy to think of you out at Winchelsea to help Abigail care for her, but there is your future to be considered."

"Playing God, Mr Purchis? I'll consider my own future, thank you. As for Saul Gordon, I don't much like being in *this* house with him, let alone in *his*. Unless you actually turn me out of Winchelsea, which you have every right to do, I would like to stay there."

"But, Mercy . . ." He wanted to say something, give some warning about Francis, but she left him with a firm little click of the door between his study and the house. No use . . .

Back at Winchelsea, he found himself even more anxious to be gone. It was curious how life there had changed. On his own instructions, Sam was taking his orders from Francis now, and seeing how smoothly things continued to go on the estate under this new management, he could not help wondering if he had been flattering himself with a mere illusion of indispensability. And, as bad or worse, now that he had time to spend in the big, cool house, he found himself out of things there too. Giles Habersham rode out most days to sit with Abigail on the porch or walk with her under the shade of the ilex avenue, and Mercy seemed to spend most of her time either working on the extensive new wardrobe Mrs Mayfield thought necessary for her Charleston visit, or eagerly listening to Frank's talk of his day's work in the fields.

Not, of course, that Frank actually worked, but he rode about and played the part of the master, better, Hart found himself thinking, than he had ever done. Perhaps the servants actually preferred a man who merely sat his horse and gave orders, rather than getting down into the dirt and working with them. It was all uncomfortable together, and he was delighted when the last stitch was set in what Frank laughingly called Mrs Mayfield's trousseau, and his own small boxes were packed and ready.

"Yes?" He had been packing his books and looked up at the light knock on his door.

"Hart." It was Mercy, looking unusually shy, with a pile of something in her arms. "I do hope you won't mind it; I have been making you some shirts on the English style. I am sure you will find the other students all mighty fine in Cambridge."

"Why, Mercy!" Once again that maddening blush. "How very good of you. It's true, I'm afraid I haven't given much thought to what I am to wear."

"No!" She laughed at him over the shirts in her arms, looking at the piles of books. "And you are not to pack these underneath your Johnson's *Dictionary* either, or I will come up to Cambridge and haunt you."

"I wish you could." He took the shirts from her. "But, Mercy, there are a dozen—"

"Of course there are a dozen," she said tartly. "What would Purchis of Winchelsea be doing with less?" And then, suddenly flushing to the roots of her hair at an impatient shout from somewhere down the hall, "Yes, Mrs Mayfield, I will be with you directly." She paused for a moment, her hand on the door, half in, half out of the room. "Hart?"

"Yes?"

"If I should ever think of somewhere that press might be, what should I do?"

"Nothing." He dropped the shirts unceremoniously onto a chair and moved over to take her hand in his hard one.

"Mercy, it seems to have been forgotten. For God's sake, let it remain so. Speak of it to no one. No one, I tell you. Not even"—now his colour was as high as hers—"not even to Francis."

"No?"

"No." Here at last was his chance for a word of warning. But how to put it? "Frank's—oh, everything I want to be, but, Mercy, he does keep odd company. And you're a girl of sense—you know how it is, with men. Sometimes, I think, at Tondee's—"

"The talk flows free. Father used to say men were worse gossips than women. But Francis would never speak of me, Hart. Never." And with this firm, revealing phrase, she left him.

Hart and his aunt left for Charleston a few days later, and he was relieved to find the Mayfield house there undamaged, and his aunt's man of business ready with a list of possible tenants. In South Carolina, even more than in Georgia, the mobs had been roused by the news of the Boston Port Bill, and people who had lived contentedly all their lives on remote plantations were now eager to move into the comparative safety and undoubted luxury of Charleston. Anne Mayfield was able to choose the most eligible of three possible tenants, and Hart found himself free to take the next week's packet for Boston, or rather for Salem.

It was a strange, disturbing journey. He had promised his mother—and, indeed, himself—that he would be cautious in what he said and did. He would watch, and listen, and say as little as possible until he was established in his new life. This was made easier for him by his youthful appearance. In Savannah he had been Purchis of Winchelsea, and treated with deference. On board ship he found himself merely a boy on his way to college. Easy enough for a fair-haired young man who still needed to shave only once a week, and whose voice would occasionally betray him, to keep quiet and listen to his elders talk.

But what he heard appalled him. If there were any Loyalists on the packet, they were keeping as quiet as he was. In Savannah the upper classes at least had always insisted that whatever they might think of Parliament and its vagaries, they were loyal subjects of King George III. There were no Loyalist toasts on the packet. If toasts were drunk, they were to the Continental Congress that had been summoned for the fifth of September at Philadelphia, and to the ill-treated citizens of Boston.

Worst of all, the more Hart heard of what happened in Boston, the more it shook him. What right had Parliament, weeks away over the sea, to take a decision that must mean ruin for a whole city? And it seemed more and more likely that a British garrison was to be imposed on the city, almost as if it was a hostile one, captured in time of war. He was glad to stay quiet and listen, but it was a very sober young man indeed who disembarked at Salem for the land journey to Harvard College.

Once there, he threw himself into his studies with an enthusiasm that won him golden opinions from his tutors. There was little enough to distract him. As Aunt Mayfield had warned him, the other students tended to be both younger and less experienced than himself. After running his own plantation, he inevitably felt himself a man among boys and could not bring himself to join in the frolics, the drinking and swimming parties, or the riding excursions with which they enlivened their studies. They, for their part, laughed at his Southern drawl and suspected his Southern loyalties. Georgia was the only one of the thirteen colonies that had not sent representatives to the Continental Congress at Philadelphia. Busy planning a non-importation agreement that would hit Great Britain where it hurt, in her trade, the Congress still had time to resent Georgia's indifference. As a Georgian, Hart found himself inevitably suspect among the radical youth of Harvard.

He did his best to write cheerfully to his mother, describing everything that was comic and different about his college life, without hinting at its loneliness, but she must have guessed at it, for she was soon writing to urge that he visit Abigail's cousins at Lexington. Abigail had written to them about him and had had a warmly hospitable reply. "Only," went on his mother's fine scrawl, "Abigail is not quite sure about their politics. You will be careful, my dear boy. . . ."

Careful! As if he was ever anything else. He tucked the letter rather irritably under a pile of books he had just fetched from the library, and reopened his Locke.

He was reading Locke three days later when he heard a light tapping on his door. It was a rare enough occurrence to be surprising. At his "Come in," the door was pushed open to reveal a strange young man older than himself and dressed with the rigorous plainness affected by so many New Englanders.

"Purchis?" The young man advanced with hand outstretched. "I'm your cousin from Lexington. Well!" He had a delightful full-throated laugh. "Courtesy cousin, if you like. Cousin Abigail wrote us about you, and I am here to welcome you to New England on behalf of all the family. Mark Paston, and most entirely at your service."

Hart took the outstretched hand. There was something irresistible both about the stranger's friendly greeting and about his unmistakable, fair-haired, blue-eyed likeness to Abigail. "I'm delighted to see you," he said. "You're very like your cousin."

"Am I? Poor girl. But what's this?" He reached out a friendly hand to take the book from Hart. "You're never reading Locke's *Second Treatise on Government!* What kind of Loyalist does that make you? My mother told me I was on no account to talk politics with you, and I always do what my mother tells me, but what am I to do when I find you reading such dangerous stuff?" He laughed again and handed back the book. "There will be time at home for politics, whatever Mother says. Right now, where's your hat, your greatcoat, your valise? I'm kidnapping you, carrying you off to the wilds of Lexington for a visit. My mother told me to bring you, and I warn you, what Mrs Paston says, goes." And then, seeing Hart hesitate, "Do come, cousin. I'm just back from a trip to Boston and I need some good company to take the taste of things there out of my mouth. The chaise is outside; it is but to pack a shirt or two, and we're on our way. I'll return you, all right and tight when you feel you must get back to your studies." And, as a clincher, "Bring your Locke, if you like, and we'll discuss him over the Madeira tonight. Come on, don't make me face my mother empty-handed; she's a Tartar when she's crossed and will slap all my sisters in turn out of very disappointment."

Hart could not help laughing. "How many sisters have you?"

"Seven, God help me. But no need to look so scared. I'll not let them plague you. In fact, the two eldest are married and the others are still in the nursery. But with Father dead, you can see how much I need male society. So come, pack up and let's go."

Half an hour later, Hart did indeed find himself riding in the chaise of this compelling new cousin of his, and very happy to be doing so. It was high autumn now, with the leaves bright on the trees, and the weeks of lonely study lay heavy behind him. Brimful of new ideas, he had been starved for someone to discuss them with, and when Mark Paston trailed a provocative remark about Locke and the social contract, he leapt at it and they were soon arguing away like old friends. Once, Mark Paston pulled him up short. He had said something that indicated his assumption that a constitutional monarchy was the only rational form of government, and Mark held up a warning hand. "All very well with me, cousin," he said, "but don't, I beg of you, say things like that in Lexington. We're pretty fierce there, you know. There's not a Loyalist dog of a Tory left in the place." And then, laughing that irresistible laugh of his, "If you could just see your own face! Don't worry, I won't let them eat you, and to tell the truth, I rather think you will find yourself more nearly agreeing with us desperate radicals than you expect."

"But won't I be an embarrassment to you?"

"Not a bit of it. A brand from the burning, more like. And besides, my position is such that I can carry it off. Jonas Clarke is my godfather and my best friend."

"Jonas Clarke?"

"You've not heard of him? He's our pastor in Lexington and the leader of the radicals there. And for good measure his wife is cousin to John Hancock, your treasurer at Harvard and another leading radical, as you must know. And Hancock and Sam Adams are firm friends. They've both approved everything we've done in Lexington so far."

"And what's that?"

"Organised a Committee of Safety, of which I'm proud to be a member, and begun to enrol our own militia. You see before you one of Lexington's Minutemen."

"Oh?"

"Cousin, have you talked to no one at Harvard?"

"Well"—it was painful to admit it—"very little."

"But you must know that the military governor, General Gage, has cancelled the legislative session of the Court of Massachusetts?"

"I did hear something." It had not, at the time, seemed to concern him very much.

"Well, when he did that, on top of all the repression that the citizens of Boston had suffered, we decided it was time to look to our defences. Minutemen, cousin, are volunteer soldiers ready to come out at a moment's notice. We are to have a citizens' army at last, and then let General Gage look about him! Look!" He pointed with his whip at a snug, white-painted farmhouse, set under a hill among flaming autumn leaves and neat stone-walled fields. "Don't you think we've made something here in New England that is worth fighting for?"

"But surely it's all a misunderstanding." He began to wish he was sure of it himself.

"That's as may be, but if so, it's one that is likely to cost Great Britain dear. But forgive me, cousin, I'll quit preaching at you. Tell, instead, something about Cousin Abigail."

Hart laughed. "I was just thinking about her and wondering what in the world she would say if she could hear our talk. If you think me a diehard Tory, what would you make of her, I wonder?"

"Well," said Mark tolerantly, "I reckon things are different for you, down in Georgia. I'm not one of those who want to quarrel with you for failing to send representatives to the Congress. Everyone knows you've been the spoiled darlings of government so long, it's hard for you to see the light. But see it you will, mark my words." And then, with one of his deep, warm bursts of laughter, "Lord, if I'm not back to politics. I cry you a thousand pardons, cousin! But, see, we're almost home." He slowed his horse for a moment at the top of the hill and pointed with his whip. "There, on the left is Munroe's Tavern—he's our sergeant of Minutemen, and a good one—and then the Mulliken house—she's a widow, poor thing—and just across the road, see, where the sumac is? That shabby old shingled house is the Paston mansion." He called an encouragement to his horse and they started down the hill. "Needs a coat of paint, don't it, but the living's friendly and the welcome warm for you, Cousin Hart. And, my gracious, hold your hat; the girls have spotted us." An attic window had been thrown open and two laughing, curly-headed girls were leaning out and waving their handkerchiefs.

"Mark!" cried one. "You're home at last!"

"And you brought him," said the other, then both withdrew their heads, closed the window with a bang, and vanished.

"The twins," explained Mark as the horse turned off the road towards the little house. "You'll get used to them." As he jumped down from the chaise, the door of the house flew open and the twins bounced out and flung themselves upon him.

They were followed by a plump, smiling, middle-aged woman dressed in brown homespun. "You brought him, Mark. I'm so pleased." She held out a welcoming hand to Hart as a boy appeared from round the side of the house to take charge of the horse and ask, quickly, what was the news from Boston.

"Not good," said Mark. "It's going to be a hard winter there, I'm afraid, what with British tyranny and mob violence. Yes, yes . . ." He fended off the twins. "I did my best with your commissions, but you'll be disappointed just the same. Things are even tighter in Boston than I had supposed. I managed to find the stocking needles, but you'll have to make your own silk mitts." And then, as their faces fell, "And if that's the worst privation you suffer, you'll be two lucky girls." He kissed his mother robustly on the cheek. "How are you, Mother, and how have the imps been behaving?"

"Well, and well. Come into the house, the two of you, and get warm after your drive. You must be starved with cold. I put back dinner in the hope you'd be here, Mark, and it will be on the table directly."

It was a frugal enough meal of boiled beef and dumplings, but made up in quality for what it lacked in variety. Aunt Anne Mayfield, thought Hart, would have been insulted by it; for his part, he was delighted both with the good, plain fare, washed down by sweet cyder, and the friendly family talk, in which even the youngest of the five girls joined. In Savannah, she and her next sister would have been upstairs with their black nurse; here they were very much part of the family, and he found he liked it.

Nor did he mind the volleys of questions with which the fifteen-year-old twins plied him. Sitting one on each side of him at table, they cross-examined him mercilessly about what they seemed to think the barbarous customs of Georgia. When they came to the question of slavery, he found himself remembering his first meeting with Mercy. "No," he told them. "We do not have slaves at Winchelsea, only servants, who, I hope, love us."

"Do they eat with you?" This was Ruth, older by half an hour than her sister, Naomi. She spiced the question with a significant glance for the other end of the big table, where the boy, Paul, was sitting tucking away a vast slice of apple pie.

"Well, no," said Hart.

Mark pushed back his chair. "Time you girls were back at your lessons," he said. "And gave your cousin a bit of peace. You'll get used to them, Cousin Hart, never fear."

"But I like it." Hart too rose to see the ladies out of the room. "It makes me realise what I missed through being an only child. You're lucky, Cousin Mark."

"I know," said Mark Paston.

7

"I'm worried to death about that boy." At Winchelsea, Mrs Purchis threw Hart's latest letter crossly on to her worktable. "He writes eternally about those Paston cousins of yours, Abigail, and they sound nothing but a parcel of arrant rebels to me."

"Not the children, surely?" As usual, Abigail did her best to soothe her aunt, and as usual, she failed.

"On the contrary—they're the worst of the lot!" She picked up the letter again. "Those twins! No conduct whatsoever, ridiculous names, and they dare to twit my son with the institution of slavery. They remind him of you, he says." A furious glance included Mercy in the general condemnation. "Imagine asking him if our servants eat with us!"

"Well, I eat with you." The guilt of her secret engagement had made Mercy wretchedly aware of her anomalous position in the household. Sometimes she actually found herself wondering if she should not have accepted that invitation of Saul Gordon's. But, even backed by Mrs Purchis, there had been something strange about it. Was it a nurse for his wife he wanted, or a substitute for her? Or, in his frugal way, both? She was not sure and had no intention of finding out.

And, luckily, Mrs Purchis had lost all interest in the scheme when Abigail became engaged to Giles Habersham. "I should hope so, too," she said now, "as indispensable as you are! What I should do without you when dear Abigail leaves us is more than I can imagine." She turned to Abigail, mercifully distracted from the subject of Hart's letter. "Have you and Giles agreed to name the day yet, child?"

Abigail laughed, sighed, blushed, and shook her fair curls. "No, Aunt. I have a perfect slow coach for a lover! He says we mustn't consider our own happiness at a time like this. His visit this morning was to tell me that Sir James has asked him to go on a special mission to England. He came, he said, for my permission, but I knew my place too well not to give it!"

"Why not marry him and go too?" asked Mercy.

"If only I could! We did speak of it a little, but he says the conditions on board ship will be too rough at this time of year, and besides, until he returns and Sir James finds him some more permanent office, he is hardly in a position to support a wife."

"If I were you, I'd go just the same," said Mercy stoutly. "Even if it meant washing the captain's shirts for your passage."

"I believe you would."

"Of course I would, but then it's different for me. I was brought up hard. You and Giles must know what is best for you."

"I hope so." Abigail looked down thoughtfully at the small ruby on her engagement finger.

"Naturally they do," intervened Mrs Purchis. "If dear Abigail had a dowry, everything would be different. I wish we could do more for you, my dear, but Francis says we'll be lucky if we break even this year, the way things are going."

"Dear Aunt." Abigail jumped up to kiss her. "Don't mind it! I only wish I could be the help to you that Mercy is."

"I wish I had the strength I used to have." Mrs Purchis had failed visibly since Hart had left, and had been glad to let much of the domestic management at Winchelsea slip into Mercy's capable hands. "As for you, child, you have enough to do with your trousseau. Let Mercy make herself useful; she likes it."

"Of course I do," said Mercy warmly. But Mrs Purchis' very kindness exacerbated her sense of guilt, and she made an excuse to meet Francis "by accident" that evening as he rode home from Savannah.

"You're out late." He dismounted as he saw her waiting for him halfway down the ilex avenue.

"Yes, I must speak to you, Francis."

"Must?"

"Yes. I've picked some flowers for my father's grave. Will you come with me?"

"Well." He looked doubtfully at the great white bulk of Winchelsea, illuminated now in the glow of a brilliantly setting sun. "We'd best not be long. It will be dusk soon."

"Dear Francis." She smiled up at him. "Please. I'm so unhappy."

"Unhappy? Why?" But he looped his horse's reins over his arm and turned to walk beside her towards the family lot at the back of the house.

Well, why? A trace of impatience in his tone made it hard for her to begin. "Mrs Purchis is so kind . . ." she started, hesitantly.

"Well, of course she's kind." No question about the impatience in his tone now. "Old and ailing as she is, she knows her luck in getting you for unpaid housekeeper."

"I'd do anything for her," said Mercy. "That's just why I so hate to deceive her. Francis, could we not tell her? About our engagement?"

"No!" It came out with the force of an explosion. "Dear Mercy." He had seen her face whiten. "We've been through all this before. You know it's impossible. You agreed . . ."

"Yes, but I didn't understand what it would be like. Deceiving people who have been so good to me . . ."

"I know." They had reached the graveyard now, and he tied his horse to a tree while she bent to lay the flowers on her father's grave. "It's hard. But if it's hard on you, Mercy, think how much harder it is on me. Loving you as I do, how can I bear to keep my happiness secret!" He turned for a quick, careful look at the trees that hid the house before he gathered her into his arms. "You'd been forgetting!" It was almost reproachful as he released her from the long, hard embrace.

"How could I?" But it was true. She had forgotten how the whole centre of her shook under the force of his kiss.

"Francis!" Despite herself, her arms were round his neck, her body worshipped him.

"That's better." He let her go at last, gently, laughing a little. "Inconstant puss." His tone cherished and mocked her. "Must we meet thus, every night, just to remind you of me? I doubt it would be safe for either of us."

"No." She looked up at him gravely, aware that the light was ebbing from the tops of the trees. "But, Francis, there was something else. About Abigail. Is there really no money for a dowry? I thought, from something Mr Gordon said . . ."

"Saul Gordon! That penny-lover! You'd believe him against me! Mercy! Is this your love? Your confidence in me?" He let her go so suddenly that she reeled and steadied herself with a hand against the Judas tree that grew beside her father's grave. "It's all of a piece," he went on, more angrily than ever. "You've never trusted me! If you did, you would tell me where your father hid that press of his."

"But, Francis, I don't know!"

"Don't know! Won't tell? Like to keep me dangling, looking a fool to my friends. . . ."

"Which friends, Francis?"

But he had turned angrily away to untie his horse. "Must get back. You know how quick the dark falls. I care for your good name, if you don't." And indeed, as they looked towards the big house they saw here and there the first flickers of light from indoors. "No time for more." Francis bent for one of his quick, hard kisses. "Go in at the front, love, while I go by the stables—and have some sense, do."

It was their first quarrel. Crying herself to sleep that night, she resolved it should be their last. But when she woke next morning it was to learn that Francis had ridden off, very early, to Savannah, and then to Charleston on some errand of his mother's. There was no message for her. How could there be?

He stayed in Charleston over Christmas, which was celebrated quietly enough at Winchelsea, since Hart was spending the vacation with the Pastons, and Giles Habersham had left on the long voyage to England. Naturally, Mercy had known that Francis would not be able to write to her, but had at least expected some trivial, significant Christmas gift. Instead, there were presents for all the family except her, and a long letter to his mother describing a party at which he had met "a very rich Miss Doone."

His next letter, proudly read aloud by his mamma, had further references to Miss Doone and a request that sounded oddly like a command. He thought it advisable that the ladies go into Savannah for the celebration of the Queen's birthday on January 18. "I know it is what Sir James Wright would wish."

"I suppose it is." Martha Purchis sounded doubtful.

"Frank says he will meet us there," said Anne Mayfield, as if that settled it, and indeed, it seemed to do so. Mercy and Abigail exchanged one long, troubled glance. They had never said a word about it to each other, but both knew that each of them found it disconcerting to see the extent to which Francis now behaved like the master of Winchelsea. Nothing she felt could blind clear-eyed Mercy to this, and Abigail had no cause to love him.

"I wish Hart would come home," she said now, secretly convinced that he would see she got her dowry.

But Hart was having what he affronted his mother by describing as "One of the best Christmases of my life. They do things quite differently in New England."

His letter found them in Savannah, where the Queen's birthday had been celebrated quietly enough by Sir James Wright and with scant courtesy by the radicals of Tondee's Tavern, who had grown more and more aggressive as the news came in of the sufferings of their fellows in Boston. Despite the generous supplies sent to the unemployed there by the other colonies, there was cold and hunger in Boston that winter, and conditions were inevitably exacerbated by the presence of British troops camped on the Common, and their officers billeted often on unwilling hosts. Perpetual small incidents threatened to blow up into large ones, and every time a letter came south, there were details of some new piece of oppression by the soldiers.

"I expect they get plenty of provocation," said Mercy.

"Yes," agreed Abigail. "There was something Hart said in his last letter about little boys throwing snowballs with nails in them."

"What's that?" Francis had come quietly into the room.

"We were talking about Boston," explained Abigail. "Something Hart said about boys throwing frozen snowballs at the soldiers."

"With nails in." Mercy had hoped in vain for a word alone with Francis, who had arrived the day before.

73

"He's crazy!" Now Francis sounded really angry. "Does he not know that most of the mail from Boston gets opened by the radicals in Charleston when it's landed from the packet? He'll get us all into trouble writing things like that!"

"Writing the truth?" asked Mercy.

"You can't be serious," chimed in Abigail. "They cannot possibly be opening private mail?"

"No? Then why, pray, did Sir James Wright take the trouble to send your beloved Giles all the way to England with his letters? You've not heard from him yet, I suppose?"

"No. It's much too soon, unless his ship had spoken another on the way over."

"Of course." Carelessly, "Stupid of me. Forgotten how recently he had left. I have been so much occupied in Charleston that the time seems long."

"Pleasantly occupied?" His mother broke one of the long silences in which she would sit, staring at nothing, so that one tended to forget she was in the room.

"Vastly so. Were it not for the duty I owe Hart at Winchelsea, I should urge that you and I go back there, get rid of our tenants, and enjoy ourselves for a change. Social life here in Savannah is positively primitive compared with Charleston. Why, at the Doones' the other night we sat down sixty to supper, after a ball as good as you could hope for in London."

"And what, pray, have you been using for money?" asked his mother with unwonted sharpness.

"Dear Mamma." He moved over to lean on the back of her chair and gaze down upon her with mocking affection. "Always so captious. Don't forget that my kind cousin now pays me a handsome—and well-earned—salary for my labours in the field. Besides, to tell truth, I had a good run at the tables over Christmas."

"Oh, Francis," wailed his mother, "you're never gambling again! Oh, where is my vinaigrette!"

"What else is there to do in life?" He said it, across his mother's back, with a strange, hard glance for Mercy. And then, half-concealing a yawn, "How do we propose to entertain ourselves tonight? If at all."

"We dine out. Have you forgotten? With the McCartneys. Your Aunt Purchis insists that we go, though she is not well enough. I hope you will find it sufficiently entertaining after the gaieties of Charleston. Mary McCartney said there would be dancing for the young people."

"Ten couples! And the butler scraping away on his fiddle. I'd as lief be out ruralising at Winchelsea."

"The McCartney girls are very charming," said his mother.

"Dear Mamma!" Tolerantly, "What a good friend you are! Oh, I suppose Bridget's well enough in her freckled way, but I doubt Claire will ever see thirty again. No wonder if their mother has taken to entertaining all Savannah."

"All Savannah accepts her invitations," reminded Mrs Mayfield. "They remember, if you don't, Francis, that there's a dollar for every freckle."

"It would have to be a thousand to tempt me. But, never look downcast, Mamma, I'll trip it with the best of their ten couples tonight. Particularly, if Cousin Abigail will honour me with the first dance? And"—slowly turning towards Mercy —"Miss Phillips with the second?"

So, at last, she was to have her chance to speak to him alone. The February evening was mild, even for Savannah, and the McCartneys' ballroom oppressively hot from the scores of candles glittering in candelabra along the walls. The doors were soon thrown open onto a paved terrace overlooking the Common and young couples danced their way out into the half darkness. "Scandalous." Francis guided Mercy skilfully through the doors as the music of their dance came to an end. "But pleasant." He led her to the far end of the terrace, lifted the hand that did not wear his ring, and kissed it. "I've a pardon to beg, Mercy," he said. "I've behaved like a brute to you, but it's for your protection. Besides, how can I help it, when you hurt me so by your lack of confidence in me?"

"But, Francis . . ."

"Hush!" He looked quickly round. "Must be careful, love . . . must bear with me while I play the gallant to my Charleston Misses Doone and those freckle-dollared Mc-Cartneys. It's for your own comfort I do it. What would happen to you, do you think, if my mother and aunt were to guess at what's between us? Don't imagine that Hart could be any protection to you, way off in Harvard, and taken up with those Pastons. You'd be out in the street, my dear, and enemies enough waiting for you."

"Enemies?"

"Don't think those savages who killed your father have forgotten you, do you? You've convinced me, at least, that you truly don't know about that press of his. But if I, who love you and want to trust you, am still sometimes a prey to doubt, what do you imagine the Liberty Boys think? Don't walk alone here in Savannah."

"I never do."

"Of course not. My aunt would not allow it, or I should have warned you against it long since. In Winchelsea you are safe enough, so long as the slaves stay faithful."

"Slaves?"

"Servants, then." Laughing, "Suits my cousin to call them so." He looked up quickly at the sound of one shot, fired somewhere over towards the river. "Oh, my God!"

"What is it?"

"Trouble. Been on edge all evening; half expecting it. Lot of talk earlier at Tondee's. Hoped I'd calmed them down."

"But what is it?"

"That fool of a customs collector seized a cargo of Andrew Wells' for failure to pay dues. Eight hogsheads of molasses and six of French sugar. All impounded down at the dock. Know who Wells is?"

"No."

"Brother-in-law to that madman Sam Adams who's behind all the trouble in Boston. Wells was preaching mayhem and murder at Tondee's this afternoon. Mercy—" Once again he looked round to make sure they could not be overheard.

"Yes?"

"Now is the time to show you trust me. Love me. That I can trust you."

"Yes?" she said again.

"Must go. My duty. Stop them if it's not too late. But I'd much rather not be seen in it."

"No?"

"No." Impatiently, "I know it's hard for a female to understand, but these are dangerous times. One must act for the best, but secretly, carefully. . . ."

"Yes. So what would you have me do?"

"Hide somewhere in the garden here till I return, so that we can say we were together all the time."

"But your mother—"

"Will scold, if it comes out. Very likely will not. I took the precaution of asking no other ladies to dance, save Abigail, and you, if I know Savannah, are not heavily engaged."

"No." She admitted it defiantly. "Your Savannah young

76

men know me for what I am."

"Ah, love, but so do I. An ally in a million." He bent, quickly, to kiss her full on the lips, then vaulted the low wall that bounded the terrace and was gone.

Mercy looked about her. He had led her to the end of the terrace farthest from the lighted double doors, and they had been standing concealed in the entrance of a small summer pavilion that backed against the wall on the corner of Whitaker Street and the Common. Luckily for her the musicians had struck up again and the other couples were moving back towards the doors. She retreated quickly into the darkness of the pavilion where a stone bench was arranged to command a summer view of the Common. For her, it had the advantage of being concealed from the terrace. She sat down, gathering her light-coloured skirts closely about her, so that they should not betray her to some couple who might decide to stay out for the dance. If she was discovered, she thought coldly, explanation would be unnecessary. Francis had been brutally correct in what he said about her position.

The gentlemen of Savannah knew her for the indentured man's daughter she was. That was why Saul Gordon had been able to make his dubious offer. Only Hart, and Giles Habersham, and of course, Francis were invariably courteous to her. The other young blades of Savannah had a way of looking straight through her that she tried hard to find comic. But, tonight, if she was found sitting here alone, it would simply be assumed that she had been ashamed of being partnerless. Normally, on such an occasion, she would have joined the older ladies at the card tables, for she had achieved something of a reputation for her skill at whist and was much sought after as what was usually called a "lucky" partner. But tonight Francis was here. Had been here.

There had not been another shot, but now, intensely listening as the musicians paused for a moment, she heard a sound with which she had grown all too familiar since that first, dreadful day. Francis had been right. The mob was out, and in force. Worse still, she rather thought they were coming towards the Common. Towards this house, where Mrs McCartney, a widow with two daughters to marry off, entertained Whig and Tory alike?

Ought she to give the alarm? The noise of the mob was

perceptibly nearer now. It was beginning to be possible to distinguish individual shouts from the general ominous roar. "Death to taxes," she heard, and "Down with the Collector," and, oddly, "May they swim to hell." The crowd was very near now. To give the alarm would be to fail Francis, and yet— Those lighted windows were an invitation to violence.

She rose to her feet, shaking a little from remembered reaction to the horrible, half-human noise, then paused, as a group of men's figures appeared in the light of the house doors. They, too, had obviously heard the approaching tumult. One of them turned back indoors, and one by one, the lights began to go out in the house. The musicians missed a note and stopped. In the ballroom someone was saying something, doubtless urging silence, caution, but, just the same, the terrace was already filling up with silent figures, men and women, watching, listening. The mob must be as near as South Broad Street now, coming fast along Whitaker.

The terrace was crowded. She chose a moment when a particularly loud cry of "Death to the British," held the attention of the couples nearest to her, and slipped quietly out of the pavilion, to mingle with the crowd. Her story, if she was challenged, must be that she had come out with Francis, who had left her for a moment to find out what was happening.

The mob debouched onto the Common, torches flaring, a fife tauntingly playing "Yankee Doodle"—a great burst of shouting, and then a queer, horrid, waiting silence. "What's the crime?" shouted a voice. A gentleman's voice.

The silence prolonged itself for a moment, then the answer came with a roar, "Treason to the people of Savannah."

"What's the verdict?"

Again that stretching silence, while on the terrace near her people whispered to each other, anxious, irresolute. More torches had been brought onto the Common, and Mercy, straining her eyes, could see, not far from the house, a group of people round a horse that had something laid crossways over the saddle. Something? Someone? She was shaking all over now, remembering her father.

"Death!" came a voice. A few others took up the cry. In the flaring, uncertain light of the torches, Mercy could see that the group who seemed to be leading the crowd were dressed as sailors, with blackened, featureless faces. The other men had hats pulled down or collars turned up so as to be almost equally unrecognisable. Now, she thought, the first voice spoke again. Certainly it was again a gentleman's. "No, no. Not worth death. A mere tide waiter. Tarring and feathering will teach him, and his like, a lesson. Besides, we've an audience." He waved a hand towards the McCartney house. "Let us show the ladies and gentlemen of Savannah that the Sons of Liberty deal in justice, not tyranny. Where's the tar"—he hurried on, over-riding a few scattered cries of "Death"—"and the feathers?"

At one point in his speech, Mercy's teeth had clenched so hard together that her whole head throbbed. Almost fainting, she put out a hand to steady herself against the terrace wall, then stood, an automaton, watching the horrible business go forward. The tar was ready; the man was stripped palely naked; a gasp, part horror part pleasure, went up from the crowd and was echoed shockingly by the watchers on the terrace.

"How about *them*?" called a rough voice. "We don't want no haudience!" A rock, thrown from the edge of the crowd broke a window, showering the watchers on the terrace with glass.

"Inside! All of you!" Francis appeared beside Mercy. "It's not safe here. Quick!"

"But that poor man," objected one of the gentlemen. The ladies were already scurrying indoors, with little squeaks of mixed horror and fright as they shook fragments of glass off muslin skirts.

"If we try to help him, they'll kill him." Francis' voice rose above the tumult. "He's lucky to get away with tarring and feathering, with the mob in the temper it is. If we intervene, we'll only make matters worse. Like as not they'll burn down this house, and God knows what would happen to the ladies."

"You're right," said one voice. "We must think of the ladies," chimed in another. "Who is he, I wonder?" asked a third.

"Some poor devil from the docks, I'm afraid," said Francis. "There was a lot of wild talk at Tondee's today about that cargo of Andrew Wells' that got sequestrated. It looks as if the mob has taken the law into its own hands."

"Oh, is that it?" The men were lingering out in the protective darkness, their faces invisible to each other despite the glow of torches that showed the mob still horribly busy on

79

the Common. "Well, fair enough, maybe," put in another speaker. "Poor Andrew. If you ask me, Sir James picked on him because of that New England cousin of his, Sam Adams."

"Well, Sir James made a mistake," said another voice.

"Looks like it," said Francis. "But come, gentlemen, best get indoors and comfort the ladies. The sooner all is shuttered and quiet here, the better." And as if to give point to his words, a glaring torch, flung over the terrace wall, lit up horrified faces for a moment, then sputtered out on the paving stones. It started a new rush indoors, and Francis was hard put to it to protect Mercy from the shoving and pushing of the "gentlemen" of Savannah.

Inside, chaos. Mrs McCartney was swooning on one of a pair of sofas and Anne Mayfield on the other. Young ladies were crying and wringing their hands, while the card players, who had been in a back room, had crowded in to see what was the matter, the room's only illumination provided by the light that streamed in with them. The three musicians had dropped their instruments and were gazing with a kind of open-mouthed relish at the scene.

"Quick!" Francis turned on them. "You there, close the shutters and look sharp about it. Mrs McCartney, may I send for someone to clear up the glass? I am afraid one of the young ladies might hurt herself. And we need a taper to relight the candles as soon as the shutters are closed. You will take charge, ma'am, with your usual strong common sense, I am sure."

"Yes. Yes, of course." Mrs McCartney dropped her vinaigrette and sat up straight on the sofa. "You, James," she called a footman who had been standing by the doorway apparently enjoying the scene, "fetch a light, quick, and one of the girls to clear up in here."

"And perhaps a glass of something for the company?" suggested Francis. "I know it's a little early."

"Yes, indeed!" As she gave the necessary orders, the last shutter banged to and the footman started relighting the candles. People began to talk again, low and anxious, only to be silenced as the steady roar from outside suddenly rose to that subhuman shriek Mercy remembered so well. Faces, already pale, turned ashen. Mrs Mayfield fell back into her swoon.

"You there," said Francis to the musicians, "strike up, can't you! Something lively."

"It's not decent." Mercy turned on him.

"Have you a better idea?"

"No." She had to admit it. "But . . ."

"Later," he interrupted swiftly. "Go and revive my mother, for God's sake, and stop her making an exhibition of herself. If you can."

Mercy found Abigail there before her, offering her vinaigrette and the cherry bounce that servants were now handing round to the ladies, while the gentlemen retired, one by one, to the downstairs room where stronger stuff awaited them. "It's monstrous," said Mercy.

"Yes," agreed Abigail. "But Francis is quite right. There is nothing in the world we can do. There, Aunt Anne, take a sip of that and you will feel better."

"What happened?" Mrs Mayfield made a little business of "recovering consciousness" and gazed round her in apparent puzzlement.

"The mob is out, Aunt. They're tarring and feathering a poor man on the Common."

"Horrible!" Mrs Mayfield shuddered artistically and took a good pull at her cherry bounce. "Barbarians." Another sip. "Brutes. That poor man." And then, on a note of genuine misery, "I don't feel well. I want to go home!"

"Not yet, I'm afraid." Francis had just re-entered the room. "I don't suppose you want to encounter the mob yourself. I've been out to reconnoitre. The worst is over, I think, and they're beginning to drift away, but we must trespass on Mrs McCartney's hospitality awhile longer, I'm afraid." He bowed across to where she still sat on the other sofa.

"No, indeed!" She, too, was feeling rather the better for her cherry bounce. "You mustn't leave me and the girls with no one but the servants to protect us. But is it all over, Mr Mayfield? Is the poor man . . ." She left the sentence unfinished.

"I couldn't get near enough to see just what they've done to him, but he'll be lucky if they don't end up riding him out of town on a rail."

"Oh, the poor thing." And then, on a quite different note, "But at least it should get them away from here."

"Yes." A quick glance for Mercy recognized her sublime selfishness. "I rather hope it should."

Half an hour later, the Common was quiet, with only the smouldering end of a torch here and there to show what had happened. It was still early, by Savannah standards, but there was no life left in Mrs McCartney's party, and her guests were soon summoning their carriages, despite her pleas that someone stay and protect her and her "poor defenceless girls."

"No need to fret, ma'am." Crisis seemed to suit Francis. "Lightning doesn't strike twice. You're probably safer here than we will be on our way home. Who knows, we may yet encounter the mob."

8

They got home unmolested, though the embers of torches, still glowing in the sand of South Broad Street and Broughton, suggested that the mob had indeed paraded their unfortunate victim through the town. And Francis, out early next morning, came back with a grave face. "I'm afraid the tarring and feathering wasn't the worst of it," he told the two girls. "There were two sailors on guard at the dock with the tide waiter. The mob threw them in the river. One of them couldn't swim."

"You mean—" Mercy looked as if she had not slept.

"He's vanished. Drowned, for sure. A hanging business if they can identify the ringleaders of the mob."

"Will they be able to?" This time it was Abigail who asked the question.

"I doubt it. The survivor swears the men who manhandled him had their faces so blackened he had no chance of recognizing them. But they were gentlemen, he says. And"—with an ironical laugh—"in the confusion, the sugar and molasses that caused the trouble seem to have vanished. Sir James has offered a fifty-pound reward for information. I wish him luck."

"Murder," said Mercy.

"Mr Wells?" asked Abigail.

"I don't believe I'd even speculate about it, if I were you, cousin. These are strange times."

"What of the poor tide waiter?" Mercy made herself ask the question.

"Vanished, poor man, and do you wonder. What with the pain and the shame, I doubt we'll see him in town again."

"Horrible," said Abigail. "Ah, there's Aunt Martha's bell at last. I wondered if she and your mother would ever wake this morning. I'll just see how they are."

"Do, there's a good cousin, while I persuade Mercy here to pay a visit of sympathy to Mrs McCartney. I think we should, don't you?"

"It would be more to the point to condole with that poor tide waiter," said Mercy more tartly than she had intended.

"He wouldn't thank you. Mrs McCartney will."

"She'd rather have Abigail." They were alone now.

"Yes, love, I know, but I would rather have you. And if I know anything, Abigail will be busy all morning with the two old tabbies upstairs. Oh, yes"—he smiled at her shocked face—"I know one of them's my mother, but if we can't be honest with each other, you and I—"

It warned her what to expect. He had chosen to drive her himself in his gig and had no sooner got her comfortably settled beside him that he was back at the old theme of her father's press. "Must understand now, Mercy, what a risk you run. The mob have not tarred and feathered a woman yet, but"—he paused—"I'm afraid they would enjoy it."

"I wish you had given me an engagement ring."

"Why?" She had surprised him, as she intended.

"So that I could throw it in your face. If you will not believe me in this, how can I trust you with myself?"

"How can you not? Surely you must realise that all this winter I have used such influence as I have at Tondee's Tavern to protect you? If I withdraw it"—he flicked his horse with the whip—"you'll not be riding like a lady in a gig, but like a harlot, out of town on a rail. I can save you, Mercy Phillips, or destroy you. Only, I must have your help. If your father truly did not tell you where he had hidden that wretched press, surely you know him—knew him—well enough to make some kind of guess?"

"Oh." Wearily, "If it's guesses you want . . . I hadn't thought to waste your time with something so vague and so unpromising."

"No?" He slowed the horse again, turning towards her eagerly. "But?"

"Well, those last few days, when the news from town was so bad, Father set me to work cleaning the house. He said we might have to flee at any minute, and we must leave all things in order behind us. He was like that, Father—"

"Yes?" Impatiently now. They had reached South Broad Street.

"The press was hidden behind a stack of wood in the barn. He went out every day while I was cleaning and scouring. I watched when I could. He took a spade and went down towards the river . . . every day, for three days, four? I don't rightly remember. Then, one night when the moon was at the full, I woke and found him gone. He was back in the morning. I said nothing. Why should I? Only—"

"Yes?"

"Next day I went to the barn for wood. The press was gone."

"You didn't ask him?" Furiously.

"If he had wanted me to know, he would have told me."

It was unanswerable, or at least he found it so. "Mercy." He slowed the horse at the McCartneys' door. "If I've spoken harshly, it's out of anxiety for you. You'll forgive me? Forget?"

She looked up at him with wide eyes. "You know I can't help myself, Francis."

"That's my girl." He jumped down, swung her to the ground, and called a boy to hold his horse.

Mrs Purchis insisted that they go back to Winchelsea next day, and Mercy was glad of it. She rather thought Francis had frightened his aunt into the move, and thought him wise. And back on the plantation, she respected the energy with which he threw himself into improving the warning system Hart had set up the year before. Extraordinary to think that it was almost a year since her father's death. Visiting his grave under its flowering Judas tree in the quiet family lot by the river, to dress the sunken rectangle with fresh leaves and a few sprays of wild jasmine, she looked up and saw Francis riding towards her on his way back from the rice fields.

"Hoped I'd find you here." He looped his horse's reins round a branch of the Judas tree. "See how I study your habits, little sphinx. You've been avoiding me. Frightened of the old tabbies?"

"A little." She yielded herself to his hard embrace, aware, as she did so, that he had made sure they were out of sight of the house.

"No need." He laughed. "I can manage them." He looked down at the sunken grave. "Pity we can't give him a head-stone, but better not. No use asking for trouble. Reminding the mob. D'you know what I think's kept them away this winter?"

"No. What?"

"The absurd letters Hart writes about his visits to those Pastons. Everyone who knows anything is aware there's not a Loyalist left in Lexington. Every time my idiot aunt reads one of Hart's letters aloud, full of philosophical talk she can't understand, don't you think it's reported right back to Tondee's?" This time his laugh was harsher. "Used to flatter myself I had some influence with them on my own account, but now, sometimes, I wonder if they don't bear with me as Hart's cousin. It wouldn't altogether surprise me if he were to receive a summons home, if things got worse."

"Hart? A summons from the Whigs? But, Francis, you know as well as I do that everything he writes confirms he is still a Loyalist at heart. It's just—"

"Just that he likes those Pastons more than a little? Two young girls hanging on every word he says? A clever friend older than himself, leading him by the nose until he doesn't know what he is saying, still less thinking? Sometimes, Mercy, I wonder if I shouldn't send for him home myself?"

"But would he come?"

"Ah, there's the rub. Besides, we're doing well enough as we are, it seems to me."

"And to me. I'd never have thought—" She stopped.

"That an idle good-for-nothing like me could turn such a neat hand to the plough? Well, dear Mercy, you must know what the inducement is. Shall I not be an excellent farmer when you and I are Darby and Joaning it in the West?"

"It's hard to believe." She looked up at him wide-eyed. "Oh, Francis, will it be very long?"

"Who knows? Maybe!" He bent for a quick, light, teasing kiss. "Maybe not! Maybe you'll be a married lady when Miss Abigail is still wearing the willow for that slow-top Giles of hers. Don't try to tell me he couldn't have been back here long since if he really wished it."

"She says he feels he's too usefully occupied among the

85

British Whigs who sympathize with our troubles."

" 'She says!' " Scornfully—then, "Hush! There's someone coming." He moved quickly away from her and was bent, re-arranging a spray of jasmine, when Abigail joined them.

"There you are, Mercy. I thought—I was afraid I'd find you here. Would you very much mind coming in? Mrs McCartney is come out to visit us from town, and my aunts want you for a fourth at whist. You know what a dunder-head I am!"

"Mrs McCartney? All the way from Savannah?" said Francis sharply. "What news brings her?"

"Nothing to speak of."

"You mean, nothing she's spoken of. Well, let's go and greet this venturesome lady." He looped the reins of his horse over one arm and used the other to guide Abigail away from the burial ground. Turning to look back, he saw Mercy bend to pick up the sprig of jasmine he had touched, and smiled.

At the house, he found himself proved right. Mrs Mc-Cartney was indeed the bearer of news. A ship had docked from France with a cargo of silks and laces, of which she thought her dear friends would want early information. And with a coy glance for Francis, "What I expect will interest Mr Mayfield more, Sir James has dissolved the Assembly."

"He has, has he? Why, pray?"

"Because he's had enough, I think. That Georgia Provincial Congress the rebels made bold to call has elected three delegates to the Continental Congress, *and* voted to join the non-importation association. So you see, dear Martha, dear Anne, you would be well advised to come into town and stock up on some elegant trifles before it is too late. I doubt, once we are known to belong to the non-importation lot, the British won't let French ships, or any others, land here."

"But why dissolve the Assembly?" asked Francis.

"Well." She made big eyes at him over her fan. " 'Tis like he thought they might approve what the rebels had done. You know as well as I do that many of the Assembly members are on the rebels' Provincial Congress too." She was looking unusually handsome today, Mercy thought, and then realised why. She had discarded the mourning she habitually wore for her husband, and looked, as a result, at least a generation younger than Mrs Purchis and Mrs Mayfield. She must have been married out of the cradle to have two grown daughters. "The girls are down at the wharf already." She spoke of them now. "Hoping for the first choice. You will find them monstrous fine when you next do us the honour of calling, Mr Mayfield."

"They will be hard put to it to outshine their handsome mamma, Mrs McCartney. It's good to see you in colours again at last."

She smiled, blushed a little, and flirted her fan. "La, Mr Mayfield, only fancy your noticing. To tell the truth"—she leaned forward to include them all in the confession—"I thought, since the non-importation forbids mourning, as requiring imported goods, it might seem a patriotic gesture to leave my blacks. And it has been some little time since my poor dear Mr McCartney—" She left the sentence unfinished, drooping elegantly in her chair, and Mrs Purchis took the cue to ring and order refreshments. "You will need a glass of cordial before we begin our game."

But Mrs McCartney, accepting the cordial, declined the game of whist. "In truth, my dear creature, I have stayed a monstrous time already and must be on my way or I'll be benighted. Just think if I should encounter the mob in my way across the Common! God knows what they may not be up to tonight, with the Assembly dissolved."

"You're right." Francis stood up. "What escort did you bring?"

"Why, just my coachman, my faithful footman, and an outrider."

"Not enough." He put down his glass. "Should have apologised for joining you in my riding clothes, but now I'm glad of it. With your good leave, I'll see you safe home. No need to look so anxious, Mamma. I'll spend the night in town, do some business with Gordon in the morning, and be home for dinner, with the latest news and such silks and laces as you ladies trust me to buy."

This was a clincher so far as the two older ladies were concerned, and if Mercy thought he was more eager for news than for silks and laces, she kept her thoughts, as usual, to herself.

In Cambridge, it had been an unusually mild winter. Hart was lucky, the Pastons told him, to have his first experience of a New England winter such an easy one. "Why, here you are for your spring vacation," Mrs Paston greeted him on a fine April Saturday, "and the ground's thawed already

87

and the spring ploughing well begun. Poor Mark has had to leave his books to help."

"Then I will go and join him," said Hart. "I'd like to see how you manage this bleak New England soil of yours."

"Bleak!" She laughed up at him. "Just because it has a few rocks in it. And see how useful they are for our walls. You'll find Mark in the pasture beyond the Common, the one by Jonas Clarke's house. Unless he's sneaked in for the latest news from Jonas. He's got Mr Adams and Mr Hancock staying with him, has Jonas Clarke, while the Provincial Congress meet in Concord. I don't know how Lucy Clarke manages, with those eight children and dear knows how many guests besides. In fact"—she had ushered him into the big main room of the house as they talked—"if you do reckon to go and join Mark, I might make bold to ask if you'd take some of my cookies to Lucy as you go. She must be hard put to it, with things the way they are. Would you mind?" She had suddenly remembered the Southern gentleman they used to think him.

"Mind? Of course not." Hart, too, remembered a time when he would have thought this an extraordinary commission. "In fact"—he had put his grip in the small downstairs room he always used, and now turned back to her—"I'm as bad as Mark, I'm afraid. I'll be glad of an excuse to go and hear the latest news from Concord. Besides, I'd like to see Mr Adams and Mr Hancock; I've heard so much about them."

"I dare swear you have!" Once again, laughter creased the familiar lines across her weather-beaten face, and he found himself wondering what Mark's father had been like. "Don't tell the twins you heard me swearing," she went on. "I'd never live it down. They're at the dame school. Village school's closed. Economy!" She sniffed. "I don't call it economy to stint the children of their learning. There." As she talked, she had been deftly packing fresh-baked cookies into a home-made flat wicker basket. "With my kind love, for Lucy. And I'll expect you and Mark for dinner, and no excuses. If the Minutemen need drilling, let Captain Parker do it, and let Mark take an evening off for once, in honour of his guest."

"I'll do my best, ma'am." Hart took the basket and set off down the familiar road to the Common. As he passed Widow Mulliken's house, young Nathaniel raised a friendly hand in greeting, and Hart, shouting a "good day," thought how pleasant it was to have near neighbours, as one did in New England. It was very different from the remote plantation life of Georgia. But he did not much want to think about Georgia. He would talk about his mother's letter presently, when he and Mark had a moment alone. And, thinking this, he thought all over again how lucky he was to have found such a cousin and such a friend.

Reaching the Common, he took the right fork of the road by Buckman's Tavern and paused for a moment outside its stables to look across to the silent school and wonder which of the village dames was teaching the Paston twins. At the next corner, where the Bedford road turned off, he shouted a greeting to Ruth Harrington, who was hanging out her washing between the blossoming apple trees beside her house. She called back a cheerful answer and added, "If you find my Jonathan up at Clarke's, send him home with a flea in his ear for me, Mr Purchis. All these politics are mighty grand, I reckon, but we've got the boy to feed and the spring planting not started yet."

"I'll tell him," Hart called back. "And I'll give him a hand, too, when Mark can spare me."

"Thanks." She turned back to her clothes line, and he strode on towards the Clarke house, and the meadow that Mark had hired from Jonas Clarke, because the minister was too busy to farm it. No sign of life there, so he crossed the road towards the Clarke house, only to see Mark emerging from it.

"Hart!" Mark shook his hand warmly. "It's good to see you. What's the news from Harvard?"

"Not much. Everyone's gone home. And what from Concord?"

"This and that. Next time the British come out on one of those marches of theirs, we're to call out the Minutemen and keep an eye on them. Good training for the men, I reckon, and might teach the British something."

"Mark! You wouldn't attack them!"

"Lord, no, it's just a gesture. Defensive only, the order is, unless they should be fools enough to attack."

"Which they won't," said Hart positively. "You know how cool General Gage has played it all winter. I'm sure he's hoping for a settlement that will leave us all friends again."

"Let's hope you're right," said Mark. "So long as it really is that. It's going to take a good deal to satisfy men like

Sam Adams, I can tell you."

"I know." No need to go back over the long winter's discussions, which had left them such good friends and, Hart sometimes thought, so surprisingly close in their beliefs. Up here in New England, things seemed different, somehow. He must remember to ask Mark's advice about how to answer that disturbing, angry letter of his mother's. She actually seemed to think that his loyalty to the Crown was in doubt. Absurd. He did look at things differently, perhaps, but he remained a loyal subject of King George, and so did Mark, who was often scandalised by Sam Adams' revolutionary pronouncements.

The next day, Sunday, April 16, saw an unusual amount of activity in Lexington. Mrs Paston, who did not believe in Sunday travel, was scandalised. "They keep riding by," she told the young men. "I don't see how I can teach the children to keep the Sabbath if they see so many breaking it. I've a good mind to speak to Jonas Clarke. They're all going to his house."

"It must be urgent," said Mark, "or he'd not allow it. I'll walk along there later on." He did not invite Hart to join him.

The rumour was soon all over the village. The British were planning one of their armed excursions into the countryside. There were various explanations of this. They were coming to arrest Mr Adams and Mr Hancock. No, they were coming to seize the stores of powder and provisions that had been carefully gathered and hoarded in Concord throughout the winter. Or, no again, they were simply making one of their occasional displays of force.

"But this time," said Mark, "we are going to watch and follow them. How glad I am you're here, Hart. I'd not much like to leave Mother and the girls on their own if they do call out the Minutemen."

"Absurd," said Mrs Paston. "As if any harm could come to us! But"—recognising Mark's tactful intention—"that's not to say I won't be happier with a man about the place."

Two days later, a breathless messenger tapped at the door of the Paston House, just when Mark and Hart, who had done a long day's ploughing, were beginning to think of bed. "The British are coming," he told Mark, and then qualified it with "I think. All events, Sergeant Munroe's got a guard at the Clarke house, and we're to rally on the Common."

"Right!" Mark was already reaching for his musket, powder-horn, and cartridge box from their place behind the door. "I won't rouse Mother." He turned to Hart after the messenger had hurried on to the next house. "No need to fret her, and it's most likely just another rumour."

"Right." But it was strange to be left alone in the house with only the sleeping women above stairs. Strange and sad. Those were his friends who were gathering on the Common. Mark and Nat Mulliken and Jonathan Harrington and Captain Parker. He heard footsteps hurrying by and wondered which other of their neighbours had been roused and gone to join his friends and do his duty as he saw it. Strange to think how horrified his mother would be if she could know that he was sitting here, watching over the Paston women, while Mark attended what she would think a treasonable assembly.

It was very quiet in the house, and getting cold. He put more wood on the fire, determined that he would stay up until Mark returned, and fetched Hume's *History of England* from his room. But he could not concentrate. From time to time, the sound of a horse passing on the road took him to the window, but it was too dark by now, with the moon not yet risen, to make out faces. Lunatic to think the British would come tonight. And yet there was still much more activity than usual on the road.

Time dragged. The old clock in the kitchen struck midnight, then one, then two. The moon was up now and he longed to walk a little way towards the Common to see what was happening. But Mark had left him in charge here. He turned another page, then realised he had not taken in a word. Was that the sound of voices? He hurried to the door and, looking out, saw a little group of men approaching, the muskets they carried making strange shapes in the moonlight.

"False alarm." Mark had seen him standing in the lighted doorway. "There's not a sign of the British. Good night, boys. Let out a holler if you find the redcoats camped up at Munroe's Tavern."

This raised a laugh from the other men who lived farther down the Boston road. "Phew, I'm frozen." Mark closed the door and moved over to the fire. "Thanks for keeping it up for me. Get any work done?" He had noticed Hume lying on the table.

"Not much. Is it really all a false alarm?"

"Seems so. Not a word from our scouts. Parker's left a guard on the Clarke house, and the men from farther out are stopping the night at Buckman's Tavern, but the rest of us are stood down. If anything should come up, young Bill Diamond will summon us with that drum he reckons so much to. Too late to go to bed now." He pulled his favourite chair to the fire. "I reckon I'll see the night out down here, just in case, but there's no need for you to."

"Oh, I'll stay." They were both tired and sat there in companionable silence, dozing and waking in the mellow light of the fire. The clock had struck four and, outside, a first bird was chirping in salute to a pre-dawn change in the quality of the darkness, when Mark stirred and sat bolt upright in his chair.

"What was that?" He moved a little stiffly over to open the door and peer out into misty darkness. It came again, unmistakable, the sharp tap of a drum. "Bill Diamond. They must be coming after all. And most of us dispersed. We'll make a poor show of it, I'm afraid. Don't let the girls do anything stupid, Hart, if they should wake." As he spoke he had quickly collected his equipment. "See you at breakfast. Tell Ma some of her griddle-cakes wouldn't come amiss." He shut the door quietly and was gone.

It was getting lighter momently. The relentless beat of the drum continued, and Hart was not surprised to hear footsteps in the bedroom above. "What is it?" Mrs Paston opened the door at the foot of the attic stair, her hair bundled up under her cap, a shawl held closely round her long flannel nightdress.

"The British really seem to be coming." Hart quickly told her of the night's events.

"And you've been guarding us. Thanks. Well, I'd best get dressed and go to work on those griddle-cakes. Mark will be fair famished after this night's alarms. I hope the British don't loiter. I sunppose they're for Concord?"

"I don't know. Mark said something about a guard at the Clarke house."

"They'd never come all this way just for that old windbag Sam Adams. Dear God, what's that?"

A new noise. A kind of dull counterpoint to that agitated

drumming. The sound of marching feet? And another drum? "So soon?" Pulling her shawl more closely round her, she stared at him, eyes dilated with what he recognised, anxiously, as fear. "Hart! It sounds like a whole army. It could mean trouble."

"Surely not. Just a demonstration." He looked longingly at the door. "They'll be here any minute. Do you think . . ."

"Yes! Run, quick! The back way. Tell them to be careful —tell them it's a whole army. They'll be tired, the British, marching all night. Tired men act stupid sometimes. I wish it was day." She saw him hesitate. "Go on, Hart, please. They won't hurt us, that's one thing certain—women and children. Not the British."

"No." When he opened the door, the thud of marching feet sounded alarmingly near, the tap of a drum, the rattle of harness; he was across the road, making for the path that skirted the hill behind Mulliken's and cut a corner off the road to the Common. Lucky he knew it so well. There were lights in the Loring and Merriam houses. He cut behind them, splashed through the Vine Brook, and emerged, panting, just across the road from Buckman's Tavern. Now, the urgent tap of William Diamond's drum almost drowned that other, more menacing sound of marching feet.

Torches flared here and there on the Common. People hurried to and fro. The door of Buckman's Tavern was open, casting its beam of light on to the confused scene and making faces harder to distinguish. Where was Mark? He must give his warning, and only Mark was sure to listen. Captain Parker was shouting, trying to urge his men into line. Into line? Why? No—two lines. Absurd, ridiculous. About two dozen men, or maybe three, forming up to challenge the armed might of Great Britain. *They'll laugh at us*, he thought, and then, *Us?*

Where was Mark? Somewhere in that awkwardly forming line, but where? Speak to Captain Parker? Too late. As he had hesitated, the marching feet had caught up with him. It was hypnotic—the beat of the blood, the pulse of the heart. Instinctively, he retreated to the shadowed entrance of Malt Lane as the British tide surged out onto the Common. There were orders now, snapped out. "Disperse . . . don't fire!" Parker's voice, thank God. And an English voice, too, "Don't fire . . . surround them!"

Horsemen galloped past the end of the lane, cutting behind

the Meeting House. The Minutemen on the Common were dispersing, slowly. It was lighter, but he could still not make out faces. And all the time the measured tramp of marching feet, the menacing drum, shaking the nerves, troubling the blood. He had not thought it would be like this.

Red and white uniforms were between him and Buckman's now. No hope of finding Mark. No use anyway. The red and white tide flowed smoothly out on the Common, dawn light catching, here and there, the polished tip of a bayonet. He was so near he could smell the soldiers' fatigue, hear their grunted curses as they spread out to form into line on the edge of the Common. And then, crashing across the dawn, one shot. Who fired it? He had no idea. He had thrown himself on his face in the mud of Malt Lane as the British infantry let out a ragged volley of fire and went in with the bayonet.

When he sat up, sick with disgust at himself, it was over. A British drum was beating. Furious British officers were cursing their men back into line. On the Common, some men lay still, others were moving, shakily, this way or that. It was much lighter now. He recognised Jonathan Harrington as he crawled across the Common towards his own house. He ought to help him. He must find Mark. If the British attacked him as he searched, he thought he would be glad. He had proved himself the coward Mercy had once called him. Redcoats were swarming all over the Common now; an officer was beating back a party who threatened to break into the Meeting House. Horrible. The British. So who am I?

A rebel. And, on the thought, a voice, a whisper, Mark's. "Hart? Thank God." The redcoats were so busy around the Meeting House that they had not noticed him come staggering across the Common.

"You're hurt?" Hart went to meet him, got an arm under his, and felt him shudder with the pain of it.

"In the side. As I turned to go. Obeying orders. Get me home, Hart, if you can."

"Soon." Very gently, he eased Mark to the ground, cradled his head in his lap, and watched as the British slowly drew off, drew together, reformed in marching order, and then, unbelievably, fired a triumphant volley, gave three cheers, and marched off down the Concord road. Could he be crying? Yes. Coward again. A tear fell on Mark's face.

"Don't mind it so much." Mark's eyes flickered open. "It

had to come. Not all their fault. Ask . . . ask Jonas. But first, Hart, get me home."

He got him home, to die there, as Jonathan Harrington had, on his own doorstep, and Mrs Paston, dry-eyed, closed his eyes, and said, yes, she and the girls would indeed be grateful if Hart would take them to her cousins' secluded house five miles from the road. "They'll be back," she agreed. "The British have to come back from Concord."

9

It was May. The huge magnolia down by the bend in the river was covered in blossom, and Indian corn was a foot high in the fields. Mercy had her choice of catalpa, dogwood, or garden roses for her father's grave, but the flowers withered fast in the hot sun. It was strange to see the seasons coming round again at Winchelsea and to feel how much she was at home there. Hard to remember the frightened girl who crept about, afraid of masters and servants alike.

That was a year ago. Now her anxieties, or most of them, were shared ones. There had been no letter from Hart for over two months, and Mrs Purchis was beginning to fret herself ill over him, while Jem, who had been furious at being left behind by the master from whom he had never been parted, mooched about the plantation, grey-faced with worry. "It's too long, Miss Mercy." He reached up to pull down a high branch of catalpa for her. "He'd never leave Madam Purchis so long without a letter."

"That's what we think. Mr Francis has gone into Savannah to find out if there has been one of those hold-ups of mail at Charleston. Poor Miss Abigail hasn't heard from England either." Now she was friends with the servants, she was cheerfully aware there was not much they did not know about the family's affairs. Except for her engagement to Francis. She hoped, passionately, no one knew of that.

"That'll be Mr Francis." Jem's words seemed to echo her thoughts as the familiar signal sounded from the drive entrance. "I'll take your flowers, Miss Mercy, and put them on the grave."

"Thank you, Jem." Did he expect her to go to meet Francis? And if so, why? Instead, she took the quickest path back to the house and joined Abigail, who was pretending to read in their little downstairs room. "Frank's coming, I think. They've signalled from the gate."

"At last!" Abigail jumped up eagerly. "He's come back so quick, there must be letters."

But Francis' face, when they met him in the hall, was so grave that the two girls clutched each other's hands. "Where's my aunt?" He had not even paused to greet them.

"In the drawing-room, I think," Abigail told them. "But, what is it, Frank?"

"I'd rather tell it once and for all. Come up with me? And, Mercy, send for cordials."

"It's bad?" She hesitated a moment to ask the question.

"War, I think. And for us, perhaps worse. There's a messenger rode in this morning. Exhausted. They've been riding south in relays. Hurry, Mercy, my aunt must be told before some gossiping neighbour comes to mock her with sympathy."

"Dear God, not Hart?"

"Who knows? The news, so far, is general. As bad as possible. The time for individual grief comes later." He was flushed with his swift ride and with a suppressed excitement Mercy recognised from previous crises. Hurrying to do his bidding, she thought of Hart, the boy who had rescued her, the man who had welcomed her to his home, and swallowed a great knot of tears.

In the drawing-room, she found that Francis had just succeeded in rousing his mother from her morning lethargy. "It's news, Mamma. Bad news for us all. Worse, I am afraid, for you, Aunt Purchis." He turned at sight of Mercy, who had brought the cordial and tray of glasses herself. "Good. Pour a glass for my aunt."

"For me? What is it?" Martha Purchis had gone very white. "Not Hart?"

"Must devoutly hope not. But bad, just the same. Where did he say he was spending the spring vacation?"

"With the Pastons, of course, at Lexington. You know that as well as I do. Francis, *tell* me!"

"There's been fighting. At Lexington and at Concord. The

96

British marched out of Boston, God knows why, and when they reached Lexington, fired on the Minutemen on the Common there. Madness! Left eight dead, they say—more wounded."

"Dear God." Martha Purchis' breath was coming in hard gasps. "The names of the dead?"

"Some known. Some not yet. Mark Paston was one."

"Hart!" As Martha Purchis fell, fainting from the sofa, Mercy leapt forward to catch her.

"You should know better than to break it to her so sharply," she turned furiously on Francis. "Send for her maid, with those drops of hers. Why did you not tell me to have them ready?"

"I'll go," said Abigail. "Quicker."

"I'm a fool." Francis hurried to help Mercy support his aunt on the sofa. "Haven't rightly known what I was doing since I heard the news." A quick look at his aunt reassured him that she was unconscious. "I've not told her the worst yet. I'm so afraid someone else will come . . ."

"There's worse?" Mercy had taken Anne Mayfield's vinaigrette and was holding it under Martha Purchis' nose.

"Much worse. The British must have been out of their minds. They marched on to Concord, leaving the dead and wounded behind them. The news travelled ahead of them. There was fighting, savage fighting, at Concord too. They seized some ammunition, burned some carriages, and began to withdraw. They were attacked every step of the way, from behind walls and trees, from houses. At Lexington, they found a relief party under Lord Percy. He had made Munroe's Tavern his headquarters and drawn his troops up in square on the Common. They opened their ranks and their exhausted comrades staggered in. Percy rested them for a while. Then . . . is she still unconscious?"

"I'm afraid so. I wish Abigail would come with the drops. But what happened then?"

"He burned Munroe's Tavern and the houses round it. Said they might be used by snipers to fire on his rearguard."

"The houses round it? But . . . the Pastons'?"

"Must have been one of them, from everything Hart has said."

"And the people in them?" asked Anne Mayfield.

"Who knows? The message has been passed on, from mouth to mouth, all the way from Lexington. With so much of general disaster, there's been no time for individuals. Except we do know that Sam Adams and John Hancock, who were staying with the Reverend Clarke at Lexington, got clean away. Some say that it was to arrest them that the British marched. Ah, there you are at last, Abigail. But where are my aunt's drops?"

"I don't know." Abigail had returned empty-handed. "I looked for them everywhere. They are always by her bed. What shall we do?"

"I've some." Mercy was on her feet now. "The doctor gave them to my father. I always carried them with me. His trouble seemed very like your poor aunt's." She was out of the room already, running upstairs. When she returned, Martha Purchis was still unconscious and Francis was pacing anxiously about the room. "May I?" she asked.

"Suppose they are not right. Might kill her."

"Look at her now," said Mercy. It was unanswerable. Mrs Purchis' breathing had become shallow and rapid, and there was a blueish tinge to her face.

"Go ahead, child," Anne Mayfield spoke with unusual decision. "Try them. Let the responsibility be mine."

"Thank you." Mercy wrestled for a moment with the stiff cork of the bottle, then shook three drops onto her handkerchief and held it under Mrs Purchis' nose. The result was almost instantaneous. Her breathing eased, her colour improved, and she was soon moving restlessly in a return to consciousness.

Opening her eyes at last, "Hart?" she said.

"You mustn't fret, Mrs Purchis." Mercy took her cold hands and began to rub them gently. "Think how cross Hart will be when he gets home and finds you've worried yourself ill over him."

"When he gets home? But I thought Francis said . . ."

"Only that poor Mark Paston was dead. Which is terrible enough, but remember, Hart would never have joined those Minutemen. I expect, if he was there when the trouble started, he escorted poor Mrs Paston and the girls to safety. That would be like Hart, wouldn't it? And something else I'd expect him to do is come home as fast as he can, as soon as he can leave Mrs Paston. At a time like this, he'll know his place is here. And he mustn't find you looking so wretched. I think bed, don't you, Abigail?"

"Yes, indeed." Abigail moved forward to help get he

unt shakily to her feet. "I wish I could imagine what happened to those drops."

They found them, after they had got Mrs Purchis safely into bed with a hot brick at her feet. The bottle had fallen off the table, rolled into a dark corner, and broken there, its precious drops seeping out to stain the polished wood floor. Thank God you had your father's," said Abigail.

"Amen to that. But we'd best send for the doctor, just the same."

"Francis can tell him. He's riding back to Savannah after dinner. It was good of him to come out and tell us."

"Yes," said Mercy, "but I could wish he had done it more carefully."

Dr Flinn did not arrive until next day, and then he was so full of news he hardly had time for his patient. "She'll do well enough," he told Mercy and Abigail. "Yes, child, you took a terrible chance with those drops of your father's but they did the trick, so we'll say no more about it. I've brought you two bottles of her own, as you asked."

"Two?" Abigail sounded surprised.

"In case of accidents," explained Mercy. "But, Doctor, what's the news?"

"Nothing more from the North, I'm afraid. I know how anxious you ladies must be for news of young Hart. But we've had stirring times in town, I can tell you. Ah"—he looked with approval at the assortment of cold meats, fruit, and cheese laid ready for him, and reached out a loving hand for the claret bottle—"it's always a pleasure to come Winchelsea, dear ladies. Will you take a glass with me?" And as they shook their heads, pouring his own. "You've not heard about the powder magazine?"

"No." Anne Mayfield did not sound much interested, but the two girls leaned forward eagerly as he carved away the breast of a smoked turkey.

"Yesterday." He wiped his hands on his damask napkin, took a good pull at the claret, pronounced it delicious, ate a huge mouthful of cold turkey and spiced watermelon, and smiled benignly round at their attentive faces. "A group of gentlemen." Another approving sip of claret. "Not disguised this time. Mr Habersham—Joseph, of course—and Mr Jones junior. And Edward Telfair and I don't know how many others— Where was I?" He was silent for a moment dealing

99

with a huge mouthful of home-cured ham.

"A group of radical gentlemen," prompted Mercy.

"Yes, quite so. Very radical indeed in their behavior. If you'll believe it, ladies, they marched—well, walked along the bluff to the powder magazine at the east end of town. I drink their healths." He did so, with a wary, considering look at his hostesses. "Do you know, they found it, by some strange chance, totally unguarded. So, in they marched, cool as you please, broke open the doors—or found them open. I don't rightly know. Down to the cellar where the ammunition is . . . was stored, and off they go with six hundred pounds of gunpowder. I reckon there's not a cellar or attic in town today but has its share, and poor Sir James can offer what reward he pleases for evidence. He won't get it—nor yet his powder back. Far as I know, some of it's on its way to Beaufort already, for safe keeping, and some on the long haul north, where it's most needed. Poor Sir James and his hundred-fifty-pound reward! I reckon he might as well give it to charity at once."

"But you mean the guilty men are known?" Anne Mayfield was never a fast thinker.

"Known and applauded, ma'am. The word is not 'guilty' it's 'heroes.' "

"Oh." She took it in slowly. "And my Francis?"

"Was not there, ma'am, I'm sorry to tell you." He rose, dabbing at greasy lips with the napkin. "With your good leave, I must be on my way. There are a few 'accident' cases round here that I must visit."

"Accident?" asked Mrs Mayfield.

"You could call them that. Fools who thought they might like to collect Sir James's reward. They're none of them well enough, this morning, to go into town. Odd, ain't it? I hope your son will bear their fate in mind, Mrs Mayfield."

"What did he mean?" Anne Mayfield asked querulously after he had taken his leave.

"He meant to frighten us," said Mercy.

"He succeeded," said Abigail. "I wish Giles were here."

"I think you should thank God he is not," said Mercy. "It's Hart I'd like to see. The mob must have been out this way last night. Thank God, they didn't come here."

"You mean those 'accidents'?" Abigail was very white. "What can Sir James be doing?"

"His best, I have no doubt, poor man—and not worth

much by the sound of it. If he can't even keep sentries on duty at the powder magazine . . ."

"You mean, he can't protect his friends?" Mrs Mayfield had been taking it in slowly. "What are we going to do?" Her voice rose to a dangerous note of hysteria. "Francis shouldn't have left us like this."

"I expect Francis knows what he is doing," said Mercy.

"Well, I wish he had thought fit to tell me," grumbled his mother. "What in the world do we do if the mob comes here tonight?"

"Everything they tell us," said Mercy.

"Shame." Abigail turned on her.

"Suit yourself." As Mercy spoke, Mrs Mayfield rose and tottered from the room. "Be a martyr if you wish it, but see to it that you don't involve the rest of us. For my part, I intend to survive this, and if a little shouting of 'liberty' will do it, then shout I will. No, never priss up your mouth at me! Be honest, now. As things stand, can you tell me there is a pennyworth to choose between the two sides?"

"Mercy? But your father! They killed him. The rebels."

"The mob killed him. He hated mobs, whatever they called themselves. Whig or Tory, what's the odds! Look at our 'civilised' masters, the British. What were they but a mob when they attacked the Lexington Minutemen? Mark Paston is dead, Abigail, and others with him. Hart may be."

"I won't believe it." Abigail was crying helplessly. "Oh, how I wish he would come home."

"So do I. And be sure, love, he will. In the meanwhile, it behoves you and me to act with sense. I think we should say something to the servants, don't you?"

"Yes," gasped Abigail through her tears. "But what?"

They were saved the decision by Francis' return. "It's open revolt." He helped himself to a glass of the claret the doctor had left. "I wish I knew what to do for the best."

The admission, so unlike him, earned him a sharp look from Mercy. "What do you mean?"

"I've temporised as long as I can. Now, the cards are on the table—the sides are being drawn—I must declare myself."

"As what?"

"How can you ask that? As the Loyalist I have always been. Only, if I do so, I endanger this household most horribly. It wants only for Giles Habersham to come back, and we are all ruined. But what can I do? A man must act up to his conscience at a time like this."

"Yes, indeed," said Abigail eagerly. "To tell truth, Francis, I have sometimes had my doubts about you, this winter past. I ask your pardon; I should have known you better. As for the danger to us, you must not think of that."

"No?" said Mercy. "But what about your aunts? Are they to suffer for Francis' conscience? Tell truth, Francis. What purpose will be served by your declaring yourself, as you call it, and drawing down who knows what kind of vengeance on this house?"

"Why, the greatest of all. How can you be so wilfully stupid? You must see that now is the time when men of influence must use it. There are plenty of honest Loyalists in Georgia, but this news may panic them into flight, or a pretence of conformity. It is a time when one must stand up and be counted."

"Whatever the cost?"

"Whatever the cost."

"To yourself, yes," said Mercy. "I think your mother and aunt have a right to be consulted about the cost to them."

"And you?"

"Oh, I count for nothing." The exchange between them was all the sharper because of Abigail's presence. "But as for you . . . you should, I think, consider your Cousin Hart and your position as substitute master of Winchelsea. If you come out as a Loyalist and get the house burned down, where does that leave Hart, quite aside from the rest of us?"

"My dear Mercy." His tone was patient, as to a child. "You are as bad as my aunt. Can you not bring yourself to face the facts? All China to a Lombard orange, Hart is dead. Which means, to all intents and purposes, that I am master of Winchelsea."

"Oh? Might not your aunt have something to say to that? And your cousin, here, who is Purchis, where you are not?"

"Oh, don't!" Abigail could bear it no longer. "Are not things bad enough without you two quarreling?"

"She's right." Francis reached a plate from the sideboard and carved himself a slice of ham. "Join me in a glass of claret, ladies, and let's kiss and be friends." His smile, behind Abigail's back for Mercy underlined the words.

But they had reminded her that the doctor had been gone some time and still no servant had appeared to clear away his luncheon. "It is time we talked to the servants," sh returned to the subject. "What are they thinking of, to leave things thus?"

"My convenience, as it happens," said Francis. "But I take your point. They, too, will need their minds settling."

"I doubt if your coming out as a Loyalist will have a very settling effect."

"You'll be surprised." He finished his glass of wine and poured another. "Tory to the backbone, most of them."

"And loyal to Winchelsea," said Abigail.

"I hope so." Mercy looked up. "What's that?"

The sound of a horse, ridden hard. "Where the hell *are* the servants?" Francis strode to the window. "What's happened to Hart's famous warning system?" And then, "Good God! It *is* Hart!"

The three of them reached the front portico as the lathered horse came to a weary halt. Hart himself was white with fatigue under a caked layer of dust and sat for a long moment, swaying in the saddle, gazing at them blankly.

"Hart! By all that's wonderful." Francis hurried forward to help him alight and then steady him as he swayed with fatigue. "We were afraid—"

"Right to be." He looked about him. "But where are the servants? Were you not warned I was coming?"

"No. Things are at sixes and sevens here, cousin. It makes it all the better to see you. But come in and rest. You look worn out."

"I am." He had an exhausted smile for Abigail and Mercy. "I've ridden day and moonlight, when I could. Better that than thinking. You've heard the news?"

"Yes. Past believing. Is it really so bad?"

"Worse. They came out from Boston, the British. I was staying with the Pastons. There were—oh—seven hundred of them. Something like that. The Lexington Minutemen were waiting for them, drawn up on the Common—forty men—fifty? I don't know. A demonstration, nothing more. The British fired on them, Francis, went for them with the bayonet—their officers couldn't stop them. I saw it all. I'll never forgive myself. I hid. And then Mark found me. He was dying. Shot in the side, as he obeyed the order to disperse."

"I can't believe it," said Abigail. "Cousin Mark—"

"You've got to." He turned on her, and Mercy saw new lines deep in his drawn face. "Everything's changed, Abigail.

Everything's different now. Because that wasn't even all. They gave three cheers, the British, and marched off to Concord, and there was fighting there too. I expect you've heard."

"Something," said Francis. "It sounds a barbarous enough business. An Englishman scalped, the retiring column fired on from behind walls—Indian tactics. I do trust you had nothing to do with that, Hart."

"They wouldn't let me. By the time I'd got Mrs Paston and the girls safe to her cousin's house, they had their plans made. I asked . . . I *begged* to join them." His challenging glance raked their faces. "Jonas Clarke and Dr Warren said, no, I must come home, tell you what happened, tell everyone. Make you understand. It's war. D'you know what they did to the houses round Munroe's Tavern? Burned them in cold blood. The Pastons were safe away, thank God, and the other women and children, but they'll have a hard winter of it, specially the Pastons with no man to look out for them. And Ruth Harrington, whose husband was shot on the Common and crawled home to die under her window."

"But why?" Mercy was searching the face of this exhausted man for signs of the boy who had ridden away, the boy who had saved her life.

"God knows." His tired eyes, meeting hers, were the same as ever. "It's past understanding. But it's happened. Nothing will ever be the same again." He turned as a group of servants came hurrying round the corner of the house. "Well!" The furious blue eyes condemned them. "And where have you been, pray?"

They were all round him, with loving, outstretched hands and cries of "Welcome home," and Mercy, watching, thought how instantly Frank's brief authority had snuffed out. And no wonder. Haggard, dirty, sweat-stained, Hart towered over the little crowd, the focus of all eyes, the man of the moment, while Francis stood on one side, elegant as always, faintly petulant, totally ignored.

Now Sam, the overseer, came forward to take Hart warmly by the hand and explain, "There was a servants' meeting called, Mr Hart. We was ordered to go. We thought, best obey, for the ladies sake."

"Quite right. You shall tell me about it later. We have much to talk about. All of us."

"Yes, sir, Mr Hart. You, there, Jem, take the master's

horse; you girls, into the kitchen and get to work. And a hot brick in Mr Hart's bed, first thing."

"Not bed." Hart shook a weary head. "Hot water. I must see my mother. How is she?"

"Anxious," said Mercy.

"Overjoyed." Martha Purchis had appeared at the top of the steps. "Oh, my dear boy!" She tottered down them and fell into his arms.

"But you've been ill!" He looked down at her white face and swansdown-trimmed negligee. "What's happened?"

"It was the news." Francis spoke up as they moved into the house, Hart supporting his mother. "I told it something too quickly, like a fool that I was. But you ought not to be up, Aunt Martha."

"No. Nor letting me dirty your pretty gown." Hart led his mother to a sofa in the morning room. "Rest there, Mamma, while I make myself fit to be seen. I'll be with you directly. Ah"—he had seen the table of cold meats—"food. Now that I could do with. No, don't clear"—to a servant who had just timidly entered the room—"bring clean things and another bottle. Mercy, give my mother a glass of cordial." He paused at the door. "I'll be back directly."

"He's grown up." Martha Purchis was gratefully sipping her cordial.

"Yes," agreed Abigail. "His voice has changed."

"More than his voice, I think," said Mercy.

"Madness to have let him go!" Francis turned on Martha Purchis. "Do you realise, Aunt, that your son has come back a flaming rebel! What do you propose to do about that?"

"Why, Frank, I believe I shall say that that has to be his own affair. Do you know, I believe I could eat a morsel of that cold turkey myself. And here, in good time, comes the new bottle." Her tone reminded Francis that politics were not discussed in front of the servants, though it was a rule, Mercy thought drily, more honoured in the breach than the observance. She wondered if the curly-headed girl who was neatly changing plates and glasses would hurry out to the servants' quarters at the back of the house with a story to be sent to Savannah. She did not like the idea of that servants' meeting either.

"Abigail?"

"Yes?"

"Do you think Sally would tell you what went on at that meeting?"

"I don't know," Abigail said it slowly, looking anxious. "We used to talk—oh, about everything, but lately I've felt she was . . . careful."

"Yes, I know what you mean. Oh well." More cheerfully, "I expect Sam will tell Hart."

Sam would. Hart had been surprised to find him waiting with the hot water in his bedroom. "You, Sam?"

"Yes, sir, me. We have to talk, and quick. You didn't stop in Savannah."

"No." Only afterwards did Hart realise that it had not been a question. "I had the boatman set me ashore at the east end of town and came direct. I wanted to know what had happened here. Thanks." Sam had helped him out of coat and sweat-stained shirt.

"So you don't know about the powder?"

"Powder? No? What about it?"

"A parcel of gentlemen took and broke into the magazine. Yesterday. No disguise. Broad daylight. And nothing Sir James can do, but shout treason and offer a reward. Couple of people out this way thought they might try for it. A hundred and fifty pounds is a lot of money."

"Yes?" Hart was busy with sponge and hot water.

"The mob was out last night. The informers don't feel so like going to Sir James this morning."

"I see. You're never going to shave me, Sam?"

"Someone's got to, sir, before you face the ladies again, and your hand's shaking too much."

"Thank you. For everything, Sam. I've been . . . anxious."

"You've had a right to be. I'm glad you're back, Mr Hart, and that's the truth. These are bad times. And Mr Francis hasn't helped much."

"Oh?" Hart looked up quickly and met Sam's eyes in the glass.

"The mob nearly came here last night." He had worked up a good lather and now reached for the razor. "Mr. Francis, he didn't go along with the other gentlemen to the powder magazine. So, there was talk, last night, *and* about Miss Phillips and that press of her father's no one's ever found. Luckily, someone spoke up, loud and clear about you, Mr Hart."

"Me?" He ran an appreciative hand along his smooth chin.

"Yes." Now he met Hart's eyes in the glass with a faintly apologetic grin. "Seems like word's got around about your doings up at the North. And the word is maybe you're not quite such a fire-breathing Tory as you used to be?" Now it was a question and, Hart recognised, a hopeful one.

"My God, no." Hart pulled on the clean shirt Sam had found for him and reached out a still-shaking hand for a cravat. "After what I saw at Lexington? I helped bury the dead, Sam. My friends. No, I'm no Tory, if that's what you need to know."

"It surely is, sir. I'll pass the word around, quick, while you break it to the ladies."

"It's like that, is it?"

"It's like that, sir." He had found a broadcloth coat that Hart had left behind, and held it out for him.

Shrugging into it. "Good God!" said Hart.

"You've grown, sir, I saw it right away. It's a tight fit, but you'll do."

"I'll have to." Hart surveyed the straining seams ruefully in the glass. "Thanks, Sam. For it all."

Sam smiled at him. "It's only what we owe Purchis of Winchelsea, sir. Some of us remember. But"—a warning note —"not all."

"I'll remember." He adjusted his ruffles with a quick flick of the wrist and smiled oddly at Sam. "They wear homespun in New England. I find I prefer it."

"We'll come to it here, sir. Lucky if it's only that."

In the morning room, Hart found his mother happily eating her first square meal, she told him, since the news of Lexington. Francis, pacing up and down the room, turned to greet him with a hard look. "We were afraid you had fallen asleep, cousin."

"Just making myself fit to be seen. Dear Mother, you look better, and so shall I be, when I have had something to eat." He moved over to the table to help himself, while Mercy poured and passed him a glass of wine. "Thanks, Mercy." His eyes rested on her thoughtfully. "You look worn out. I hadn't thought you could be thinner. What's the matter?"

"Oh, nothing . . . everything," she said. "These times try us all."

"There's not time for all this talk," Francis exploded.

"While you sit there in your clean linen, drinking your wine, Hart Purchis, the mob may be on its way to Winchelsea."

Hart looked at him squarely across his lifted glass. "If it is, cousin, it seems it will be on your account."

"On mine?"

"Yes. Where were you, Frank, when that powder was taken?"

"You've heard?" Surprised, "I was dining with Sir James."

"One dinner too many, I think. I'm glad you are all here." He looked round them. "Because I have something to tell you." He lifted his glass. "I've turned my coat. Will you drink with me? A vengeance for Lexington!"

"Hart Purchis, you can't be serious!" Anne Mayfield put down her glass with a little click on the table. "To think that I should see this day . . . a Purchis talking treason."

"A Purchis facing facts, Aunt. This quarrel with Great Britain is none of my seeking, but by God they've gone too far now. What they did at Lexington made free men of us Americans, and I'm glad at least some people down here in the South have seen it."

"Some fools," said Francis. "Hotheads, rebels."

"Not rebels anymore, Frank. Patriots. The British have broken the social contract that bound us to them. They don't want us as citizens, they want us as slaves. It's been clear in everything they have done in Boston this winter. And I'll tell you one more thing." He turned on Francis, who had sat very silent, twisting his empty glass in his hands. "If you had seen the way they treated the Loyalists up in Boston, you'd be wondering about your own position. Oh, friendly enough, and all that, but as master to subject, as tyrant to slave. Swallow that, and you can swallow anything."

"Hart, you don't understand. You must be patient with the British. You haven't been there. How can you see, what a small issue this has seemed to them? Now, I'm sure, you will find a change in their handling of the business."

"A change? I expect you're right. But not for the better. So, who will drink my toast?" He looked round them, blue eyes bright and challenging.

"I will," said Mercy.

"And I," said his mother. "Though I don't pretend to understand . . ."

"Not I," said Abigail. "I'm sorry, Hart."

Francis had gone very white. "What happens to those

who refuse, Hart? Are we to be exiled from Winchelsea?"

"No. No, of course not." He looked suddenly young again. "I'm sorry. I should not have insisted. If we, who are family, cannot behave like civilised people, what hope is there for us all? Of course you must stay—all three of you." He managed a smile for Anne Mayfield. "Only I must ask you to be careful what you say and do. There are bad times coming, and whatever any one of us does, may harm us all."

"You mean"—Francis looked at him very straight—"you don't want Winchelsea burned down."

"No. Nor my mother and aunt, nor the girls, molested."

"Right," said Francis. "Then here's a toast we can all drink: to Winchelsea!"

10

"What did you mean by agreeing to drink Hart's rebel toast?" It had been some days before Francis contrived to find Mercy alone on her evening pilgrimage to her father's grave.

"That I agree with him, I suppose. What did you mean, Frank, when you proposed the toast to Winchelsea?"

"Why, just what I said." He turned to look through the delicate leaves of the Judas tree towards the big white house behind its screen of dark ilexes. "Long may it stand to shelter us all."

"Amen to that. So you are going to do as Hart asks and be careful?"

"Naturally. It's common sense. No time yet for bonnets over the windmill. Hart's right; there are bad times coming, but what will come of them is anybody's guess. There may yet be a day when it is the Loyalists in the family who are the saving of Winchelsea."

"Do you really think so?"

"I think the world's turned upside down." He began to whistle the popular march, then stopped short at sight of her face. "I'm sorry. I quite forgot where we were."

"No matter. Father wouldn't mind. I only wish I knew what he would say today."

"I know what he'd say. You forget, Mercy, what a Loyalist he was. He was Phil Anglius, wasn't he? Died for his beliefs. He'd call you a fool of a rebel, as bad as my little cousin Hart."

Mercy tried to laugh it off. "You could hardly call Hart little!"

"In mind, dearest Mercy, in mind. Like all the others. Just because Sir James has been left with only a hundred or so troops and can do nothing for the moment, they are letting themselves forget about the British Navy. And the garrison at St Augustine in East Florida. I wonder which will get here first, to shock some sense into them. And who will be the saviour of Winchelsea then? In the meantime, since Hart must needs go and play at rebellion in Savannah, it seems my duty, still, to stay here and keep the estate going." He laughed. "And how that brute Sam hates taking orders from me! He'll pay for his surly looks when the British come. As they will, my little love, as they will." His fingers moved, warmly caressing, in the palm of her hand. "I long to tell the world of my happiness, but dare not yet, since my Loyalist taint might endanger you. When the British fleet sails up the river, then will be the time to come forward and claim you as my bride."

"And Winchelsea?"

"Why, Mercy, what can you mean? If Hart survives the troubles to come, which, with my help, please God he will, he is master of Winchelsea. Remember, love, you and I are to build our own future in the West."

"Yes." Doubtfully, "But may not poor Hart lose Winchelsea if the British do win? And might not you be the obvious—"

"Hush, love." He put a warm finger on her lips. "Those words are dangerous."

She moved a little away from him. "It seems to me that everything is dangerous. The servants go on having meetings, I think."

"I'm sure of it. They'll pay for it when the British come. As for that dog, Sam, hanging's too good for him. Hush!" His head went up, listening. "They're signalling from the gate. It must be Hart. Better not let him find us together, love." He bent to snatch a kiss. "You go the short way; I'll meet Hart."

"Be careful, Francis.

"I'm always careful." He threw it back over his shoulder as he left her.

Alone, she sighed, bent to re-arrange the flowers on her father's grave, and then moved slowly towards the house. The familiar signal had brought Abigail out onto the broad stoop and the two girls stood and watched as Hart rode up, with Francis walking beside him.

"Council of Safety!" Francis' voice floated mockingly towards them. "President Bulloch! Provincial Congress! A lot of boys playing at politics!"

"Be careful, Frank." Hart looked quickly about to make sure none of the servants was in earshot. "Mind what you say. They tarred and feathered young Hopkins for making fun of the new Council of Safety. Started at the Liberty Pole by Tondee's Tavern and rode him in an illuminated cart all through the town. Oh, why can we not live up to the grandeur of our cause!"

"Mob rule, cousin. You asked for it. You'd better like it. Or pretend to. After all, they're not sure of you yet, are they? Can't be, or you'd have been elected to their precious Council of Safety."

"I begin to be glad I was not," admitted Hart. "Except that I might perhaps have some kind of sobering influence."

"Not with your background, Purchis of Winchelsea. They must be amazed to find you among them at all. But what other news is there in town?"

"There's a rumour." Hart looked drawn with anxiety, and Mercy thought he was now coming to its nub.

"There are always rumours," said Francis lightly. "What's this one?"

"That there's been a battle at Boston."

"A battle? A real one? You can't be serious! That rabble you call an army can never have been so mad as to attack the armed might of Great Britain." And then, seeing that Hart was unconvinced, "But if they have, rejoice, little cousin, our troubles must be nearly over. One real encounter between British regulars and those rebel ragamuffins and the revolutionaries must see the writing on the wall. It was all very fine to dodge, and lurk, and shoot down a retreating column, man by man, from behind trees and walls and from inside the safety of houses. Let them just meet the British lines and they'll learn their lesson soon enough. Mark my words, Hart, if your rumour is confirmed, it will be with news of a rout."

"We should know soon enough," said Hart. "I left Jem in town with orders to ride out directly if there was anything certain."

Jem came cantering up the drive two days later in a state of such breathless excitement, what with the news that he carried and his hard ride from Savannah, that it was some time before they could make head or tail of his panting, ungrammatical sentences. There had most certainly been a battle outside Boston on a bit of rising ground called Bunker Hill—or was it Breed's Hill? He seemed not to be sure. But, anyway, the Americans had dug themselves in there at night and been attacked by the British next day.

"But how?" asked Francis sharply. "How did the British let them get dug in?"

"I don't know, sir. But seems like they woke up in the morning, and there was these lines kind of looking down on them. So, 'course they had to do something 'bout it. It was a bloody dreadful fight, they do say. The British, they come up the hill, over and over again, drums beating, fifes playing, and was thrown back down again, right into the sea. Dunnamany they lost."

"Thrown back?" said Francis. "The British line. Impossible."

"You'd have thought it impossible for them to have let the rebels entrench themselves on Bunker Hill," said Hart. "If you knew the lie of the land as I do. Once they had let that happen, I should have thought anything was possible."

"Of course, we must defer to your superior knowledge." The sneer in Francis' voice was a little too pronounced for comfort. And then, sharply, to Jem, "But, naturally, they beat the Americans in the end?"

"Well, yes, sir, that they did, 'cos our lot done run out of powder, but everyone in Savannah's saying that a few more battles like that one and that British General Gage will sure be needing to send home for more men. They're drinking 'Liberty or Death' at Tondee's Tavern today. Oh, I clean forgot, Mr Gordon, he sent you a letter, sir." He handed it to Hart.

"Thanks, Jem. Go get your horse rubbed down and yourself a drink. You've earned it."

"Thank you, sir." He dug his heels in the tired horse's sides and moved off towards the house.

"We must not quarrel in front of the servants, Frank."

Hart was opening the letter.

"No, sir, Mr Purchis." And then, impulsively, "I'm sorry, Hart, this news has quite upset me. It sounds too much like war."

"It *is* war." Hart had been quickly skimming through the closely written pages. " 'War to the death,' Gordon says. Jem had it pretty well right. A most bloody engagement, and the British line thrown back twice."

"But they won in the end?"

"Well, yes. So it seems." Hart had turned to the last page, where the handwriting degenerated into a scrawl. "They took the position, but with what Gordon describes as 'immense losses, much greater than ours.' "

"Yours," said Francis. "Don't include me in any of your rebel calculations, cousin."

"I may have to," Hart told him. "President Bulloch has asked me to vouch for you, Frank."

"And you did! Of course you did! Oh, kind and generous cousin. Oh, patient and loving cousin."

"That's enough." There was a note in Hart's voice Mercy had not heard before. "These are hard times, Frank. Let us do our best not to make them harder. If we cannot be friends here at Winchelsea, God help us all. Mercy"—he turned to the two girls with an effort at a smile and change of subject—"I came past your house, your father's house, on the way back from town today. Did you know that someone had been digging between there and the river?"

"No. Have they?"

"Yes. I wondered if they could be searching for that vanished press of your father's. Poor Mr Johnston—" Having given him time to cool off, Hart turned to include Francis in the conversation. "I reckon he's got problems enough without having Mr Phillips' press found. He's in deep trouble with the Council of Safety for taking so long to print the news of Lexington and Concord."

"Three weeks," said Mercy. "Yes, it was a long time. I wonder how long he will take over Bunker Hill. And how much longer he can contrive to continue his policy of publishing both Sir James' proclamations and those of the Provincial Congress. These are bad times for neutrals."

"Bad times for traitors," said Francis.

"Traitors?" Hart flushed angrily along tanned cheekbones. "What do you mean by that?"

"Why, anything you care to think, little cousin. Turncoats, then. 'Gentlemen' who send loyal petitions to George the Third with one hand and elect themselves a president with the other. President Bulloch indeed. And you expect me to thank you for being so gracious as to vouch for me to him."

"Don't call me little cousin," said Hart.

Next morning, he and Francis quarrelled. Abigail and Mercy were sitting in their little downstairs parlour, Mercy mending sheets and Abigail reading aloud. "Oh, dear." Abigail put down *Sir Charles Grandison* at the sound of raised voices in the next room. "They sound dreadfully angry. Do you think they might fight?"

"Cousins? Surely they would not . . ." But Mercy, too, put down her work and cocked her head, listening anxiously.

"I'd never have thought it possible," agreed Abigail. "But now . . . With this terrible political difference. And you know what the point of honour is like, among our Southern gentlemen. They'll kill each other for a nothing, a trifle."

"Yes." Mercy had gone very white. "You're right, Abigail. We must fetch your aunts. Quick. Or, rather, you fetch them." The voices had suddenly grown much louder and she thought she heard the word "dowry." "I'm going in there to interrupt them."

"Do you dare?"

"Of course I dare. Do you fetch the others. Quick!" As Abigail ran upstairs, she hurried down the hall and threw open the door of the room Hart used as study and office combined. The two young men were on their feet, glaring at each other. A chair, pushed over by the desk, showed that Hart had just jumped up. Francis was leaning against the window-ledge, smiling. "Afraid, little cousin?" His tone was mocking. "So you should be."

"Francis! Hart!" Mercy moved forward between them, as Hart's hand came up to strike that sneering face. It caught her on the cheek. "Are you out of your senses?" She put her own hand to the smarting place. Hart had struck hard. Should she faint? No time for that. As angry as they were, they might well leave her to lie and fight it out across her body. "Your mothers are coming." She kept her place firmly between them. "I'll accept your apology later, Hart. In the meantime, what sort of a scene do you intend to present? They'll be here directly." She was saying anything, nothing, simply to give them time to cool off.

114

It seemed to be working. "Mercy, I ask you a thousand pardons," said Hart.

"Granted. It was my fault I came between you and the fly you were trying to swat."

"Fly?" For a moment he did not understand the way out she was offering him. Then, "Just so. You must forgive me, Mercy."

"Fly!" Francis took a step forward. "It's a fly with a sting, little cousin, as you shall discover."

"Francis"—she held out a pleading hand to him—"for the love of—" She left a pause long enough to suggest that she was going to speak of their secret engagement, then concluded with, "God. Remember who you are, and where. Ah." She turned with a sigh of relief as the three other ladies came crowding into the room.

"What is it?" asked Martha Purchis. "What are you two boys fighting about?" Quite unintentionally, her tone of the anxious parent reduced the whole thing to absurdity.

"What indeed!" Francis managed a rueful laugh. "I cry you a million pardons, cousin. Only, you must understand that what you said about Abigail's dowry came a little near the bone with me."

"My dowry?" asked Abigail, puzzled. "What's that to the purpose?"

"Why, everything," said Francis, as Hart stayed silent, apparently slower to collect himself. "Hart here seemed to imply that I failed in my duty to you when I refused to advance it from the estate. For a moment I thought he was suggesting something worse."

"Nothing of the kind." Hart had himself in hand now. "Of course you acted most scrupulously for the best. I only feel sad"—he turned to Abigail—"that I was not here to make funds available so that you could marry Giles Habersham before he sailed for England. I am afraid it may be a long day now . . ." And then, back to Francis, "Frank, I hope you did not for a moment imagine that I was suggesting you had not, always, acted for the best interests of Winchelsea." He held out his hand. "If anything I said could have been so construed, I beg you will forgive me."

"Handsomely spoken," said Anne Mayfield. Was her look for Francis a warning one? "Nobody could possibly quarrel with that, Francis."

"No." Francis had taken Hart's hand in both of his. "What

fools we nearly were. We owe our thanks to Miss Phillips for saving us from a great absurdity." And then, quietly to Mercy, as they all began to talk at once, "You'd best get away and do something about your face before anyone notices."

Since both mothers were now roundly abusing their own sons, and Abigail was doing her best to pacify them, Mercy found it easy enough to escape from the room and hurry upstairs to survey her rapidly reddening cheek in the glass. She pulled a face at herself and ran down the hall to Mrs Mayfield's room, where it was easy to borrow masking cream and powder from a heap of other aids to beauty. Returning to Hart's study, she found that a kind of uneasy calm had settled on the party there. *Everyone*, she thought, *was beginning to realise just how near to disaster they had been*. She had brought her broad-brimmed straw hat with her. "I am just going to walk down with some flowers for my father's grave," she told anyone who cared to listen.

Francis joined her there a little while later. "Whew," he said. "That was a near thing, love. If you hadn't come in just then, I don't like to think what would have happened."

"No more do I," she said. "Oh, don't for a moment think I was anxious for your life, my dearest. I know that you'd have made mincement of poor Hart, and were in a mood to do so, too. But I would have hated to see you hanged for murder."

"Murder?" He took her up on it sharply.

"Well, yes. Had you not thought? If you, a known Loyalist, were to kill a radical convert like Hart—and one from whom you are like to inherit too—it might go hard with you. I've never seen a lynching, nor want to." She shuddered and rather thought he did too.

He took her hand. "And with my inheritance would have gone yours, eh? You're a cold-blooded, quick-witted little piece, aren't you, love, and I admire you for it. Had it all summed up in the moment of opening that door, didn't you?"

"Well," demurely, "yes." No need to add that she had had it all summed up before that. "But, Francis, I remain anxious about you. Do you think it is safe for you to stay here? Suppose Hart were to decide to get rid of you."

"Hart! Get rid of *me*?" His astonishment was almost ludicrous.

"He's not the fool you let yourself think. And"—she

116

paused expressively—"he has friends. Who may not want a Loyalist in a position of power here at Winchelsea. Dear Francis"—she raised pleading eyes to his—"for my sake, go back to Savannah. I truly think you will be safer there. If only you would sign their Articles of Association!

"Never! And as for safety!" He dismissed it. "But, it's true, I had begun to think that I might be more useful in town. I'm nothing but a cipher here on the plantation now that Hart is home. That black bastard Sam smiles and says, 'Yes, sir,' and does just as he pleases. And as for Hart—he and I are oil and vinegar since he has been away. What nearly happened today might come at any time. You're right, love. Had it not been for you, I'd have gone the moment I could, but how could I tear myself away?" He raised her two hands and kissed them roughly, one after the other. "Now, with your leave, I will go. But my heart stays here."

He rode into town the next morning and returned a few days later with an announcement that surprised even Mercy. He had been invited to stay with the McCartneys. "They feel their position," he explained, "out there near the Common with no man in the house. No need to look so disapproving, Mamma. I know it is a little out of the way, but so are these times. And you have Hart here, amply able to take care of you."

"Yes," doubtfully. "But, Frank, you are never going to propose for one of those freckle-faced girls after all?"

"Good God, no. You must be aware I've seen metal more attractive." A quick side glance for Mercy before he went on, "What do you hear from Mrs Doone, by the way?"

"Nothing good. Since the news of Bunker Hill, the mob has been out in Charleston with a vengeance. I tremble for our house, Frank."

"And for our friends," he said drily. "Don't look so anxious, ma'am. I'll get myself domesticated with the McCartneys and then ride north and make sure all is well in Charleston."

"And pay a call on the Doones?"

"Well, ma'am, what do you think?" Once again he managed a private glance and smile for Mercy.

Saying good-bye to her, later, down by her father's grave, he had a note of apology. "You mustn't mind my mother. She can't help being an inveterate match-maker." He laughed. "It's only a miracle she hasn't got on to us long since. And, frankly, another reason why, alas, I think I am best away. You're wonderfully patient, love." It did not surprise him.

"What else can I be?" She looked up at him wistfully. "But, Frank, how long do you think . . ."

"God knows. This news from the North has set all to sixes and sevens. With Hart home, I had hoped the time might be coming when I could apply for a grant of land in the West, but, Mercy, I cannot risk you there now, with the mob on the rampage, and very likely the Indians too. Have you heard anything, by the way, about that powder ship of Captain Maitland's that's supposed to be due from England?"

"Not a word."

"I'm worried about Hart," he explained. "There's all kinds of talk in town about what they mean to do. Ask help from South Carolina—commission a schooner to take Maitland's ship . . . madness . . . patent treason. And I did hear that Bowen was to captain the schooner, with Joseph Habersham as second in command. Well, they're old friends of Hart's, and he's a damned useful man on board ship."

"Is he?"

"Oh, yes. We grew up on and off the river, he and I, but I lost the taste for it when I went to England. Hart knows every creek and channel between here and Tybee. I can't imagine anyone I'd rather have aboard on a mad venture like that. Or anything I'd less like to see Hart involved in. That really would be treason to the Crown. Worse even than signing that damned rebellious Association. So, Mercy, if you should hear anything—anything at all to make you anxious—you would send for me, would you not?"

"Dear Francis, who else?"

Hart was away a good deal during the next few days, and his mother and aunt began to complain and wish for Francis back. "Why should he protect the McCartneys when we need it just as much or more?" wailed Mrs Mayfield. "My nerves won't stand much more. For all the use Hart is . . ."

"I wish we knew what he was doing," said Martha Purchis.

They learned a few days later when Sir James Wright paid them a stiff-necked, angry visit. He had asked for Hart, but showed no surprise at finding him absent. "I feared as much." He kissed Mrs Purchis' hand. "I'm afraid you will live to regret sending that boy of yours north, ma'am."

"Oh, Sir James, I do already! But why today in particular?"

"You've not heard? Those madmen have taken Captain

Maitland's ship. The powder's vanished without trace. God knows how Captain Stuart is going to pacify the Indians for whom it was meant. I'm only grateful you and I both have our estates on this side of town, ma'am. When the Indians start attacking, as I fear they will, it is bound to be from the west. Though, mind you, the mob will doubtless turn out to help protect Winchelsea from the redskins if they come, which is more than it will my plantation."

"Sir James, you're not suggesting— You don't think Hart was involved?"

"Well." He looked about him. "Where *is* Mr Purchis?"

When Hart returned, much later that night, it was to face a barrage of questions from his mother and aunt, so that Mercy had merely to stay quiet and listen. "So you've heard of our little foray." Hart was looking tired, sunburnt, and exalted, like someone a little drunk, perhaps with success.

" 'Little foray?' " His mother was horrified. "Hart, you mean you admit it!"

"I boast of it, ma'am. And so may you. The first ship commissioned by the patriots, and the first British ship taken. I think we have made history today. Savannah may be only a tiny port compared to Charleston or New York, but we have shown that we have teeth as good as theirs. If the powder seized from the magazine here in Savannah last spring was really used to good effect at Bunker Hill, along with the cannon captured at Ticonderoga, I wonder where today's haul may not explode into action."

"But what have you done with it?" asked Abigail.

"Ask no question, cousin, and I'll tell you no lies. What's the news of Francis, Aunt Anne?"

"He was here the other day," said Mrs Mayfield. "Asking after you. I think he was afraid you might involve yourself in this mad venture."

"So he knew about it?"

"I suspect everyone in town knew about it," said Mercy. "The servants certainly did. Sam came back from Savannah talking of nothing else."

"Yes," said Mrs Purchis. "And that reminds me, I must speak to Sam. His manner to Sir James was quite the outside of enough. There was a kind of gloating smile about him that made me itch to strike him."

"Mamma!" Hart's tone was unusually sharp. "Hush!" And

then, as she looked at him in angry amazement, "As to Sam, leave him to me. I'll deal with him. Sir James is an old friend and must be treated with respect in this house, but you must see, ma'am, that nothing is as it used to be."

"Hart!" She was close to tears. "I see it, and I hate it." She rose and tottered from the room, followed by Mrs Mayfield and Abigail.

"Mercy." Hart held out a hand to detain her as she was folding up her work. "I never did get a chance to apologise, to thank you. Your face, I was so sorry—is it better?"

"It was nothing." She tucked the shirt she had been sewing into her workbox and stood up.

"You're so tiny." He reached out a tentative, apologetic hand to touch the cheek he had struck, saw her flush, and withdrew it. "You've lost weight, Mercy, while I've been away. Are you quite well? Do we treat you right at Winchelsea? My mother? Aunt Anne?" And then, "There's been no more talk, I hope, of your going to Saul Gordon's?"

"Not . . . not just lately. But I'm afraid Mrs Gordon's very ill, poor woman."

"No affair of yours. This is your home, Mercy, and I want you to remember it, whatever happens. And if you should ever need a friend, someone to advise you, someone to talk to, I'd like to be a brother to you, Mercy."

"Thank you. I'll not forget." Her eyes were full of tears.

11

Sir James Wright's visit to Winchelsea proved his last. As summer wore into autumn he became more and more of a cipher, reduced to watching impotently and writing increasingly desperate letters to his unresponsive masters in England, while the rebellious Provincial Congress and Council of Safety took control of the colony. By Christmas, the militia had been purged of all Loyalist officers, and last of all, in December, the Loyalist Chief Justice, Anthony Stokes, was replaced by a Court of Appeals.

At Winchelsea, time passed quietly enough. Hart and Sam were busy trying to domesticate a flock of sheep that Hart had bought in accordance with the Articles of Association he had signed. The colony had prohibited the importation of anything but a short list of such essentials as gunpowder and arms, and, as a result, wool for homespun was at a premium. Country-bred Mercy was dubious about the sheep, menaced by everything from poisonous snakes to alligators, but she and Abigail were learning to spin, just the same, from an old lady who remembered Sir James Oglethorpe and the early days of the colony.

"Ridiculous not to know how." Abigail was sucking a sore finger. "What an idle butterfly I have always been. You're worth ten of me, Mercy. I just wish I could help Hart the way you do over those sheep of his."

Mercy laughed. "Fine lot of help I am. I let him make their pen too small and they are out of fodder already. He talks of taking the boat downriver towards Tybee the next fine day to look for some."

"Making hay while the sun shines? Mercy, shall we go too! I never thought I could get so tired of being cooped up here at Winchelsea."

"Dear Abigail." Mercy reached out an impulsive hand to clasp hers over the wool it held. "Do let's go. We'll make a picnic outing of it. It will do us both good. I'll tell Hart he needs my advice about what the sheep will eat!"

But when she approached Hart, he looked grave. "It's hardly the time to be talking of picnics. Suppose we were to encounter one of the Tory privateers that are raiding the coast up from St Augustine?"

"But they've never been up this far, surely? I thought the mouth of the Altamaha was about their limit? And, Hart, I do think Abigail needs a change of some kind. Something to take her mind off her troubles. She's pining, you know."

"For Giles Habersham? I was afraid so. No news since last summer. But then, with all our mail coming through Charleston, that's no great wonder. Just the same, I'm not surprised she looks wretched. I wish to God Frank had given her that dowry and she had married Giles before he left."

"She could have married him anyway," said Mercy.

"And been a burden to him? Not Abigail. She's a Purchis— too proud for that."

"Pride's an expensive commodity."

"Too high for these hard times? You may be right at that. You often seem to be." His smile illuminated a tanned face now much graver than his years warranted. "Very well, wise councillor, let us have your picnic, if the weather will just oblige us."

Two days later, Mercy woke early to the sunshine of one of the fine spring mornings she had learned to hope for even in January in the two years she had lived at Winchelsea. The birds were all singing as if it was April, and she lay in bed for a while, wishing she knew their different voices. Then, hearing the morning routine begin in the stable yard round the corner, she jumped out of bed and hurried to her window. Hart always got up when the men did, and she was just in time to see him come round the corner of the house, the fair hair that would curl gleaming in the sunshine, the shirt open at his bronzed neck. He was giving the day's orders to Sam, but, as if aware of her gaze, looked up quickly towards her window, so that she had to beat a hasty retreat and found herself blushing hotly as she changed her frilled nightgown for a plain, grey dress.

Had he seen her watching him? Greeting him, half an hour later, when he came in from his morning round, she was still not sure. There was always a healthy glow about Hart. "You're bright and early." He smiled at her, then, his face clouding, "The sheep have been trying to break out again."

"Hungry, poor things. Hart, let's go downriver today."

"And leave care behind? Well, why not? And it's true, we do need that fodder. Wake Abigail, Mercy, while I order out the boat."

It was all delightful. Even Abigail lost some of her drawn look as she took her place under the awning of the plantation's big rowing boat and breathed deep of the morning breeze. The rowers were already in their places, and when Jem, the helmsman, gave the command, they burst into song and plunged their oars into the water. But the tune they chose sent a cold little premonitory shiver down Mercy's spine. It was "The World Turned Upside Down."

She soon forgot that moment of almost superstitious dread as the men's steady rowing took the boat downstream, against the tide, into country she had never seen before. Here, golden grass high on either bank told how Savannah had got its name, and promised a good harvest for Hart's sheep. "We could stop here, I suppose." Hart must have followed her thoughts. "But I know a place downriver a little where the landing will be easier for you girls, and there's a cleared hillock where you two can sit and enjoy the sun while we get in the hay."

"Delicious," said Mercy. "You're good to us, Hart."

"Nonsense. It was your idea." A quick, boy's blush coloured his brown cheek-bones. "There's our hill!" He pointed ahead, and Mercy, who had felt her own face flush and turned away to hide it, saw the little knoll rising out of a patch of scrub.

At an order from Jem, the rowers slowed their pace and pulled into a cove pitted with alligator holes, from which a faint track led uphill. "No one here today. It's often used as a lookout point," Hart explained as he helped the two girls to land, "but I doubt if anyone's come here hay-making." While the men tied up the boat, he led the way uphill. "You get a fine view of Tybee," he promised. "Watch out for the poison ivy." And then, "Dear God!" He had emerged onto the bare top of the little hill and turned to look seawards.

"What is it?" Hurrying after him, Mercy turned, like him, to look out to sea, and saw, as he did, the sails on the horizon. "What are they?"

"Ships of the line. One, two. . . . You've sharp eyes. How many do you make it, Mercy?"

She screwed up her eyes, gazing into morning sun. Were the ships getting larger? "Three of them, I think. Hart, what are they?"

"They must be British. We've nothing that size, God help us. And coming closer, I think. Do you?"

"Yes." She was sure of it now.

"Into Tybee inlet. Maybe upriver to Savannah. And nothing in the world to stop them. Jem!" He hurried back to the top of the path. "Back on board, and out oars, quick! We've got to warn them in town." He turned to explain to the two girls. "Our outing's over."

"Hart!" Abigail had been standing, hands clasped, gazing at the ships. "Are you sure it's the British? Just think, Giles may be on board."

"And death and destruction for us all." There was a note in his voice Mercy had never heard before. "Hurry, girls, there's not a moment to be lost." And then, as they emerged on to the little beach, "Well done, men. There's a guinea for each of you if you get us home in an hour. The enemy's out there."

"Enemy?" asked Abigail and Jem in unison.

"The British."

They made it to Winchelsea in just under the hour, and he men collapsed exhausted on their oars as Hart jumped ashore and promised them their guineas as soon as he got back from town. Jem was already running ahead to order but his horse, and he turned, with a brief apology to the girls, to follow. "Start packing up," he called back over his shoulder. "We'll likely have to move into town."

When the girls reached the house, they found Anne Mayfield in hysterics and Martha Purchis dolefully trying to comfort her. There would be no help from them in the packing, but then Mercy had hardly expected it. She and Abigail worked with a will, but Mercy knew that all the time Abigail's thoughts were elsewhere. By evening, everything was ready for a move, if it should prove necessary, and the two of them went out for a badly needed breath of air. "Let's go down to the river," said Abigail.

"If you like. But we won't be able to see anything on our backwater. If they come, it will be up the Savannah River. Thank God, Winchelsea's not even visible from the Wilmington."

Abigail looked at her out of eyes ringed with exhaustion. "You may thank God, Mercy, but what do I do? Those are my friends, out there. Giles may be on board. And Hart calls them the enemy."

"Dear, you must face it. To Hart—and to me—they are the enemy."

"And to Francis?" asked Abigail.

"Oh, Francis!" Could Abigail suspect their secret engagement? "His loyalty's a matter of course. But, Abigail, whatever happens, let us promise that we will never quarrel, you and I. Things are bad enough without that."

"Yes." She held out both hands, then pulled Mercy towards her for a solemn kiss. "Whatever happens."

"It's a bargain. But, Abigail, I think we should turn back. Your aunts will be worrying, and there's so much to do."

"Just a little farther." Abigail set a swift pace as they walked along the wooded path above the creek. Presently she stopped. "Can you keep a secret?"

"I think so." She seemed to do nothing else.

"Well, then, come this way. It gets you down to the water much quicker." She turned off the path to push her way past the big magnolia that stood above the bend of the creek and, following her, Mercy saw an abandoned track, just visible, leading down through thick bushes toward the water.

"It's the old landing stage," Abigail explained. "It was given up when they built the new boat. The creek's too shallow here. The others have all forgotten it, but I come here sometimes." She paused, her colour high, and Mercy thought she had not always come alone.

It was quiet in the bushes, and Mercy was suddenly aware of a soft, secret rustling somewhere ahead of them. A large animal? Wild boar? Alligator? Or man? She caught Abigail's hand. "Hush!" Finger on lips. "Listen," she whispered, sure now. "Someone's coming."

"Oh, thank God!" Abigail started swiftly forward.

"But Abigail, it may be anyone . . . Indians . . . the British." Even the desperate whisper seemed too loud.

Abigail turned to give her a long, strange look. "Nobody knows of this place but us."

"Us?" Her question was answered by a soft, cautious call from somewhere ahead of them. Unmistakably, it was the one used by the servants when a member of the family turned into the drive.

Abigail's eyes shone with tears. "It is," she whispered, then raised her voice, in a low, clear reply. A few moments later, she was running forward into Giles Habersham's outstretched arms. "Oh, Giles, you came." She was laughing and crying all at once. "I knew you would."

"Of course I came." He raised his head from the long kiss to smile wryly at Mercy. "Your servant, Miss Phillips. I'm glad I know you for so true a friend."

"True friend, maybe," answered Mercy. "But not a lunatic. You are mad to come, Mr Habersham. Things have changed here since you've been away. If you were caught—"

"But we come as friends, Miss Phillips. That's what I have come to tell you."

"Friends? The British? After Lexington?"

He turned to face her, his arm round Abigail's waist. "A terrible business. But, forgive me, you have only heard one side of the story."

"It was enough."

"Mercy," Abigail flung out an appealing hand. "You promised not to quarrel with me."

"I don't remember promising not to quarrel with Mr

Habersham. But there's no time to waste. When you say you are come as friends, Mr Habersham, what precisely do you mean?"

"Why, merely that we wish to send into town for provisions and fresh water, and, of course, a word with Sir James Wright. You surely could not imagine that we are come to attack Savannah?"

"After Lexington," she told him, "I can imagine anything."

"Rebels who shoot retreating men from safe hiding places? But we'll not quarrel, Miss Phillips. You're right. There is no time for that. I must go back to my ship before dark. Abigail, my heart's dearest, you will believe me when I tell you there is not the slightest hint of danger to you, or to Savannah."

She was crying quietly, but managed a smile as she looked up at him. "Of course I do, my darling."

"And you will tell me how things are here."

"No." Mercy's voice was uncompromising. "That she will not do. We have promised not to quarrel, Abigail, and I will keep my word. But if you let Mr Habersham turn you into a spy, I will go straight to the house and raise the alarm."

"A spy!" Abigail turned on her indignantly. "Are you out of your mind?"

"Well, then, a traitor, if you prefer it. Hart and his mother have given you shelter for years. Do you owe them nothing?"

"But all we need is to understand each other," pleaded Giles Habersham, "and then, I promise you, Miss Phillips, all our troubles would be over."

"I wish I could believe you. Tell me, who gave you leave to come and a boat to bring you?"

"Why, Captain Barclay. Our commander."

"And why did he do so? Out of mere philanthropy? To make the course of true love smooth?"

"Well, he did hope—"

"For news. Precisely. You will have to disappoint him, Mr Habersham. Or, if you wish, you may tell him, with my compliments, that Georgia is united as never before."

"Against its King?"

"No. Against his oppressive ministers and neglectful Parliament. Abigail, dear, it will be dark soon. We must go."

"No! Giles!" She turned in his arm to look up at him pleadingly. "Take me with you."

"Dearest. I cannot. The *Scarborough* is a man-of-war. I am

126

a soldier under orders. If we were only married, it would be a different matter."

"A soldier?" Mercy looked him up and down. "Where, then, is your uniform, Mr Habersham?"

He coloured. "I was told . . . advised not to wear it."

"And still you say you are not a spy? Your very life is in danger if you are caught. And I would not like to think of our fate either, if the mob were to hear of this visit."

"Mob rule, Miss Phillips? Is that your splendid unity? But you are right, just the same. Abigail, my darling, I must go. But first, one word alone?" A pleading glance at Mercy.

"No," she said. "You must see, both of you, that I cannot consent to that. I, too, am deep in debt to Hart Purchis, for my very life. You cannot ask me to let you betray him."

"Betray!" His hand went down to where his sword should have been. "Miss Phillips, if you were a man—"

"A fortunate thing I am not, or you would compound your offence against Abigail and her family. As it is, I think you should go, Mr Habersham. And do not come back."

"Mercy!" exclaimed Abigail. "How can you!" And then, pleadingly, "Giles, you see how I am placed. Take me away, please."

"My darling, I cannot. Besides, these troubles will soon be over. No need to risk the discomforts of life on board ship. I cannot believe that Georgia will not heed the call of duty."

"I hope that's not what you are going to report to Captain Barclay," said Mercy. "Because if you do, you will be gravely misleading him." She was interrupted by a soft whistle from the waterside.

"I must go. My darling." He bent over Abigail for a long, silent kiss that sent a horrid flame of jealousy through Mercy, compelled to stand there and watch. "May I come back?" It was to Mercy that he put the question.

"No, Mr. Habersham. Only openly. In your British uniform. I shall tell Hart the minute he gets back from town and ask him to put a guard down by the water. To come back like this will be to ruin us all."

"You're ruthless."

"I'm honest, or try to be." She watched their long farewell, her eyes misting with tears, partly for them, partly for herself. Then, as Giles Habersham turned away to plunge down the path to the shore, she held out her hand to Abigail. "Dear, I am so sorry."

"Don't speak to me now." Abigail's face was white and hard. "I expect you're right, Mercy, but don't speak to me now."

Back at the house, they found chaos reigning. A messenger from Hart had just arrived, urging that they join him in Savannah next day. Abigail and Mercy had been looked for and found missing. Deciding at once that they had been abducted by a marauding band of British soldiers, Anne Mayfield had gone into strong hysterics and Martha Purchis was busy trying to bring her round with sal volatile and burnt feathers. Inevitably, both of them turned on the two girls.

"Well," Martha Purchis attacked first, while her sister gulped her way back to silence, "if that isn't the outside of enough. Here we are, threatened with attack, assault, battery, rape, and I don't know what worse, and you two choose to vanish. And out in the twilight too, with not so much as a shawl to keep out the cold. If you don't both catch your deaths and keep us here, in mortal danger, it's more than you deserve."

"I'm sorry, ma'am." Mercy spoke for them both. "We just went out for a breath of evening air and stayed longer than we meant. But at least all is ready for our move tomorrow."

"Yes, that's the main thing," said Mrs Purchis.

But in the morning, Abigail was ill, just as her aunt had predicted and took gloomy pleasure in telling her. Only Mercy suspected that it was unhappiness, rather than the cold evening air that had confined her to bed with alternate bouts of convulsive hot and cold shivers.

"But what shall we do?" wailed Anne Mayfield for the fifth time.

Mercy had been thinking hard. Although she had recognised Giles Habersham as a mere tool in the hands of his commanding officer, she was sure she could believe his promise that no harm would come to Winchelsea. Captain Barclay would have more sense than to alienate a family he must know to be so gravely divided already. They were probably quite as safe at Winchelsea as at Savannah. She put Abigail's hot hand back on the coverlet and looked up at Martha Purchis. "I think you and Mrs Mayfield should go into town," she said. "I will bring Abigail as soon as she is better. In the meantime, I am sure Sam and the servants will take good care of us."

"Alone? Unchaperoned? Impossible!" But Martha Purchis looked pitifully ready to be persuaded to leave them, and Mercy soon contrived to do so.

"There, dear." She returned to the sick room. "They are gone at last. Now you can rest."

"Thank you, Mercy. For everything." Neither of them would refer to their mutual silence about the meeting with Giles. Abigail slid off into sleep, and Mercy hoped that she would wake feeling better, but instead, towards evening, she began to toss and turn restlessly and mutter to herself. The words grew gradually clearer as Mercy sat anxiously by her bed. "Giles! Take me with you. Please take me with you." And then, sitting suddenly bolt upright, "The *Scarborough*. I won't mind life on board. Truly I won't.

"Hush, dear." Mercy pushed her gently back under the bedclothes, grateful that she had sent Sally away. Anyone who heard must guess at the secret meeting with Giles Habersham. Impossible to summon the doctor, as she had meant to do if Abigail was not better by morning. This illness was a burden she would have to bear alone.

Hart rode out a few days later to ask after Abigail, but Mercy would not let him see her. "Her mind's still wandering," she explained. "It wouldn't be right, Hart."

"What does Dr Flinn say?"

"I haven't sent for him."

"What? Are you out of your mind?"

"Far from it. I'm afraid of what she might say. I know the doctor's a good friend of yours, but he's a staunch Whig too. Poor Abigail . . . I think it's as much the long strain as anything. She's been so good and quiet about it, I think we have not quite understood what she suffered."

"About Giles Habersham?"

"Yes. Hart—" She must tell him about Giles' visit. But he had turned away as the big English grandfather clock in the hall struck the hour. "I must get back. There's all hell loose in Savannah today. They've arrested Sir James."

"No!"

"Yes. The die is cast, I think." No wonder he looked exhausted. "Joseph Habersham took a body of militia and arrested Sir James as he sat with what he still insists on calling his council. They ran for it. Oh, he's merely under house arrest, on parole, but God knows what the British commander will do. He's been refused the supplies he asked for. Well,

129

why should we supply British ships? We're going to be short enough ourselves. Besides—"

"Yes. The thin end of the wedge. But poor Sir James. What will he do, Hart?"

"God knows. Mercy, I must go back. Take care of Abigail. And of yourself. I think you should be safe enough here. The British swear that they are come in peace, and even if the worst should happen, why should they come down this backwater?"

"That's what I thought. But just the same, I wish we could see the main river. Then at least I'd know . . ."

His laugh accentuated the fatigue lines on his face. "That's like you. But I promise, whatever happens, I'll let you know; come myself if there's danger. I wish, now, that I hadn't sent for you all to Savannah. I'm not sure my mother and aunt wouldn't be safer out here, but there's no moving them now."

"No. I can imagine. Hart, what's the news of Francis?"

"He's keeping very quiet. No need to worry about him. I hope. He's at the McCartneys' still. But"—he looked more anxious than ever—"there's talk of making it obligatory to sign the Association. This visit by the British fleet could not have come at a worse time. It has inflamed passions that were hot enough already."

"And if he won't sign?"

"Exile." Hart looked wretched. "Confiscation of property. Not that he has any of that, poor Frank. I must go, Mercy. I promised Aunt Anne I would ride back by way of McCartneys' house and do my best to persuade him to sign. Better if he does so before it's made obligatory."

"Yes. Hart—" Once again she started to tell him about Giles Habersham's visit, and once again he interrupted her.

"Dear Mercy." He picked up her hand and kissed it. "Try not to worry. We need your strength. I don't know how we'd manage without you. Now, I must go. Give my love to Abigail and take care of her for us all. And," oddly, he repeated it, "don't worry, Mercy."

She laughed. "Absurd advice. But I'll do my best." Impossible, of course. She ought to have told him about Giles' visit. As she sat by Abigail's restless bed in the waning light, her thoughts kept circling back to that disused, secret landing stage. The enemy knew of its existence. Giles Habersham had not come alone. Suppose, frustrated in their demand for supplies and angry at Sir James' arrest, the British should decide to raid plantations along the river. They could land at the disused wharf and be practically at the house without warning. It did not bear thinking of. She rang and sent for Sam.

"Yes, Miss Mercy?" In a world where so much was in doubt it was a blessed relief to know how certainly she could trust him.

"Sam, Miss Abigail took me down to a disused wharf by the river the other day. Do you know it?"

"Yes, ma'am. The old one. Mr. Hart's father used it all the time, but the new boat's too big. I reckon it must have rotted away long since."

"Very likely." She had not seen the wharf itself. "But, Sam, if there's a cove where a boat could land, should we not have a guard on it, just in case?"

"We certainly should. I'll see to it right away. I'll send Pete. He's one I *can* trust."

"Not to do anything, Sam. Just to warn us. In case—" What exactly did she mean?

"That's right." At least he seemed to understand her. "I've got a man at the other wharf, day and night, since the British ships came. And at the drive entrance. Mr Hart must have clean forgot the old wharf. Well, no wonder, the things he's got on his mind."

Back at Abigail's bedside, Mercy thought she noticed a slight change for the better, and thanked God for it. If the British should raid the plantation, she did not intend to be there to see. Somehow the arrest of Sir James Wright seemed to have changed everything. "The die is cast," Hart had said, and she was afraid he was right. When the British heard of it, as they soon must, anything might happen.

Next morning, Abigail was perceptibly better, and Mercy felt able to begin to plan for an escape, if it should be necessary. Sam had been thinking about it too. "If they come by the new wharf, we'll have quite a bit of time from the warning," he told her. "If you can have your things ready, you can be away in the carriage before they so much as see the drive. If they come by the old wharf, it ain't so easy, but if we have all ready, I reckon you could still do it. It's if they come all ways that we're in trouble."

"Yes." She had thought of this too in the long watches by Abigail's bed. "We might hide in the house, I suppose."

It was not an idea she liked.

"No, ma'am. Remember what they did to those houses at Lexington? You don't want to be hiding in no burning house."

"No." She looked at him hopelessly out of dark-ringed eyes. "I don't dare move Miss Abigail for another day or two. Not unless they come."

"I know, Miss Mercy. So I've been thinking, if you're not scared, you could hide, the two of you, in the family grave. Lord knows it's big enough. I've been down there the last two nights, fixing the door so you can open it easy and shut it tight. The air's a mite close, but nothing to hurt you. There ain't been a burial there," he explained, "since the first Mr and Mrs Purchis. You wouldn't mind, would you, miss?"

"Sam, you're a marvel. Of course I'd not mind. I'm so grateful." And then, quickly. "Who else knows?"

"No one. I thought, best that way. There's a lot of talk goes on, from house to house these days. I reckon the only safe secret is one no one knows. I've put food there and some blankets. If there's an alarm from all three look-outs at once, you and Miss Abigail just get down there as quick and quiet as you can. I'll let you know when all's safe. If I can."

"Yes." They both knew that he might not be alive to do so.

12

Abigail continued to progress steadily, but with her strength, all her anxieties returned, and she pined for news even more obviously than Mercy did. And still there was none. The British ships had made no move, Sir James remained under house arrest, the Provincial Assembly was debating what to do next, and Hart wrote that he could not leave Savannah for the moment. "Keep good watch," he ended his letter, and Mercy, reporting this to Sam, thought he looked anxious.

"The men is getting restive, ma'am," he said. "I'll be right down glad when you and Miss Abigail move into town. I never thought I'd see the day I had to say it, but there's not more than three or four, here on the plantation, I can rightly trust anymore. Talk is the British will free the slaves; they want them to turn against their masters."

"No!"

"Yes, ma'am. 'Course, I told the boys, we ain't slaves, but 'What's the difference?' said they. It's hard to make them see. I'm ashamed, ma'am. After all the kindness we've had."

"Don't mind it, Sam. And don't worry too much. I'll take Miss Abigail into town tomorrow."

"That's good." His huge smile split his face. "That's mortal good news, Miss Mercy." It was strange, how, these days, he alternated between calling her "miss" and "ma'am."

That afternoon Mercy persuaded Abigail to come out of doors for the first time, and sit, warmly wrapped in shawls, on the screened porch. "The air will do you good." She pulled a footstool close to Abigail's rocking chair. "And you'll need all your strength for the trip to town tomorrow."

"But I don't want to go to town!" Abigail was gazing through the screen of ilex trees towards the family lot, and, beyond it, the thicket of scrub and jasmine and wild vine that masked the river bank.

"Abigail, dear." Mercy tried to sound more patient than she felt. "Please. Giles won't come back. I warned him. And he must know how horribly it would endanger us all."

"He might come to fetch me. If he did and found me gone, Mercy, I couldn't bear it."

"But, dear, he told you—he's under orders, he can't. And, Abigail, you've heard how the British treat their Loyalist allies. As inferiors. They laugh at them, use them, and treat them like dirt. He'll never expose you to that."

"I don't believe it. And even if it were true, I'd want to share it. If only I had gone with him when he first asked." And then, breathless, "Look! Mercy! It's he—it must be!"

A man's figure had emerged from the scrub that hid the river, and was moving very cautiously around the wooded edge of the little graveyard, taking advantage of every bit of cover. If they had not seen him when he first emerged, Mercy doubted if they would have noticed his stealthy progress. "But what's happened to the guard at the wharf?" she exclaimed. And then, straining her eyes, "Abigail, it's not Giles."

"No." Abigail's voice was dead. "I think it's Francis."

Mercy moved closer to the screen. "You're right. But—why?" He had paused at the near side of the graveyard and was gazing cautiously towards the house. She raised her hand in a curious gesture, half warning, half salute, and he stopped in his tracks, then put a hand to his mouth, urging silence, and came swiftly towards them.

"Francis!" Mercy greeted him, low-voiced. The very look of him spelt danger. "Come in, quick!"

"Thank God it's you. And Abigail." His smile for her was perfunctory. "You've got to hide me, Mercy. The mob are after me."

"The mob! Francis, why?"

"I wouldn't sign their piddling Association. I, Francis Mayfield. To put my signature along with that scum!"

"Hart has."

"That's Hart's business. But, Mercy, there's no time. They'll be here any moment. I gave them the slip on the river, but they're bound to come here. They mustn't find me."

"You led them *here!*" Abigail turned on him. "And expect us to hide you and face them!"

"Pshaw." Uneasily, "They'll never hurt you. Two girls on their own. Not in a thousand years. Just tell them you've not seen me. Suggest I might have gone to Brewton Hill or Sir James' place. But first hide me, Mercy." He turned back to her. "It's death if they catch me."

"Death?" She had never liked him so little. "Just a suit of tar and feathers, surely? I wish I knew what has happened to Pete. You didn't see him, Francis? He was on guard down at the wharf. Should have been. If he's not there, we'll get no warning if the mob comes that way."

"You'll be warned all right. You should hear them! They're in full cry, out for blood. Mercy, where am I going to *hide?*"

"In the family lot." He was probably right. If they were caught sheltering him, they had no chance, any of them. If he was not found, there was still hope. And now, far off, from the direction of the main river, she did indeed begin to hear the familiar, terrifying sound of the mob. "They're in boats?"

"Yes, little ones. All kinds. All speeds. How do you mean, the family lot?"

"In the tomb. Sam made it ready for us. He's told no one." She anticipated his objection. "There are blankets and food. He's fixed the door so you can shut it from inside. Hurry! If they find you here, we are all lost. Will they know about the old landing?"

"I don't know." Something wrong in his tone. "You're sure there's food?" And as she nodded, speechless with anxiety. "Then I'll be on my way. Let me know when it's safe to come out. Good luck, girls." He was gone as silently as he had come.

"How could he?" exclaimed Abigail.

"No time for that now. There's something terribly wrong, and I don't know what it is. Stay there, dear, and keep a lookout. I must find Sam."

"Ring for him."

"No." She must not talk to Sam in front of Abigail, and risk alarming her still more. She looked white and drawn enough already, her newly regained strength visibly ebbing.

Sam met her in the wide main hall of the house. "Miss Mercy! Do you hear them? On the river. Coming fast. And Moses—he's at the drive entrance—he's just signalled. There must be more coming by land."

"So we can't get away?" She had wondered whether they should not leave Francis to his fate and make a bolt for it. After all, Abigail must come first. But was she strong enough?

"I don't think so, ma'am. Unless from the old wharf. Pete's there. We can count on him. We'd have heard from him if there was trouble that way. There's a little boat there, ready. I could take you and Miss Abigail if you want to run for it. We could hide down-creek somewhere till it's over."

"Till they've burned Winchelsea, Sam?"

"You and Miss Abigail are more inportant than Winchelsea, miss, and so Mr Hart would be the first to say." He was grey with fatigue and worry. "But, it's true they'd likely do you no harm, two young ladies. If only we knew why they was coming."

Mercy was not going to tell him about Francis. What he did not know, he could not be made to tell. "I think we'd best stay." She had made her decision. "If they caught us trying to get away, we really would be in trouble."

"Yes." It was what he had been thinking. "I've let you down, ma'am. not getting a warning to you sooner. I wish I knew what had happened to the men at the wharves."

"So do I, Sam." Half her reason for not trying to escape by the old wharf was fear of what they might find there.

"You'll not hide in the graveyard?"

"And leave you to face them? No!"

135

"I wouldn't have to. I'd just mix with them; it's what the others are doing, I'm afraid."

"All of them?"

"Looks like it. There's none left. I'm ashamed." And then "Listen! They've landed. They'll be here in ten minutes. How are you going to meet them?"

"On the front steps. Alone. I'll tell them about Miss Abigail. You stay with her, Sam."

"But will they listen to you?" The mob were singing raggedly now, as if they were tiring and needed to keep their spirits up.

"I hope so, but just in case, fetch me one of Mr Hart's duelling pistols."

"Miss!"

"I won't use it. Or only to fire in the air. It might give me a moment's silence. Hurry, Sam."

But still he lingered. "Do you know how? Suppose you shot one of them, by mistake."

"Of course I know how! My father taught me, years ago. If I'd had a pistol the first time I met the mob, I'd have killed as many as I could. But not this time, Sam. There's Miss Abigail to think of. So hurry."

Five minutes later, she stood on Winchelsea's high portico, the pistol loaded and ready in her right hand. Sam had joined Abigail at the back of the house, promising that if the worst should happen he would try and get her away into the bushes. The mob was very close. Mercy thought that the two parties, from the road and from the river, had met. They had stopped singing, and instead she could hear voices raised in what sounded like argument. Was this hopeful? Impossible to tell. But at least her greatest fear—that they might spread out and attack the house from all sides at once—was not going to be realised. They came round the curve of the drive in a ragged body, then halted at sight of her, a growing crowd of angry figures, some with sticks, some with stones, a few, she was afraid, armed.

Many years ago, watching a dress rehearsal at Drury Lane, she had heard the great Mr Garrick teach a young actress how to throw her voice to the back of the theatre. She took a deep breath. "What do you want, gentlemen? There's no one here but Miss Purchis and me, and she's ill. What can I do for you?" As she spoke, she was desperately scanning the faces, hoping to recognize someone among the leaders.

"It's the printer's daughter," came a voice from the back
f the crowd. "Him as hid his press so snug we never found
. I know what we can do with her." And as another voice
aimed in with an obscene suggestion, the crowd surged
rward.

"Stop!" But still they came on. She raised the pistol she
ad concealed among her skirts and fired into the air. It
ave her the moment's quiet she needed. "Are you men or
avages?" Her voice came fuller and clearer now, compelling
em to silence. "You, or your friends, killed my father. You
oubtless burned his press with his house. Kill me too, if
ou like, and you kill as hearty a rebel as yourselves." Now, at
st, she recognised a face in the crowd. "You, there, John
tubbs, you know Hart Purchis. What will he say to this
ay's work? Or his friends on the Provincial Assembly, Mr
labersham, Mr Jones, and the others. Kill me, fire the house,
ad you give the British out there—" She pointed away
wards Tybee, and was glad to see heads turn obediently in
at direction. "You give them the excuse they need to
tack Savannah."

"It's true." John Stubbs spoke up. "Mr Purchis is a good
iend of ours, since Lexington. We didn't reckon to hurt his
ouse, did we, brothers?"

The mood of the crowd had changed. There were cries of
'Course not" and "Hurray for Mr Purchis." But then, more
enacing, "Just give us the traitor and we're on our way."

"Traitor? What traitor?"

"Francis Mayfield." It came back as a growl, from many
oices, and she wondered if he could hear it, round at the
de of the house, where he huddled in the Purchis tomb.

"Him as played us off so neat and sweet," came one voice.

"Running with the hare and hunting with the hounds,"
aimed in another.

"Such a fine Liberty Boy." This was John Stubbs. "Till it
me time to declare himself and sign the Association, and
en, 'Oh, dear me, no.' His conscience won't allow that.
raitor's too good a word for him. We wondered who kept
owing our plans, didn't we, boys? And now we know."
nother angry growl answered him. "So, miss, just let us
him."

"But he's not here." For a breathing space, as Stubbs spoke
e damning words, she had been horribly tempted to betray
rancis. It had all been true, every unspeakable suspicion

137

that had haunted her since that day at McCartneys' whe
she thought she recognized him as the mob's leader. He ha
indeed been playing off the two sides against each other, wit
the stake, of course, Winchelsea. Well, it would serve hi
right if he was to cause its burning. No time for this no
"Why do you think to find him here?" she asked as th
crowd began to murmur angrily again, like the hornets' ne
it was. "He's not been here for weeks. You should look fo
him at Mrs McCartney's house."

"We did," said John Stubbs. "Searched the house prope
we did, and nothing there but those two girls, screaming an
carrying on."

"You didn't hurt them?" How strange—they were almo
conversing.

" 'Course not. There's no harm in them, bar silliness. The
said Mr Francis had gone, and their mother too. And it wa
true, there wasn't a bit of his stuff about the place. So the
we picked up his trail in town and followed it here. Whe
is he? And the old woman?"

"Mrs McCartney? I've not seen her since before Christmas
Here at last was truth. "Think, man. He'd never have broug
her here. Ten to one they've gone to Sir James Wright
plantation. Or the British ships. Best hurry if you want
catch him before he gets clean away. But before you go,
beg you will search this house, just in case he has got i
We've been round at the side, Miss Purchis and I. Th
servants are all run. He might have come this way and b
hiding. If he's the traitor you say, I don't want him he
at Winchelsea. Please." Seeing them hesitate, debating amor
themselves, she made it more urgent. "Don't leave till you'
searched!"

"That great house!" One of the mob's leaders spat on th
ground. "We've no time for that. It's true, he's likely go
down the Wilmington River to the British ships. Not a m
ment to lose. After him, boys. After the traitor! You, the la
party, go take a look at Sir James's plantation; we're
downriver."

Mercy leaned against the porch rail, shivering convulsivel
and watched them go as swiftly as they had come, b
quieter now, and, she thought, even more dangerous. T
suggestion that Francis might actually have joined the enem
had stirred the blood-lust in them. Lucky for him that
was well hidden.

"Well done, ma'am." Sam emerged quietly from the front door. "I never thought you'd manage them. But what now?"

"I don't know." The words came out slowly, jerkily, as reaction began to set in.

"You can't go to Savannah." Sam confirmed what she had feared. "Go by river, you'll likely meet the mob someplace; go by road, the same's true. Either way, I'd have to take you, and someone ought to stay and mind the house."

"Do you think the servants will come back?" She thought she had seen two or three familiar faces, hanging well to the back of the mob.

"I don't know, miss. If Mr Hart came home, they might. Either way, if I was you and Miss Abigail, I reckon I'd stay here tonight, till the mob's safe home, and go in town tomorrow as you planned. Right now, maybe you'll keep Miss Abigail company while I go and talk to Moses at the drive entrance. I'm afraid I saw the man from the new wharf in the mob, but I'm right down anxious about Pete. He'd never have run. I just don't understand it."

"Yes. Do that, Sam, but don't be too long about it." She shivered again and looked up at the sky, from which a little brightness had drained away. "I doubt we couldn't get to Savannah before nightfall anyway, and if there's one thing we don't want, it's a meeting with that mob in the dark."

"You're right, miss. Specially if they don't catch Mr Francis. which, please God, they won't. But what was that they kept shouting? It sounded like 'traitor' to me."

"Oh, a lot of nonsense." She had been thinking hard about what she would say. "Just because he wouldn't sign their association they're out for his blood." She left him and walked through the dark, strangely silent house to find Abigail still sitting where she had left her on the porch.

"Mercy! Have they really gone? How did you manage? Are we safe? And poor Francis?"

"I think so. I urged them to search the house for him, of course they refused. Who wants to be guided by a woman? They're off to look for him at Sir James' and downriver as far as they dare go towards the British ships. By the time they draw a blank there it will be nearly dark. They'll head for home, I hope."

"Dear God, so do I! But what are we going to do about Francis?"

"Leave him where he is. He's got food and blankets, and

the nights aren't too cold. We dare not do anything else
Sam mustn't know he's here, for his own sake as well a
ours. And, besides, the other servants may come back, now
the danger's over. Suppose they found him here."

"Yes. But, poor Frank."

"Poor Frank's alive."

"Why, Mercy, how can you be so hard. Do you know . .
I half thought you were fond of Frank."

"Did you, dear? Well, perhaps I was, just a little. I'm no
sure we are going to have time to be fond of people in th
days that are coming."

"Oh, Mercy, do you think it's so bad?"

"As bad as can be. I wish now I'd made Giles Habersham
take you away with him."

"As if you could have," said Abigail. And then, "So do I.'

"Well." Mercy had allowed herself the luxury of collaps
ing onto a rocking chair, but now got wearily to her feet
" 'Talk pays no toll,' as my father used to say. We'd best g
indoors and make sure we know where lamps and food are
before night falls. I doubt the servants will be back today
Except Sam and his two stalwarts." And how she hoped the
would.

It was good for Abigail to be occupied in cleaning ne
glected lamps and fitting new candles into their holder
Mercy, relieved to find ample stores of food in the big, coo
larder at the darkest end of the cellar, could think of nothin
but Sam as she cut great slices off a home-cured ham an
looked out a jar of Abigail's favourite water-melon pickl
By now he must have relieved Moses at the drive entranc
and, presumably, sent him back to the house. He could not b
expected to stand watch all night. He would be back soon
and she must be ready for him and his questions. Sam woul
no doubt cut across the rice-fields to the old wharf, sinc
that way took him past the new wharf and he could mak
sure that all was safe there. She did not think the leader
of the mob would have had the wits to leave a man on guar
but anything was possible. And, as for the old wharf—anothe
long shudder made her put down her load and lean for
moment against a huge kitchen table—what would Sam fin
there?

"Mercy!" Abigail's anxious voice from upstairs. "I ca
hear someone coming."

"Here I am." Mercy left the ham on the marble sla

and hurried up the steep cellar stairs. "Who is it?" She saw Abigail at the front door, peering out.

"Only Moses. Well, of all things!" Her voice was shrill with anger. "He's coming in the front way. I'll give him a piece of my mind for that!"

"No, you won't," said Mercy. "You'll thank God that he's coming at all."

Moses had little to report. The mob had not molested him, either going or coming, and he said he thought some of them were about ready to give up and go back to Savannah. "They wanted me to go too."

"But you didn't, said Mercy. "Thank you, Moses. Mr Hart will be grateful."

"Mr Hart taught me to read," said Moses. "I'll go light the lamps, Miss Mercy. It will be dark soon."

"Yes. I wish Sam would come. He cut across the fields, did he?"

"Yes, ma'am. He said he was going to both wharves. He's worried about Pete."

"And so am I. But worrying won't help. Abigail, dear, you must eat something and get to bed. Tomorrow's another day, and not an easy one, I'm afraid."

She had just seen Abigail safely tucked up with a hot brick at her feet when she heard Moses greeting Sam, and hurried down to join them. One look at Sam's face told her she had been right to be afraid.

"He's dead," said Sam. "They killed him. Pete."

"How?"

"Hit from behind. I don't know how they managed to land without him hearing. The noise they were making. I suppose he was listening to the other lot, up at the new wharf. But, why, miss? Why did they go for to do it?" He was painfully close to tears. "Pete was a good friend of mine."

"I know. I'm sorry." Please God he would never discover how much worse it was than he thought.

"I couldn't even bury him, just had to leave him there. My friend Pete."

"You and Moses must do it first thing in the morning. Now, we're all worn out, but you two are in the worst case. I'll keep watch till midnight, then wake you, Sam. You take your turn, then wake Moses."

"But, miss—"

"No argument, Sam. Please."

"You should 'a been a man." It was capitulation, and she breathed a sigh of relief.

Half an hour later, with the house quiet as death and the moon rising, she let herself quietly out of the library window. There was just enough light to show her the well-known way to her father's grave and, beyond it, the big family one. "Francis?" she whispered at the crack of its door.

"And about time too." He pulled it angrily open. "I thought you'd never come."

"You're lucky I did."

"And what, pray, do you mean by that?" But for all the bravado of his tone, she thought he knew.

"Sam's been down to the old wharf," she said.

"So?"

"He found Pete's body. Stupid, Francis. You should have hidden it."

"There was no time." And then, aware of how fatally he had betrayed himself, "I had to kill him! He was bound to have made a noise, given one of those absurd signals, brought them down on me. I couldn't risk it."

"No, I don't suppose *you* could. And nor can you risk staying here. In the morning, the servants will be back. If they learn you've been here, they'll put two and two together, soon or late. And everyone loved Pete. Your life wouldn't be worth five minutes' purchase. You'd best be off to the King's ships, Francis. They are the only place for you now."

"You won't tell?"

"That's all you care about? No, I won't tell. I can't. I lied to the mob. If they were to find out, they'd be back for me. You're safe enough from me, Francis."

"I know I am. Dearest Mercy." He found her hand in the dark and made to raise it to his lips.

She snatched it away. "No. There's blood on it."

"A slave's."

"A man's. And—I must go. Sam will be waking, looking for me. You'll have to walk, Francis. If you take the boat, he'll know."

"You think of everything. Dearest Mercy." Once again he tried to pull her to him.

"No, I tell you. There's no time, Francis. If you don't value your own life, value mine. I must go. I don't suppose we will meet again. Good luck, Francis. I think you are going to need it."

"Mercy!" But she had pulled away and was hurrying along the familiar path back to the house.

13

After that, the night passed quietly, and Mercy even slept for part of it, while Sam and Moses stood watch in turn. But at first light, she got up, threw her clothes on, and went down to find Moses peering out at a fine morning. "I think you should wake Sam," she told him. "And go and bury poor Pete, quick. I don't want Miss Abigail to know. It would only make her worse." If it sounded heartless, she could not help it, and she knew well enough that it was the kind of attitude many a white employer would take.

As soon as they had gone, she hurried out to the grave-yard, picking a quick bunch of early spring flowers as she went. They must be her excuse if anyone should find her there. Laying them on her father's well-tended grave, she breathed a quick prayer, then moved over to the family tomb. As she had expected, Francis had left unmistakable signs of his presence: blankets rumpled, a half-gnawn crust of bread, and even, final folly, a monogrammed handkerchief. The bread she could not replace, but it might easily have been eaten by chipmunks. She retrieved the handkerchief, tidied the blankets, and was back in the house in time to hear a faint call from Abigail's room.

She made her stay in bed and fetched hot milk and stale cornbread for them both. Abigail was quiet this morning, and looked drawn, listening.

It was hard not to listen. And, at last, they both heard the sound of horse's hooves, far off, muffled by the crushed shell-surface of the drive. "What now?" Mercy hurried to throw open the window and lean out. Then, "It's Hart!" she exclaimed. "Thank God. I'll go down to him. No need to hurry yourself, Abigail." She must have a moment alone with Hart to tell him about Pete's death. And about Francis?

By the time she got downstairs, Hart had ridden round

to the stable yard and dismounted. "Mercy!" He saw her. "Thank God. You're not hurt?" He came towards her, hands outstretched, then stopped, collected himself, looked about him. "Where is everyone? The mob's been. I've seen their traces all the way, been mad with worry. They didn't hurt you, Mercy? You're . . . you're all right?"

"Of course." She stood there, looking up at his anxious face and fighting the temptation to throw herself into his arms, and cry, and cry, and cry. How horrified he would be. "The servants have run." She made her voice cool. "Except Sam and Moses. They'll be back soon. Pete was killed last night, Hart. They're burying him."

"Killed?" It hit him hard. "Pete? We grew up together, he and Jem and I. But, Mercy, why now? Why here? Surely not your father's press after all this time?"

"No. They were after Francis. Said he'd refused to sign the Association. I talked to them a bit, and they went away."

"Admirable Mercy! You talked to the mob and they went away! Without burning the house, or hurting anyone, except poor Pete." It was the inevitable assumption, and she found she was not going to disabuse him. Francis was gone. Pete was dead. What use to make bad worse! Hart's tanned face was fine-drawn with exhaustion already.

His next words explained it. "Sir James has broken his parole."

"No!"

"Yes. He slipped out of his house by the back way. There was a boat waiting to take him to his friend Mulryne's at Bonaventure. I imagine that by now he's safe on board the *Scarborough*. I trusted him, Mercy. I advised Joseph Habersham to accept his parole. These times make traitors of us all."

"Oh, poor man," said Mercy. "How wretched he must feel."

Hart had finished attending to his horse and now turned angrily towards the house. "Don't waste your pity on him. He's not worth it. Anyone who will break parole— And, Mercy, I'm afraid there's worse news—for us."

"Oh?" She thought she knew what was coming.

"Francis. I'm not surprised the mob was after him. But he would never have brought them here! Not even Francis. Mercy, I'm ashamed to have to tell you: he's been playing a double game all along. When he refused to sign the Association, it all came out. How he had collaborated with

144

both Tories and Whigs, informing on either as it suited him. I . . . I can't understand it, Mercy. Oh, at first, perhaps, it was a game to him, the kind of gamble he enjoyed. Dressing up, playing the two sides against each other, convincing himself he was acting for the best. But, later, when it became serious— Mercy, how could he? Why would he? Frank . . . my cousin . . . a Purchis."

"Oh, Hart." She could not help a shaken little laugh. "Is that the worst of it? That he's family?"

"Dear Mercy." Suddenly he bent to take both her hands in his. "I'm glad you can laugh about it, take it so well. You're gallant. And you'll see, he'll settle down, now he's been forced into the open. He was always a Loyalist at heart."

"Do you think so?" Something about his tone puzzled her, and she decided this was no time to tell him of her own far more unpleasant suspicion that in fact Francis had been playing his double game for the stake of Winchelsea itself. Mrs Purchis' curiously mislaid medicine drops, that attempt to provoke Hart to a duel—what had they been but moves in a gambler's game to eliminate the lives standing between him and Winchelsea? But how could she bear to try and convince Hart of this? Convincing herself had been bad enough, with memory of those Judas kisses still scorching her.

"I've not told Abigail about Pete's death." She changed the subject. "She's not well enough, and she'll be down directly. Will you go and warn the men to say nothing?"

"Of course. You think of everything. And then I am going to close this house, leave Sam in charge, and take you to stay in town until things are quieter."

"If they ever are."

Abigail protested passionately against the move to Savannah, and earned a long, sad look from Hart. "You've seen Giles Habersham. I heard he was with the British. And did not choose to tell me." His look of reproach was more for Mercy than for Abigail.

"I tried," Mercy began, but Abigail interrupted her.

"Yes, I did see him," she said defiantly. "And begged him to take me away. But he would not. It seems there's no room for human feelings in the world anymore. We must all be things until this war is over."

"I'm glad you see that it is war," said Hart. "The British still seem to think it can all be settled with a few fair words. But they are wrong, as they will find in the end. And, Abi-

145

gail, for the moment I truly think you have a better chance of meeting Giles openly, at Savannah, as a British emissary, than in some hole and corner way here at Winchelsea." He turned on Mercy. "I cannot think how *you* could have connived at it."

"Connived!" Abigail took him up angrily. "She wouldn't let us have a single moment alone together. You're all against me."

"Abigail." Hart's patient tone was strained. "This is not the time for such refining. Please, come to Savannah. I need your help. And Mercy's. My Aunt Mayfield is in such a fret about Francis that I am afraid she is making my mother worse."

"Hart, I'm a brute. Of course I will come."

Back in Savannah, life achieved a dour routine of its own. Sir James wrote of peace and olive branches from the British ships that stayed, threatening and unsupplied, off Tybee, and the Council of Safety ignored him and looked to its defences. Busy with the militia, Hart was hardly home at all, and the house on Oglethorpe Square was a sad enough place. Mrs Mayfield spent most of her time in her room, mourning her son as if he was dead, though he was, in fact, known to be safe on board the British ship *Cherokee*.

"Oh, Mercy," said Abigail, "why didn't I make him take me with him!"

"Francis? You can't be serious!"

"He took Mrs McCartney."

"Abigail!" Mercy looked at her with something between love and exasperation. There was a kind of obstinate innocence about her that had so far proved impermeable to the truth about Francis. Well, of course, with his mother in the house, they did not talk about him much. Hart did not talk about anything, and Mercy sometimes suspected him of making excuses to stay away from home, and could hardly blame him.

Mrs Purchis missed him, and grumbled, and seemed, for some reason, to take it out on Mercy, who could do nothing right these days. Too ill to run the house herself, Mrs Purchis nevertheless seemed to resent the automatic way the servants turned to Mercy for orders. It was she, now, who went to the market in Ellis Square every morning to buy the provisions that grew dearer each week, and therefore it was on her that Mrs Purchis' wrath fell as the cost of living rose. Martha Purchis had never been short of money in her life, and the prospect frightened her. Mercy would have been sorry for her, ill as she was, if there had not seemed something personal, almost spiteful about her complaints. If Abigail had been better, she would have been tempted to turn the house-keeping over to her and apply for a post in one of Savannah's dame schools, but Abigail had had no word from Giles Habersham and crept about the house like a ghost.

Deeply sorry for her, Mercy could not help, sometimes, comparing their positions. Giles loved Abigail; they were engaged. In the end, surely, all would come right for them. But what future lay ahead for her? She tried not to think of the past, of Francis' long betrayal. Had he ever loved her? It would be easier to bear if he had. Sometimes she thought so; sometimes, waking from a dream when she had melted once more into that hot embrace of his, she thought she could not bear herself.

If Hart were home more, it would be easier. Sight of him, somehow, put those old nightmares to flight. But instead of Hart, there was Saul Gordon, whose wife had finally died that winter. Inevitably, with Hart busy both with the Council of Safety and with the militia, Saul Gordon had taken over what estate business there still was. He spent most of his time in the little office next door and made a habit of sidling into the main living room with each new rumour, specially, it seemed for her. There was a sense of breathless waiting in the air, as the days passed, and still those threatening ships lay out of sight but never out of mind at Tybee. Rumours flew through the streets and squares like wildfire, but there was no solid news. James Johnston, the printer of *The Georgia Gazette*, had given up the struggle to be fair to both sides. In his issue of February 7, he had announced both the arrival of the British ships and the appointment of the popular patriot Colonel Lachlan McIntosh to the command of a new battalion of Continental Troops. The February issue was his last for a long time. The financial crisis had hit him as it had everyone, but worse still were the threats of the Council of Safety.

"He's gone, and I can't blame him." Hart had brought the news on one of his quick visits to collect his equipment for infantry drill. "With a wife and five children, he could hardly risk a visit from the mob."

"Poor man," said Mercy. "But what of the *Gazette*? People need to be kept informed."

"They do indeed. Trouble is"—he laughed ruefully—"we've no printer. They've even sent after Johnston to ask him to come back and keep up the *Gazette*, but he won't, and it's not surprising. Strange, isn't it, that after all the fuss about your father's press, now we have a press and no printer."

"Very strange." Mercy was going to say something more when Mrs Purchis joined them.

"Hart! I thought you gone long since. You'll be late for that drill of yours. What are you thinking of, Mercy, to keep him gossiping here?"

"My fault, ma'am." Hart smiled down at his mother, and it made Mercy realise that she had shrunk a little that winter. "I was telling Mercy about the *Gazette*. But you are up very early for an invalid!"

"Someone has to take thought for economy these days. I should have thought you would be out back with cook by now, Mercy, instead of gossiping here."

"So I should be," agreed Mercy. "It is so hard to convince her that we must be saving with things like salt." She smiled at Hart. "Don't work too hard, Hart."

"What would we do without her?" said Hart warmly, after she had left them.

His mother sniffed. "Very well indeed, if you ask me. It would do Abigail good to pull herself together and do the job that is rightly hers."

"Poor Abigail." He looked at the clock and bent quickly to kiss her. "Mother, I must go."

"Good-bye, dear boy." She looked after him thoughtfully, then sat down to write a note.

A few days later the McCartney sisters called in Oglethorpe Square. "Dear Mrs Purchis," said Bridget effusively, "and dear Mrs Mayfield. How lucky we are to find you both at home. And Miss Abigail"—she kissed her on both cheeks—"and Miss Phillips, of course." Dismissing her, she turned back to Martha Purchis. "Ma'am, we are come as humble petitioners, as beggars, if you like." And then, laughing and jingling her diamond bracelet, "Well, not exactly that, but with a proposition rather. Ma'am"—she leant forward earnestly as Mercy rang the bell and ordered tea—"we're scared out there on the edge of the Common, plumb scared.

Two girls on our own, now Ma's gone; it ain't nice and it ain't safe. Claire was saying to me only last night, weren't you, Claire? What if the mob comes back, you said. I'll never forget that last time, when they came after Mr Mayfield." She shuddered. And then, colouring and turning to Mrs Mayfield, "Forgive me, ma'am. Perhaps the less said about that, the better. Mrs Purchis"—she laid a pleading hand on Martha Purchis' plum-coloured skirts—"may we . . . could you possibly . . . might we come and stay? We'd"—she opened her jewelled fan and looked coyly over it—"we'd wish to help pay our way. We know how things are these days—everyone does—butter twice what it was last year, and as for rum . . . not that we buy it, of course, except for the gentlemen. But, how I'm running on. Mrs Purchis, please, just till the British ships go away?"

Mercy had watched Mrs Purchis with interest through this surprising speech and wondered whether, in fact, it had surprised her. She certainly gave her consent with unusual graciousness, and the two sisters and a formidable collection of baggage were installed in the best guest-chamber that same evening.

"It will mean more work for you, dear Miss Phillips." Saul Gordon had caught her in the yard as she went out the back way to market. "But nobody thinks of you. You must let me help you in any way I can."

"Why, thank you. But short of finding me a bushel of salt, I don't know what you can do for me."

"Your wish is my command." He produced the salt that same evening, and she wished she had not asked for it.

Hart had welcomed the McCartney girls hospitably and, Mercy thought, spent more time at home now their cheerful presence was added to the household. Well, no wonder. Abigail talked less and less, and Mercy herself, busier than ever, hardly had time for more than a few words with him, but Miss Bridget and Miss Claire would listen to him forever.

He came home one night late in February looking unusually grave, and Bridget was on to him at once. "Dear Mr Hart, you look quite fagged out. Come here and sit by me, and Miss Phillips will order you a glass of your favourite punch to warm you." She gathered up blue satin skirts lovingly to make room for him on the small sofa beside her. And then, "Don't look at this old thing! We found a boxful in the attic at home, Claire and I. It's so out of fashion, it

149

makes you laugh, but it's bright and will help to keep our spirits up."

"And that we need." He sat down beside her. "There's a rumour going round town today that I don't much like."

"Oh?" She leaned closer to him, and Mercy, handing him his glass of punch, was aware of the heady perfume she wore. "Is it a secret, Mr Hart, or may a mere woman hear it?"

"I'm afraid everyone will hear it. Thank you, Mercy. That's what I needed." He took a long pull at the punch. "It's the rice ships," he explained, "over at the wharves on Hutchinson Island. Their captains are tired of being bottled up by the British—seems some of them reckon to sail and be 'captured.' The Council of Safety has ordered their rigging dismantled and their rudders shipped, but God knows whether they will be obeyed. Our merchants still seem to think of pockets first and country last."

"Well, it's hard for them." Bridget smiled at him over her fan. "If they sell to the Council, they'll be paid in Georgia paper, and you know what that's worth!"

"Just because of people like those same merchants," said Hart angrily. And then, as she made big, shocked eyes at him over her fan, "Forgive me, Miss Bridget, but you must try to understand."

"I'll try, if you will just explain."

The explanation took most of the evening, and Mercy, listening with interest, thought it unlikely that Bridget understood a word of it, but she sounded as if she did, and it was good to see Hart so animated, and Mrs Purchis nodding approval from her corner. It was odd, after this unusually sociable evening, to go to bed, so strangely depressed.

She slept badly and was waked very early by the sound of agitated knocking on the porch door below. Hurrying down in her grey dressing gown, she found Hart before her, in shirt and breeches, talking to a breathless messenger. "It's the British!" He turned to Mercy. "The *Hinchinbrook* has managed to sound her way up the back river behind Hutchinson Island in the night. She's grounded off Rae's Hall."

"Too far upstream to harm the town," said the messenger. "We'll show them! Major Habersham wants you, Mr Purchis. He's taking a picked band of riflemen to attack from the shore. If only we had the boats, he says, we could take her."

"Yes. If only. Mercy"—he turned to her with a smile—"I'm glad you're here. I count on you to keep things quiet. Don't

150

let my mother worry and look after Bridget and Claire."

Had he coloured when he spoke of the McCartney girls? No time for such imaginings. "You'll take care of yourself, Hart?" She had found his jacket for him. "And send a message if you think I should take them all down to the cellars."

"No need yet. The *Hinchinbrook*'s well out of range up there above the island. I just wish I understood. Thanks, Mercy." He pulled on his jacket, gave her a quick smile, and was gone.

It was still very early and no one else was stirring. Mercy hurried down the steep cellar steps to make sure everything was ready there in case they had to take refuge from a bombardment. Like Hart, she wished she understood. Why had the British sent this one ship, and by such a circuitous route? She puzzled away at the problem all through a long morning devoted to soothing the nervous terrors of the household. The McCartney girls urged that they all move to their house, which was so much farther from the river.

"Suppose the *Hinchinbrook* floats clear on the tide and comes down this side of Hutchinson Island," shuddered Miss Bridget. "We'd be in easy range of their guns! Mrs Purchis, Mrs Mayfield, do let us go!"

"No." Martha Purchis was firm. "Hart's up there with the riflemen. He'll see she doesn't come any nearer. And, besides, what if he came home and found us gone!"

"That's quite true. Dear Mrs Purchis, you are absolutely right," said Bridget. "We must show ourselves worthy of him, of course."

The mention of Hutchinson Island had sent a frightening thought flashing through Mercy's mind. The rice ships! Suppose this was all a ruse of some kind to free them. "I must go to the Council of Safety," she said.

"You?" Bridget's tone was almost a sneer. "They don't reckon much on females. And I expect they've a good deal on their minds today."

"I must go just the same." Mercy picked up her bonnet.

But Bridget proved right. It was a vain errand. The Council of Safety was indeed in session, but no plea of hers could gain her admittance. "They're busy, ma'am," said the man on duty at the door. "They've got matters of state to see to." And then more kindly, "No need to look so frit. You go home and look to your children."

"I'm not frightened," she said angrily. "Or—not for myself. Won't you just send my name in? To Mr Bulloch, or Mr Glen, or Mr Jackson even? Tell them it's urgent."

"So are their affairs, ma'am. Now, be a sensible girl and don't kick up a rumpus." He gave her a sudden, sharp look. "Ain't you the British gal whose father worked with Johnston the printer? If I were you, I'd stay home and quiet today. You don't want to run into the kind of trouble your pa did! Lucky to have a roof over your head, if you ask me. Now, you cut along or I'll call the guard and you'll be in real trouble."

"Will you take them in a note?"

"No, I will not. Now git, ma'am."

She had been away too long already, but must take time to go back by way of the bluff. A handful of loiterers were gazing first upstream to where the masts of the *Hinchinbrook* were just visible beyond a bend of the river, and then across to Hutchinson Island. All seemed quiet there. "What's happening?" she asked a fatherly-looking man in a respectable black broadcloth.

"Nothing to see," he told her. "Couple of the ships over there are taking down their rigging like they've been told to. See, there and there." He pointed. "And there's been firing upriver. I reckon the men on the *Hinchinbrook* are good and sorry they ever left Tybee. Storm in a teacup, looks to me. Just the same, I'd go home if I was you, ma'am. Things is rough in town today. No time for ladies to be walking the streets."

"No. Thank you." She took one last long anxious gaze at the quiet ships docked by Hutchinson Island and decided she had let her imagination run away with her.

Back at the house in Oglethorpe Square, she found the two Misses McCartney deep in a game of whist with Mrs Purchis and Mrs Mayfield. "Well?" Bridget McCartney gave her a challenging glance. "And what did the Council of Safety have to say?"

"You were right." Mercy did not enjoy admitting it. "They would not see me."

Hart returned late, exhausted and discouraged. "Oh, we did them a little damage, but nothing to signify. If we'd had a few boats, it would have been another story, but they are well informed. I have no doubt they knew we were helpless. We kept the decks swept clean with rifle fire until the tide rose and she floated clear. And that was that! I just wish I understood."

"Hart!" Mercy had tried in vain to catch his attention, but inevitably the whole household of females had surrounded him on his return. "I had an idea. I tried to tell the Council of Safety, but they wouldn't see me. Suppose it was all a feint? A ruse to distract attention from what they're really planning?"

He had not heard her. Bridget McCartney had summoned him to her across the room with an imperious gesture. Why had she ever thought both McCartney girls plain? Had it merely been because they had always been overshadowed by their handsome mother, or had Bridget come into late bloom? She suddenly felt too exhausted for further effort. And, after all, she had been to the bluff, she had seen Hutchinson Island, lying quiet in evening light, the rice ships moored in their accustomed places—very likely it really was all her imagination.

"Come, dear." Abigail was beside her. "You're tired out and so is Hart. He won't go to bed till we do. Shall we set the example?"

Next morning, the same strange quiet held Savannah. The *Hinchinbrook* had vanished in the night. "A flash in the pan." Hart was eating a yeoman's breakfast. "I think the British still don't like to admit they are fighting us. But they are! No use Sir James's talking of olive branches now." He finished his last draught of rather dubious coffee and rose to his feet. "I must be off to the Council of Safety. And that reminds me, Mercy, what's this Bridget McCartney tells me of your running off to them yesterday?"

"Nothing. A folly, I suppose. I told you last night. I had an idea the British might have sent the *Hinchinbrook* to distract attention. That she might even have grounded on purpose. They wouldn't see me."

"The Council of Safety?"

"Yes. I'm sorry, Hart, I suppose I was foolish to go."

"Well, perhaps not quite so strongly sensible as usual." He rose quickly to his feet as the Misses McCartney appeared in the breakfast-room doorway. "Good morning, Miss Bridget, Miss Claire. I trust you are none the worse for yesterday's alarms. You certainly do not look it!"

"Not the least in the world." Miss Bridget swam towards him, her beautifully fitted gown of finest blue worsted bringing out red highlights in her hair. "We feel so safe, dear Mr Purchis, under your protection. I just hope we are not too great a burden on your household." A glance at Mercy suggested that this was to her account.

"Good heavens, no. It's our great pleasure to have you, is it not, Mercy?"

"Why, of course." In her plain grey homespun, she felt herself relegated to the position of a domestic servant and was glad when Abigail joined them, just as soberly attired.

"Dear me." Miss Bridget stroked her blue dress lovingly. "You make me feel quite ashamed to be so bright, Miss Purchis, but so long as our old gowns last, we feel it our duty to show the flag by appearing as well-dressed as possible. Only God shall know how we suffer inwardly, when we think of our poor mamma."

"I am sure it does you the greatest credit," said Hart with more good manners than sense. "But I must take my leave of you ladies."

"You'll send word if there's any news?" asked Mercy.

"Naturally. But I expect none. Unless it be another of Sir James' 'olive branches.' The more I think of it, the more I think the *Hinchinbrook*'s appearance yesterday must have been a mere show of strength, designed to frighten us into submission."

"I do hope you are right." She regretted the scepticism of her tone as soon as the words were uttered.

"Of course he's right." Miss Bridget seized on it. "The gentlemen usually are, Miss Phillips."

But not this time. In the course of the morning, two sailors rowed over from Hutchinson Island. They had escaped from the rice ships at the risk of their lives and reported that while all attention had been centered on the *Hinchinbrook*, another British ship had anchored behind the island and a force of British soldiers had marched across and captured not only the ships but also the detachment of men from Savannah who had been seeing to the dismantling of their rigging.

Hart brought this news as he hurried from the Council of Safety's meeting to join Colonel McIntosh and his detachment of three hundred men who were throwing up a breastwork on Yamacraw Bluff to protect three four-pounder guns trained on the shipping. "You were right, Mercy," he told her, "and I was wrong. They've pulled the wool over our eyes finely, but they'll regret it. As if arresting our captain and his men wasn't bad enough, they have taken Roberts and Demeré, who went over under flag of truce to negotiate for their release. Will you warn the other ladies that I expect fire to be opened very soon? Poor Miss McCartney, she will be wishing she'd stayed safe on the other side of town, though I truly do not think the British will fire in this direction. They are more likely to concentrate on the gun emplacement on the bluff."

"Yes. But do you not wish to tell the Misses McCartney yourself? They are in the parlour."

He looked tempted. "No. There's no time. Take care of them, Mercy. They've been through so much."

"Yes." Mercy hurried round the house making sure that the buckets of water she had ordered were all full and ready. "At least there is plenty of sand!" She had met Saul Gordon, who was making a similar check.

"Yes. Dear Miss Phillips, let me tell you how I admire your calm."

"No time for anything else." *Or for flattering speeches,* she thought, joining the rest of the party in the main living room. "Dear God!" As she closed the door behind her, the house shook with the first gunfire from the bluff. They looked at each other, white-faced. None of them had ever heard guns fired in anger before. They waited, silent, breathless, for the answering fire from the island, and when it came, exchanged glances of shamefaced, unspoken relief. Wherever the balls were falling, it was nowhere near.

"May I join you ladies?" Saul Gordon peered round his office door, white-faced and sweating. "I find I cannot concentrate."

"And that's no wonder," said Mercy in a blessed moment of silence. "Abigail, dear, would you feel like giving us a tune on your spinet?"

"A tune!" She was silent for a moment as another blast from Yamacraw shook the house, then, surprisingly, smiled a ghost of the old delightful smile that was so like Hart's. "Well, why not! Shall it be a hymn or a song?"

"Oh, a song. One we all know."

"Ridiculous!" said Bridget, but Abigail had opened the spinet and started to play one of the choruses from *Acis and Galatea,* "Oh, lovelier than the cherry." Mercy, picking up the tune, heard Saul Gordon follow her in a surprisingly strong bass, and then the others join in one by one.

It made the continuing gunfire a little easier to bear, but

at last Abigail started on "Greensleeves"—"Alas, my love, you do me wrong"—and burst into tears, her head in her arms.

"I shall go mad," said Bridget. "This noise is killing me."

"It's probably killing men too." Mercy spoke more drily than she had intended. "But I think it's slackening." She picked up a black shawl she had knitted for herself, which combined with her homespun dress to make her look like any countrywoman in town for the day. "I'm going out to see what's happening."

"You'll never dare!" protested Miss Claire.

"She should be safe enough looking like that," said Miss Bridget. "But don't loiter, Miss Phillips. I long for news of dear Mr Purchis."

"I doubt if I shall be able to bring that," Mercy told her. "I merely mean to go down to the bluff here, not up to Yamacraw. They will hardly want females there." She wound the shawl firmly round her head, crossed its ends in front, and tied them at the back, then slipped out through the back yard and down across Bay Street to the bluff.

It was crowded with people, white-faced, watching, listening, whispering to each other, oddly, between the deafening sounds of gunfire. But these were slackening. Fire still from the ships on Hutchinson Island, but none from Yamacraw. Why? She worked her way gently forward through the crowd, listening to a phrase here and there. "Fired on Captain Screven," said a voice. "Nearly sank their boat," said another. "They'll pay for it now. Yes! Look! There comes the fireship!"

Mercy reached the edge of the bluff and looked across the wide, grey river to the flat marshy land beyond. No way, from here, to tell it was an island. But no doubt about the frenzied activity on the decks of the ships that lay there. Red and white figures swarmed on them. "What are they doing?" she turned to ask the man nearest her in the crowd.

"Trying to turn their guns on our fireship, the *Inverness*." Intent on what was happening, he did not even turn to look at her. "That's why we've stopped firing, see, for fear of hitting her. Look, there she comes! A floating powder-keg. Thank God I'm not on board."

"Who is?" Mercy could see white sails now, outlined against the farther bank of the river, as the small ship swooped down towards the anchored merchant vessels.

"Volunteers." His eyes were still fixed on the ship's rapid progress. "Captain Bowen, Lieutenant James Jackson. The men who took that powder ship of Captain Maitland's."

"Not Mr Purchis?"

"Surely! They sent for him special, from Yamacraw. He's a dab hand with a boat, is Hart Purchis."

"Is it very dangerous?" She clasped her shawl with hands that would shake.

"Dangerous? What do you think! Look!" There had been a shift in the red and white pattern on the anchored ships. "Listen! They're firing on her. Please God they've got no rifles." The water round the *Inverness* churned white; she heard the sharp crack of musketry fire. "Dangerous!" he said again. "Wouldn't you think it a mite dangerous to hold a candle to a barrel of powder? They've got her full as she'll hold of dry rice and deerskins, and they're going to turn her loose across the river. That's why they need Mr Purchis, who knows the currents and ways of our Savannah like the back of his hand. And, by God, there she goes."

The *Inverness* had swung suddenly towards the ships on the farther bank and surged forward, all sails set, a sinister plume of smoke rising from her deck, and men leaping into the water from her stern.

Men. Who? "I can't see," she cried, straining her eyes.

"Not faces," he agreed "Much too far. But no need to fret, ma'am. Our boats are picking them up, see! Most of them, that is. Risky business. Looks like one of them's got caught by the current. Won't fetch up till Tybee, most like. I wouldn't choose to go swimming in our Savannah."

Impossible even to try and recognise the figures that were being hauled into waiting row-boats. Mercy followed the one, lost drifting head with aching eyes. Hart was a strong swimmer, but suppose he had been wounded in the volley of fire poured into the fireship when the British belatedly realised what was happening.

"Look at her go!" exclaimed the first stranger.

"Straight for them, by golly," said the other. It might have been some game of skill they were watching, Mercy thought furiously, not a matter of life and death.

"Ho! And look at that." Another man pushed rudely forward in front of Mercy. "The redcoats are running for it. Look at them! Straight into the marsh. They'll get their feet wet surely!"

Peering round him, Mercy saw that chaos had broken out on Hutchinson Island. Two of the ships had managed to get under way and were escaping up river, out of range of the now-flaming fireship, but as she watched, flames passed rapidly from one to the next of those that were still anchored. She could not hear, but could imagine, the terrified screams of the small figures she saw leaping overboard—anywhere away from the swiftly advancing fire. "They must be dry as tinder," said the man nearest her. "Waiting to sail all this time! The damned redcoats will remember this day for a while. Just look at them wallowing through the marsh. Back to their ships with a flea in their ear, mud on their boots, and lucky to get there! And darkness coming soon. There'll be plenty drowned in the creeks before morning."

14

Slipping back into the house on Oglethorpe Square as quietly as she had left it, Mercy found a scene of confusion. Saul Gordon had just arrived with the news that Hart was on the fireship, and this had been the signal for competitive hysterics on the part of Mrs Mayfield and Miss Bridget. While Claire and Abigail were doing the best they could with sal volatile, burnt feathers, and sympathy, Mrs Purchis was sitting bolt upright in a chair, her face rigid, fighting for composure.

Mercy, who knew how bad anxiety was for her, flashed a furious look at Saul Gordon and hastened to reassure her that all but one of the men had got safely back on board the boats.

"That will be Hart." His mother spoke with a kind of dry despair. "I've had a feeling in my bones all day. Oh, why did this horrible war have to happen? Why must we fight our own kith and kin? And how in the world do we think we are ever going to beat them? If it isn't today, it will be tomorrow. I shall lose my son, my home, everything!"

"But not the cause!" Bridget sat up and dried her tears.

"Dear Mrs Purchis, we must not be unworthy of your gallant son! Just think how horrified he would be if he were to hear you say such things." She crossed the room and sat down by Mrs Purchis on her sofa, holding her hand and whispering consolation.

"Mercy." Abigail's voice was low and strained. "The British. Could you see?"

"Only their red coats and white breeches, dear. I'm sorry. I expect most of them got away across the marsh, and some were safe enough on board the ships that got clear."

"They are bound to have sent Giles," said Abigail. "He knows the island so well. Oh, Mercy, suppose he and Hart should have met!"

"Impossible." This at least was true. "It was all long range," she explained. "No hand-to-hand fighting."

"They might have killed each other just the same," said Abigail, and Mercy could not deny it.

Instead, she applied herself to persuading her companions into a more cheerful frame of mind, and even managed to get them to eat a little supper, pointing out that when he returned Hart would not wish to find them already mourning him as dead. It won her a look of reluctant respect from Mrs Purchis and a moan of "quite heartless," from Bridget, but even she found herself able to toy with a few smoked oysters and drink a glass of Madeira.

"Admirable Miss Phillips." Saul Gordon had taken advantage of the general confusion to join them at their supper. "What would we do without you?"

"Very well, I expect." Her tone was sharp with irritation and anxiety. He must know as well as she did that Hart should have been home long since. And there he sat, his white hands tucking smoked oysters into the too-red lips as if nothing in the world was the matter. Hours passed. Minutes? How could she tell. Internally, she was still shaking from present anxiety and remembered violence. The mob had been bad enough. This precisely ordered murder was far worse. Brothers, cousins, friends . . .

The porch door banged at last, and she jumped to her feet as Hart appeared, his fair hair curling wildly where it had dried, his shirt and breeches clinging to him. "That's good." He surveyed the cheerful scene. "You got my message then."

"Message! Nothing of the kind!" Flown with relief and Madeira, his mother turned on him angrily. "No thanks to you that I have not had one of my attacks."

"I'm sorry." He looked past her to Bridget. "I sent a boy to say I had to go straight to the Council of Safety."

"Of course," said Mercy. "We should have thought of that."

"The conquering hero." Bridget raised her glass. "To your victory, Mr Purchis."

"Nothing of the kind." His tone to her was sharper than usual. "A skirmish, that's all. Both sides will be claiming victory tomorrow, no doubt. What worries me is what will come of it." He reached out absent-mindedly and helped himself to a roll. "Tempers are high at the Council of Safety. I'm afraid we may make bad worse."

"Can it be worse?" asked Mercy.

"You're famished, you poor man," said Bridget. "What are we thinking of to keep you talking here! What he needs is hot soup," she told Mercy. "Not questions."

"And dry clothes," put in his mother. "What a figure you cut, to be sure, Hart. Do you mean to tell me you've been talking to the Council of Safety like that! I don't know what your father would say if he could see you now."

"They would not have listened to me if I had looked like Solomon himself," said Hart bitterly, but refused to be drawn further.

As he had predicted, morning saw both British and Americans claiming victory, and each with some semblance of truth. The British had indeed captured some of the rice ships they needed so badly, though Governor Wright was undoubtedly exaggerating when he wrote Lord Dartmouth that they had taken fourteen or fifteen of them. Similarly, the Americans inflated the losses they had inflicted on the British, and, an inevitable aftermath of the fighting, the mob was out in force. A group of Governor Wright's councillors who were still in town were lucky to be arrested, and many Tory merchants saw their danger in time and took refuge with the British fleet.

Hart, who had arranged for a guard to be put on the McCartney house, continued silent and anxious, and returned from the meetings of the Council of Safety in such a black mood that only Bridget dared speak to him and even she did not like to ask what was the matter. They learned at last towards the end of the month when he announced curtly, one evening, that he was to go on duty next day. "You will know where soon enough," he told his anxious mother. "But there is no need for alarm, and no hope of glory."

He left at dawn and returned long after dark, grey-faced and uncommunicative. "Yes," he said curtly, in answer to Bridget's bold question, "we've been on a punitive raid, down to Tybee. Destroyed the houses the British have been using there. It was the only answer the Council of Safety could think of to the British attack on the rice ships. Horrible. The mob's not much worse. "Oh"—as Bridget began to protest— "we didn't tar and feather anyone, but turned helpless women and children out of doors and burned their homes before their very eyes."

"Oh, the poor things," exclaimed Mercy. "What will they do?"

"Go aboard the British ships. What else *can* they do? And their men will follow them. We've made enemies enough to-day! And the Indians with us, enjoying it all. That's why I agreed to go." He needed to explain it. "I was afraid they might get out of hand."

"Never, with you there." Bridget smiled up at him admiringly.

"Not this time," he said. "Archibald Bulloch had his men well in control, I'll say that for him. We were even able to spare one house where a woman and her children were lying sick, but what will she do, poor creature, with her neighbours all gone? We might just as well have killed her and been done with it."

"I told you it was a wicked war," said his mother. "Can it not be stopped, Hart?"

"No! It's not our decision anymore, Mother. The British Parliament have settled it for us. No more olive branches now. They've passed a Prohibitory Act announcing to the world that a state of war exists between us: our ships are to be prizes, our goods confiscated. We have it in their own letter to Governor Wright, which they sent here, thinking him still in control. He has their gracious permission to confiscate the property of 'rebels.' No, Mother, no more talk of reconciliation now, it's independence or slavery." He turned to his cousin. "Abigail, I think you should stay at home for a few days. I am afraid your sympathies are too well known for your safety."

"It's as bad as that?" asked Mercy.

"Quite as bad. We learned too much for comfort in the

161

course of that unspeakable raid on Tybee. Both Giles and Francis distinguished themselves on Hutchinson Island. They are dead men now, if they set foot in Savannah. You must try to forget Giles, Abigail, and"—he turned to the McCartney sisters—"Miss Bridget, Miss Claire, I am sorry to have to say it, but I think you should do your best to put your mother out of your minds."

"I should think so!" said Bridget.

"Poor mother," said Claire.

"And what about my Francis?" asked Mrs Mayfield.

"Aunt Anne, I'm sorry." His glance shifted, for an instant, between her and Mercy. "Francis is in the worst case of all. You must face it. We must all do so."

"My child! My only son!" Anne Mayfield burst into noisy sobs, and the McCartney girls moved to either side to try and comfort her, and finally to lead her, still sobbing, from the room.

Abigail was gazing steadily at Hart. "I will never forget Giles," she said. "If he had only let me go with him when I asked. Hart, you don't think . . ."

"No. It's too late. The sides are drawn; the die is cast. Since James Johnston's nephews slipped away to the British ships, there's a close guard kept on the river. It wouldn't be safe for you—and it wouldn't be safe for us if you were caught."

"No!" She flared out at him. "Not since you harbour Bridget and Claire McCartney, whose mother is known to be with the British. Of course you cannot let me follow my heart when you have so prejudiced our safety already. If the mob do come here, it's more likely to be on their account than on mine. Ask Miss Bridget and Miss Claire if they have not had letters from their mother! And what questions she asks! And then ask yourself what kind of guests you are entertaining. Giles would never—" She rose and ran from the room, choking on tears as she went.

"I'm sorry." Hart turned with a sigh to Mercy. "If only she had been able to marry him in the first place. But, now, you'll do your best to comfort her, Mercy, will you not?"

"Naturally." Her voice was dry. "But I think you should also bear in mind what she said about Mrs McCartney. No —" She saw him flush up angrily, but went firmly on. "I know you think it none of my business, but I have met the mob twice, and that is enough, I don't propose to be tarred and feathered if I can help it. And, Hart"—how could she put it?—"Bridget and Claire are dear girls, but Bridget is young, and Claire . . . well, not very wise. Abigail's right, you know. They might, in their innocence, write something to their mother that she would pass on to Francis."

"To Francis?" She had astonished him. "Mercy! You mean you know . . ."

"That they went together? I'm not a child, I can see what's in front of my nose. I suppose she took her jewels with her. You could live a long time on those diamonds of hers."

"Mercy!"

She had shocked him, she saw, as much as she had wilfully hurt herself. What did he think, what guess about her and Francis? She did not think she wanted to know.

A few days later, Savannah was celebrating the news that the British ships had vanished from the river's mouth. The immediate danger was past, and for Abigail and the McCartney girls there was an end to sickening hope deferred. There had been no last messages from either Giles Habersham or Mrs McCartney, but Mercy had been accosted in the street by a barefoot vagabond of a boy and handed, to her amazement, a long, loving letter from Francis.

It explained everything. His love for her. His desperation. The appalling financial embarrassment that had followed on Hart's return from the North, and the consequent ceasing of his salary. And, above all, glowing through every line, his passionate belief in the justice of the Loyalist cause. "If I have seemed to behave not quite as you felt I should, dearest Mercy, you must understand that my duty to my King outweighs every other consideration. 'I could not love thee, dear, so much, loved I not honour more.' " And with this resounding conclusion, he was her devoted Francis, "until happier days."

Of Mrs McCartney there was no word, unless the reference to his financial embarrassment was meant to dispose of her. Mercy read and reread the letter, arguing, as she did so, with her conscience. She had made bold to lecture Hart about possible communication between the McCartney girls and their mother. Was she now going to keep Francis' letter secret from him?

She rather thought she was. It gave little information that was not already freely available in town. Everyone knew that

Sir James Wright had sailed for Halifax on learning that the British had abandoned all thought of a further attack on Savannah. And Francis knew no more than anyone else where they would next attack. There was only one line in the long letter that pricked her conscience. Mentioning Halifax as their destination, he said, "I hope to God we do not find Howe there already."

If this meant what she thought it might, it was news indeed. General Howe had replaced General Gage in command at Boston after the British setback at Bunker Hill. Was it possible that the ragged army with which Congress' new commander in chief, General Washington, was besieging Boston, might actually succeed in throwing out the British? It seemed so wildly unlikely she decided to say nothing about it. If there was to be good news from Boston, it would come in its own good time.

The first hint that she might have been right in what seemed a wild enough conjecture came in a letter received from one of Mark Paston's sisters, who were staying with cousins in Cambridge, now that General Washington had his siege headquarters there. "Ruth thinks something is afoot," Hart said when he had finished the closely written letter. "I hope to God she's right. We need good news badly enough, after this winter's fiasco at Quebec."

A few days later, Christ Church bells were ringing to celebrate the amazing news of the British evacuation of Boston. The Virginian general that Congress had made its commander in chief had successfully stolen the same kind of march on the British that had been attempted the year before at Bunker Hill. Waking to find captured British guns staring down at him from Dorchester Heights, General Howe had characteristically taken his time over evacuating Boston, but had finally sailed away northward on March 17. The whole of Massachusetts was free at last.

"But it won't bring Mark Paston back to life," said Hart. "Nor all the other brave men who have died for our liberty. George Walton writes from Philadelphia that Mr Jefferson is working night and day drafting a document that will set out the principles of our cause. I wish with all my heart it could be finished and signed before we let this victory at Boston lull us back into a dream of easy freedom. Walton says there are still too many people at Philadelphia who think we can wipe out the bloodshed of this last year and resume negoations with England as if nothing had happened. I almost wish the British would strike again, to clear their minds for them."

His wish was granted all too soon. A messenger came sweating into town one hot June afternoon with the news that a British fleet was attacking Charleston.

"Dear God, my house!" wailed Mrs Mayfield. "Down by the harbour as it is, there's not a chance of its surviving."

"Not much chance for Charleston," said Hart grimly. "The messenger says their defences are far from complete. Colonel Moultrie is fortifying Sullivan's Island, to defend the harbour, but it sounds like a forlorn hope to me. And, make no mistake, if Charleston falls, we are bound to be next. I am afraid the British must think they have enough Loyalist sympathisers down here in the south so that it's worth giving them a rallying point. They've showed their teeth once, the damned Loyalists, and got their comeuppance at Moore's Creek. Please God Charleston holds out."

Miraculously, Charleston did. Gallantry on the American side combined with muddle, incompetence, and sheer bad luck on the British, and soon Savannahians were drinking the health of two new heroes, Colonel Moultrie, who had insisted on holding Fort Sullivan and had done so against what seemed overwhelming odds, and Lieutenant Jasper, who had gallantly saved the endangered garrison flag. Designed by Colonel Moultrie himself, it consisted of a blue field with a white crescent on which was embroidered the one word, *liberty*. By a curious coincidence, Governor Rutledge visited the fort to congratulate Moultrie, Jasper, and its other defenders on the Fourth of July, unaware of another dramatic declaration of liberty taking place farther north.

News of the signing of the Declaration of Independence did not reach Savannah until the tenth of August, when it was solemnly read aloud four times by President Bulloch, first to the Provincial Council, then outside the Provincial Assembly, then at the Liberty Pole, and finally in the Trustees' Garden.

"I wish they had invited ladies to their celebrations," said Bridget McCartney petulantly, taking Mercy's arm and leaning on it heavily as they turned homewards along Bay Street from the final reading in the Trustees' Garden. "It would be mighty pleasant to dine out there in the cool of the cedar trees, on a day like this."

"Pleasant for us, perhaps." Mercy managed to disengage herself. "But the gentlemen may enjoy themselves more freely without us."

"You mean they will drink too much," said Bridget. "No Mr Purchis. I have never seen him disguised yet. Anyway. have his promise—" She stopped, colouring.

"And besides," agreed Mercy, "he is responsible for the arrangements for the mock funeral of George the Third this evening. I am afraid his position as right-hand man to Colonel McIntosh is likely to be an arduous one."

"No more so than he is amply able to handle. I expect marvellous things tonight, and so I told him. And he promises too, that he will be here to escort us. It's a pity there are so many of us females, poor man."

"I do not propose to go." Abigail had been very quiet.

"Oh, fie! Now more than ever, child, we must seem a united household. You do not wish to bring down one of the mob's visitations on your poor cousin, I trust."

"I don't see why we should seem a household at all." Abigail turned on her. "I heard Hart telling you only the other day that he thought it quite safe for you to return to your own home now. In fact, if I were you, I would be inclined to go there today and make sure you show proper illuminations tonight, or you might be visited by the mob yourselves."

"Oh." Bridget had not thought of this. "I wonder if the slaves would be so foolish—"

"I never knew servants who would take the liberty of burning their mistresses' candles without permission."

Mercy had been amazed and delighted at Abigail's sudden attack on Bridget, whose visit had struck her, too, as having scandalously outlasted itself. If Hart was not careful, he would find a state of engagement existing between himself and Bridget, and, try as she would, she could not decide whether he was aware of this hazard. She rather thought not. He was so busy these days with his duties with the militia and the new responsibility to his friend Colonel McIntosh that he had little time or thought to spare for what went on in the house on Oglethorpe Square.

"I have it." Bridget had made up her mind. "You will go home, Claire, and see to the illuminations. It is my duty to support dear Mr Purchis tonight, but I'm sure either Miss Purchis or Miss Phillips will accompany you."

"I will go gladly." Abigail seized on it, and Mercy was

166

elieved for her. It had been indescribably painful for her, he knew, to listen to the Declaration of Independence read, and would be still more so to have to attend the mock funeral of the King for whom she still felt such love and loyalty.

What she had not expected was that Bridget would assume that this division of their forces was to be a permanent one. "It will be much easier for Miss Abigail to be a little more out of the way of things," she explained to Hart as they returned from the mock funeral that night. "I hope you will think I have contrived well for her. She will be the greatest comfort to my poor silly Claire, who has never been able to manage for herself, and of whom I am afraid the slaves take quite shameless advantage. Such a set of worthless wretches . . . I don't know how you contrive to have yours so well behaved, Mr Purchis."

"Perhaps because they are not slaves, but servants," he said.

"Oh, la!" She flirted her fan at him. "Do you take me for a simpleton, Mr Purchis! You know as well as I do that they all ran from Winchelsea when the British ships appeared off Tybee."

"All but two. And all but a few came back when the British left. And, what's more," Hart warmed to the theme, "they'd taken my flock of sheep with them for safety and brought them back unharmed."

"Well, almost," put in Mercy. "You remember, Hart, they did admit to having eaten one when they got hungry hiding out in the swamp."

"As if they couldn't have caught themselves fish and to spare," said Bridget. "And, anyway, the British never did visit Winchelsea, did they?" There was something in her tone that Mercy did not quite like.

"No. We were lucky." Hart seemed to have noticed nothing. "I wouldn't be surprised if my cousin Francis and my cousin's friend Giles Habersham had put in a word for us." He sighed. "And I cannot help being both grateful and ashamed."

"I am sure your feelings do you the greatest credit, Mr Purchis." Bridget, who had made sure of his arm, leaving Mercy to walk a little behind them, and in their dust, gave his hand an approving pat as they turned in at the garden gate of the Purchis house. She paused and looked up at the stars, visible again now the town's illuminations had dwindled and died. "The air is so sweet tonight, and I am so happy with the day's good news, I think I will stay out a little longer. You will keep me company, will you not, Mr Purchis and let me tell you how well you handled your heavy duties today? I am sure there's no need to keep Miss Phillips from her well-earned rest."

Dismissed, Mercy moved towards the porch door, but found Hart following her. "The air is sweet indeed," he said "but I am afraid my day's duties are not yet done. As you know, Colonel McIntosh is but just returned from Charleston where he has been concerting measures for our mutual defence. We expect General Lee momentarily with a detachment of Virginia and North Carolina troops, with whom we are to mount an operation against St Augustine. It's true that if we could capture that British base it would make the greatest difference to the safety of the southern part of Georgia but I could wish the expedition had been undertaken with longer notice and at a more propitious time of year. As it is, there is everything to procure for it, and I must get to work at once. Today's celebrations were necessary, of course but they've not exactly helped us forward with our plans."

They hardly saw Hart for the next few days, which culminated with the arrival of General Lee and a ceremonial review of his troops on the green at Yamacraw Bluff. It all looked impressive enough, but Hart caught Mercy for an anxious aside. "Don't let my mother and the other ladies be too hopeful," he told her. "You'll not repeat this, I know, and I would say it to no one else, but I wish we had a less impulsive commander. The troops are sickening already as a result of marching at this unsuitable time of year, and we have no medical supplies. Mercy, if the worst should happen, I rely on you and Gordon to look after things here."

"Hart!" But he had turned away to join the troops that were to leave almost at once for Fort Sunbury, where, she knew, he was to try and organise boat transport for the southern journey through the sheltered inner sea passage the British navy could not reach. It was cold comfort to have been picked out for his confidence when the information was so alarming. She had noticed soldiers falling out of their ranks in the course of the review, obviously stricken with the summer sickness bred in the effluvia of the hot, damp rice fields. Hart was normally a healthy man, but he had been working so hard. . . .

She was joined by Bridget McCartney, looking elegant, if hot, in a silk gown Mercy suspected of being smuggled goods. "A striking sight, is it not?" said Bridget. "General Lee tells me he expects to be master of St Augustine and indeed of all East Florida before the British know what is happening to them. Does he not make a gallant figure? I wish we could persuade Mr Purchis to be a little more point device in his uniform."

"Mr Purchis says that comfort is all important to a fighting man. He thinks it one of our greatest advantages over the British troops in those great red woollen coats of theirs."

Bridget pressed her arm. "I like you the better for defending your benefactor. Will you be able to manage the house while he's away? I feel it my duty to return to my poor Claire now the town is so full of troops."

Mercy was delighted to hear it, and not at all surprised when Abigail returned home next day. "Miss McCartney pressed me to stay," she told Mercy, "but to tell truth, I did not much want to. I'm fond of poor Claire, for all her silliness, but, do you know, Mercy, I am ashamed to confess it, but I cannot quite like Bridget."

"Don't be ashamed," said Mercy. "I'm proud of you for trying. We shall do very well without them. If only Hart were safe."

"But it's to be a walkover, this campaign, is it not? Bridget was sure of it. She had it from General Lee himself."

"Then we must hope General Lee is right."

As the hot August days drew on and barefoot slaves hesitated to set even their hardened feet on the baking sand of the streets, disquieting news began to trickle back from Sunbury. Officers and men alike were ill, and the death rate had reached fourteen or fifteen a day.

"And this without even encountering the enemy," Mercy told Abigail bitterly, then looked up, irritated, as Saul Gordon pushed open the office door and peered at them round it.

"Just as well if they do not, I am afraid, Miss Phillips. Ah, lemonade! Delicious." He advanced on the cool jug from which she was helping Abigail. "Miss Mercy, may I beg a word of advice from you? In the office, not to trouble Miss Abigail."

"Advice from me?"

"It's about the sheep," he explained with one of his sidelong apologetic glances for Abigail. "Mr Purchis told me to come to you if there was any trouble about them." As he spoke, he bowed ceremoniously to Abigail and ushered Mercy into the office. "I have had a message from Sam." He closed the office door behind him. "It seems they are suffering gravely from this heat."

"Are not we all," said Mercy. "I wonder. Do you think they should be shorn a second time? It might help them, and we could do with the wool to send north. Our troops will freeze in Boston this winter."

"Not Boston, Miss Phillips. Had you not heard? The word is that the British fleet has appeared off New York, and General Washington has marched to its defence. But I'm sure you are right as usual. I'll do what you say about the sheep." His soft, white hand picked up the pen on his desk and put it down again. "Miss Phillips, as you know, my poor wife died this winter. I shall miss and mourn her forever." His hand went to his heart under the silky black broadcloth he now wore. "But she'd been ill a long time." Businesslike now, "A man suffers, and survives, and looks about him. I am a poor man, but"—he looked down at the black broadcloth—"not, perhaps, quite so poor as I was. And not without ambition. If I'm not very much mistaken, there are fortunes to be made from this war, and I intend to make one. Miss Phillips, will you share it with me?"

"Good gracious!" She gazed at him in honest amazement, and was aware, and angry, that her amazement surprised him. He had been sure of her answer. It made it that much easier. "Mr Gordon, forgive me, I had no idea. You have quite taken my breath away." If not entirely true, it was the nearest she could get to courtesy.

"I do not wonder," he said. "Situated as you are—forgive my plain speaking—it must come as a surprise to receive such an offer. A dependent and not always, ahem, in the easiest of circumstances . . . yours is not a happy lot, Miss Phillips, and I have been filled with admiration at how you have borne it, and how you have, if I may say so, reduced this house to a state of order. It's no wonder that Mr Purchis has come to depend on you, but there will be changes soon, if I am not very much mistaken, and then think what an asylum my little house must be to you. And there is much to do there, Miss Phillips. I will be plain with you. Since my poor wife died, I have been quite at sixes and sevens, lacking a woman's domestic hand. We could be much for each other, you and I."

"Mr Gordon." She was hesitating how best to deal with this remarkable offer, when a sound in the main house made her turn. "It's Mr Purchis! Forgive me, Mr Gordon, if I say it cannot be."

"Cannot?" But he, too, turned towards the door into the main house as it was flung open to reveal Hart, dust-streaked, exhausted, hair, shirt and breeches clinging to him with sweat.

"There you are, Mercy, thank God. General Lee sleeps here tonight. The best bedroom, everything, dinner—he'll be here in an hour or so."

"Defeat?" She must ask it.

"No. A recall, and a most timely one, if the reason for it was not so black. General Howe has outwitted Washington and taken New York. The town has burned to the ground, and Washington saved his army by a miracle. No time now for mad ventures down here in the South. We are fighting for our lives."

15

If Mercy had hoped that Hart's dramatic interruption had settled the question between Saul Gordon and herself, she was to be disappointed. Authority had changed the overseer from an insignificant man to one who liked to domineer, at least over women. Mercy sometimes sensed the hint of a sneer under his elaborate courtesy to Mrs Purchis and Mrs Mayfield. Abigail he tended to ignore, but worst of all was his manner to herself. In some curious way he contrived at once to relegate her to the position of housekeeper, as opposed to member of the family, and to imply a bond between them. Manager and housekeeper, what could be more logical? And yet there was nothing she could put a finger on, nothing to which she could actually object.

"Hart," she said one dark February morning when he had come in equally depressed by the news from the North and by the slowness with which the fortification of Savannah was going on. "Could we not go back to Winchelsea? It's hard on Abigail, here in town."

"I know." There were no Loyalists in Savannah now, or rather, those who were kept very quiet. But everyone knew of Abigail's engagement to Giles Habersham, and everyone also knew that Giles was in a British regiment at New York, where the British garrison was passing a comfortable winter, while George Washington did his best to hold his army together in the bleak New Jersey countryside. And the messenger who brought news of Giles had also reported that Francis was now attached to the staff of the British General Cornwallis and was in winter quarters with him at New Brunswick, threatening Philadelphia. As Bridget McCartney said, it was lucky for the family in Oglethorpe Square that Hart was such a prominent patriot. "Though, mind you, it weakens his position with the Council of Safety," she added, and Mercy knew it was true.

"Do let's go," she said now, seeing that Hart was actually considering it. "Surely the rice crop is as important as anything these days, and then there's the lambing to be thought of."

"Yes. Food for George Washington's soldiers and wool for their uniforms. I never did thank you properly for that second shearing, Mercy, and all the work you did getting the wool spun and made up. I like to think that some of the soldiers in that freezing camp at Morristown are wearing Winchelsea homespun. I wish we could go out there. Now that we've finished drafting the Georgia Constitution, I seem to have less and less influence with the Council of Safety. Since Lachlan McIntosh drove the British back to St Augustine, people seem to think the threat to Savannah is over. As if it ever will be while the British navy keeps control of the sea. And secret enemies enough here, I'm afraid, to betray us when the moment comes. There's talk of another southern offensive, but I don't feel much more hopeful about it than I did of the last one. Not while President Bulloch continues so unwell. What is the use of the Council of Safety giving him absolute power, when everyone knows he's a sick man?"

"Is he so bad?"

"I'm anxious about him. But you will say nothing of this,

172

Mercy. In the meantime, we'll think about Winchelsea, but I believe I must stay in town until there is better news of Bulloch." He gave her a quick, considering look. "Would you like me to send Gordon out to see to the lambing?"

"Oh, *yes!* Thank you, Hart." Through the long, gloomy winter, Saul Gordon's attentions to her had become so heavy-handedly obvious that it had been impossible for anyone to ignore them. "Though," she felt in honour bound to go on, "I cannot think he will be much use."

"No. But there's nothing for him to do here, now that the blockade and the non-importation agreement have put an end to trade. A bit of cross-country trade with Charleston and some upriver traffic with Purrysburg is about the extent of our business."

"And worthless paper all you get for your hard work."

"Don't call it that!" He flushed angrily. "I'm surprised at you, Mercy. I thought you at least understood. . . ."

"I'm sorry. But how can I help understanding that you are working yourself to death for no pay and not much thanks."

But he had picked up the broad-brimmed hat that was beginning to show its age. "I'll be out for dinner. Miss McCartney is having trouble with those slaves of hers again, and I promised I'd ride over as soon as I could find the time. I'll give her your compliments, of course."

"If you wish." Left alone, she picked up the woollen stocking she had been knitting and threw it as hard as she could across the room.

"I beg your pardon!" Saul Gordon had opened the office door just in time to catch the prickly bundle full in the face. "My dear Miss Phillips!" And then, with one of his quick, knowing looks, "Alas, am I too late to catch Mr Purchis?" He was busy winding up her wool with those soft white hands, and now handed the stocking back to her with an attempt at a courtly bow. "Always at your good works, I see."

"Thank you. Yes, Mr Purchis is gone out." Wild horses would not make her say where. She began to knit again, savagely, as if each movement of the needles were stabbing an enemy to the heart. "If only I was a man!" She regretted the words as she spoke them.

"I am so very glad you are not. Miss Phillips, it is some months since I last had the honour to address you. Let me . . . allow . . . bear with me while I speak once again about

173

the matter that lies so close to my heart." He laid his white hand on the appropriate area of his glossy black coat. "Dear Miss Phillips, let me, for once, speak frankly to you." And then, with a sudden and disconcerting change of tone, "It's no use at all, you know. You must see that by now. You're the housekeeper—worth your weight in gold, invaluable, whatever you like, and invisible. So . . . marry me. Show the lot of them. Let them see what a prize they've undervalued. And, talking of prizes, I've not spent this winter too unprofitably myself. If you remember, when I last had the honour to address you, I admitted to my hopes. Well, my dear young . . . my dear Miss Mercy, they are more than hopes now. I told you there was money to be made, did I not? Well!" He blew out his chest with a deep, satisfied breath. "I'm thinking of setting up my own plantation, Miss Mercy."

"You will call me Miss Phillips!"

"I will call you anything you please if you will only let me call you mine."

"Never! Do you think you can buy me, Mr. Gordon, with the blood-money you have made out of this war?"

"Blood-money? Nonsense." How enormously he had changed in the course of the winter. "Just because Mr Purchis chooses to act the spendthrift and take worthless paper for his produce, there's no need for everyone else to be so stupid. Even in times like this, Miss Phillips, money breeds money if you treat it right. Mark my words, by the time the British recapture Savannah, I'll be a rich man and Hart Purchis will come begging to me."

"The British recapture Savannah! Are you out of your mind, Mr Gordon?"

"No, just a little saner than most, as you will come to see sooner or later. In the meanwhile, never forget that I am your devoted slave. I've bought a new house, by the way." He threw it in as an afterthought. "Down on the Bay. A Tory house, going so cheap I couldn't resist it. But it seems forlorn enough without a mistress."

"Then you had better look for one elsewhere."

"Dearest Miss Phillips. Never. We Gordons are men of single mind, and I tell you the time will come when you will be glad and proud to call yourself Mrs. Gordon."

President Bulloch died suddenly that February, and Button Gwinnett, one of the signers of the Declaration of Independence, was elected in his place. "It's only a temporary appointment," Hart explained. "Until the new Assembly meets. But I am afraid not much good will come of it. Gwinnett has hated my friend Lachlan McIntosh ever since McIntosh was made commander of our troops on the Continental Establishment last September. I think Gwinnett wanted the job himself. God knows why. He may be a politician, but he's no general. He's making it pretty clear he wants no truck with McIntosh or his friends. He's planning an expedition of his own against St Augustine, and Lachlan and I am most significantly not included. To tell the truth, I don't much like the feel of things here in Savannah these days. It's hard to tell fair-weather friend from foe. . . . Too many turncoats and too many profiteers in high places. There are even rumours about how poor Bulloch died. But for goodness sake don't speak of that!"

"As bad as that?" asked Mercy. She wished she knew whether he had been referring, among others, to the McCartney girls, who were keeping open house now for the members of the Council of Safety, the stigma of their mother's flight to the British apparently quite forgotten in the lavishness of their entertainment.

Bridget called at the house in Oglethorpe Square a few days after Bulloch's funeral to chide Mercy and Abigail for being, as she put it, "Quite strangers. I missed you at my soirée the other night."

"I'm sorry." Abigail's little chin went up. "It was our night to sew for the militia." `

"You!" Bridget pantomimed amazement. "Sewing for a parcel of rebels!"

"They are men, just the same," said Abigail. "And need shirts. I only hope some patriot lady would do as much for my Giles if he were to need it, which, please God, he does not."

"What do you hear from him?" asked Bridget.

"Why, nothing. And you from your mother?"

Bridget coloured angrily. "Nothing, of course! Do you think Claire and I would communicate with a traitor? We have quite washed our hands of her and so I trust she knows." She rose to her feet. "I have kept you two ladies from your good works long enough. Give my regards to poor Mr Purchis. His nose is badly out of joint these days, is it not? He and his rumbustious friend McIntosh are quite out of favour with our new President. Mr Gwinnett blames McIntosh for all our disasters in the south."

"And one cannot wonder Mr Gwinnett feels strongly about them," said Mercy, "considering his plantation is down at Sunbury."

Bridget closed her fan with an angry snap. "It's easy to be cool and level-headed when one's estate is here in the environs of Savannah. I think Mr Purchis would be wise to retire to his, and so you may tell him with my regards."

Left alone, Abigail and Mercy looked at each other for a moment in silence, then, "Well!" said Mercy.

Abigail laughed. "Very well, if you ask me. She has decided to fly for higher game now Hart's star is no longer in the ascendant. Oh, Mercy, do you know what I sometimes dream, sometimes let myself hope? I love Hart so dearly; I'd give anything to see him happy." She shook back her fair curls and looked up at Mercy. "Sometimes I wish the Mc-Cartney girls had gone with their mother."

"I don't know what you're talking about," said Mercy.

"No? Then I'm sorry I spoke." She sat down at her spinet and played a few notes.

As Abigail's fingers wandered into a Bach prelude, Mercy subsided into wretched thought. First Saul Gordon, now Abigail. Had everyone seen that she loved Hart before she even recognized it herself? And Hart cared nothing for her—or, rather, cared as one would for the stray animal one had rescued. He would always be a brother to her, as he had promised. No more. No less. And not enough. At all costs, she must get away from this house, where, try how she would —and she had tried hard since that talk with Saul Gordon— there was no avoiding daily contact, the daily calm courtesy that fed and starved her.

And yet, how could she leave? Abigail was much stronger these days, it was true, but she had been brought up to be a young lady, to be marriageable, to be accomplished. She could no more go to market and fight for her share of whatever provisions were available than Mercy could have spent all those hours reading Richardson's novels or playing Bach on the spinet.

In the end, the problem was solved for her by Hart himself, who surprised her by changing his mind, leaving the family and Saul Gordon in Savannah, and spending most of his time at Winchelsea. If only he had taken Saul Gordon with him. Did he, too, as his mother so obviously did, expect her to yield in the end to Gordon's advances? Intolerable thought. She wished now that she had spoken more firmly about Gordon, who had passed from words to soft, quick touches with those damp hands of his. And how could she avoid him? With Hart away, they must work together. If she left the office door open when she had to talk to him, he made a ceremonious point of closing it. Handing her the week's housekeeping money, he would detain her hand, raise it for a soft, wet kiss. She longed to strike him. But he was indispensable too.

She had escaped from one such encounter, feeling a little sick, to take a breath of air in the back yard under the protection of the servants' friendly eyes, when her spirits rose incorrigibly at sight of Hart riding in at the gate.

"Mercy! What a stroke of luck!" He jumped to the ground and handed Thunder's reins to Jem. "I was hoping for a word with you." His fair face was flushed; he looked, for once, younger than his years. "Come round to the garden?" He pushed open the little gate for her, then paused under a flowering dogwood, his face dappled with shade from its leaves. "I seem never to see you alone."

"You've been away. And we're both busy." She felt he must hear the beat of her heart. What could be coming?

"Yes. That's it. That's just it. I'm glad of this chance." He bent to remove a trail of Spanish moss from a battered little cupid on the terrace. "I've just been to see the McCartneys."

"Oh?"

"Yes. Found them alone for once. Miss Bridget read me a lecture. About you."

"About me?"

"I'm grateful to her." He was twisting the Spanish moss round his wrist. "I should have thought . . . I'm ashamed . . . she's quite shocked to think that we do not pay you a salary for all you do for us."

"A salary? Me!" Which did she hate most? Herself, for that absurd moment of delusive hope, or Bridget? But Hart was looking down at her, kind, friendly, puzzled. She made an immense effort. "Are you trying to make a stranger of me, Hart? You must know that whatever I do about the house, I do out of my great gratitude and affection for you all."

"Indeed I do, and most grateful we are, but the fact is

that you have become the linch-pin round which the whole household revolves."

"You mean the housekeeper." She had herself in hand now. "That, no doubt, is how Miss Bridget describes me."

"Well, yes . . . housekeeper, dear friend, and valued confidante is how I would prefer to put it."

"Thank you." Miraculously, her voice was steady. "But, Hart, what should I need? I've always felt anxious that I was not properly earning the pin money you insisted on giving me when first you took me in."

"Earning it! That trifling sum! Mercy, you must let me do what I feel is right about this."

"Must I?" She thought it over for a minute, coldly, hating herself, very nearly hating him. Then, "Very well, if you insist, but it shall be on my own terms."

"And they are?" She had surprised him.

"Cash or kind, Hart. I don't care which, but I have no mind to set my curls with Georgia paper. Settle it with Mr Gordon. I am sure he will think of a proper way." She had shocked him into silence and seized the chance to leave him, merely throwing over her shoulder, "I must remember to thank Miss Bridget for her kind thought."

Next afternoon, Saul Gordon invited her ceremoniously into the office. "So you're the salaried housekeeper now." She thought he eyed her with a new respect, and for once he kept his hands to himself. "And in cash or kind, Mr Purchis tells me. No Georgia money for you, Miss Mercy?"

Mrs Purchis grumbled about what she called Hart's absurd extravagance, but Mercy could see she was relieved at this new state of affairs. Young plantation owners did not marry their paid housekeepers.

Private misery lost itself in public crisis when Button Gwinnett's divided army came staggering back from the south, with hardly even an honourable defeat to boast of and the usual toll of sickness and unnecessary death. "If he thinks he'll be re-elected president and commander in chief after that debacle, he's crazy." Hart had come in from Winchelsea for the election of the President of the Assembly on the first Tuesday in May. "Yes, Mother," he answered Mrs Purchis' question. "All's well at Winchelsea. The lambing's over, and the rice looks better than ever." He looked at the big clock and rose to his feet. "I must go. Every vote is going to count today."

"A lot of fuss about politics," said Mrs Purchis comfortably. "Mercy, wind my wool for me."

William, the coachman, brought the first rumour, tapping anxiously at the back door to ask for Mercy. "Miss?" She had stepped out into the yard to join him, imagining that one of the servants was ill and needed her. "There's a story running round town. I thought you ought to know. But not Madam Purchis. Not yet. It may be all just talk."

"What is it, William?"

"Talk of a duel, miss. Mr Gwinnett and General McIntosh. And seconds, miss. You know how they often fight, seconds and all. Twelve paces . . . sure death . . . right here in town, the Jewish Graveyard? I don't know. But, miss, the master . . . where is he?"

"Oh, dear God!" If McIntosh had fought, Hart was bound to be involved. "But, William, why?"

"I don't know, miss. May be all talk. Don't fret too much."

Absurd advice. She lifted her head, listening. "There's a carriage stopping outside. Perhaps it is Mr Hart." But a carriage would mean he was wounded. Dead? Twelve paces . . . murder.

Back in the house, she found Bridget McCartney. "Do so hope it's not true, dear Mrs Purchis," she was saying. "But so impulsive, poor Mr Hart."

"Mercy!" Martha Purchis turned to her. "Have you heard anything? About a duel?"

"Rumour!" said Bridget. "More than that, I'm afraid. When Treutlen was elected president, McIntosh had the gall to turn on Gwinnett and call him a scoundrel. In front of everyone. Of course there's been a duel. Both of them gravely wounded. Like to die. It will mean a murder charge. For the survivor. And the seconds."

"The seconds?" asked Mercy. "Who were they?"

"I don't know. But if Mr Hart was not involved, where is he?"

"Mercy." Mrs Purchis was ash-white. "My drops. Quick!"

"Here." Mercy always carried them in her pocket now. By the time she had administered them, Abigail was showing Bridget out with a cold courtesy Mercy admired. Together they put Martha Purchis to bed, explained the situation to Mrs Mayfield, and waited.

The clock struck ten, eleven. Outside, the night was silent as death. "Mercy," said Abigail. "Dear Mercy, you don't need to pretend with me."

"Oh!" She was on the floor, her head in Abigail's lap, crying, and crying, and crying. It was Abigail, in the end, who insisted they both go to bed, leaving a servant on the watch for news. "We'll need all our strength in the morning."

"Yes." Shakily, "Thank you, Abigail. Only, you know, and so do I, that whatever happens, there's no hope for me."

"If only he's alive," said Abigail, and Mercy knew herself rebuked.

She thought she would not sleep, but did, dreamlessly, and woke to find Abigail shaking her. "He's not hurt! Mercy, he's not hurt!"

"Not hurt! Thank God. But—"

"He stayed to help nurse McIntosh. Bridget was right about that. They're both badly wounded. He and Gwinnett. No hope for Gwinnett. McIntosh may live. It's trouble, Mercy, for Hart, terrible trouble."

"How could he?" asked Mercy.

"How could he not? McIntosh was his friend—is his friend. You know what our Southern gentlemen are like. He had no choice."

"Monstrous. Father said duelling—" She stopped, swallowing tears. What use was that?

A few days later, Button Gwinnett died. "It will go hard with McIntosh." Bridget McCartney was paying one of her daily calls of "sympathy" that always made Mrs Purchis worse. "He must stand trial, of course! If I'd been he, I'd have been well across river by now, and Hart too."

"Nothing of the kind!" Martha Purchis pulled herself more upright on the sofa. "Hart will stay, of course, and face what must be faced. I just wish he would come home!"

"He feels he has a duty to Colonel McIntosh," said Mercy, but she wished it too.

"Acquitted!" Dr Flinn brought the news. "Gloriously acquitted by Judge Glen. I have no doubt we will see young Hart home soon, and then we'll be better, won't we, ma'am?"

"I'm sure I hope so." But Mrs Purchis sounded as doubtful as Mercy felt. Though McIntosh had been acquitted, there was still a strong party against him in town. Mercy had heard that the mob had visited Lachlan McIntosh's house and been turned away by a furious speech from Hart. No need to wonder who had stirred them up. McIntosh had plenty of enemies in high places.

"We mustn't hope too much, ma'am," she told Mrs Purchis after the doctor had left.

"No, dear." Illness had made Martha Purchis gentle. "I think hope is the most dangerous indulgence of all." And then, suddenly brightening, "What's that? It sounds like . . ."

It was Hart. Much thinner, he was very grave, unusually pale from his sojourn by his friend's sickbed. "Dear mother." He bent to kiss her. "I was sorry to hear you were ill. And so glad"—a sober smile for Mercy—"that I knew you were here to nurse her. I dared not come sooner. You understood?"

"No," said Martha Purchis.

"Yes," said Mercy.

"Dr Flinn says you're better, Mother. I met him . . . I asked him. . . ." His look, for Mercy, was an appeal.

"I'm much better, dear boy, now you are here. Now we shall all be happy again. You'll dine tonight, Hart? We'll celebrate?"

He gave her a strange look. "Yes, Mother, we'll celebrate." He bent to kiss her, then stood up. "Now I must call on Miss Bridget, who, I hear, has been a most faithful caller while you've been unwell."

"Faithful, yes," said his mother. "Cheering, no." But Hart had drawn Mercy aside and did not hear her.

"Make a party of it, Mercy. Champagne? Have we any left? I've news, or shall have."

The best damask napkins. The cut glass they never used. A few sun-drenched roses for the silver centrepiece Oglethorpe had given the first Purchis of Winchelsea. "Make a party of it. . . . I've news, or shall have." The words rang in her head all day. He was going to call on Bridget McCartney. He would have news. Perhaps he would bring her with him. She smiled savagely to herself and went out to confer with the cook. Market was over for the day. The winter's supply of smoked and salt food from Winchelsea was long since exhausted. "Make a party of it!"

"Miss Mercy." William had emerged from his hut at the far corner of the yard. "You want some fresh fish? Give Jem and me the afternoon off, and you'll have your party."

"Delicious." Hart had not brought Bridget McCartney. He finished his second helping of devilled crab and smiled round the table. "It's good to be home."

"And good to have you, Hart." His mother raised her glass. "To stay this time, I hope. No more running off to Winchelsea."

"Oh, Mother." His tone was at once apology and warning. "I'm sorry . . . I should have told you at once." And then a quick aside to Mercy, "Have you her drops?" And as she nodded, speechless, he went on. "Lachlan McIntosh goes north," he told them. "His friends advise it. He can do no good here, after what's happened. And, Mother, the same is true of me, I am afraid. I have said I'll go too."

"And leave us defenceless!" Anne Mayfield turned on him, while his mother sat rigid, fighting for composure. "Of all the obstinate, inconsiderate, cross-grained boys . . ." She was working rapidly towards one of her bouts of hysteria.

"Hush!" said Martha Purchis. "No, dear"—to Mercy—"I don't need my drops. I'm not quite a fool." She turned with a travesty of a smile to Hart. "I saw this coming. Purchis of Winchelsea must do his duty, and you're right, there's no place for you here. Not now. And as for us, a household of women, we have nothing to fear, and Saul Gordon to protect us. But, Hart, have you no other news? No good news for me?"

He looked at her squarely. "No, ma'am. I don't think these are times for good news."

And what did that mean, Mercy asked herself for the hundredth time, sleepless in her bed. That he had proposed and been refused, or decided not to propose? She would never know. Did she want to know? He was going away. That was a good thing. That was what she had wanted. She put her head under the pillow for fear that Abigail, in the room next door, might hear her sobs.

16

It was strange to be sewing shirts again, as she had three years ago before Hart went to Harvard. It seemed much longer than that. It seemed a lifetime. A disastrous one. When there was no chance of hearing that firm tread or listening for the voice that seemed to grow deeper and graver every day, might she manage to achieve some kind of pretence at quietness? Not peace, never happiness, but surely she might hope to be quiet?

They were all going to Winchelsea at the end of June, and Mercy was glad of it. Hart and his mother would both be better away from the gossiping tongues and sly glances of Savannah. "It may be the last visit for a long time," Hart warned. "I'm afraid, with things as they are since that last disastrous expedition of poor Gwinnett's, it's altogether too far from town and too near the sea for your safety, Mother. You'll not go when I'm not here?" It was as much order as request.

"Of course not. But, Hart, do you know when——"

"Not for some time. I must wait for my posting. I'd much rather wait at Winchelsea."

"So would I," agreed his mother. "Hardly anyone came to our sewing circle last night, I can't get up a hand of whist, and even the McCartney girls seem to be avoiding us now."

"They've other interests," said Hart shortly. "I called this afternoon and found Joseph Wood there, and two of those cousins of his who all have such profitable appointments since he's crept into power. I wish we may not be carrying democracy too far."

"Can one?" asked Mercy.

"I begin to think so. As to Miss Bridget"—the heavy brows drew together—"she sent a message to you, Mother. As I was leaving. To say how sorry she is not to be able to visit you."

"Not able? And what is stopping her, pray?"

"She came out on to the porch with me, on purpose to explain . . . to apologise . . . She feels it very much, she says. . . . It's because of their mother . . . and . . . and Francis and Giles. She thinks two households, so tainted with loyalism, had better not be seen to associate."

"Well!" Martha Purchis drew herself up. "Of all the un-grateful hussies. When I think what we've done for those girls. I should like to give them a good piece of my mind, but I suppose they would be 'not at home' if I were to call."

"I don't know." He looked and sounded wretched.

"Hart." Abigail had turned very white. "I said this before, when the Loyalists were proscribed in October, and I say it again. You have only to say the word, and I go."

"Dear Abigail." He crossed the room quickly to take her hand. "So long as I have a house, its protection is yours. Thank God, as you are a woman and without property, there is no need for you to take the patriotic oath."

"No." She sat down again, her hands limp in her lap. "But I know what harm my abstaining does you with Joseph Wood and his creatures."

"Hush!" He surprised them all. "I know it seems odd that someone like Joe Wood, who has actually been taken to court as a dishonest man, should be sent to represent us at the Continental Congress. We cannot help thinking these things, but, Abigail, I think we should not speak of them."

She looked up at him sadly. "You'll be glad to get away, won't you, to the North, and your hero, Washington."

The day before they were due to leave for Winchelsea, they were amazed by a visit from Bridget McCartney.

"Dear Mrs Purchis!" Bridget was at her most winning. "I am come as a suppliant to you."

"A suppliant?" Martha Purchis had received her with a cool dignity Mercy admired.

"Yes. Claire and I have minded so much, these last weeks, that we have not seen you."

"There was nothing to stop you," said Mrs Purchis.

"Only our wish not to make matters worse than they were already for Hart," explained Bridget. "If you but knew, Mrs Purchis, how we have been pleading his case with our friends, but now my poor Claire is not well. Above all things she needs a breath of country air, and what better excuse could there be for us to visit you at Winchelsea?"

"At Winchelsea?" Martha Purchis did not try to conceal her amazement.

"Dear Mrs Purchis, I could not bear to let Hart go north, to such a danger, without saying a real good-bye, and how can I, here in Savannah, where even the walls have ears?"

Martha Purchis looked round her handsome sitting-room as if wondering whether this was true. "You and Claire actually want to come and stay?"

"Do you not know that the time we spent here in Savannah with you was one of the happiest of our lives?" Bridget looked down thoughtfully at her diamond bracelets. She was wearing two today, Mercy noticed. "We owe so much to you all, and most especially to Hart. Dear Purchis, just for a few days, just to say good-bye."

"I said yes," Martha Purchis told her son that night. "It seemed only civil."

"Just so long as the Woods don't come to call," said Hart. Impossible to tell how he felt about the proposed visit. The days when one could read his thoughts in his face were long gone.

For Mercy, the visit was the last straw. Bad enough that Saul Gordon was coming, but now this. "I shall be glad when it's over," she told Abigail.

"If only it is well over," said Abigail. "And no harm done. Do you know, Mercy, I cannot quite like this visit of the McCartneys."

Mercy laughed. "Oh, Abigail, I do so agree with you."

She remembered Abigail's words when the McCartneys arrived. Claire did indeed look far from well and had been glad to be urged to spend her mornings in bed, but Bridget showed herself remarkably friendly and actually insisted on accompanying Mercy on her morning visit to her father's grave. She talked all the way volubly, about fresh country air and the blessed quiet after Savannah, but when they reached the low wall that surrounded the family lot, she paused. "You will wish to be alone with your memories. I will explore a little farther along the path towards the river." She took a deep breath and started again. "It is so *good* to be away from the heat and bustle of town, but a breath of river air will be best of all. I will see you back at the house."

"Be sure and keep to the path," advised Mercy.

"I shall indeed. I have no wish to lose myself in Hart's jungle. Besides"—she lifted muslin skirts to reveal the softest of white kid slippers—"I am hardly shod for it."

Mercy was glad to be left alone to put her morning-gathered flowers on her father's grave, but ashamed to find herself thinking more of Bridget than of him. And yet . . . she put her flowers in the porous clay container the estate potter had given her and stood for a moment looking down at them. What would her father have thought of this curious visit of the McCartney sisters, and odder still, of Bridget's behaviour this morning? He would have questioned it, as he questioned everything. *"Cui bono?"* he would have asked. "Who gains what by it?" Well, she smiled down at his grave as if she were actually answering him. Bridget obviously intended to gain Hart if she could. Or did she? She had certainly managed to suggest this to Mrs Purchis so as to get invited, but Mercy was not so sure, suspecting her of flying at higher, more political game. So, why this visit? Perhaps the game had eluded her and Hart was to be second best? Odious thought. And, somehow, she did not think her father would be satisfied with it. Following his mind with her own, she decided that he would question the purpose of this morning's walk. Bridget McCartney never walked if she could ride, never rode if she could drive. So what was she doing in her soft little kid shoes, looking for a breeze by the river?

Go and see, said her imagined father. She rose to her feet and walked across the graveyard to the river path. No sign of Bridget. She must have walked fast indeed to have vanished in either direction. Mercy looked back at the grave under its Judas tree and then across to the family tomb where Francis had hidden. He had killed poor Pete at the disused wharf. And that wharf was reached by a concealed path behind the big magnolia at the corner of the dike. Impossible, surely, that Bridget could have found this, or ventured down it, through what she had called "Hart's jungle," in those soft slippers. But, already, Mercy was walking swiftly towards the place where the path branched off. Impossible or not, she was going to make sure.

Reaching the magnolia she stood for a few minutes in the hot sun, wondering what to do. Nobody who did not know could possibly tell that a path started here. And how should Bridget know? The answer came instantly. Through Francis or through her mother. Was this the reason for the visit? Was she down there, at the cold wharf now, keeping some treasonable assignation? She shivered in the hot sun, thinking of Pete's death. If Bridget was meeting someone down at the wharf, they would not be alone. Madness to challenge them single-handed. But she must do something. Straining her ears, she could almost imagine she heard voices. It was not far down the path; the shrubbery was thick with a rich June growth of wild bay and myrtle; if she went, very quietly, a little way . . .

"Miss Mercy!" She turned to see Saul Gordan hurrying towards her along the dike. "I have found you at last! Mr Purchis is asking for you urgently."

"Oh? Where?"

"By the sheep pens. I hate to ask you to hurry, in this heat, but just the same—"

What should she do? Take Saul Gordon into her confidence? Ask him to go down to the old wharf, see if Bridget was really talking to . . . to whom? Francis? It was possible. Francis had served at the unsuccessful British assault on Charleston the year before. That was all they knew. He could be anywhere. Here? Delivering a secret message to Bridget from her mother?

Saul Gordon stood there, innocuous in his black suit, sweating in the sun. She trusted him less even than Francis or Bridget. Danger was thick in the hot air. "Very well," she made it casual, "I will go to Mr Purchis at once."

It was a half-mile walk to the sheep field, and when she arrived, there was no one there. And the sheep looked contented enough, munching stolidly at the alfalfa Hart had had planted for them. Mercy gazed at them, puzzled, undecided, wondering whether she had imagined that moment of terror. Should she go back to the old wharf? No. Too late, useless. She must find Hart. She hurried back across the sheep field to the house.

Arriving, hot and flushed, she found Bridget there already, sitting on the porch, gently rocking in one of the big estate-made chairs. Her slippers, very evident as she pushed herself off the ground, shone white as they had this morning.

But were they the same slippers? "Did you enjoy your walk?" asked Mercy.

"Vastly." She was gently waving a broad-brimmed chip hat to create her own breeze. "I went as far as that big magnolia on the river path and then cut through the orange grove to the house. I shall do it every day and become a perfect amazon. But you look hot, Miss Phillips. You must not court sunstroke running about in the heat of the day. You had best go indoors and rest a while. Look, here comes Mr Purchis. Shall I venture out into the sun to meet him? I really believe I will. Besides, it will give you time to make yourself a little presentable, my dear creature. You would hardly wish your employer to see you looking as you do now." She rose, picked up a white, frilled parasol that lay on the porch floor beside her, and drifted out through the screen door and down the steps towards Hart's approaching figure.

That parasol. Bridget had not had it when they started out to the family lot together. So, she had been up to her

187

room to fetch it and might at the same time have changed a muddy pair of slippers for the spotless ones she was now wearing. Mercy fell into step beside her. "Mr Purchis was looking for me."

"So that's why you've been hurrying." Bridget's amused stare took in every detail of her hot face and crumpled dress. "You have the most devoted housekeeper, Hart," she greeted him. "You send for her and she courts heatstroke seeking you out."

"Sent for you?" Hart looked puzzled for a moment, and then, "Oh, the sheep. I am so sorry, I didn't mean Gordon to send you to me. I merely wanted to ask—"

"Some dreadful question about pitch and shearing?" Bridget interrupted him. "If it's not of the first urgency, I think you should send Miss Phillips indoors for a while before you trouble her about anything. She looks quite exhausted with heat and hurry and should not be standing here in the sun."

Bridget, on the other hand, had a glow about her. Standing on the porch, watching, frustrated, as she took Hart's arm and strolled away, the frilled parasol shading both her dark head and his fair one, Mercy recognised it. It was the look Abigail had worn the day she met Giles down by the old wharf. Bridget had been meeting a lover. Not Hart. A sudden uncontrollable surge of happiness greeted this realisation. The glow had been there before Hart joined them. The lover was part of the conspiracy, part of the secret of the old wharf. And Saul Gordon must be in it too. This was baffling . . . frightening . . . but why else would he have turned Hart's casual request into an urgent summons? He had wanted her away from the path to the old wharf, and he had known just how to achieve it. But why? What possible connection could there be between him and Bridget? A sinister one, that was certain. She did not think she had imagined that moment of terror on the river bank. If she had not obeyed Saul Gordon, what would have happened to her?

Every moment's delay in telling Hart might be disastrous. But when he came back from his stroll with Bridget, Saul Gordon intercepted him in front of the house and they went straight to the study together. Too late now for any hope of catching Bridget's secret lover. Besides, if it had by any extraordinary chance been Francis, would Hart *want* to catch him?

She tried to distract herself by taking down a dose of calomel to old Amy's grand-daughter Delilah, and Jem found her in the alley between the servants' houses. "Mr Hart wants to see you, Miss Mercy."

"Oh good! Thanks, Jem."

"I hope it's good, miss. Something's wrong, I reckon. Something's badly wrong. You'd best be ready."

"Why, thank you, Jem." Over and over again, she was touched by these instances of the servants' friendliness towards her. But what could be the matter? Mrs Purchis perhaps? She had been making a gallant attempt to appear normal, but there was no doubt that Hart's plan of going north again had hit her hard.

Hart was in his study, and, most unusually, doing nothing. The frown thickened across his heavy brows. "Mercy!" No smile. "Sit down, this may take some time and you have had a busy day."

"No busier than usual." She tried to make it light.

"No need to remind me of how indispensable you have made yourself." He had never spoken to her like this before. "I know it all too well. That is why, dearly though I would like to, I cannot send you packing to Savannah . . . or farther . . . to the British, where you belong."

"Hart! What are you saying?"

"That I know it all. God, when I think of the excuses I have made for you, I could put myself in the stocks for a fool, a gull. How you must have laughed at me!"

"I? Laugh at you? Hart, what are you talking about?"

"About your secret engagement to Francis, of course. Yes, well may you gape at me. You thought yourself so clever, didn't you, pulling the wool over my eyes so finely. Did you ever stop to think what a discovery would do to us all? But he's very charming, I can understand how. . . . When he wrote me about it, I . . . I think I was sorry for you. I waited for you to tell me. I was sure you would. I thought we trusted each other, you and I. And instead you go babbling of it to Bridget McCartney! No!" He was sitting, looming over her, on the edge of his desk, and put up a peremptory hand to stop her as she made to speak. "Let me just get it over with. Even that, I suppose I might have understood: woman to woman. It must have been lonely for you all this time with no news." He laughed; *at himself*, she thought. "Come to think of it, no doubt Abigail knows too, thinks you a heroine out of one of those romances of hers, gossips with you about your Loyalist lovers when you are alone. Only I, who am responsible for you, for us all, must be kept in the dark."

"But, Hart—"

"No!" In anger, his voice got lower and lower, yet more and more distinct. "If that had been all, if it had been merely the private treachery . . . but this of today. You look surprised? You didn't know you and your lover were seen? Shameless . . . he told me . . . Saul Gordon . . . he described —You were too well occupied, no doubt, to notice him skulking in the bushes, watching, enjoying. So, what secrets of our defence plans were you letting Francis worm out of you, Mercy? Someone who's capable of giving orders, as if from me, that the old wharf be left unguarded is capable of anything. Putting us all at risk! What do you care for the breach of trust, the danger to the family who've sheltered you? And now . . . now, for all our sakes, I must bribe Saul Gordon to silence. You see what depths you've brought me to! Oh, no need to look so anxious: he's well and truly bribed; your secret is safe enough. But what am I going to do with you, Mercy? If only you'd gone with him, with Francis, when you had the chance . . . then I could mourn you as dead—forget you. But what am I to *do*?"

"You might let me speak." And yet, what could she say? The fatal strand of truth was so interwoven in his whole furious indictment that it was hard to know where to begin. "Francis wrote to you?" she asked now, and knew it at once for a mistake.

"When the British sailed away last spring. At the same time as he wrote you. He said so. The same boy brought both letters. He asked me to protect you, to care for you as his affianced bride. I waited for you to tell me, Mercy. Can you imagine how I felt when you warned me about the letters that Abigail might be writing to Giles Habersham, when all the time I knew—"

"But, Hart, it wasn't like that!" If only she had told him of her suspicions of Francis at the time. What hope had she of convincing him now?

"No? Then what was it like, this traitor's romance of yours?" And then, furiously, as the study door opened, "I said I was not to be disturbed!"

"It's your orders, Mr Hart. They've come. Marked urgent."

Jem handed them over and withdrew, with an anxious glance at Mercy.

Hart broke the seal, read quickly, and looked up, coldly considering now, at Mercy. "Well, there it is. I am to report to General Washington. At once. Pity you can't let Francis know that, isn't it? Or have you some arrangement? Some means of sending news after him? Very likely. So, what am I to *do* with you?" He looked at his watch as she strove in vain for a way to cut through the web of lies. "I must leave tonight. There's no time. I'll have to trust you, Mercy, this once more. It's against my judgement, but I don't think you'd wilfully hurt my mother. And it's no use—she can't manage without you. Will you promise me, on your word of honour —no, on the memory of your father—that you will not communicate with Francis again?"

"But I haven't—" Useless. His face was closed against her. "Hart," she tried once more. "It's not true—any of it—I didn't see him."

"Not let him hug and kiss you, down there by the water, with Saul Gordon licking his lips in the bushes? No use, Mercy. He's not got the imagination to make that up. You're going to have trouble with him, and from that I can't protect you. Keep close to Abigail. That's the best advice I can give you, but try not to corrupt her, Mercy."

"Hart!"

But he had opened the study door and there were Bridget and Claire, dressed for dinner. "At last," said Bridget. "We were really beginning to feel we could be patient no longer. Is it news, Hart? Is it your orders?"

"Yes. I must speak to my mother." He left Mercy without another glance, and left the house, much later that evening, without the chance of another word.

17

Reaching the sanctuary of her room after Hart had gone, Mercy stopped on the threshold. There, lying on her worktable, were the shirts she had made for him. She moved stiffly across the room to pick one up and finger the carefully embroidered button-holes. What should she have done? What could she have done? It had been so cunning, the mixture of truth and falsehood, that even in retrospect she did not see what possible chance she would have had of convincing Hart. Not with so little time . . .

And that was frightening, too. Who could have known that Hart's orders would arrive tonight? Someone with swift information from Savannah. Saul Gordon? It all began, horribly, and too late, to make a kind of sense. Saul Gordon and Bridget McCartney . . . Saul aware of Bridget's secret assignation, perhaps even posted on the river bank to make sure she was not caught . . . getting rid of Mercy and hurrying down, to meet Bridget and— It had to be Francis. From the start, the whole thing had had the stamp of his devilish ingenuity. Francis thinking fast, thinking of the best way to discredit her with Hart.

But there was more to it than that. Francis had patiently, subtly laid the ground for today's scene when he wrote to Hart about their "secret engagement." Oh, God, if only she had told Hart about Francis' letter. As she looked back, it seemed madness. At the time, had she still without knowing it, been to some extent under Francis' spell? Hard to imagine that once those hot embraces of his could blind her to reason, to common sense. *Now*, she thought coldly, *he is doing the same thing to Bridget McCartney*. The scene Saul Gordon had described to Hart had been real enough, he had just switched heroines. It was the very ring of truth about it that had shocked Hart into those broken, horrified phrases, into instant belief.

Francis—so Winchelsea. He meant to be master here. He had as good as told her so, in the old days, when he was sure of her. When had he decided she was a threat to him? Begun to suspect she was not quite the enamoured slave she pretended? And taken a quick chance to weave his fatal web of lies around her. As for his accomplices, Bridget's stake in the game was obvious. She must have been promised the position of mistress of Winchelsea. Whether she would achieve it was another question. Her mother, who had thrown reputation to the winds for Francis' sake, might prove a formidable rival. Or would she die, conveniently, and leave the way clear for her daughter? With Francis, anything was possible.

Terrifying to feel herself alone against someone at once so ruthless and so clever. The bribe held out to Saul Gordon was obvious enough: herself. Discredited, turned away from Winchelsea, without character or prospects, what would she have done? Not turned to Saul Gordon. She knew that, but Francis could not, any more than he could have expected that characteristic generosity of Hart's that had left her still in her place, still safe at Winchelsea.

Now she was crying. At the time she had been angry, desperate, unable to se how extraordinarily kind, granted what he believed against her, Hart had been. To his certain knowledge, she had deceived him twice, dreadfully: once when she concealed her engagemnt to Francis and, worst of all that letter of his, and again when she failed to tell him about Giles Habersham's visit. No wonder that he had believed the worst of her. And yet, believing it, he had still not turned her away. It was cold comfort, but the best she had.

Work was comfort too. Hart had left orders that the household was to move into Savannah as soon as possible, and this kept her blessedly busy making arrangements for her spinners and weavers, giving orders for the autumn pickling, preserving, and smoking of food that was extra important in these days of increasing shortages, and helping Mrs Purchis decide which of the servants should go into town with them and which stay dangerously at Winchelsea.

That it was dangerous, there could be no doubt. Since Button Gwinnett's abortive expedition that spring, things on the southern borders had gone from bad to worse. Bridget McCartney made the situation sufficiently clear when she sent for their carriage the morning after Hart left. "You may wish to be scalped in your beds, or raped by British seamen, or simply carried off into God knows what kind of servitude by the Indians like that fourteen-year-old daughter of Joe McCrea's, but now Hart has gone, I'm taking no more chances." To do her justice, Bridget urged Martha Purchis to go with them, leaving Mercy to close the house, but it was Anne Mayfield who accepted, explaining that her nerves would not stand another night of Winchelsea's whippoorwill-haunted silence.

"And good riddance, if you ask me." Martha Purchis surprised Mercy by turning to her with this valediction as the carriage bowled away between the ilex trees. "Oh, not poor Anne, of course. But if I never see those McCartney girls again, it will be too soon. And quite spoiled our last days with poor Hart. Oh, Mercy, when do you think we will hear from him?"

"He promised to write from Charleston." Saul Gordon had joined them on the porch. "You will doubtless find a letter waiting for you when we get back to town, Mrs Purchis. I think we should be able to set forward by the end of the week, do not you, Miss Mercy?"

"I can certainly be ready by then." With so much wretchedness, there had been a faint, ironic amusement in watching Saul Gordon's bafflement when Hart rode away leaving Mercy still in her position of—what had Hart called her? "Housekeeper, dear friend, and valued confidante." He would not call her that now. But housekeeper she still was, and it baffled Saul Gordon and added a twinge of caution, for which she was grateful, to his advances.

Or was he perhaps flying at higher game? He did not propose to her once all that autumn and, curiously, this began to make her anxious. Hade he other plans for her? She had scorned him once; now she feared him.

Sometimes she wondered if Bridget McCartney did too. The McCartney sisters had apparently forgotten about the Loyalist taint of the Oglethorpe Square household and were frequent visitors again, but when Saul Gordon appeared, Bridget tended to cut their visits short. But then, he hardly compared favourably with the officers and politicians who frequented the McCartney house.

Mrs Purchis lived, visibly, from one of Hart's letters to the next. He had been disappointed at first because he was not sent to join Lachlan McIntosh, who was commanding in the western district of Virginia and Pennsylvania, but his mother was glad of it, and so in the end was Hart, who wrote exultantly that he was serving with his hero, the commander in chief, George Washington. "Much better," said Martha Purchis. "That way, the old sad business of the duel will be forgotten sooner."

She changed her tune a few days later when the bad news of Washington's defeat by Howe at Brandywine began to trickle through, but at least a scrawled note from Hart reassured her that he was hurt only in his pride. "It was a bad, muddled business, and the less said of it the better." She read this passage aloud to the family over dinner, and Saul Gordon seized on it.

"Congress must be packing their bags." Was there a note of pleasure in his voice? "There's no defending Philadelphia now."

He was right, but the bad news of the evacuation of Congress to York was soon balanced by the amazing report that a whole British army under General Burgoyne had been forced to surrender to the American General Gates at Saratoga. Dr Flinn called it the best news since Bunker Hill. "It may mean allies for us," he explained to Bridget McCartney, who had arrived just as he was leaving.

"Allies?" she asked brightly. "Oh, you mean the French! Just think, if they were to come in on our side, it might mean a beginning of trade again, might it not?"

"More like a continuation," he told her. "It's been an open secret that they've been helping us with arms and ammunition all along. But to have them publicly on our side, their fleet to trounce the British, that would be something." He turned back to Mrs Purchis. "Now, ma'am, you are to quit worrying about that boy of yours and take care of yourself. General Gates may be the hero of the hour, but I'll back George Washington to take care of his men through thick and thin. Look how he got them across the river and safe away from New York."

"A splendid man in a retreat," said Saul Gordon. "I wonder where he will retreat to next."

"Dear Mrs Purchis." Bridget jumped up to press the older woman's hand. "No need to look so anxious. Whatever the men suffer on a retreat, the officers are sure to be taken care of."

"I wish she wouldn't call me 'Dear Mrs Purchis," said Martha Purchis later.

"She almost sounded pleased that George Washington was in trouble," said Abigail. And then, "Oh, I know, Mercy, so ought I to be, but how can I when Hart is there?"

"If only we would hear from him," said his mother.

Hart's letters, when they came, told little, since there was always a chance they might fall into enemy hands. The most important thing for his mother as the unlucky autumn campaign continued, was that he was well and unhurt. Ending with loving messages for them all, he contrived to omit

Mercy's name, or to send a message so formal as to be almost as bad as omission. But her suffering over this dwindled to unimportance when, with December, the letters stopped altogether.

Mrs Purchis would not be comforted. Anxiety made her ill and illness made her bad-tempered. "Why would he not stay home?" she wailed. "And look after the estate. We'll be bankrupt by spring at this rate." She turned on Mercy. "And you go on taking your salary in kind, when Hart made Mr Gordon promise to sell our goods for Georgia paper. And we all know what that's worth!"

She was interrupted by a beaming servant with, at last, a letter from Hart. "He's well enough," she read it eagerly. "But cold. Those dreadful Northern winters. My poor Hart." And then, impatiently, "It's not so much a letter, more a list of things he wants. And such a scrawl, too! Anyone would think he had never learned to write. And as for the paper—"

"What does he want?" asked Mercy.

"Why, everything! Here." She threw the letter across the table. "The most personal words in it are 'My dear mother.' No reason why you should not read it."

It was indeed a scrawl, but Mercy, working her way patiently through the straggling, ill-written lines, presently found the explanation Mrs Purchis had overlooked. "He wrote it on his lap," she said. "By firelight. And, Mrs Purchis, he says his hands are cold and apologises for making such a mull of it. What kind of a winter camp can it be where the officers have cold hands?" She was running a quick eye down the list of things Hart wanted sent. Blankets, knitted stockings, shoes . . . " 'Some of the men have to face these arctic conditions barefoot.' " she read aloud, slowly, puzzling out the words. "And food . . . it's unbelievable," she said. "There must be supplies up North."

"Oh, yes," said Mrs Purchis. "He says something about that. You must have missed it." She took the letter back. "Here it is, in the margin, something about the country people preferring to sell to the British for hard money."

"It's scandalous," said Mercy. "And there is General Howe wining and dining Mrs Loring in Philadelphia."

"I wonder if Mrs McCartney is there too," said Abigail. "Mercy, if there's mail from the North—Would you feel you could call on the McCartney girls? They might have heard something. You know they don't like me to visit them,

196

but they would be glad to hear of Hart's letter and perhaps they might have news too." She had still had no word from Giles Habersham, and Mercy suffered with her.

"Very well," she said now, reluctantly. "I don't suppose they will be almighty pleased to see me, but I will go if you would like me to, Abigail."

"Oh, thank you!"

"But only after I have gone through Hart's list with Mr Gordon to see what we can contrive."

Mr. Gordon was not helpful. "My dear Miss Mercy." He had put on weight in the course of the winter. "In the excitement of the moment, we must not lose sight of Mr Purchis' best interests. Naturally, he is shocked by his first experience of a winter camp. He is very young, Miss Mercy, and quite untried as a soldier." His soft white finger tapped the list she had copied out from Hart's letter. "From this, you would think he wished to feed and clothe George Washington's army single-handed."

"Or that things there are very bad indeed," said Mercy. "I must have your answer, Mr Gordon. Are you going to set these commissions in hand or must I?"

"I am going to do my duty to my employer and to my country. I am going to take this remarkable list of Mr Purchis' down to the Assembly. There is talk of another expedition against St Augustine as soon as the weather permits. I think we will find they decide such supplies as we can collect will be better employed there. By all reports, George Washington has lost as many soldiers by desertion as he has by illness in the course of this unlucky winter at Valley Forge. Come spring, I imagine General Howe will walk out of Philadelphia and trounce him. Then, perhaps, we will get a commander in chief we can trust."

"Oh?" Mercy gave him a straight look. "Mr Purchis seems to trust General Washington. He says in his letter that he's amazed how few desertions there are, considering the appalling conditions and the fact that many of the men's time was up at Christmas. There was something he said—" She had the letter in her pocket and now fetched it out. "Yes. Here it is: 'We've a German officer called Steuben. He drills us in the snow. Those of us who have shoes. I think General Howe is in for a surprise when the spring comes.' Does that sound like a dwindling army to you, Mr Gordon? Or one that will be trounced come spring?"

197

He favoured her with a patronising smile. "You and Mr Hart were always optimists. But I am afraid in this case he is letting his hopes guide his reason. At all events"—he picked up the list she had copied so carefully—"this must go to the Assembly. I will, of course, let you know what they say when they have decided."

Mercy found small comfort at the McCartney house. Bridget and Claire did not admit to having heard from their mother, but seemed curiously well informed about affairs in the North. "General Howe continues to live in the best society at Philadelphia, I understand," said Bridget. "Monstrous! But human nature, I am afraid. And as for that ragtag and bobtail George Washington is trying to hold together at Valley Forge, it is hard to hope much for them."

"Except that Hart Purchis may survive." Claire spoke up for once.

"Oh, that's of course. But an untried soldier like him will never be sent into any position of trust or danger. I do not think we need trouble ourselves excessively for Hart. He will be home, I wager, a wiser man, in time for our spring campaign against East Florida, from which I hear great things are expected."

"So they have been before," said Mercy.

"Defeatist talk, Miss Phillips? What a fortunate thing none of our friends from the Assembly is here yet. You, from your household, must be just a mite extra careful these days. You have heard, perhaps, of the attainder proceedings against James Johnston?"

"Yes. The man they begged only last year to come back and keep the *Gazette* running for them."

"The one who refused to do so. Let him but show the tip of his nose here in Savannah and he's a dead man. I do wish you could persuade Miss Abigail to take the patriotic oath. She must see what harm she does you all."

"What harm can she do?"

"Who knows? Who can tell whether she is not in treasonable correspondence with her fiancé, or her cousin, for the matter of that? A little bird told me Frank Mayfield was in Philadelphia with Howe. How strange it would be, would it not, if he and Hart were to meet on the field of battle."

"Horrible," said Mercy. "Did your little bird say anything about Giles Habersham?"

"No. Miss Abigail does not hear from him?"

"Not a word. I suppose he fears to compromise her."

"As well he may. These are terrible times." She rang the hand bell that stood on the table beside her. "Let me give you a little light refreshment before you go?"

It was an offer that half expected the answer no, and this combined with a still-unanswered question to make Mercy accept. The summons was answered almost at once by two neatly clad maids with all the apparatus for a lavish collation. Wielding the heavy silver teapot, Bridget urged Mercy to help herself to one of a surprising variety of pastries and sugar cakes. "Do not stint yourself, my dear creature. I warn you, it will all be swept up by our gallant legislators, who tend to visit me in the intervals of their labours. They will be surprised, I doubt, to find you here."

If it was intended as a suggestion that she leave, Mercy chose to ignore it, merely congratulating Bridget on her cook's hand with pastry. "We have found it impossible to get light enough flour."

"I imagine you might." There was the slightest possible emphasis on the word "you." "When the gentlemen come, I would not talk too much about Hart, if I were you. He is not altogether popular, I am afraid, in certain quarters, poor Hart. Ah!" There were sounds of arrival. "Here come the gentlemen. I rely on you, my dear."

When the first arrivals proved to be Joseph Wood, a son, and a cousin, Mercy wished she had gone when the going was good. They were followed by several more of the less reliable members of the Assembly, and all of them entered the McCartney house with the freedom of habitués. Pouncing on delicate little pastries, cramming their mouths hungrily with the devilled oysters that now made their appearance, they talked loud and angrily about the increasing shortage of food in Savannah. "It's all the farmers' fault," said one of the Wood connection. "They are holding out for higher prices."

"Which will come soon enough," said Miss Bridget. "Do you know that I had to pay ten shillings a pound for butter in the market the other day. And fifteen for best candles. I burn nothing else, naturally."

"Naturally," agreed Joseph Wood. "But, dear lady, you surely never attend the common market yourself?"

"Oh, no!" She smiled and flirted her fan at him. "Only

199

figuratively speaking, of course. I am afraid I am not so bold as Miss Phillips here, who, I believe, goes there regularly, shopping basket, umbrella, and all."

"Yes." Mercy rose to her feet. "And that reminds me that I have duties to attend to at home. We are making candles today. Thank you for my delicious tea, Miss Bridget. Goodbye, Miss Claire." A rather blind general curtsey got her safely out of the room before she could say anything she might regret. The sight of these well-fed, prosperous men, in their imported clothes, gorging themselves from the McCartney cornucopia, while Hart and his men went cold and hungry at Valley Forge, had almost been too much for her discretion.

"William, let me drive!" The coachman had brought the light whisky round at sight of her. "I'm in a bad temper!"

"So long as you don't frit the horse, ma'am." William handed her the reins and moved over on the seat. "But you'd never do that." She and William had been firm friends since she had cured his wife Amy of a fever by a ruthless combination of blisters and jalap. She had then further cemented the friendship by persuading Mrs Purchis to let old Amy accompany William to Savannah, explaining that she was one of her best stocking knitters and must be kept at work.

She turned the whisky towards the Common. "I need a breath of air after that, William. We'll go the long way home."

"Such company for a lady like you. I watched them come. And those servants. Ma'am, I was plumb glad to see you come away. I don't like the way they talk. Lot of no-good trash! I was almost at fisticuffs with Mr Wood's man. He was saying such things about Mr Hart!"

"William, you mustn't!" This was a hazard she had not thought of. "Our household's in trouble enough without you kicking up a row. Promise me?"

"Very good, ma'am, if you say so, but the Lord knows there will come a day of reckoning and that man of Mr Wood's will be sorry he was born. And dressed up fit to bust, too." He looked down gloomily at his own homespuns. "Ma'am, it don't seem right."

She laughed. "You should have seen Miss Bridget and Miss Claire, William, fine as fivepence in imported lutestring and declaring it was a little old bolt of cloth they'd found in the attic. That attic of theirs—"

"Ma'am." William turned to her earnestly. "Talking of attics—I wanted to speak to you about the cellar."

"The cellar?"

"Yes, ma'am. Our cellar in Oglethorpe Square. You know how it is. The big one under the big house, and the little one right beside it, under the office. That we don' use."

"No." Puzzled. "Because there's no way through, and plenty of room in the new one." The big, cool cellar of the main house was invaluable for keeping stores brought in from Winchelsea.

"That's it. I was down there the other day, fetching up salt pork for cook. I had kind of a mosey round. There's a place in the tabby wall where the builder must a' started to make a door through and then changed his mind. Give me half a day down there on my own and I could take it right through. Funny thing"—he threw it off casually—"I'm the only one of the folks knows about that other cellar. Before their time, 'twas that it was last used, and the only door being from Mr Hart's office. Well, you can see. Actually"—more casual than ever—"Mr Gordon, he don't know neither. The door from the office, it's at the back of a big old cupboard nobody's used since the little house was lived in. Full of cobwebs it is, and black as tophet. He look in and then he come out quick and send for water to wash those white hands of his. He don' know. I reckon Mrs Purchis must a' known once, but bet your last dollar she's forgotten. And that's it. So if I made a kind of a secret entrance in the corner of the big cellar, then, come trouble, you and the other ladies could nip in, I'd close up after you—"

She shivered. "You think trouble's coming, William?"

"Trouble do come, ma'am, as the sparks fly upwards, and we'd be foolish not to be ready for it. Mr Hart, he told me before he went to look out for you ladies, and I'm agoing to do it. I'd hide the door through," he explained. "It's at the dark end of the big cellar, away from the grating. Easy enough to mask it with a layer of tabby. Just give me a day clear to do it."

"It would stick to the wood?" She knew about tabby, the curious compound of sand and shells of which so much of Savannah was built.

"Not in the usual way, ma'am, it wouldn't, but my pa, he had a mortal good way of making it. I reckon his way it would stick. If you'll let me try, ma'am? Only, secret like?

Then you'd have two ways in and no one the wiser."

"Yes. I'll fix it. And—thank you, William."

The Assembly issued a decree a few days later, banning the export of flour, rice, and a list of other commodities, and Mercy had to be content with sending Hart a consignment of shoes, stockings, and the coarse shirts she and Abigail had been stitching at all winter. She was lucky. Captain Smythe, who commanded the packet, was an old seagoing friend of Hart's.

"Don't fret, ma'am." He had come himself to arrange about the shipment. "I owe Hart Purchis my life. I'll see he gets it all. And bring you an answer back too, if I can."

He was as good as his word, and this time Hart wrote jubilantly. The long, grim winter was over, the men were in good heart, and best of all was the news of the alliance with France. All Savannah was *en fête*, with hastily constructed French flags flying beside the new American Stars and Stripes that Congress had authorised the summer before. "It seems odd," said Mercy thoughtfully, "to be drinking toasts to the King of France just when we are trying to get free from the King of England."

"It's all of a piece." There had been no letter for Abigail, and she looked pinched about the face. "With men like Joe Wood for leaders, what better can you expect by way of allies! Of course, Britain's old enemy is happy to seize this chance to do her harm. I expect soon we will hear that Spain has come in too."

"I wonder what it will mean for George Washington and his army."

"And for us down here," Mr Gordon had come quietly through the office door. "I would rather have news of our expedition against East Florida than all your packets from the North. We shall never be safe until St Augustine is taken."

"If only our men don't all die of the fever first," said Mercy. Once again the venture, planned from spring, had been delayed until the heat was as great a hazard as the enemy. By July, the expedition was back in Savannah, full of mutual recrimination but maintaining, with some show of truth, that they had scotched the Loyalist plan of invading Georgia.

There was other news too. The French alliance had indeed altered the British government's plans. For both British and

French, the rich West Indies were infinitely more important than the thirteen rebellious colonies. The British Generals Howe and Clinton had been ordered to evacuate Philadelphia, concentrate their forces in New York, and detach as many troops as possible for service against the West Indies. George Washington had attacked the British army as it retreated from Philadelphia, and the longest and one of the most fiercely contested actions of the war had been fought in intense heat at Monmouth Courthouse. Both armies suffered heavy losses, from sunstroke as well as from wounds; both claimed victory. But the British made their way safely to New York. And they took Hart Purchis with them as a prisoner. The news, received with that of the battle, put out the lights in Oglethorpe Square.

"But we must illuminate," said Mercy, white-faced. "Mrs Purchis, you know we must. Otherwise the mob—"

"Quite heartless," said Martha Purchis. "Very well, give the orders; waste my precious supply of candles. Now my son is as good as dead, it's all one what happens to me."

"Dear Aunt Martha." Abigail had put aside her own sorrow to try and cheer her aunt. "Comfort yourself with the thought that he covered himself with glory, and that as an officer he should surely be well treated and, let us hope, exchanged." Sudden colour flooded her face. "I have never done it before, but I could perhaps write to Giles in care of the Loyalist headquarters in New York? I am sure he'd do everything in his power to help Hart, if only he knew what had happened."

"Oh, my dear Abigail." Her aunt rose shakily from her chair to kiss her. "Do it today—do it at once. And, Sister, might not you also write to Francis? Intercession from him must come even more forcibly than from Giles since he is Hart's own cousin."

"But how should I do it?" asked Anne Mayfield fretfully. "You know he has never troubled to write to me."

Mercy remembered the letter she had received, so secretly, from Francis, with its instructions as to how he could be reached in a crisis. Was this, she wondered, the kind of crisis he had meant? Coldly, she thought perhaps it was. "I think the letter to Giles should be enough," she said. "From something Miss Bridget said the other day I am fairly confident that he is in New York, and, perhaps, better placed with the British to help Hart." It was the nearest she could get to a reference to Francis' double-dealing, which must surely have left him suspect with British and patriots alike.

Anne Mayfield drew herself up with a creak of satin and whalebone. "I suppose I may write to my own son, if I so desire, without permission from you, Miss Phillips? It shall be done today. We might as well use all this candle-light we are proposing to waste."

It was a long time since Mercy had put on her peasant's shawl and gone out among the Savannah crowds. Well, she thought ruefully, taking the shawl from her empty closet, her ordinary clothes were shabby enough by now. But, still, the shawl tight over her head did give her a comfortable feeling of anonymity as she made her way out of the back entrance of the house and across lots to Bay Street. Here a cheerful crowd was celebrating the good news and waiting for dark and the illuminations it would bring. Nobody had done much work today, and as she looked downriver towards the crumbling fortifications at the Trustees' Garden, she remembered an anxious question in Hart's last letter. Had work begun yet on re-fortifying Savannah?

She was not going to let herself cry. She pushed her way briskly through the crowd and emerged at last on the bluff where she could look down at the quays. Yes, there was the packet that had brought the news, and as she had let herself hope, it was the one with Hart's friend Smythe for captain.

The path down the bluff was steep, and the quay no place for an unaccompanied lady. Perhaps she should have sent William? Too late now. She walked boldly up the packet's swaying gang-plank and asked a grinning sailor for a word with Captain Smythe.

The fact that she knew his name helped, but still the man looked doubtful. "Who shall I say, miss? He's kind of busy."

"Tell him Miss Phillips." She was wondering if Captain Smythe would even remember her name, when the sailor suddenly reached out to terrify her with a rum-flavoured embrace.

"I'd a' known you anywhere," he said thickly, letting her go again. "You and that father of yours, bless him, that talked all the time. Whatever happened to him, miss? Did he get sold all right and tight and has he worked out his free-dom by now?"

"No." She did not remember the man, but he must have

been on the ship that brought her father and herself to America. Logical enough that he should now be working in the coastways trade. "The mob killed him." She looked up at the man's blotched, sympathetic face. "And now I need help. Your captain knows me. Please——"

Five minutes later, Mercy was explaining the situation to Captain Smythe. He looked sympathetic, anxious, doubtful. "It's true," he answered her final appeal. "By all accounts things are bad as can be for prisoners up in New York. On hulks in the harbour, they are, and off dead more often than alive. You think these letters you speak of might help Mr Purchis?"

"I hope one of them might."

"Yes." He studied her thoughtfully across the tiny, cluttered cabin. "I ought not to trust you," he said at last. "One ought to trust no one these days. But Hart Purchis saved me from certain death year before last. God, there's a swimmer. He never told you?"

"No."

"No, I reckon he wouldn't. He and I were aboard the fireship that was sent out against those varmints of rice ship captains. Time come to jump clear, we both jumped, he landed nice and tidy, close to the boat that was to pick us up. I landed out in the current headed straight for Tybee, drowning, or the British. I could hear them in the boat, shouting, 'No time, can't go for him, must get away.' And I heard Hart Purchis, too, damning them for cowards. I'm not a very good swimmer. I was in trouble when he grabbed me. I'd not have lasted five minutes. No, ma'am, I reckon anything you want doing for Hart Purchis, I'll do."

"Thank you." She smiled at him, and for the first time he thought her a pretty girl instead of an anxious woman. "I'll tell you——"

She gave him the letters next day, at the open market, where they had arranged to meet. It was very quick, very definite, as they had planned it. "This one for Mr. Habersham"—she handed it to him—"and this to Mr Mayfield."

"Ma'am, you may count on me. One delivered. One not." He raised his voice. "Rum at sixty shillings a gallon. Double last year! What's a man to do?"

18

The waiting was worst of all. Impossible to tell how long it might take for Captain Smythe to find a safe messenger to cross the no-man's-land that now encircled British-held New York. Everybody knew there was a lively traffic in information across what was known as the debatable ground. It was only too easy for a reliable Loyalist in New York to turn into a true-blue patriot on the way over. Always provided he survived the dangerous frontier, where marauding bands tended not to make much distinction between rebel and Loyalist. All they wanted was loot.

It was the same on the southern and western borders of Georgia. Every day brought its new story of horror and bloodshed. "And it's not only the Indians," said Abigail mournfully. "It seems as if it is worst of all when it's within families. Dear Mercy, we will never quarrel, you and I."

"No." They had agreed it long ago, that time Giles came back. "Oh, God, I do hope your letter has reached Giles by now and that he is able to do something."

"Or Francis," said Abigail.

"Yes." Mercy changed the subject. "Abigail, I think we should move everything we possibly can in town from Winchelsea. Will you help me persuade Mr Gordon? Or get your mother and aunt to do so? He calls it defeatist thinking. All he seems to care about is what the Assembly will say. I care more what Hart will think when he gets home." She would not let herself say "if." "Imagine how angry he would be if the servants out there were attacked."

"You think that possible?"

"Dear, I keep telling you anything is possible. Now they've sacked Commodore Bowen for non-cooperation on that disastrous expedition against St Augustine, we've no naval defences whatever. Remember the last time the British fleet came to Tybee and upriver? What's to stop them doing it again? Not any fortifications the Assembly have built, and not the militia, now it's harvest time. They always go home to get in their crops. And as for the Continental troops: well, you know Governor Houston and Colonel Williamson are hardly speaking since the debacle at Sunbury. It's a miracle they've not fought a duel."

"Oh well," said Abigail. "The British seem just as ineffective. Did you hear the rhyme they are quoting from the London *Evening Post*? How does it go?

> *Here we go up, up, up*
> *And here we go down, down, downy*
> *Then we go backwards and forwards*
> *And here we go round, round, roundy.*

"Yes. While cousins and brothers kill each other in the backwoods, it almost seems as if the American and British armies do not really want to fight it out."

"Can you wonder?" said Abigail.

It was late in October, with the harvest all in, but still Gordon refused to give orders to bring in at least the domestic staff from Winchelsea. He shrugged off Mercy's protests. "I was out there myself just the other day. Everything as right as can be. I don't know why you indulge yourself in these alarmist fancies, Miss Mercy. It is like a female, I know, but not like you. And talking of the ladies." Archly. "You will never imagine who I met taking their promenade out there."

"No, I suppose I probably will not."

"Who but Miss Bridget and Miss Claire! They feel no danger in driving out there to call on friends and take a peep, as they described it, at Winchelsea on the way back. I cannot imagine what makes you so timorous."

"Common sense perhaps." But she wished she knew what had taken the McCartneys to Winchelsea.

She was wakened, very early, a few mornings later by the news that the packet was in and that Captain Smythe wished to speak to her. "I came myself." His greeting was unceremonious and she did not trouble to apologise for her thrown-on clothes. "It's good news, I hope. I have him on board."

"Hart! Oh, God bless you."

"Don't say that yet. I've done my best. But, Miss Phillips, he was a dying man when he came on board. He'd been on one of those stinking hulks they call prison ships. All through the summer in New York Harbour. Please God, his exchange came through just in time. The passage has certainly done him good. Fresh air, the little food we could get him to take, but you've a nursing job on your hands, and not a light one. I'm on my way to report to the Assembly, but I thought you'd want to start making arrangements for getting him home. My men have orders to help any way they can. He should not stay down there in the harbour a minute longer than need be."

"He's bad?"

"Very bad."

"Wounds?"

"Nothing to signify. If they'd been tended. Miss Phillips, if I had a British prisoner here, at this moment, I think I'd strangle him with my two hands."

"No!"

"Wait till you see him. I should warn you, he won't know you." He picked up hat and cane. "And—good luck."

"I haven't thanked you."

"No need. And no time."

Saul Gordon was away on one of his visits of inspection to Winchelsea, and Mercy was glad of it. She rang, sent for William, gave her orders, and then hurried upstairs to wake Abigail and break the news. "Will you tell his mother and aunt while I go down to the quay and fetch him. Don't let them hope too much, Abigail."

"No? Oh, Mercy!" And then, making herself be practical, "His room. Have you given orders for it?"

"No use. Captain Smythe says we cannot possibly get him up the stairs." Her mind had been nibbling at this problem. "Only one thing for it," she said now. "Abigail, have them set up a cot bed in the office. It's the only way."

"Mr Gordon won't like it."

"No, he won't, will he?"

Nothing Smythe had said had prepared her for the reality of Hart's condition. Gaunt as a skeleton, pale as a ghost, he lay in his ship's cot, hands twitching at the blankets, lips constantly in movement, saying something unintelligible. But a blessing, for the moment, that he did not recognise her. It made the undignified business of getting him ashore and up the bluff a little easier.

And, arrived in Oglethorpe Square, she was relieved to find that not even the news of Hart's arrival had got the two older ladies up and dressed yet. She was able to get him into the room Abigail had had prepared with a minimum of muss and confusion.

"I've sent for the doctor." Like the servants who had helped get Hart to bed, Abigail was crying quietly. "He should be here directly."

"Bless you. I should have thought of that."

Dr Flinn was less discouraging than Mercy had feared. He had met Captain Smythe in Broughton Street, he told her, and had a preliminary report from him. "I do not wish to raise your hopes unduly, Miss Phillips, but from what Smythe said, I think a very pronounced change for the better must have taken place on the voyage down. We have found this, you know, on each of our unlucky expeditions southwards. The fever cases and the wounded alike tend to improve enormously in the course of the voyage back through the inner channel. It's the fresh air, I suppose, or something." He rolled up his shirt-sleeves. "And now, if you'll leave me, I'll examine these wounds of his."

"Had I not better stay," said Mercy. "I intend to look after the nursing myself."

"You do?" She had surprised him. "Would it not be more suitable if one of the servants—"

"It might be more suitable, but it would be a great deal less satisfactory. One cannot trust them to keep things clean, and my father always said that cleanliness was half the battle when treating wounds."

"Your father spoke like a sensible man. Very well then, so long as you promise not to faint or have hysterics."

"I don't think I know how," said Mercy.

"He's been lucky." Dr Flinn summed it up when the examination was over. "A good constitution, and he must have been hard as nails when it happened to him. And only superficial wounds. I'd say they must have nearly healed on the march from Monmouth up to New York. Impossible to tell, of course, but that's the way it looks to me. And then broken out again owing to the frightful conditions on the hulk. Another few weeks of that and it would have been gangrene, and death. As it is, rest and care, Miss Phillips. Keep the wounds clean and dry. I hope you haven't given all your linen for bandages. I know how generous you and Miss Abigail have been."

"No, I'm afraid I saved some for our own emergencies."

"And very sensible too. I'll call again tomorrow. Oh"—he was putting on his black coat—"no excitement whatever, Miss Phillips. No tears, no scenes of joyful reunion."

"It's hardly the occasion for that," she said. "Yet. But, Dr Flinn, would you add to your kindness by seeing Mrs Purchis and explaining to her? She would take it better from you, I know." It was going to be difficult to keep Hart quiet in this room, which opened off the main family living room, but it must be done. "Could you perhaps suggest the possibility that it might be a fever?" she asked. "Maybe catching?"

He had known them all a long time. "An excellent idea. I'll go through straightaway."

Left alone with her patient, Mercy stood for a long moment, letting herself imagine he seemed a little better, now that his wounds had been dressed. Then she went over to the back door of the office and looked out into the yard, where, as always, a group of the servants' children were playing under the catalpa trees. She sent one of them for William, and when he came, she asked him to put a bolt onto the door that led from the office into the big ground-floor room. "Mr Hart must have absolute quiet," she said.

"Yes, miss." He hesitated for a moment. "My Amy say she'd be right down proud if you'd let her help nurse the master. She don't reckon much to fevers, she says."

Agreeing gratefully, she was amazed as always at the speed with which family news travelled among the servants. Equally, and of course, it would be all over Savannah. When William returned and put on the bolt, she sent him off to hunt the house for screens to mask the door from the outside. "We must keep him quiet at all costs," she explained. "And we are bound to have visitors. Miss Abigail will have to see them, since I have exposed myself to the fever. I shall go to and fro by the back way."

"Yes, miss. I surely hope the rain don't start. But if it do, I'll think of something."

"I'm sure you will."

It was peaceful, nursing Hart. Since she would not allow either the front door of the office or the one into the house next door to be opened, she could only see people in the back yard, and it was not many who would come round through the servants' quarters. Captain Smythe came, to be thanked once again, and wish her luck, and Dr Flinn came daily, and, daily, allowed a little more hope. "But it will be a long business," he warned her. "And I think I should tell you that, even if he does recover, I fear some permanent damage to the muscle of his right arm. He must have thrown up his arm to protect his head, and the sabre caught him in an awkward place. Well." He was making ready to go. "It's the end of fighting for him, which may be no bad thing."

"Doctor, you speak as if you thought he would recover."

"That's true," he said. "I think I do. Thanks to you, Miss Phillips. And if you can go on keeping him quiet. I shall be glad when his mind stops wandering."

"So shall I. Though, mind you, it makes him easier to nurse."

"Yes." Dr Flinn had grown very fond of her. "I think you must expect trouble when he does come round. He won't a bit like your nursing him, you know."

"Of course he won't." And that was an understatement if ever there was one. What in the world would Hart say when he found who was nursing him? But that, like all the others, was a bridge she would cross when she came to it. She smiled at Dr Flinn. "I am rather hoping that by then he will be well enough so I can let Amy and her daughter take over and pretend they have been nursing him all the time."

"You think of everything, Miss Phillips. I shan't worry myself about you. Except, I wish you will not over-tire yourself. Do you get out at all?"

"Oh, yes, in the evenings, when I am less likely to frighten people with thoughts of the fever." In fact, she now habitually put on her peasant's shawl and went down to take the air on the bluff and gather what news she could.

When she returned that evening, it was to crisis. Saul Gordon had arrived from Winchelsea, Amy told her, and was furious at finding himself turned out of the office. "You can hear him," said the old woman, and it was true. The angry voice in the next room penetrated through screens and door alike.

"I'll go and speak to him," said Mercy. "Let me out the front way, Amy, it's quicker. But lock up tight behind me." Luckily, she and Dr Flinn had agreed that very morning that the pretext of the fever could now be abandoned, since the nine days' wonder of Hart's return had been superseded by new rumours of a possible invasion from St Augustine.

Her appearance, for the first time, in the family living room caused an apprehensive stir in the agitated little group there. Saul Gordon had been haranguing the two older ladies while Abigail listened and looked anxious. Now they all turned to stare at Mercy. "Is this wise?" Mrs Purchis took a step backward and picked up her fan from the table.

"Yes. And necessary. You are disturbing my patient, Mr Gordon, with your shouting."

"Your patient is in my office," he said angrily.

"I think you forget, Mr Gordon, that my patient is your employer."

"That's as may be," said Gordon.

Before she could take him up on it, Mrs Purchis interrupted, "Keep away," she exclaimed, as Mercy took a step forward. "Do you want us all dying and the whole house quarantined! Things are quite bad enough as it is, with hardly a soul coming near us since the news of Hart's fever got about."

"My apologies." Mercy's voice was dry. "I quite forgot to mention that Dr Flinn pronounced Hart clear of the fever when he called today. But he still needs quiet. No visitors, the doctor says, until his mind is clear." Which, please God, would be soon.

"Oh!" Saul Gordon pounced on it. "So he's still out of his mind, is he? And it's you, I take it, that I have to thank for this high-handed decision to turn me out of my office?"

"I'm afraid so. Did no one explain that I had all your papers moved, with the greatest care, to a room at the back?"

"Entered from the slaves' quarters! I thank you, yes, they did explain. And as for tampering with my papers in my absence! Mrs Purchis"—he turned angrily back to her—"since your son is out of his mind and likely to remain so, and since you let this young person rule the roost here, I have no option but to offer you my resignation."

"Mr Gordon! You'd never do that after all your years with us!"

"On the contrary." He drew himself up to his full five feet four inches. "I have quite made up my mind. Frankly, I have had good offers of employment and refused them out of loyalty to you. This high-handed behaviour on your housekeeper's part has made up my mind for me. I will but collect my papers from the slave's hovel where she has had them put and take my leave of you."

"No, you will not," said Mercy. Something in his tone as he spoke of the papers had alerted her. "They are not your

212

papers, Mr Gordon, but Mr Purchis'. For your own sake, I know you will wish an independent observer to be by as you remove what is yours and leave what is his. I suggest we send for Mr Purchis' lawyer."

"He's out of town." But the fight had gone out of Saul Gordon.

"Then we will wait until he comes back. In the meantime, the papers will remain locked up and I shall keep the key. Naturally, Mr Gordon, you must do what you think best about your own affairs. If you really wish to leave, I do not imagine that Mrs Purchis will try to prevent you. Indeed, ma'am"—she turned to Martha Purchis—"with business so quiet and the harvest safe in at Winchelsea, I am sure Sam and I could see to things between us until Hart recovers."

"If he recovers." But Saul Gordon's tone had changed. "Of course, I will not abandon you at this anxious time, ma'am. If you will give me the keys to my new quarters, Miss Phillips, I will start setting things to rights there."

For a moment, she was tempted to refuse. She was more certain than ever, now, that there was something very wrong among those papers, but looking at the relieved faces of the three other women she knew that this was a battle she was bound to lose, and gave way with good grace. Only, afterwards, sitting in the quiet of Hart's room was there time to wonder whether it was evidence of public or of private treachery that Saul Gordon was, doubtless, this very moment destroying.

She was sitting by the bed, gently rubbing Hart's limp right hand, when his left one touched hers. Looking quickly to his face, she saw his deep-sunk blue eyes, fixed on her, rational at last. "Mercy!" It was between a sigh and a whisper. "I'm home?"

"Yes, thank God. And getting stronger every day."

"Day!" He tried to sit up, but she put a gentle hand on his chest to hold him down. "How long have I been ill?"

"A long time. Captain Smythe brought you home a month ago."

"A month! Dear God. Then it's—"

"November. No, Hart!" He had tried again to sit up. "You're not strong enough."

"Then *you* must go." He let himself fall back among the pillows. "To the Assembly . . . warn them . . . the British are going to attack down here in the South. It's the last thing

I remember. While I was waiting for the exchange to go through. Hearing them laughing and talking about it. Plenty of Loyalists, they said, ready to help when they landed. Up by land from St Augustine, down by water from New York. Mercy, how are the fortifications?"

"Don't worry, Hart." She dared not tell him that nothing had been done about repairing them. "Lie and rest. I will go to the Assembly directly." This time they *must* believe her. Better, of course, if she could get a man to go, but nothing would make her trust Saul Gordon with the message, and Dr Flinn had left town. She sent Amy to sit with Hart and hurried out, to find the streets unusually crowded.

"What's the matter?" she asked the first neighbour she met.

"Matter enough. The British are out from St Augustine. They've burned Midway Meeting House and are raping and looting all the way up to Sunbury. My father lives down there."

"I'm sorry." She said it mechanically. So half of Hart's warning had come true. Would this make it harder or easier to persuade the Assembly of the truth of the other half?

It made it impossible. The Assemble was in emergency session; messengers were rushing to and fro, each one with a new bulletin of bad new. The best she could do was write Hart's warning, have it sent in to Governor Houston, go home, and hope for the best. She found Hart heavily asleep, with Amy sitting beside him. "He's rambling in his mind again," said Amy. "He keeps talking about Mr Francis. Saying the strangest things." And then, "Don't you worry, Miss Mercy, I won't say a thing. Not even to William."

19

"Francis!" Mercy had dozed off in her chair by the bed, but Hart's voice woke her. "You must know me! I can't have changed so much! Oh . . . filthy . . . stinking . . . these vile hulks, but, Frank, I'm your cousin, your Cousin Hart. What do you mean? Complete stranger? It's not possible, Frank!" The final shout tailed off horribly into a groan.

"Hush." Mercy reached out and took his good hand. "It's all over, Hart. You're home—you're safe in Savannah."

"Judas!" he said. "My cousin Judas. But why? I saw it in your eye. I knew you recognized me. How could you not? And left me there to rot. Why, Francis? It made me wonder. . . ." He sat bolt upright in bed. "When did you start to lie to me, Francis? Cousin Francis . . . Lies . . . all lies? If only it were . . . Mercy?"

"Yes?" But did he recognise her?

"Tell me it was lies . . . I thought . . . all winter, freezing there at Valley Forge . . . I thought about you . . . not a traitor, Mercy? Anything else . . . not a traitor? Not you?"

"No. A fool, maybe, but not a traitor. Hart, you must rest." She reached for the laudanum Dr Flinn had left for him. "Drink this. Trust me. Rest."

"Poison? Cousin Judas?" But he drank it obediently and was soon deeply asleep.

Amy watched by him for the second half of the night and reported in the morning that he seemed calmer. "He's asking for you, Miss Mercy."

"Good." Mercy had brought a bowl of gruel and sat down by the bed. "Good morning, Hart. I have brought your breakfast."

His eyes were clearer today; she thought there was real recognition in them. "Food." He took a mouthful obediently. "We were hungry all the time. Fought each other for . . . for horrors. I remember—"

"Don't remember, Hart." Another spoonful. "Try to forget. You're home now, in Savannah—safe."

"No! Not safe. Nothing's safe. Nothing's sure anymore. Savannah's betrayed. The British are coming. Mercy, have you been to the Assembly?"

"Yes." It was only half the truth, but Hart needed rest, for both body and mind, and she meant him to get it. She longed to know whether he remembered anything of their strange conversation the night before, but knew she must not speak of it. At least he was treating her as friend and nurse, and with that, for the moment, she must be satisfied.

Dr Flinn called next afternoon and was encouraging about Hart's improvement. "His mind is clearing steadily now, but you must not let him worry himself over these imaginings of him. Do you know he told me that he had seen his cousin Francis some time during his illness? If Frank Mayfield had known poor Hart had got among the common soldiers on the hulks, he'd have had him out of there in no time and treated like the officer he was. It's all delusion, but I advise you to let him think the Assembly is acting on his advice. We mustn't have him worrying himself worse again."

"No, indeed. Doctor, how long before you think he will be well enough to be moved?"

"Moved? What need? Oh, you were thinking of a change of air out at Winchelsea? I'm not sure I would recommend it, but I suppose in two months or so, if you took him easily, by water."

"I see." If only she was still in charge of the nursing, but now Hart was conscious, she had had to yield most of it to Amy and her daughter, and was afraid that his progress had slowed down as a result of their loving but erratic ministrations. Nor did the inevitable daily visits from his mother and aunt help much. They always left him white and exhausted, but when Mercy suggested that the visits be kept short, Mrs Purchis lost her temper, as she did too often these days.

"I'll thank you to let me know what's best for my own son! As if setting Mr Gordon against us was not bad enough! I warn you, Miss Phillips, that when Hart is a little stronger I mean to get a new housekeeper who understands her position in the family rather better than you do."

"Aunt Martha!" Abigail had been a horrified spectator and now began a protest, only to be rounded on by her aunt.

"No, child! Do you not see how she has insinuated herself into the management of things that should properly be yours, granted the uncertain state of my health. And has made a pretty penny of it, I have no doubt, with her salary paid in cash or kind, and who knows what saved here and there out of the housekeeping. I warn you"—back to Mercy—"I have promised Mr Gordon that as soon as Hart is well there is to be a thorough investigation into what has been going on in this house, and I hope we will find that the records are straight."

So did Mercy, but did not expect it. She had made, she realised, a dangerous enemy in Saul Gordon. But she had more urgent things to think about. The news from the south grew worse every day. The British had surrounded Sunbury now and ordered it to yield, and though Colonel John Mc-

Intosh's reply, "Come and take it!" had already become a catchword in Savannah, the fact remained that if Sunbury should fall, little or nothing stood between the enemy and Savannah itself, with its inadequate fortifications and handful of guns bearing only on the river. And still, every day came the unspeakable stories of pillage, rapine, and revenge. Rebel against Loyalist. Brother against brother. Father against son. If Savannah should be taken, Hart must not be there to be recaptured. Neither his mind nor his body would stand another spell of imprisonment.

"William!" She had contrived to find the coachman alone in the stables at the far end of the lot, where he was busy polishing the family carriage and singing a doleful tune as he did so:

> Where'er they march the buildings burn
> Large stacks of rice to ashes turn. . . .

"Yes, ma'am?" He turned at the sound of her voice.

"I need your help. For Mr Hart. Just in case—"

"Yes, ma'am. You think, the cellar?"

"No, I don't. It would be bad for him, and besides, we don't know how long—"

"We sure don't. But is he well enough to ride, ma'am?"

"No. It will have to be by boat. Can you have one ready, below the bluff, out of sight? All the time, William. With men you can trust to man her?"

"Ours?" Doubtfully, "I reckon I'd not be sure which might choose to tell Mr Gordon. And I don't trust him nohow. But there's Jem, of course, and he and I've got friends among other families might be glad of a chance to get clear. That's what it will be, won't it?"

"Yes, that's what it will be. I can pay, thank God. In cash." She had not spent a penny of her wages.

"That's good. Will you be coming?"

"No." They both knew it would add immeasurably to the danger of the escape.

William told her three days later that it was all arranged. "You don't need to fret 'bout nothing, ma'am. You give the signal; Jem and I take him down to the wharf; they'll be ready."

"God bless you, William."

Hart could walk very feebly across the little room now,

217

but he was still obviously not well enough to be worried about business. Nothing more had been said about a new housekeeper, but Mrs Purchis' manner warned Mercy that she was merely biding her time, and Saul Gordon was his plump, confident self again. He was spending a great deal of time at the McCartney house, where he met many of the leading members of the Assembly, of whom he now spoke familiarly by their first names. He came back from there one Friday early in December with a budget of good news. The British attack on Sunbury had failed. "Now I hope we'll hear no more panic talk of bringing the slaves in from Winchelsea." The statement was general, but aimed, she knew, at Mercy. She hated his habit of calling the servants slaves, often in front of them, but until Hart was well enough to take charge of his own affairs, there was nothing she could do about it. And at least Gordon volunteered to ride out to Winchelsea to make sure that all went well there and to bring back some badly needed supplies. "We'll get a fancy price for our seed-corn next year, ma'am," Mercy heard him tell Mrs Purchis. "With all the destruction down south, it will be at a premium. Oh, I know there's talk of fixing prices, but you can rely on me to see you right."

"I don't know what I'd do without you," she told him with a side glance for Mercy, who beat a retreat, as she often did, into Hart's room, where she could be sure of a welcome.

But when she told him of the British retreat from Sunbury, he merely frowned anxiously. "I don't believe it. Oh, they may have retired for the moment, but those were mere skirmishing parties. It is something very much more serious that I fear. Mercy, I *must* get my strength back so that I can go and speak to the Assembly myself. Take me out of doors. That will do me more good than anything."

"Not in the street."

"No, in the yard. Walking up and down there will be better than crawling to and fro in this wretched little room." And then warmly, "Not that I'm not immensely grateful for all you've done, but I begin to think if I have to spend much longer staring at these four walls, I'll go mad."

"You'll never do that."

"No? I was afraid—sometimes—in the hulks. Men did, you know, killed themselves—jumped overboard, defied the guards into killing them. It was—" He was beginning to shake. "Mercy, I can't tell you how horrible it was."

"Don't think about it. Come out into the fresh air instead."

In the yard, children were playing, chickens scratching in the dust, and a bright line of washing hung to dry in winter sunshine.

At the sight of Hart and Mercy the children came crowding round, with beaming faces and cries of welcome. Hart's hand went automatically to his pocket. "I wish I had something for them," he said.

"They don't need anything beyond the sight of you. But they mustn't tire you. Delilah"—she smiled across the bobbing black heads at William's grand-daughter—"Mr Hart's not well yet. He needs quiet."

"Sure thing, Miss Mercy. He shall have it. Come down to the stables, you all, and my grandpa will show you how he shoes a horse."

They ran after her, laughing and chattering, and Hart, leaning gratefully on Mercy's arm, began a slow pacing to and fro. She had just begun to feel him tire when the door of Gordon's office opened and he came across the yard towards them. She had thought him already gone to Winchelsea and cursed herself for her carelessness as he made an elaborate business of welcoming Hart home and enquiring after his health. "It is good to see you looking so much more the thing, sir. I hope you are rid of your delusions."

"Delusions?" Hart's voice was both angry and anxious.

"This wild idea about a two-pronged British attack. It caused a bit of panic in town when Miss Mercy chose to spread it around. The last thing we want. I have it from the Assembly that they would much prefer you talked no more about it. Either of you. This is no time to let the mob be stirred up by a sick boy's fancies."

"You choose to lecture me." Hart's arm, in Mercy's, was rigid with anger. "You forget your place, Mr Gordon. Now you will do an errand for me. You will go to your friends at the Assembly and tell them I am neither a boy nor suffering from delusions. I was man enough to fight for our freedom and am sane enough to wonder just what advantage there might be to you in having my warnings ignored. Have you sold out to the British by any chance, Mr Gordon? Are you one of Savannah's secret Loyalists? The Assembly would like to know about that, would they not? I suggest you make your best haste to them and deliver my message."

"If you insist, Mr Purchis, I must naturally do as I am bid,

219

but I should warn you it will do you no good with them. I fear it will merely convince them that you are still very far from being yourself and are being led by the nose by a clever woman. But that is another story."

"And not an edifying one as you would tell it. I still have my hearing good as ever, Mr Gordon. There is talk, is there not, of a great accounting when I am well enough? Well, be sure your figures can stand up to it. I know Miss Phillips' will. Now go."

Mercy could feel the effort by which he kept himself rigidly erect until Gordon had left the yard. Then, "Mercy," he said, "I'm not well; help me indoors." As he leaned more and more heavily on her arm, she cast a wild look at the nearest of the servants' huts, and instantly William was there, putting his strong arm round Hart's waist, helping to guide his shaky steps towards the office door. "Delilah told me," he said to Mercy across Hart's sagging body. "That's a good girl, that one." He was almost carrying Hart by the time they got him back into his room and had to lift him bodily onto his bed, where he lay, white-faced, half conscious, breathing heavily. "That Mr Gordon could hardly have done worse if he'd done it a purpose." He summed up her own suspicions. "I'll send Amy to you right away."

"And fetch the doctor, William."

Dr Flinn was angry, and Mercy did not blame him. "Quiet, I told you. I even persuaded Mrs Purchis not to fuss at him, and you have to let that rat Gordon at him. We'll just have to pray God it don't mean brain fever. I'll give him a stiff dose of laudanum for tonight, and someone had best sit up with him, just in case. In the morning, we'll see. I'll come straight over from the hospital." Like Savannah's few other doctors, he spent every minute he could in the hospital tending the sick and wounded from Sunbury.

"Mercy!" She had dozed off in her chair, but woke, somewhere in the dead hours of the night, at Hart's voice.

"Yes!" She reached out and found his hot hand in the darkness.

"Do *you* think I'm mad? Suffering from delusions?"

"No, Hart. I almost wish I did. It's not a pleasant prospect you hold out."

His shaky laugh was enormously comforting. "No. Proper Jonah I am. Or Cassandra, more like. But how can I blame them for not believing me, when I can hardly believe myself? Mercy, there's worse than I told you. That's why I keep wondering if it *is* all delusion. But I swear to God, as I lay there half conscious, on that stinking pallet in the hulks, I heard Frank's voice. He pretended not to know me. 'Him?' he said. 'Good God, no. Never saw him in my life.' Mercy, was I—am I very much changed? Could Frank not have recognised me?"

"Impossible. But he might have denied you. Betrayed you. Left you there to die." They were into it now, and she thought it best to go on, get it clear at last between them.

"Frank? You believe that? That he could have betrayed me, denied me? A traitor to me as well as to his country? Francis? My Cousin Francis? Mercy, it's time we talked about that day, the day I left." He reached out with his left hand to grasp her right one in a grip that hurt. "After Frank denied me, left me there to die in my own dirt, I began to think, to wonder. Mercy, what really happened that day?"

"I don't know exactly. But not what they told you. Bridget met someone down at the old wharf, and Saul Gordon knew about it, sent me off on a wild-goose chase after you, when he thought I might catch them. Hart, I think it has to have been Francis. Who else would have known enough to set up that convincing story against me? I don't blame you for believing it; it held together too horribly well."

"Francis and Bridget? And Saul Gordon named you instead? And I believed every word of his filth, just because I so badly wanted not to." His hand was gentle now, its fingers moving softly in the palm of hers. "Mercy, what a fool, what a blind, credulous fool . . ."

"No. It was my fault. After all, I had kept things from you before. Why should you trust me?" A tear dropped onto his left hand, and it came up instantly to feel for her face in the darkness and trace the wet outline of her eyes.

"Mercy. Tell me it's not too late. I've been so stupid."

"Not stupid. Trusting. The way I'd have you be. Easy for me to mistrust Francis. I hadn't grown up with him; he's not my family."

"But you did love him, engage yourself to him secretly. It wasn't all lies?" He hoped to hear it had been.

She longed to lie to him, but would not. "No. I wish it had been. But at first I let him fool me, with his sweet talk." She would not think of those sweeter kisses. "Only, as time went on, talk and actions never seemed quite to jibe. I had seen the way he treated Abigail; I began to wonder what would happen to me. From wondering to mistrusting was an easy step. Painfully easy. And then, one night, at the Mc-Cartneys', when the mob was out, I thought I recognised him as one of the leaders. But I wasn't sure . . . I didn't know what to do. It was a terrible accusation to make, without proof."

"So you stayed engaged to him." His tone blamed her.

"Yes. Don't you see? I was afraid. For you, for all of us. I thought it safest to let him think he still had me fooled. He's deadly dangerous, your cousin Francis."

"It's hard to believe." His voice was tiring. All through the happiness of this strange, dark confrontation, she had been aware of Dr Flinn's insistence that Hart must rest, must sleep.

"Hart"—she tried to release her hand from his—"you must sleep; you must not worry; in the morning, we will talk."

He sighed, and she could hear the exhaustion in it. "Your obedient invalid. Yours indeed. Don't try to pretend to me that you did not nurse me until I recovered consciousness. That's when I began to hope. Loving hands, Mercy. Un-mistakable, loving hands." The laudanum was taking effect again. "Kiss me good night."

She bent to brush his cheek with her lips, was caught by his left hand, pulled down for a long kiss that searched, that asked, that demanded. At last, she felt a bubble of laughter well up in him. "What happiness," he said. "And I'm drugged to the gills. Dear Mercy . . ." He was asleep.

Mercy, too, dozed off in a dream of happiness, but woke very early. There was a quiet scratching at the door to the other house, and she was simultaneously aware of bustle in the street outside. It was just light enough to see that Hart was still sleeping heavily. She hurried to the door and opened it to see Abigail, white and anxious in a wrapper and slippers. "What is it?" she whispered as she half closed the door behind her. "He's deep asleep; better, I think."

"Thank God for that. There's a rumour going about town. It seems Hart may be right. They have picked up a deserter from a British ship . . . a transport . . . the *Neptune*. He says there's a whole fleet on its way from New York. Here. To take Savannah. Mercy what shall we do?"

"Nothing yet. After all, they've not been sighted. Even at

222

the very worst we've the time it will take them to come up from Tybee, and surely now the Assembly will put up some kind of defence." And then, as the oddity of it struck her, "But, Abigail, they are your friends!"

"After what they did to Hart? Mercy, they must not catch him again."

"They shan't, if I can help it. But no need to panic yet; the most important thing is to get his strength back. And bad though it is, this news may do him good. I think his fear that he was really suffering from delusions has done him more harm than anything." And that was all she was going to say, even to Abigail. "Have you sent out for news?"

"Yes, William's gone. But you look exhausted, dear. Shall I sit with Hart till he wakes?"

"No, bless you. He's got used to me, I think. It will be better for him to find me still there. And, selfishly, I'd like the pleasure of telling him he was right all the time."

"Mercy, you were never selfish in your life."

"I sometimes think I am nothing else." How true it was, she thought, settling down again on her low chair by the bed. Savannah was going to be attacked, disaster loomed for them all, and she could feel nothing but happiness. And best of all, she really did think Hart looked better this morning, was sleeping more naturally as the effect of the laudanum wore off.

He was still asleep when Dr Flinn arrived towards noon, and she joined him, finger on lips, in the next room, grateful that Mrs Purchis and Mrs Mayfield were still taking their ration of weak chocolate in bed. "He's better," she said. "I think. I hope."

"Thank God for that. Have you heard the news? He was right, and on both counts."

"Both?"

"Yes. The Assembly had just heard the news of the sea attack when a messenger rode in from the south. General Prevost is massing his troops at St Augustine. It has to mean another attack on us, and this time full-scale, led by a general. There's panic in town today. You had all best stay indoors. Especially Miss Abigail."

"Yes. But what's happening? What's being done?"

"Everything that should have been done long since. The militia are gathering. Our American General Howe is in command. I think he means to march south and intercept the enemy. Pray God he succeeds. And here in town all available hands are summoned to work on the fortifications. You had best send everyone you can spare."

"And the servants from Winchelsea. They will be far too close to the front line, if the British sail upriver. I'll send a message to Mr Gordon at once. He's out there still."

"Best have Mrs Purchis send it."

So the news of her quarrel with Gordon was public knowledge. Well, it was inevitable and probably not important. She ushered the doctor into the little office where Hart was still sleeping peacefully. "You're right." He was taking his patient's pulse. "He's better this morning than I had dared hope. Laudanum is a powerful agent."

And so is happiness. She watched a hint of a smile flicker across the sleeping face. Was he, perhaps, dreaming of her?

Hart woke soon after the doctor had left and reached out his left hand to her. "Tell me it was not a dream, Mercy."

"If it was, I dreamt it too." She let him pull her down for a long, gentle kiss. Then, "But, Hart, my darling, we must keep it secret for the moment. Until you are better and can protect me."

"Secret? I don't like secrets. I want to tell everyone. My mother, my aunt, Abigail, the world—"

"And I want you to, but not yet, my darling. Your mother will be angry, I am afraid, and you are not strong enough for scenes. Besides, there is news this morning. You were right; that was no delusion of yours. The British fleet is on its way, and General Prevost is getting ready to march up from East Florida. We're going to need all your strength soon, and all your good counsel. So, for now, you must be my obedient invalid and let me play the bullying nurse."

"They *are* coming." The weak fingers of his right hand flexed just a little on the patchwork quilt. "And I am like this! You're right. Kiss me once, my love, and then we will apply ourselves to getting me better so that I can shoot one Englishman when they attack, even if you have to load the gun and guide my hand."

"Oh, my dear . . ." Through the long kiss, she knew she must not tell him her plans for him. He would be angry with her afterwards, furiously angry, but he would be alive. She had, all the time, a vision in her mind of the British attack and of two men who would make their way to the house in

Oglethorpe Square. Francis and Giles. But Giles would stay to do his duty before he came. Francis would come direct.

Rumour blew with the sand about the streets of Savannah. General Prevost had indeed marched north from St Augustine, and the American General Howe had made a brave show as he started south to intercept him. A group of British ships had been seen off Tybee, but had been dispersed by a storm. Hope grew, as irrational as the previous terror. The British had decided to attack Charleston instead . . . to seek out the French in the West Indies . . . to go anywhere but to Savannah. People even began to make preparations for Christmas, and the Assembly was duly summoned for its January meeting.

William, returning from his stint on the fortifications to the south of the town, was gloomy. "Fewer men turn up every day," he told Mercy. "Some have run, some are busy making hideouts in their cellars, and I've no doubt, there are ladies in many houses washing out their British flags and ironing them ready for show. But our Winchelsea lot are doing us proud, ma'am, and so you can tell the master. How is he?"

"Better every day. But not well." Next time Dr Flinn came, she seized a chance to beg an extra dose of laudanum from him. "I may need it," she said.

"Oh?" He delved in his shabby black bag. "I'm trusting you, Miss Phillips."

"You may."

Next morning, bad news came thick and fast. Prevost had outmanoeuvred Howe, who had been forced to withdraw on Savannah, leaving Sunbury to hold out as best it might, and as if that was not bad enough, the British fleet was taken in full force off Tybee. "Please God they don't learn how weak our defences are," said Hart. "Our only hope lies in the kind of slow, orthodox siege military experts prescribe." He had recovered from his setback and was walking up and down the yard with Mercy and Abigail.

"Hush!" said Mercy. They were outside the hut Gordon now used as his office.

"How do you mean, hush!" Convalescence had sharpened his temper, and so had the enforced secrecy about their engagement. "Surely I can say what I like in my own back yard."

"I hope so."

That evening Gordon rode out to Winchelsea to make sure, he said, that nothing had been left behind that could be of the slightest use to the enemy if they should attack, which he, personally, made bold to doubt.

He returned three days after Christmas with the news that the British ships had crossed the bar and were anchored in the Savannah River. "They'll attack any day now. And General Howe with only six hundred and seventy men to oppose him. If I were you, ladies, I'd be packing up for a quick getaway upriver. The public records are all at Purrysburg by now and I'd feel a deal happier if you were there too. Then, if the worst should happen, you can go to Mrs Mayfield's Charleston house till happier times."

"Leave?" Martha Purchis' voice was shrill. "You think we should leave Savannah?"

"Ma'am," he said earnestly, "you've got to face facts. There's a whole fleet of the enemy. Two thousand men, they say. Some of them Germans who don't speak our language—some Loyalists who hate us. Think for a minute what will happen to you and the young ladies if it should come to a sack. You know what it's been like in the south. Why should it be different here?"

"Sister," wailed Anne Mayfield. "we must go! At once . . . or as soon as we can pack up. He's right; we can't chance it. Now you will thank God I never sold my house in Charleston."

"But what about this house?" Martha Purchis looked round the once-luxurious drawing-room that was beginning to show signs of wear and tear. "What will happen to it if we go?"

"I'll stay," said Saul Gordon. "I'll look after it for you, ma'am. You can rely on me."

Rely on him? Mercy was about to speak, when, to her relief, Abigail anticipated her. "No need, Mr Gordon. Whatever happens, I shall not go. When you talk of a sack, you forget, I think, that I am a known Loyalist. God knows I have suffered enough for it. Now, perhaps, Aunt, I can repay some of your kindness."

"Bravely spoken." Gordon's tone was scornful. "Do you really think, Miss Purchis, that in the heat of battle the enemy will stop to tell friend from foe? You must have heard stories enough of Loyalists killed by those brutes of Hessians who can't even speak English, still less read a protection."

"Mr Habersham and Mr Mayfield will have made arrangements to protect us," said Abigail. "I am sure of it. Aunt, you must see that to abandon this house is the surest way to lose it. I've a British flag upstairs. You won't mind—"

Mercy listened ruefully as they argued it out. In how many houses in Savannah, she wondered, was this same conversation going on? In the end, nothing was really decided, except that the two older ladies tottered off to pack up their possessions, "just in case," and Saul Gordon retired to his hut in the yard in a simmering, silent rage.

"He really believed we'd go." Abigail turned to Mercy, who had stayed silent throughout. "They none of them seem to have thought that we could hardly move Hart."

"No." Mercy did not intend to tell even Abigail about her plans for Hart. "I'm glad you spoke up, dear. I'll stay with you, of course. I hope it's a big Union flag."

She put on her peasant outfit that afternoon and slipped out the back way to mingle with the anxious crowds. Bay and Broughton Streets were thronged with heavily loaded carriages, all heading westwards, and she recognised many haggard, patriot faces, peering out at the crowds. The quays, too, were a scene of intense activity, and she prayed that William had a strong guard on the boat he had ready for Hart's escape. Listening to the panicky talk of the crowd, she wondered desperately what would be for the best. In a way, Abigail's decision had made things easier for her. If Abigail stayed, so would she, and if swearing allegiance to George III would save Hart's house for him, she would do it.

"Wouldn't defend it!" She heard a voice she knew and pulled her shawl more closely round her face at sight of Colonel Elbert talking angrily to a militia officer who was also an old friend of Hart's.

"Brewton Hill—Mr Girardeau's place?" She could not remember this man's name, but he sounded as anxious as Elbert. "But it's madness! If the British have any information, and we must assume they have, it's the obvious place to land, the first practicable bluff. And the rice dam would make a good defence post for us."

"That's what I said." Elbert sounded both desperate and exhausted. "Howe wouldn't listen. Well"—fairly—"it's true; he's dead short of men. He's got his line on the high ground, closer to town. We must just pray God the British don't learn about Brewton Hill."

"I'll pray God all right," said the other officer. "But I shall send my family out of town."

It was enough. Mercy turned and hurried home to make sure that William had a good guard on the Purchis boat, and then to find Mrs Purchis and urge that she and Anne Mayfield leave at once.

It was a fatal mistake. "So!" said Martha Purchis. "Just what Mr Gordon warned me would happen. You think Sister and I are going to leave you to make whatever kind of monkey you please out of Abigail and no doubt end up claiming this house, and for all I know Winchelsea as well, for your own. No, no, I know my duty. If you two chits decide to stay, I shall stay too, and mark my words, whatever happens will be all your fault."

Nothing would budge her from this decision, not even the news, next day, that the British had indeed forced a landing at Brewton Hill and started up the main road to Savannah. "Oh, my poor Winchelsea," wailed Martha Purchis. "If they're as far as Tatnall's and Governor Wright's, Winchelsea's gone."

"I heard a rumour they were using it for a hospital," said Saul Gordon.

"Thank God for that! Then they won't burn it!" said Mrs Purchis. And "You are very well informed, Mr Gordon," said Mercy.

It got her a sharp look. "Well enough informed to wish you ladies were safe away from here. Mrs Purchis, once again I beseech you. For your own sake, and most particularly, for the young ladies', order out the carriage! Go west, ma'am, go west as fast as you can! I rather think today will be your last chance."

20

Next day, the crowds were thinner, and there were no soldiers among them. Every man who could walk had been sent out to defend the thin line General Howe had stretched round the town. People talked lower, too, looking carefully over their shoulders as they did so, but Mercy, inconspicuous in her homespuns and shawl, managed to pick up a crumb of information here and there. Every available labourer was at work on the defences of the three main roads into town. At the east, where the main British attack was expected, the bridges had been burnt and a trench was being dug between the swamps on either side of the main road. "But how long that will hold them is anyone's guess," said a man with one arm in a sling. "I'm leaving tonight. If we had a soldier in charge instead of old Granny Howe, it would be something else again. Do you know what he's done?"

"No." Mercy looked sharply at this other speaker. "What's he done, friend?"

"Given 'Firmness' for the password and followed it by instructions as to how to retreat! I had that from a friend of mine who came slap back to get his wife out of town, and I'm doing the same. I don't like the way the wind's blowing today." He turned away and pushed purposefully through the crowd.

Mercy was still studying the other man. He had his coat collar pulled well up around his neck and a shabby hat down over his eyes, but just the same she was almost sure she recognised him as an assistant of Johnston the printer's and an old friend of her father's. "Mr Miles?" she said now, low and tentatively.

For a moment she thought he was going to run for it, then he swung round to face her "Who calls me that?" A sharp look, but he had known her in her poorer days. "Mercy! Mercy Phillips." He looked round quickly to make sure they were unobserved, then pressed both her hands warmly. "It's good to see you, girl. I never did get a chance to say how sorry I was . . ."

"No need. But I thought you were at the West Indies with Mr Johnston."

He smiled ruefully. "So do most people, thank God. No, I've been out of town with my wife's people, lying low." There was something wrong with his tone and she remembered that his wife came from the south of the colony.

"I hope all is well with them." It had to be said, but she was afraid of the answer.

"Dead. She and the boys. I was away. I don't talk about it. Only this: it was the British did it. One of those marauding bands up from St Augustine. I'm no Loyalist now. I'm on my way to our lines, to take one with me as I go."

"Mr Miles"—she put a quick hand on his arm—"don't. Or, before you decide, listen to me."

Twenty minutes later she was in Hart's room, mixing him his evening draft. "I'm making it a little stronger tonight," she told him. "I think we're going to need all our wits about us tomorrow."

"As bad as that?"

"Quite as bad. Hart, whatever happens, promise you'll never stop loving me."

"How could I? You're part of me, Mercy. It would be to stop loving myself."

A cold finger touched her spine, and she made herself very busy with his medicine. "Never do that."

He pulled himself up in his bed, ready to take the medicine glass from her. "I shall like myself better when I have had my turn against the British," he said. "Remember, Mercy, if they should take the town tomorrow, you're going to load my musket for me and then hide in the celler with the others."

"Let's take tomorrow as it comes, my dear." She handed him the glass into which she had poured all the laudanum Dr Flinn had given her. "For tonight, drink this, sleep well, and remember I love you with all my heart."

He raised the glass in a silent toast. "Mercy, if we survive tomorrow, marry me the next day?"

"Yes!" She watched, wide-eyed, as he swallowed the drink in one great gulp.

"Horrid!" He smiled and handed her the glass. "What poison have you been brewing for me, Mercy, my love?"

It was almost too much for her. Should she tell him? What would he do if she did? She could not risk it. "Not I," she said lightly. "Dr Flinn. He gave it to me specially for tonight."

"Laudanum. A savage dose." He gave her the ghost of a wicked smile. "I'm almost tempted to think he knows about us. Mercy, my darling, and intends to keep us respectable at all costs. Poor Dr Flinn." He held out his hand to her. "Well, if I must sleep the sleep of the drugged, kiss me good night and come hold my hand, my darling, while I go."

"Oh, Hart." As she bent to kiss him, two uncontrollable tears fell on his face. "Never stop loving me."

"Never." And then, sleepily, "You said that before. What

is it, Mercy? What's the matter?"

"Nothing, my darling. Nothing that will not keep until morning." She kept her voice calm, but her heart shook. The drug was working with terrifying speed. Could Dr Flinn have given her too strong a dose? Or had they misunderstood each other? She knew it was impossible and yet could not help being afraid. Ridiculous. She bent to kiss Hart once, gently, hungrily, in case it must last a lifetime, and went out to the yard to find William.

It seemed an age before the family were settled for the night. Mrs Purchis and Mrs Mayfield had changed their minds so many times that at last it was only exhaustion that sent them to bed, rather than out, into the carriage, and away through the dangerous darkness to the west. Abigail, too, looked worn with anxiety and was easily persuaded to follow them to bed. "I shall sit up with Hart for a while," explained Mercy. "Sleep well, my dear. God knows what tomorrow will bring."

Abigail put a distracted hand to her brow. "Mercy, it's so horrible. I don't know what to want anymore! All this time I've longed for Giles, and now, this—"

"I know." There was no comfort to offer.

To Mercy's relief, Hart's sleep, though deep, seemed natural enough. She waited until house and streets alike were quiet at last, then went out the back to where William and Jem were waiting with a litter that had been used by Abigail's mother in her last illness. It had been William's idea. "Much less noticeable than the carriage, and besides, Madam Purchis, she might take that."

Hart stirred a little and muttered something when the two men picked him up and carried him awkwardly through the narrow door and into the yard, but he did not wake. "Take good care of him, William." Mercy had already handed over the money she had promised. "And, when he wakes, give him my love. Try to make him understand."

"I'll do my best, ma'am." Mercy suspected that William understood a good deal.

"Thank you." They must not stay whispering here. "Now, good-bye, and good luck." She turned back into the little, empty room, grateful for darkness to hide the tears that streamed down her face. Would Hart ever forgive her for what she had done tonight?

She cried herself to sleep in the bed still warm from Hart's body and woke to the too-familiar sound of panicky movement in the streets. It was very early still, but when she peered cautiously out of the front window, she saw that the day's exodus had already begun. Yesterday it had been carriages, today it was handcarts, piled high with the belongings of a whole family; crying children on top and anxious women following behind. Just as well that Howe had his soldiers already in their positions. It would be difficult to move about in Savannah today.

An agitated tapping on the yard door heralded Amy. "Miss Mercy, my William's gone! I never thought I'd see the day I had to be shamed for him, but he and Jem done run in the night." Tears tracked each other down her wrinkled brown face.

"It's all right, Amy!" Mercy took her hand and led her into Hart's room. "They took Mr Hart with them. I'm sorry William didn't tell you." But he had been right, she thought.

"Oh, praise be! So they're all safe, William and Mr Hart, and Jem?"

"I hope so, Amy. They're going upriver, hoping to get to Charleston when Mr Hart is strong enough."

"Does his ma know?" asked the old woman shrewdly. And then, "Miss Mercy, if they do come, the British, what should we do in the yard?"

"Hide," said Mercy, "or run and come back when you can." She had told no one of the secret cellar William had made; she had her own plans for it. "Don't tell anyone Mr Hart's gone, Amy, not till we have to."

"Very good, Miss Mercy." The old woman suddenly seized her hand and kissed it. "Thank you for saving my William, ma'am."

"I hope I have," said Mercy.

Half an hour later Saul Gordon arrived, insisting that he see Hart.

"I'm sorry." Mercy barred the way. "He is not awake yet. I gave him a strong draft of laudanum last night on Dr Flinn's orders. I do not expect him to wake until noon."

"Wise, I suppose." Grudgingly, "Well, best put that man of his, Jem, on guard at his door so he don't get disturbed."

Or doesn't escape, thought Mercy. "Jem's run," she said. "Amy just told me. And William." Luckily, Gordon had never interested himself in the servants as people and would not appreciate the significance of this combination.

"One of the other men then," said Gordon. "I have to go out for a while. I'll be back at noon."

As he left, Abigail appeared, looking anxious. "How's Hart this morning?" she asked.

"Still asleep." Mercy instinctively postponed the moment of revelation.

"Good. My aunts are just getting up. Mercy, do you know what's happening?"

"No. Gordon's gone out—for news I expect. Abigail, would you stay here and see no one disturbs Hart while I go and see what I can find out?"

"It's not safe for you!"

"Oh, yes it is." She had brought the black shawl with her from Hart's room and now wound it round her head and shoulders and dropped into an Irish brogue. "I'm only going out for the news, surely. A plain bit of an Irish girl like me will come to no harm in the crowd."

"Good gracious!" a reluctant smile wavered across Abigail's drawn face. "I'd quite forgotten what a mimic you are! Mercy, I'm afraid for Hart. My aunts will do anything Gordon says, and I don't trust him."

"No more do I. He's put a man on duty at the back door of Hart's room. 'To see he's not disturbed.'"

"Oh! I thought I heard something. Mercy, you don't think we should wake Hart and get him out the front way?"

"I'm sure Gordon has someone watching there too. We'll know better what to do when I get back with news."

"For God's sake, be careful!"

"Believe me, I shall."

Outside, she found that the crowds had thinned and an ominous quiet fallen on the streets. And now, from the east, somewhere beyond the Trustees' Garden, she could hear the rattle of musket fire and the occasional crump of the cannon on the bluff there. That was where General Howe had his strongest defences. Perhaps, after all, there was hope for Savannah; perhaps she had let herself panic last night. If so, she had risked Hart's life, and his love for her, for nothing. They might have been married tomorrow.

Other people had heard the action beginning and were emerging from their houses to listen, half in hope, half in fear, but none of them knew any more than she did, though all agreed that the attack from the east was a good sign. "The line's mortal thin to the south and west," one old woman

233

told her. "My man said last night we were lost if General Prevost should come up from the south, but please God, the garrison's still holding down at Sunbury." She lifted her head to listen to a fresh rattle of fire from the east. "They'll hold there," she said. "The defences are good, my man says, and the men determined. But mortal tired. Most of them still ain't recovered from the march back from the south. But they know what they're fighting for!"

"Yes." Mercy turned and hurried home with this moderately good news to find Abigail in fierce argument with the two older women. "He's had a sleeping draught." She was standing against the door of Hart's room. "Mercy said he must not be disturbed."

" 'Mercy said!' " Mrs Purchis took her up on it angrily. "I'm sick to death of hearing what Mercy says! Hart's my son, isn't he? I think I have a right to consult him about what's best for us to do. Heaven help us! The firing's getting nearer! We must decide something! Soon, it may be too late." She turned and saw Mercy. "There you are at last. What's the news in town?"

"The British are attacking from the east, thank God. There seems a good chance our men will hold them. You know how hard they have worked on the lines there."

"It don't sound like the east to me," said Martha Purchis.

They looked at each other for a moment in listening silence, then, with one accord, trooped out onto the screened porch and into the neglected garden, to stand, heads up, silent, listening. The thud of a gun from the direction of the Trustees' Garden. "Oh, my poor Winchelsea," sighed Martha Purchis.

"It's well behind the British lines by now," said Anne Mayfield, "but thank God you're wrong, Sister. That's from the east all right."

"That was," said Martha Purchis, "but, listen!" This time there was no doubt about it. The roll of cannon fire was coming also from the south, from somewhere beyond the Common.

"The south road!" said Abigail. "Dear God, it must be Prevost. What shall we do? Mercy, we must wake Hart, get him away, anywhere!"

"No." While all their heads were turned southwards, Saul Gordon had entered the garden from the servants' yard at the back. "Too late for that. The servants are run already and the carriage has lost a wheel."

"Lost?" asked Mercy.

He ignored her, addressing himself to Martha Purchis. "Anyway, you run a greater risk taking to the roads than you will do in staying here." He reached into the pocket of his greatcoat and handed her a paper. "Here is your protection, signed by the British General Campbell himself. Nail that on the door, fly Miss Abigail's British flag, and you'll have no trouble when they come."

"No if?" asked Mercy.

This time he condescended to answer her. "No 'if' at all. While Campbell has kept Howe occupied, Sir James Baird and the New York Volunteers have been taking a path from Brewton Hill through the swamp that General Howe didn't trouble to defend. That firing to the south means they have turned the rebel line and are attacking from the right."

"Rebel?" said Abigail.

"How do you know?" asked Mercy.

"Those poor McCartney girls," exclaimed Anne Mayfield. "They will be right on the line of attack."

"No need to trouble yourself about them, said Saul Gordon. "They have their protection too, all right and tight. I left it there myself."

"And where did you get these fine protections?" Mercy reached out and took the document from Mrs Purchis' limp hand. "Dated yesterday. Campbell's signature. So that's where you went. You must have been mighty useful to General Campbell, Mr Gordon." And then, before he had time to answer. "There's no mention of Mr Purchis in this."

"Impossible, I'm afraid," said Saul Gordon. "A known rebel. But I have General Campbell's word for it that he will be well used. The guard who will come, very soon now, to take charge of this house will see to his arrest." He was enjoying himself hugely, Mercy thought and then saw, with horrified amazement, what Abigail was doing. She had moved quietly, while the others were all gathered round Gordon, to pick up a small stone statue of a cherub from the terrace and was now, coolly, raising it to strike Saul Gordon from behind.

"Abigail, don't!" And then, before Gordon could turn to see what Abigail was doing. "I have news for you, Mr Gordon. Mr Purchis left last night. God knows where he is now. I certainly do not. But somewhere, I hope, where he has no need of anyone's protection."

"Gone?" They all turned on her in amazement.

"Yes." If only she knew to what extent the family's safety depended on Hart's arrest. Best play safe, for all their sakes. "He went last night. I don't know when."

"Gone," said Martha Purchis. "And did not choose to say good-bye to me!"

"Gone!" Gordon turned on Mercy. "And you lied to me when I asked for him!"

"He is my employer. And, Mr Gordon, you have not yet told us what you did for General Campbell, or how he learned of the path across the swamp. I take it you have turned your coat with a vengeance."

"That's not a phrase I would use today, Miss Mercy." Before they could question him further he hurried up the porch steps and disappeared into the big living room, no doubt to make sure that Hart had really escaped.

"It's true?" Abigail had quietly put down the statue before anyone but Mercy had noticed what she was doing.

"Yes. Only"—she turned to Mrs Purchis—"for God's sake, don't tell Gordon, but Hart did not go voluntarily. I drugged him with laudanum. He was fast asleep, knew nothing about it."

"And you make him out a coward," said his mother angrily. "He'll have a score to settle with you when he gets back, Miss Phillips."

"No, Sister." Surprisingly, Anne Mayfield intervened. "Miss Phillips was quite right. Don't you see? Hart's not here to be blamed. We are. We might find our protection was worthless if we were thought to have been instrumental in spiriting him away. And come to that"—turning on Mercy—"what right had you to do so without so much as consulting his mother?"

The right of a fiancée. She longed to say it, but must not, and was saved from temptation by the furious return of Saul Gordon. "He's gone all right," he said. "Someone will pay for this. Who helped him?"

"I told you Jem and William had run," said Mercy. "Looks like they went with him."

"We knew nothing about it." Martha Purchis was clutching her protection as if she was afraid Gordon would snatch it back from her. "It's not our fault."

"I wonder," said Gordon. "But no time for that. Listen!" The cannon were silent and the sound of musket fire much

236

nearer. "They're advancing," he went on. "It won't be long now. I'd get out that Union flag if I were you, Miss Purchis. You're going to need it. I must go and look to my own house. Good luck, ladies." And with a swift, mocking bow, he was gone.

Left alone, the four women stood for a moment in horrified silence. Then, "What shall we do?" wailed Anne Mayfield.

"We'd best do as he told us, I think," said Abigail. "I'll get the flag; you get one of the men to nail the protection on the door, Mercy."

But when Mercy went out to the servants' quarters, she found only Amy. "The men has run, Miss Mercy," said the old woman. "I reckoned I'd as soon die here, if die I must. They say the British are through our lines and coming fast. You'd best hide, you ladies. My Delilah, she come back all blubbered with tears. She'd seen the British soldiers bayonetting our men while they tried to surrender. She had blood on her skirts."

"She shouldn't have been out!"

"It happened so fast, miss. They came rushing across the Common, she said, like one of the plagues in the Bible. And Howe's soldiers running like rabbits and dropping their muskets, and off to the west fast as they could. Colonel Roberts, he's holding the enemy on the west road, they say, so's our men can escape. Lucky for us, this house ain't on the main road, but you'd best be ready, just the same."

"Yes. Where does William keep his tools?"

It was horribly quiet in Oglethorpe Square. The other houses already had doors locked and shutters closed. All but one. At the far corner of the square, panic-stricken slaves were loading baggage into a chaise, their mistress, the wife of a militia officer, at once urging them to hurry and looking anxiously up and down the street in hopes of seeing her husband. Mercy ran across the square to her. "Mrs Reynolds, don't wait for your husband. The army's in full retreat. We've just heard. Go, quick, you and the children!"

"But he told me he'd come!" This was the only sure thing in a world of chaos.

"Perhaps he can't. Please, Mrs Reynolds, it's your last chance, and the children's." And, as she spoke, she knew it was already too late. Feet thudded in the sand: a detachment of soldiers marched into the square. She had got so used to the American "uniform" of slouched hat, hunter's shirt, and tattered breeches, that these men, point device in their dark green uniform, seemed almost ridiculous—toy soldiers. They certainly showed no sign of having been in battle. Had it really been so easy? Betrayed, Hart had said.

The officer gave an order, and a group of men surrounded Mrs Reynolds and began unharnessing the horse from her chaise. She screamed, once, but Mercy's eyes were for the officer. "Welcome home, Francis," she said.

"Mercy! It's good to find you." He looked up to where Abigail was hanging her British flag from a first-floor window. "And my wise Cousin Abigail. I am come to put a man on guard here, for all your safety."

Once, long ago, the look he flashed for Mercy alone would have sent shivers of excitement down her spine. Incredible. She looked up at him. "Thank you, Francis. I knew we could count on you. Your mother and aunt will be grateful, too. They are indoors."

"That's good. But I must not stay now. There are many more of our friends to be looked after. You have your protection, I'm glad to see. I am afraid things will be bad here in town for a few days. General Howe was mad not to surrender when he had the chance and save the town the horrors of a sack." Another scream from across the square gave horrible point to his words.

"Mercy, tell them, get him to tell them to stop!" Mrs Reynolds came running across the square, a child in each hand, and at the last moment recognised Francis. "Thank God, it's you, Frank. Tell them, explain to them, I have to have the chaise. Jim's not come home. I have to go to my mother's at Purrysburg."

"I'm sorry, ma'am." If he recognized her as the wife of an old friend, he concealed it very well. "We have our orders. All carts and horses to be commandeered. Besides"—more kindly—"you don't want to be out on the road today amongst those ruffians Howe calls an army. You'd not be safe."

"And I'm safe here, Francis Mayfield? If you think that—"

"Get into your house, ma'am, shut the doors, and I'll tell the man on guard here to have an eye to you."

She looked at him for a long moment, then turned and went slowly back, the children crying beside her, to where her baggage lay scattered in the sand.

"Francis!" Mercy began a protest, but he interrupted her.

"She's lucky I'm here," he said. "Otherwise they'd be

looting the house. This is no day for rebels. Jim Reynolds is dead, by the way. I saw him cut down on the Common. You'd better tell her later. He should have kept with the retreating army, not tried to come home. Now"—briskly—"where's Hart? I must take him with me, for his safety and yours."

"Hart? He's not here. We woke this morning and found him gone. And two of the men with him. God knows how he contrived it; he's hardly strong enough to walk."

"Then he can't have gone far." Nothing loving about his look now. "You wouldn't lie to me, Mercy? You wouldn't be hiding Hart by any chance?"

"No, she would not," came Abigail's clear voice from above. "Don't forget, Cousin Francis, that you are not the only Loyalist in the family."

"I forget nothing," said Francis. "And I take nothing for granted. So, I fear, we must search the house."

They found old Amy and her grand-daughter Delilah huddled together behind the hay in the coach-house. They found Mrs Purchis and Mrs Mayfield sitting white, silent, and surprisingly dignified in the big drawing-room. They found Hart's clothes in the room next door, but they found neither Hart nor, to Mercy's great relief, the secret corner of the cellar. At last Francis turned to Mercy to ask a significant question. "And where is Saul Gordon?"

"At his house on Bay Street," said Mercy. "He said he must look to his own.

"Wise," said Francis. "I'm afraid there will be no holding our men today. Those crazy Americans turned and fired on the Seventy-first Highlanders when they thought they'd surrendered. The blood and tears shed today will be on their head, and Howe's. They are looting all down Broughton Street, feathers and papers all over the place. It's lucky you're off the main track here. But I'll leave men on guard front and back. You should be safe enough if you stay indoors. I'll visit you when I can, Mother." She had thrown herself, sobbing, into his arms, and he detached himself with ungentle firmness, saluted, and was gone.

"What are we gong to do?" wailed Martha Purchis.

"What he tells us, I'm afraid." Mercy was standing from the window as Francis and his men marched off towards Whitaker Street. "Oh, my God!"

"What is it?" Abigail hurried across the room to join her.

239

And then, "The brutes." The soldiers who were unloading Mrs Reynolds' chaise had come on a case of spirits and knocked the head off a bottle. One of them had found a silver vase and filled it. They were all around Mrs Reynolds, pressing it on her, obviously urging her to drink the loyal toast.

"No!" Mercy threw open the front window and spoke savagely to the man on duty in the street.

"Sorry, ma'am." He refused to budge. "I got no orders about those rebs. Just you I'm looking after. And you stay put!"

How like Francis to have forgotten. If he had forgotten. "Abigail, keep our guard talking. Offer him a drink . . . anything. . . . I'm going to fetch Mrs Reynolds."

Abigail was still looking across the square. "I thought them my friends," she said. "Yes, quick, Mercy. Fetch her quick. Once they're drunk—"

"I know." At the moment, the soldiers crowding round Mrs Reynolds were merely amusing themselves. It would not last. As Abigail poured a glass of rum and handed it out to the soldier, Mercy picked up the protection and let herself quietly out of the little house next door. Running across the square, skirts held high from the sand, she snatched the silver vase from the soldier who was still drunkenly pressing it on Mary Reynolds. "I'll drink your toast," she said. "We're Loyalists here in the square, and here's our protection. You leave my friends alone! George the Third!" She took a pull of neat rum, coughed, spluttered, and, mercifully, amused them.

"Spunky little thing," said one.

"It's a protection all right," said another. "Can you read, Jeb?"

"Not I, but it looks like Campbell's signature. I've seen that often enough."

"Come along, dear." Mercy picked up the smallest Reynolds child, took Mary Reynolds' hand, and led the way back across the square. Strangely, absurdly, the men cheered her as she went, and then went systematically back to work looting the Reynolds house.

"I hope to God they don't set it on fire," said Mercy when they had got Mrs Reynolds and the children safely to bed at the back of the house.

Abigail was looking out of the front window. "They're

240

going away, I think. There's a British officer speaking to them." And then, as the splendid figure in scarlet and gold regimentals turned their way, "Dear God, it's Giles! Mercy, I can't . . . I won't see him . . . conquering heroes!" She lifted shabby skirts to run swiftly towards the stairs, turning as she went to answer Mercy's protest with "Tell him there's blood on his hands."

Since the two older ladies had both retired to their rooms with all the comfort that sal volatile could offer, Mercy found herself compelled to receive Giles alone. "I'm sorry," she answered his anxious question. "They are all prostrate. It's been a bad day."

"Horrible. But, Mercy, you mean Abigail won't see me? After all this time?"

"Not yet, Giles. Not today. You should have written to her. Now, you must give her time."

"How could I write? What could I say? As to time, I may not have it to give. General Howe is in full retreat and my guess is we'll be starting after him in the morning. Tell Abigail it's now or—"

"Don't say it, Giles," she interrupted him. "You don't understand what she's gone through. First Hart, coming home so ill, and then today, the things we've seen, the sounds we've heard. It's been—"

"I know, but *you're* speaking to me, Mercy."

"I'm not a Loyalist," she said. "I begin to think I'm not anything. Just a survivor, I hope. I'm sorry you're not staying in town, Giles."

"So am I. Tell Abigail I'll come when I can. Once more." The subject was closed. "Mercy, how is Hart? Am I not even to see him?

"He's not here. He went last night. Lucky for him he did. Our protection does not include him. Giles, wait a moment while I tell Abigail what you've said."

"No." He could be obstinate too. "I've stayed too long already. Give her the message exactly as I gave it to you. It's strange about Hart—I was sure—But no time for that now. I'm glad he's safe away."

"We've never thanked you for what you did for him in New York. I know his mother—"

"Or his cousin Abigail?" Bitterly, "Good-bye, Mercy. I must thank *you*, I suppose, for seeing me."

Next day, the town was quiet at last, with martial law

rigorously enforced under Colonel Innes, Sir Henry Clinton's aide-de-camp. Detachments of blue-coated Hessians, red and white British infantry, and smart, green-jacketed New York Volunteers patroled the streets, preventing looting and arresting all able-bodied men. If caught with arms, they were given a simple choice. They could swear allegiance to George III and enlist with the British army, or be sent to the stinking prison hulks downriver, and probable death. Shaken by the swift and total defeat, many chose service with the British, and soon General Campbell, who had nearly caught the battered American army on his march to take Ebenezer, had his own corps of Savannahian riflemen.

Every day brought its new rash of proclamations. Arms and supplies must be surrendered to the military storekeepers; prices were fixed and only those who had sworn the oath of allegiance might trade.

"As if there was anything to trade," wailed Martha Purchis. "With Winchelsea gone, and neither Francis nor Giles here to protect us, what shall we do?" She had received, the day before, a formal notification that Winchelsea was to continue in use as a military hospital, being confiscated as the property of a known rebel.

"It's thanks to my Francis that we have kept this house," said Anne Mayfield.

"True enough, Sister, but how can we manage with nothing coming in? Saul Gordon has given in his notice and says we have no money, no credit, nothing. Without Winchelsea, we must all starve."

"Or go to Charleston, to my house," said Anne Mayfield.

"And lose this one? And yet, if we stay here, how can we live?"

"I have a suggestion to make," said Mercy. "You know Hart insisted on paying me a salary, Mrs Purchis. I've saved it all—or almost all. If you will be guided by me, I believe we might manage to make a living in this house."

"Oh," said Mrs Purchis eagerly. "How, child?"

21

When Mercy outlined her plan, Abigail exclaimed in horror. "A gambling house! Mercy, you cannot be serious."

"Never more so. But I did not say gambling house. I said a genteel establishment where ladies and gentlemen might meet for a hand of cards. What could be more decorous? There will have to be a subscription, of course; it will be a kind of club, but not for men only like the others."

"Cards?" Mrs Purchis had brightened at the idea. "Do you think we could, Mercy? Without harming our position in society?"

"Oh, society." Mercy shrugged. "There's not much of that now, with so many people fled to the West Indies. It's survival I'm thinking of. We must do something, ma'am, or starve. My money won't last long, with this whole household to feed." Several of the servants had come creeping back by now, each with a new story of danger and escape. "Besides"—she thought of a powerful argument—"they are confiscating rebels' slaves, you know. I think, if we were to put it to Colonel Innes that we were offering hospitality to his officers, it might make a difference."

"Officers only, I do trust," said Mrs Mayfield. "I wonder what Frank would say."

Francis, visiting them that afternoon, looked at Mercy with surprised respect. "An excellent idea. Colonel Innes was speaking only this morning of the problem of entertainment. I'll approach him about it, ma'am," to Mrs Purchis. "But I think you can be sure of the necessary permissions." This was to Mercy.

"We'll need to make a few small alterations to the house," she told him. "Nothing, I'm sure, that our own people could not handle, just so long as they're not taken away."

"You think of everything, don't you? Very well, I will speak about that too. It's a good plan, Mercy. I'm pleased you're being so sensible. I was delighted to hear you had all taken the oath of allegiance."

"Well, of course," she said. "What else could we do?"

Two days later, Francis arrived with the necessary permissions, and an invitation. "Drive out with me to the McCartneys', Mercy? The air will do you good."

They must talk alone sometime. The sooner the better? "Is Mrs McCartney back?" she asked.

"No. She stays in New York. Wisely, I think. Easier for everyone." Was that all he was going to say? Apparently. "Bridget is enthusiastic about your plan for an officers' club, and most particularly asked me to bring you. They want to help."

"Then I will certainly come."

"You never answered my letter." He had dismissed his man and was driving the whisky himself.

"I did not know what to say, what to believe." She had known this conversation must come, had tried to plan for it, was still doubtful what to do for the best. "Francis, I have to say this. I know about you and Mrs McCartney. All Savannah knows."

"Devil take Savannah! Mercy, I explained in my letter. I was penniless. With the mob after me, what could I do? I made her very happy for a while. But I never forgot you for a moment, Mercy. Never shall. There's something about you that gets into a man's blood. And you"—he turned to smile down at her with all the old confident charm—"you did not take Saul Gordon."

"Never!" He actually believed her still faithful to him, thought she had rejected Saul Gordon for his sake. It was almost too good to be true. "How could I, Francis?" She made her eyes wide and wistful as she looked up at him.

"That's my girl. We'd best keep it quiet awhile longer." What pretext would he hit on this time? But he thought her his slave, and no explanations needed. He reached out a hand to pat her small brown one where it lay in her lap. "My admirable Mercy."

The Misses McCartney were expecting them, and Mercy, watching closely, saw that Bridget, too, had been well trained by Francis. One quick, flashing look, and she turned all her attention to Mercy, whom she had not met since the fall of Savannah. "So here we all are in our true colours at last." She kissed Mercy warmly, for the first time. "Sister and I are quite delighted with this plan of yours for an officers' club, and wish to help in every way we can. And one first thing—you will forgive me for speaking out, my dear creature—but"—an expressive glance swept from Mercy's shabby homespun skirts to her own dark green silk—"if you are to play hostess, you surely must dress the part."

"I know." Mercy smiled at her. "But I am ashamed to tell you how poor we are. Hart *would* sell for Georgia paper. I don't know how I am to contrive—"

"You must let us help you. Claire, dear, take Mercy upstairs; explain . . ."

Accepting bolt after bolt of smuggled silk and satin from Claire, Mercy almost found it in her heart to be sorry for Bridget, who was paying in hoarded silks for ten minutes of Francis' company. "By the way," she told him when she and her loot had been settled in the carriage, "I think I have found someone to look after the building work for us."

"Oh?" He was not much interested.

"Yes. A man called Miles. With William run, I need someone to keep the servants in order. Could you get me permission, Francis?"

"For one of those smiles? Anything."

Still no word from Hart. It was a relief to be so busy. Miles had taken charge of the alterations and created such chaos in the house that Mrs Purchis and Mrs Mayfield had been glad to go and stay with the McCartneys. Mercy and Abigail sat upstairs and sewed the unfamiliar silk and satin in anxious silence. There had been no word from Giles either.

"Mercy, you can't!" Abigail spoke up at last when Mercy tried on the bronze satin dress she had been making.

"Scandalous, ain't it?" Mercy lapsed into cockney. "I reckon it will distract them so, I'll skin them alive, those British officers."

"You'll not cheat!"

"I don't think I'll need to." It was her first satin dress. Intoxicating. She dropped herself a stately curtsey in the glass. "Your servant, ma'am."

That night, very late, William came back. Miles caught him sneaking into the yard and sent at once for Mercy.

"William." She was between tears and laughter. "You're safe! And Mr Hart?"

"At Charleston, Miss Mercy. Jem stayed. Mr Hart sent me

back. No letters. He said, too dangerous. Messages for his mother and aunt and Miss Abigail."

"And for me?"

"Nothing miss. He ain't spoken of you—not since he woke and found where he was. Not one word."

They opened the Officers' Friendly Club next day, and Mercy, bronze satin pushed low off white shoulders, was queen of the evening. "It's not exactly that she's beautiful," a British officer confided to Francis, "but there's something about her . . . ? She . . . she glows."

Francis repeated it to her, catching her for a moment behind the heavy velvet curtains she had had hung in the card room, raising her hand for a quick kiss. "You're a marvel," he said. "A witch. They're all mad for you. Mercy! Is there not somewhere we can be alone? I had no idea . . ." His hungry eyes were on the bare white shoulders.

She laughed up at him. "No more had I, Francis! I *am* enjoying myself." And then, looking past him, "Mr Gordon! This is an unexpected pleasure." Her tone was cool.

"I hope to join your club, if a mere civilian may, Miss Mercy. I was thinking—" He was unsure of himself in this elegant, uniformed crowd, scarlet, blue, and green. "I wondered . . . I have a few dozen of wine lying on my hands. I'd be most grateful if you would accept them as a . . . as a . . ."

"Gift, Mr Gordon?" A bribe. Stolen? Looted? Smuggled? "Too kind. But, come gentlemen, it is time to sit down to cards."

Abigail, severe in high-necked velvet, caught her a little later. "The servants are being much too free with the drink."

"Never mind." Mercy flashed her a sparkling smile. "Mr Gordon has just promised me several dozen he has lying on his hands. "We're a success."

Talk flowed more and more freely. The first civilised evening in this sand-hell . . . tales of the attack . . . the path through the marsh . . . so ludicrously simple . . . sympathy for brother officers, off pursuing the fleeing wreck of the American army . . . and toasts, repeated toasts, to the belle of the evening, Miss Phillips, who had thought of the club.

"You're a success." Francis caught her again towards the end of the evening. "Clever little Mercy. Ride with me tomorrow afternoon."

"Oh, Francis, I can't. I promised Mr Gordon I'd go and look at his wine."

"Let me come too! You should not be alone with him!"

"Dear Francis, if I took you too, I might not get the wine. But, look, there is Bridget McCartney all alone. Take pity on her, Frank?"

She received Saul Gordon's latest proposal across several dusty dozens of champagne and turned it off with a laugh. "I am enjoying myself far too much to consider matrimony. When the club begins to fail, when the British march away, when life becomes drab again, speak to me then, if you still wish to."

"Is that a promise?"

"If you like to think so. It's what I'm telling all the gentlemen."

"All?"

"I'm a seven days' wonder, Mr Gordon. Did you not know? Who would have thought a few yards of satin would make such a difference to a girl."

"But I loved you long ago, in your homespun."

"Why, so you did! You wanted a housekeeper then. What do you want now?" She turned, with a sharp swish of taffeta, and left him.

"Lord, how they talk." Abigail had still not heard from Giles, and looked pale and drawn these days. "I don't know how you can go on looking interested, Mercy. You'll wear yourself out. You look exhausted already. As if you weren't sleeping. And, dear, I do wish—"

"I wouldn't flirt with them? Do you remember when I first came to live with you, nobody ever danced with me but Francis—"

"And Hart," Abigail finished it for her. "I wish we would hear from Hart. His mother is fretting."

Fretting! That night, Mercy volunteered to sing for the company and brought the house down with a dramatised rendering of:

> How happy could I be with either
> Were t'other dear charmer away.

After that, there was no holding them, and she sang one of Mr Gay's songs after another, until midnight came and it was time to close the doors.

The club resounded with good news. The rebels had been roundly defeated at a place called Briar Creek, and General Prevost had launched an attack on South Carolina and even threatened Charleston itself. As, once before, there had been no Loyalists, now there were no rebels in Savannah. Or not many, and they suffered for their convictions. Those whose houses had not actually been confiscated, had officers or men billeted on them and must endure their whims. Since the alterations to the house in Oglethorpe Square had left the family's quarters sadly restricted, Francis and a couple of other officers had got themselves billeted on Mrs Reynolds. "Very handy for the club," said Francis.

Mercy, who now shared a room with Abigail, suspected that he and his two friends used to adjourn there when the club closed, taking guests with them. Female guests? It was not her affair.

The British were investing Charleston now, and still there was no word from Hart. Listening avidly to talk in the club, Mercy learned, at last, with a silent, heartfelt sigh of relief, that the attack had been abandoned and the British forces were retreating with an immense amount of loot and squads of "liberated" slaves.

Giles Habersham returned to Savannah with General Prevost. "Absurd creature," Francis told Abigail. "He does not choose to come to the club, but asked me to tell you he will call on you tomorrow morning."

It was an unlucky visit. Arriving early, Giles found tired servants still removing gouts of candle-wax from green-baize card tables. Even Mercy had overslept and greeted him heavy-eyed as she replaced packs of cards neatly in their containers. He looked about him with distaste. "It smells like a tavern. I'd not have believed it."

"You should have come last night," Mercy told him. "Then you would have seen for yourself. It's pleasant then. But, Giles, one thing she won't tell you—she's too loyal to me, to her aunts—but Abigail hates it just as much as you do. Only we have to live."

"It's all sickening together," he said. "If you had seen what I have these last few weeks, the wanton destruction— oh, by both sides. Horrible. Do you know, I think I was glad we failed to take Charleston, that I was spared another sack."

"Giles?"

"Yes?"

"Was there any news of Hart?"

"You've not heard?"

"Nothing."

"He's serving with Moultrie; was in the lines defending Charleston. That I do know. No more. But." Impatiently, "Am I not to see Abigail? And, Mercy, alone?"

"I'll fetch her. We were late to bed last night. Giles—" No use; his face was closed, impatient.

She never learnt just what they quarrelled about, but it was disastrous, final. Giles applied for a transfer to the West Indies next day, and Abigail crept about the house like a ghost and refused to appear at the club in the evening. She was missed, but not badly, not so long as Mercy was there.

Sir James Wright, returning in July to take over his interrupted duties as Royal Governor, paid an early call at the house in Oglethorpe Square. It was very elegant now, the garden trimly cared for and the ruined summerhouse in the corner repaired and repainted.

"Sir James!" Mrs Purchis had seen his carriage draw up outside the house and hurried out onto the porch to greet him. "It is so good to see you again."

"And to find you in such good heart, ma'am." He bent to kiss her hand. "You have done wonders for the morale of our officers, I hear, with this club of yours. I congratulate you."

"Thank you." She led the way into the house. "The amazing thing is"—she looked about at new paint and shining furniture—"we seem to be making money by it."

"And giving great pleasure. I would like to thank Miss Phillips."

"She is rehearsing, I think, but will join us, I am sure, directly."

"Rehearsing?"

"Did you not know? The officers are opening a theatre on Broughton Street and have asked Mercy and Abigail to take part in Mr Gay's *Beggar's Opera*. I am not quite sure about it myself, and Abigail persists in refusing, but Mercy seems quite to be enjoying herself. These are strange times, Sir James."

"Yes, ma'am." It gave him his opening. "Have you news of Hart?"

"None. One message to let us know he was safe away. Sir James, it was not right, what they did to him in New York."

"Ma'am." His embarrassed rejoinder was interrupted.

An exquisite young woman in powdered wig, crinoline, and high, red-heeled shoes had swept into the room. "Sir James." She swept into a curtsey. "We are honoured indeed."

"Can it?" He looked at her once and again. "Yes, it is . . . Miss Phillips, I am come to thank you for all you have done for us."

"Why, thank *you*, sir." Once again the extravagant curtsey. She laughed up at him, bewitching. "Forgive my costume! We are planning a small entertainment at which I hope you will honour us with your presence. We have been rehearsing. I have not enjoyed myself so much this age."

She had changed, he thought. She had grown frivolous. He had liked her better in homespun. Well, they were strange times. But it made the errand that had brought him seem even more ridiculous. "Miss Phillips." His tone was serious now.

"La, sir, how grave you sound. I hope you do not think I am leading your young men astray. We run a most genteel house, do we not, Mrs Purchis?"

"No, no, nothing like that. I'm only grateful to you for keeping them so harmlessly amused through the tedium of an occupation. But, Miss Phillips, have you heard of someone they call the Rebel Pamphleteer?

"Well, of course. Everyone talks of him. Scandalous, ain't they, his broadsheets? I vow the last one I saw quite put me to the blush with what it said about you, Sir James." And then, apologetically, "The boys will bring them."

"Boys?"

"Your charming officers, I should say. The trouble is"—she used her fan expressively—"one can't help laughing, can one?"

"I can. They are doing a great deal of harm, both here in Savannah and in the backwoods. And what I want to know is, how are they getting printed?"

She looked up at him with big eyes. "But surely everyone knows that? On Mr Johnston's press. That poor schoolmaster, Mr Hammerer, that you've got printing the *Gazette* has no kind of order to the business. I have no doubt someone gets in at night. You'd best fetch Mr Johnston back from the Indies, Sir James."

"I've sent for him. But, Miss Phillips, I am come to ask you, to remind you—I'm sorry—of that press of your father's that was never found."

"And not for lack of looking." She smiled up at him over her fan. "I surely thought it was buried out near the house where . . . where he was killed. I told Francis. Someone looked there. Didn't find it. Or"—she snapped the fan shut —"maybe they did? You'd best ask Francis, Sir James."

"And what did you mean by putting him on to me?" Francis was dangerous with rage, and she wished he had not found her alone in the summerhouse, and at dusk.

"Dear Francis, I didn't know *what* to do for the best." She looked up at him meekly. "And you always manage so cleverly. I thought best just to tell the truth and leave all to you." She made to rise from the bench where she had been sitting, but he pushed her back and stood over her, looking down.

"I wish I understood you as well as I adore you." His hands were on her shoulders now, pushing the soft muslin away from them, then moving down to cup each breast. "It's time you proved you love me," he said.

"Francis! Not now! Not here!"

"Why not? They're all upstairs, dressing. We're here, my lovely Mercy, here alone at last, thank God." The bench was rough and hard under her back as he pushed her down. "I must be sure of you." His lips were where his hands had been, his hands busy with her skirts.

"Miss Mercy?" She could never have imagined hearing Saul Gordon's voice with such pleasure.

"Damnation!" Francis' last kiss hurt the soft flesh. "What is it?" He left her on the bench and moved away to meet Gordon.

"I was looking for Miss Mercy, sir." Gordon's voice was apologetic. "I found a couple more cases of wine I thought she might like to have."

"You'll find her in the summerhouse." Francis strode off through the gate to the street, and Saul Gordon came forward, hesitantly, his pale face shining in the darkness.

"Miss Mercy. I do hope I did right." He was very carefully not looking at her.

"Quite right, thank you. And the less said about it, the better." She moved forward to meet him before he, in his turn, could corner her in the summerhouse. "It was foolish of me to be sitting out so late. It shall not happen again. I'm . . . grateful. I'll not forget."

"Thank you. But, Miss Mercy, I had been wanting a chance to speak to you . . . to warn you. He has gone, has he not?"

"Yes."

"It's precisely about Mr Francis. This Reb Pamphleteer that's making so much trouble. Had you thought it might be he? He's changed sides once. Who's to say?"

"Good God, what a horrible thought. No, it's not possible. Think, Mr Gordon, he was always a Loyalist really." She could hardly point out to Gordon that Francis changed sides only when it was to his advantage, while the Rebel Pamphleteer, whose broadsides against the occupation were convulsing Savannah, was risking his life. "Mr Gordon, for my sake, say nothing of this wild idea of yours. Think of the harm it would do us, his family, and to the club."

"Asked like that." He was developing quite a courtly air, she thought, as he kissed her hand. "How can I refuse?"

By general request, they had cleared one of the downstairs rooms for dancing, and tonight, Mercy, who usually stayed at the profitable card tables, made an excuse to go in there as the three fiddlers were striking up for a country dance. She was surrounded, at once, by hopeful partners, Francis among them.

"Am I forgiven?" He took her hand to lead her out into the circle that was forming. "I was carried away. You madden a man, Mercy."

She curtseyed low, as the dance began. Then, edging past him sideways, in the first figure, smiled up at him over her shoulder. "This once, you're forgiven, but I'm a marrying woman, Francis." They parted and met again. "And I'll thank you to remember it." And then, as he took her hand to lead her down the room, "I've a warning for you, Frank. You won't believe it, but Saul Gordon actually suspects you of being the Rebel Pamphleteer." She looked up at him anxiously. "Frank, be careful."

"You can't believe . . ." They had to part.

"Of course not." She met him in the middle of the room.

"I've sworn him to silence. Convinced him, I think, that you have always been the truest of Loyalists." She smiled at him reassuringly and passed on to a new partner.

Later that evening, she watched Francis pick a quarrel with Saul Gordon, saw the swift, angry exchange of words and then the contemptuous flick of Francis' hand that made it a fighting matter. Watching his face, from the far side of the room, she was almost sorry for Saul Gordon in his dilemma. If he fought, he proved himself a gentleman, but might end up a dead one. She thought he would fight.

William brought the news in the morning. They had fought at first light in the Jewish Graveyard within the town limits, and both been wounded, neither of them seriously. "I reckon they were both afraid of a murder charge," William explained it. "Sir James is dead set against duels."

Writing notes of condolence to both of them, she sighed with relief for a pair of problems at least postponed.

"If only we could have Frank here to nurse him," wailed Mrs Mayfield. "It doesn't seem right for the poor boy to lie ill among strangers."

"But think of the noise and bustle here, ma'am," said Mercy patiently. "Besides, he's not among strangers. Mrs Reynolds will look after him, for her children's sake."

She saw Mrs Reynolds in the square that afternoon and ran quickly out to greet her. "Is there anything we can do to help?"

Mrs Reynolds had aged since she had heard of her husband's death. Now she looked at Mercy for a long silent moment, then spat in the sand at her feet. "That's what we think of traitors like you." Bones showed through the skin of her tired face. "No need to worry about that worthless Frank Mayfield. I'll look after him. I've got to. But don't you come near me, Mercy Phillips. The Rebel Pamphleteer has a word for women like you."

In fact, the Rebel Pamphleteer was rather quiet that August. "I believe you may have been right, Miss Mercy," Sir James was paying a morning call at the house in Oglethorpe Square. "Now James Johnston is back in charge of the *Gazette*, there are fewer of those cursed revolutionary broadsheets. When can we hope to see your performance of *The Beggar's Opera* advertised?"

"Oh, any day now, Sir James. Since Frank Mayfield has resumed rehearsals, we are getting on like a house afire."

"Shocking business." It was perfunctory. "I hear Mr Gordon is out and about too."

"Yes," said Mercy. "A foolish affair, and not at all the kind of thing we want at the club. I wish you would speak to your young men, Sir James."

He sighed. "I'm afraid I have not much control over the officers, Miss Mercy, but I will certainly have a word with General Prevost."

22

For a while after the fall of Savannah, the British stranglehold on Georgia was complete, but the attack on South Carolina meant a weakening of the occupation force in Georgia, and at sea, too, though the British technically held the coast, rebel privateers could lurk in safety in secret creeks and inlets along the marshy shore.

A small boat put off from one of these on a misty evening of late August and pulled steadily northwards up the sheltered inland passage. Though the British still held Sunbury, they had been forced to abandon Augusta, and their lines of communication were badly stretched. It was easy enough for someone who had friends and knew his way to move in and out of the territory they held, and even, if he dared and if no one was likely to recognise him, to enter Savannah.

Sitting in the stern of his gig, Hart Purchis thought the risk well worth taking. He had been ill in bed all the last time he had been in Savannah, and before that had been away since he had joined George Washington's army. Not so long in years, but they had been years that changed a man. He smiled wryly to himself. Changed a boy to a man. If his experiences on the prison hulk had aged him by ten years, Mercy's treachery had made an old man of him. "Never stop loving me," she had said, handing him the draught that would make it possible to have him spirited out of town. He had asked her to marry him next day if they survived, and she had smiled, and smiled, and handed him her drugged potion.

No one would ever fool him again. He had decided that, in the black, silent rage that had endured through the dangerous journey to Charleston. Curiously enough, the rage, or the journey, or the combination of the two had immensely speeded up his recovery. When the British had made their unsuccessful attack on Charleston in May, he had been able to help build the defences, though not to fight, owing to the weakness of his right arm. That was when he had decided he would be most useful as a privateer captain. Luckily, he had found accumulated funds with his agent in Charleston and been able to buy a small sloop captured when the British retreated, and his name and reputation had ensured him a reliable crew. They had been lucky so far and had sent more than one consignment of invaluable specie to swell the empty coffers of the Continental Congress. Now, with a full bear completing the transformation from boy to man, he was ready to venture into Savannah on errands both for the Congress and for himself. Congress, or rather General Lincoln, who commanded in the South, wanted to know what help could be expected from secret rebels in Savannah, if the Americans should join with the French Admiral d'Estaing in an attack on the town.

And he, terribly, wanted to see Mercy. He had not written. He had sent no message to her. He had, quite simply, not known what to say. How could he thank her for saving his life, when, in so doing, she had lost him his honour? How could he be sure that she had not smuggled him out of town simply because he was a risk to her? How, in the face of all the lies she had told him, could he believe in her love for him? And yet, he still wanted to. He had loved her for so long. It was a habit hard to break. But, if he must, he would. That was really why he had undertaken this hazardous journey, to go to Savannah as a spy, risking certain death if he was caught.

"Quietly there." He spoke softly as the little boat rounded a point and he caught a glimpse of lights ahead. "Not a word from now on."

The oarsmen grunted in acquiescence. In fact, they had not spoken much, subdued both by the rashness of the venture and by their captain's mood. They landed him half an hour later in a deserted creek well south of Savannah, on the edge

255

of the Parish of St John's, which had always been in the forefront of the rebellion. Here, if anywhere, he would find friends to help him get into Savannah itself, and if he survived to return, he was sure of a safe hiding place here until his boat kept its rendezvous. There was nothing to be said now; everything was arranged; he shook the rowers' hard hands, slipped gently into shallow water, and waded ashore.

A week later, he helped take a load of Indian corn into Savannah, where food was still so scarce, his host had told him, that it would act as almost passport enough. "And I'm a prominent Loyalist these days! We all are. Or dead. You're my cousin from the West Indies, and no brighter than you should be. Keep quiet; you'll pass. Your voice is the only thing I'd have recognized about you. Oh—your eyes maybe, but their expression's changed."

"They've seen a good deal."

"We all have." They could see the spire of Christ Church now, rising above the trees. "Nearly there. Quiet now and look the fool I'll call you."

Hart let his shoulders sag and chewed vacantly on a tough leaf of the Indian corn. If only he knew what to expect. But though his host, John Jackson, could tell him about the political situation in Savannah, where Sir James Wright was still hoping to recall the old Loyalist Assembly and achieve some pretence of legitimate government, he knew little or nothing of social life there. "Though I think I'd have heard if anything had happened to your family."

It was cold enough comfort, Hart thought, when, after helping unload the corn in the familiar market place, he started along Julian Street towards Oglethorpe Square. It was all so extraordinarily the same. And so unbelievably different. Two Hessian privates shouldered past him, immaculate in blue uniforms with yellow facings, talking together in their native German. They were heading, he saw, for a house he had often visited. Its patriot owner had died of his wounds that hideous winter at Valley Forge, but where were his wife and children? Jackson had described the mass exodus of women, children, and slaves from Savannah after the British had taken the town. Had his friend's family been in that wretched crowd or were they perhaps still hiding somewhere in town?

No time for this kind of general anxiety. And now that he had crossed Whitaker Street, the sandy road was too crowded for comfort or safety. A carriage rolled by, smothering him in its dust, and he recognised the McCartney sisters, resplendent in bright satin, with a British officer riding beside them. So Mercy had been right in her suspicions of them.

Mercy. He quickened his pace, then made himself drop back into his halfwit's slouch as he turned off Julian Street and cut across lots so as to approach the house in Oglethorpe Square from the front. He found the square crowded with carriages and noisy with the oaths of coachmen manoeuvring to set down their passengers. The sun was in his eye, and he paused to shade them with his hand trying to make out the focus of the confusion, but already sure he knew it. Whoever lived in his house was entertaining, and doing so in style. He saw the McCartney carriage, driving away empty, and clenched his teeth. Through all his rage with Mercy it had never, somehow, occurred to him that he would not find her here, a useful ally and informant. How could he have been such a fool as to take this for granted?

"Here you!" The voice brought him out of his dreams with a jerk. The English officer who had been in attendance on the McCartney carriage had pushed his horse through the crowd to approach him. "A penny for you if you'll take my horse round to the Purchis stable! They're all asleep out front today."

"Sure will." Hart touched his shabby coonskin cap, accepted the penny, and took the reins as the officer dismounted.

"Thanks. And tell that good-for-nothing William he's to look to him better than last time, or I'll speak to Miss Phillips."

"Yes, sir!" Hart was amazed to have learned so much. It was still the Purchis house. William had got back safe, Mercy was there, and best of all, he had his reason for going into the servants' yard. He must have straightened his shoulders as he turned away, for he was stopped by an imperative. "Here, one moment!"

"Yes, sir?" He turned to peer vaguely at the red face and redder uniform across the horse's glossy back.

"You look able-bodied enough! What are you doing loitering here?"

"Who, me?" A still more vacant look as he rubbed a dirty right arm across his face, letting the hand droop limply as it would. "Earning a penny, sir! My ma won't half be pleased." A broad, vacant grin showed the teeth he had carefully blackened. "She do say I ain't bright enough to tell dinner from breakfast, but"—anxiously—"I'm good with animals, sir. I'll look to your horse, I surely will."

"Mind you do!" The officer seemed satisfied and turned away as a voice summoned him from outside the Purchis house, and Hart recognised the Loyalist of the two divided Telfair brothers. What kind of party could this be?

The familiar stableyard was thronged with men and horses. He edged himself and the officer's big bay into a corner near William's quarters and waited for a chance to speak to him privately. Here, blessedly, was the one person he could unreservedly trust. But what was going on in the house? He could hear music, now, from the big downstairs room, fiddles scraping away, and then a voice he knew too well raised in song. He had not known Mercy could sing like that. It was one of the many mocking, marching tunes that had sprung out of this war and that each side appropriated from the other. But Mercy's diction was good and her words clear. It was the British version of "Yankee Doodle" that she was singing. He listened, left hand clenched on the horse's reins as verse after taunting verse rang out and ended amid a roar of masculine applause. Sensing his fury, the horse began to fidget.

"Hey!" William's voice. "You over there, watch your horse!" And then, coming closer, "Jesus Christ!"

"You Willliam?" He made it the idiot's drawl. "The officer said you was to mind him better this time or he'd tell Miss Phillips of you." William had come round beside him, apparently to help him quiet the horse, and he added in a whisper, "William, I must see Miss Phillips. What the hell's happening here?"

"Plenty," said William. Then, louder, "Here, give me a hand stabling this brute." He led the way to the end stall, from which a small door led into his own quarters. "Quick!" William tied up the horse and pushed open the door. "This way, sir!"

"But, Amy?" Hart hesitated.

"Dead," said William. "Some soldiers got hold of Delilah. She tried to save her. We won't talk about it. No one come in here but me." The dusty, neglected cabin confirmed his words. "You'll be safe here, Mr Hart, till I can get to Miss

Mercy. But—" William had always seemed old to Hart, now he seemed antediluvian, a white-haired prophet of woe from some black bible. "Do you want to see her, sir? Is it safe?"

"What do you think?" Incredible to be asking it.

"I don't know, and that's God's truth. There's been strange things gone on in this house since the British came. Well, you've seen—"

"And heard," said Hart grimly.

"That singing. Yes. She's turned your house into a club for them. Dances with them . . . gets up plays . . . acts with them . . . and gaming tables in your office. Mr Hart, I never thought I'd see the day."

"And my mother?"

"All the ladies seem well. All dressed up like the Queen of Sheba, save only Miss Abigail, and she does nothing but sit in her room and cry, her Sally says, since Mr Habersham went away."

"He's gone?" This was bad news indeed.

"Yes, sir. Miss Abigail, she wouldn't see him at first, and then, when he came back from Charleston, they quarrelled something fierce. I reckon he didn't much like what's going on in this house either. She don't wear his ring no more. But Mr Francis is here, sir." No mistaking the note of warning in his voice. "Splendid he is in his green uniform. Thick as thieves with the British officers. And sweet as honey with Miss Mercy. He and Mr Gordon fought, a while back. About her, I reckon. They're both in there now, drinking Madam's punch, acting friends, and talking April and May to Miss Mercy. She's . . . she's changed, sir. I don't rightly know if you should let her know you're here. If you must see someone, I'd much liefer fetch Miss Abigail. Besides, I don't reckon I could get to Miss Mercy before midnight, when the officers leave."

Hart ground his teeth. "Then I'll wait till midnight." What a blessing he had arranged alternative meeting times with Jackson. "And when it gets dark, I'm going to climb up the back porch and see for myself. Is the vine still there?"

"Yes, sir, but I doubt it's safe. There's a Mr Miles Miss Mercy has put in to run things instead of Gordon. If he was to catch you. . . . He pounced on me, when I came back, gave me a bad moment. Ask me, he's sweet on her, too. They all are. I don't know what's got into her, Mr Hart, and that's God's truth."

259

"I'll be careful." Impatiently, "But before I talk to her, I must see."

"Very well, sir." William was too used to taking orders to protest further. "I'll fetch you something to eat."

The food was delicious, and sickened him. Patriots lived on messes of corn and rice meal, traitors on imported delicacies like these. It was a long time till dark, and he had nothing to do but sit and listen to the cheerful comings and goings in the yard, as servants brought or fetched their master's horses, At last, William appeared, grey faced with anxiety. "If you really must, sir, it's quiet now in the yard."

He was out and across it in a flash, feeling for the great, cord-like trunk of the old vine, climbing swiftly up, dark among the darkness to look in at the window of the back drawing-room. Velvet curtains, drawn back to let in the air, gave him a clear view. Everything was different, everything changed for the vulgar worse. Brilliant white paint, swags of gold here and there, chandeliers, imported goods. At the moment, the room was empty, but he could see through its open door to the one beyond, where scarlet coats danced with white dresses. The sound of the music came clearly through the open window. Maddening not to be able to see more. And incredibly dangerous to stay here, silhouetted against the light for anyone who looked up from the yard.

There was a buffet table of cold refreshments in the room. Wine and punch and glasses stood ready. No servants. What kind of a club was this? What precisely was this room used for? Assignations, of course. Now a green-uniformed officer guided his partner in through the open door. Red lights in the high-piled hair; bronze satin cut far too low off the white shoulders; the face tilted provocatively up at her companion. Dear God. Mercy. And Francis. Francis looking quickly back over his shoulder, leading her to the corner of the room invisible from the dancers. Francis bending for a confident kiss, his hand on her breast.

"No! Francis! It's not safe." She pulled away from him, but not in anger.

"Nonsense!" He had her again. "We're rehearsing, aren't we? I can't rehearse too often with you, my beautiful little love." But the music in the next room had stopped, and he let her go as two more couples entered the room. Saul Gordon and Bridget McCartney, a strange Hessian officer with Claire.

"One of your most brilliant evenings, Miss Mercy." Saul Gordon seemed very much at home as he poured cordial for the ladies and punch for the men. "I trust you found the new consignment of wine to your taste?"

"Dear Mr Gordon, I don't know how I could manage without you." She smiled up at him over her fan, her colour high from the recent exchange with Francis, her eyes sparkling. Another smile drew the Hessian officer into her circle, and she said something incomprehensible to him that won her a glow of gratification and made him visibly her slave. He broke into a flow of guttural German and she listened with breathless interest, while Francis and Saul Gordon glowered at each other, and Bridget and Claire carried on an artificially animated conversation of their own.

"Mr Hart, please." William's agitated whisper from below brought him back to his senses. He had seen enough. Too much. He climbed swiftly back down the vine.

"Mr Miles has just come in," whispered William. "He helps Miss Mercy lock up most nights. You must get back to my hut, sir, quick." And, once there, "Do you still want to see her, sir?"

"Yes! Fetch her as soon as you can, but don't tell her who it is. Say it's a message from Mr Habersham. That should bring her. If she's not to be trusted, I'll know what to do." His left hand felt inside his grimy shirt for the knife it had learned to use. Could he really mean to kill her?

Might there not, still, be an explanation, an excuse? Blackmail by Francis? But she had been enjoying herself. Playing the three men off against each other. Triumphant . . . beautiful . . . glowing from Francis' permitted kisses. Did she let Saul Gordon kiss her too? Press his soft hands where Francis' had been, on that exposed breast? His own hands sweated at the thought, and he looked down in surprise to see the useless fingers of his right one curling slightly, as if even they were trying for a stranglehold on that slim neck.

The knife would be surer. He loosened it in its sheath, staring out of the cabin window at the house, where windows were darkening now, one by one. Behind him, the hut door creaked, and he whirled round to see her sanding there, dimly illuminated by the lantern she carried. William had not dared give him a light, so she could not see him. "You're from Mr Habersham?" When she lifted the lantern, to try and make out his face, it picked out the red lights in her hair, green

261

stones flashing round her neck, the great expanse of white skin, the scandalous, clinging bronze dress. Francis' questing hand must have found a nipple to play with. No wonder she had had that purring look of satisfaction.

"Who are you?" His silence had disconcerted her, and she took a quick step backwards, her hand on the door-latch.

"You don't remember?" He caught her hand, with a quick recognition of its firm, strong smallness, pulled her into the room, and fastened the door behind her.

"Hart!" She took a step backwards and put the lantern down, gazing up at him, her eyes wide with tears. "Dear God, it's you at last!"

"So you actually recognise me—and back away. Wisely. I'd not have recognised you. Strumpet!"

"Hart!"

"Whore then, if you prefer it. How many of them have had you, Mercy Phillips, and what do you get for it? Besides pleasure, of course. No wonder you wanted me out of the house. Did you hope I'd die? I slept eighteen hours. Would you have thought yourself careless, or careful, if I had never waked?" His eyes, raking her satin-clad body, had now focussed on the jewels at her neck. "Whose emeralds, pray? Francis? Or Gordon? No need to ask what they bought. Dear God, and I thought to come to you for help!"

"Help?" His tirade had silenced her, but this won him a quick look and the one, breathless question.

"Help I'll not ask now. I'm a Yankee still, but not the Doodle you think me. Yes, I heard you singing it for them, heard them laugh and clap you. I saw you with them, Mercy. I climbed the vine. Saw you and Francis. The enemy. Our enemy, I thought. How long ago did you sell out to them, Mercy? Did you perhaps know I was on that hulk of theirs? Did you and Francis laugh over it? If so, you played me a pretty scene of drama when I came home, but then, I understand, you do play a pretty scene. What plays do you put on in my drawing-room, you and your English friends?" His left hand was under his shirt, feeling for the knife. "Did you ever play Desdemona, Mercy Phillips?"

"No! Hart!" Only her eyes—wide, frightened, and yet, somehow steady—were as he had remembered them. They stopped him, for a moment, hand still on the hilt of the knife, and she went on, "I don't blame you for what you think, nor for being so angry. But you must listen, Hart, before you kill me. If you do, they'll all starve."

"Starve? What do you mean?" His hand still clutched the knife.

"Idiot! Have you thought of nothing but yourself? If I'd not drugged you, got you away, you'd be dead, and serve you right, and the rest of us in prison for harbouring you. As it is, Winchelsea is gone—the British have it for a hospital, and Francis has the promise of it. Saul Gordon had sold out to the British, God knows how long ago. He proved to their satisfaction that you had no assets in Savannah. Your mother had the house, and nothing else. So I've been running it as a kind of club for British officers. They come, they enjoy themselves, they pay, they play and lose." She started to add something, then checked herself with a quick look at his set face. "We're paying our way now. Kill me, cause a scandal, get caught, and your mother, your aunt, and Abigail will be on the streets. But you're not going to kill me." She took another step backward, folded her fan, twisted its handle, and held a needle-sharp knife. "You called me strumpet, Hart Purchis, and I'll not forget. The English officers don't. I've made a joke of this, but it's a joke they remember."

"Mercy." The fingers of his right hand were moving again, was it in an attempt at murder or a longing to touch those white shoulders. What should he do, what believe?

"Well." A shrug of the tantalising shoulders. "I can't stay. I'll be missed, and for all our sakes you must not be caught here. Tell me, Purchis, have you come here only to insult me?"

"No! Mercy!" Was he asking for mercy? It almost felt like it. "I've come . . . I can't trust you!"

"You must, I think. This is more important than you and I, Hart." She twisted the hilt of her stiletto and it was a fan again. "There!" She moved a step nearer to him. "Now, even with one hand, you can kill me with the knife of yours if you still think me a traitor."

"William does."

"Of course William does! What use would I be if the very servants knew I was playing a double game. Quick, Hart. Kill me or tell me what you need to know. There's no time for talking."

More than anything in the world he wanted to touch the white shoulders, to let his hand travel down, down along the edge of that provocative satin gown. Her eyes, meeting his with that same steady gaze, knew this. "That's no answer," she said.

"No. No." He held out his empty left hand. "Mercy, I can't kill you, so I suppose I must trust you."

"Good." She took it, the fan dangling harmlessly from her wrist. "Now, what's your errand? I promise, I can get it where it should go."

"I believe you. God knows why. Two things. First. If General Lincoln and Admiral d'Estaing attack Savannah, how much help can they expect from within?"

She looked at him squarely, sadly. "Not much. I can answer that. I've watched. I know. The real patriots are gone—to Charleston, to the West Indies. It's only the turncoats who remain, and I doubt they'll turn again. There's no spirit left here. It was so quick, so sudden." A long shudder shook her. "So horrible. Men bayonetted in the streets as they tried to surrender, their wives watching. Did William tell you about Amy and Delilah?"

"Enough. And after all that, you entertain the British!"

"Oh, Hart, will you not try to understand? They're no worse than the rebels. I could tell you things they've done . . . our people. But there's no time. What I'm trying to tell you is that people here in Savannah have seen one sack, and that's enough. For God's sake, tell General Lincoln and his French admiral to take themselves somewhere else."

"Do you really mean that?"

She brushed a hand across her eyes. "No. Not really. It's loathsome, this life we're leading. You called me strumpet. It's what I feel. But at least we're alive here, surviving."

"Dancing with Francis Mayfield and Saul Gordon! Entertaining those beefy Hessian officers. When did you learn German, Mercy Phillips?"

"Father taught me." For the second time he had the impression that she was about to say more, but checked herself. "We've talked too long already. It's late. I must get back. What is your second errand?"

"There's someone I want to meet. Someone I'm surprised you have not chosen to mention. You say that everyone here in Savannah has given up hope, lost their spirit. What about the secret pamphleteer who is making the British so angry? I saw a couple of his broadsheets down—" He stopped. "Where I was staying. If you had seen them you'd know there's one true patriot here in Savannah, but I can see it's useless to ask a collaborator like you to put me in touch with him."

"Quite useless. You don't choose to tell me where you have been staying, and you are quite right. Do you think, even if I did know the pamphleteer's name, I would tell it you! But it's the best-kept secret in Savannah. Of course I've seen his pamphlets. Everyone has. They grow on the trees, like Judas blossom. We tear them up, we exclaim against him, we read them first."

"So. My errand need not be quite in vain. He's not a coward; he will urge people to fight on the right side when the time comes."

"And so warn the British that it's coming? The whole point of an attack, if there is one, must be surprise, as it was when the British came. And you want broadsheets up and down the streets announcing it? Tell your friends, if it comes, it must come fast! And if it does come, I've no doubt the Reb Pamphleteer—that's what they call him—will come out strong for the patriots. But first you must mount your attack, Hart Purchis. And for God's sake, speak to no one, no one, no one as you have to me. You're mad to have trusted me. If you get back safe, tell your general and your French admiral to send a more cautious emissary next time."

"Because I trust you!"

"These are not the times for trust. I don't know how you got into town, but if I were you, I'd find my own way out. There's a generous British bounty for the capture of people like you. It makes Judases of us all."

"So you admit it was convenient for you to have me out of the way when the British came!"

"Oh, Hart! Have you learned nothing? Do you understand nothing? Yes, William!" She moved quickly to the cabin door in answer to a low knocking.

"Mr Miles is asking for you, Miss Mercy. He's ready to lock up." He looked quickly from one to the other, relieved to find them both alive.

"I must go. William, see Mr Hart safe away. By river, I'd think, if you've men you can trust."

"They keep a close watch, Miss Mercy," said William, and at the same time, "I need no help," said Hart.

"Good." Mercy crossed the room to make a quick check of her appearance in the cracked glass that had once served

Amy, then turned to Hart. "Every inch the strumpet," she said. "Good-bye, Hart."

23

Next day Jackson was waiting at the second rendezvous, sitting slouched in the shade of his empty cart. Hart paused for a moment, Mercy's warning vivid in his mind, etched deep by his own anger at her jibes. What else could he have done but trust her? And yet, if now, or as they left Savannah, a British posse should appear to arrest him, who would be to blame? Mercy, or Jackson, who had now seen him and was waving a lazy arm in greeting?

"Trust no one" she had said. It was good counsel; all part of the general horror. William's Amy and little Delilah. Jem, who had died fighting the British at Charleston. Mercy dressed up like the whore of Babylon. Mercy and Francis. Mercy and Saul Gordon. And the stranger, Mr Miles. What did he and she do after they had locked the house?

"Let's get going," he said.

"Bad, eh?" Jackson got up, stretched mightily, and began to untether his skinny horse. "Any luck at all?"

Trust no one. "No," said Hart. "Oh yes. I'm lucky to be here and alive to meet you."

"Sure thing," said Jackson. "Let's go." And then, leisurely climbing into the rough driver's seat of the wagon, "No news of the Reb Pamphleteer then? I'd sure like to shake him by the hand. Powerful fine pieces he writes. I found one in the wagon when I got back from Tondee's. I'll show it you when we get home."

Suspicion, worse than an illness, crawled through Hart's blood all the way back to his friend's isolated farmhouse. Could Mercy have had him followed? Easily. Would she have? How could he tell? He understood nothing. "A generous British bounty," she had said, "for the capture of people like you." But she had offered him William's help, and William he knew he could trust. So, why this uneasy shiver in his bones as they emerged at last into the clearing round Jackson's farm? Everything was as usual, peaceful in the light of the setting sun. No. Everything was too quiet. The watchdog barked, it was true, cattle lowed but where were the children who should have rushed out to greet their father?

"Peaceful," he said.

"Sure is. I reckon Mina must have taken the kids over to see her ma. The less they know, the better."

"Yes." It made perfect sense and did nothing for the creeping anxiety in Hart's bones. Why had he not thought how much more valuable a capture he would be on returning from Savannah than before he went there? Trust no one. "I'm bushed." He yawned hugely as they dismounted from the wagon. "Long, useless trip."

"Tough. I'll rustle us up some grub and you can sleep it off. Pity you can't get away tonight." It was half a question.

"Yes." Thank God he had not said anything about his rendezvous with his men. "I'm sorry to put you at risk a moment longer than need be."

"I'm only sorry it's done so little good." Once again it might be a question.

Hart shrugged. "Luck of the draw. It was an idea—worth trying—no good. I'm starved. Fine welcome I got! Not a bite to eat. Nowhere to sleep. Like me to stable the horse while you find us that food?"

"Thanks!"

Was it his imagination or did the other man pause for a moment, doubtfully, on the house's shabby threshold? Suspicion breeds suspicion. Hart stopped unharnessing the tired horse and straightened up. "Anything to drink in the house? I'm dry as dust. All that waiting around!" he grumbled. "And no good come of it. Rum would be best."

"And rum you shall have." If Jackson had been wondering about the wisdom of leaving Hart outside alone, this made up his mind for him. "I didn't reckon you for a drinking man."

"I'm not, when things go right." Hart jerked the horse's bridle impatiently and led it away towards the tumble-down stable as the other man went indoors. How long did he have before he was missed. Ten minutes? Fifteen at the outside. Just the same, he tethered and fed the horse, noting with relief as he did so that the light was fading fast. When he emerged cautiously from the stable, leaving the door open to suggest he was still inside, it was into the long, dark shadow of the house, and he kept carefully within it as he edged his way out of view of the front windows. Pausing at the corner to look back, he saw a light flicker behind one of them. His friend had lit a candle. With luck, he would then pour himself a drink of the promised rum.

Memory of Mercy's naked shoulders above the clinging bronze satin tormented Hart as he made his cautious way down the path to the shore. It had seemed, at the time, an excess of caution to arrange his rendezvous with his men several creeks north of the farmhouse's own landing stage. Now, he was glad of it, and glad, too, that he had told them to come every night, just in case.

But it was going to be an awkward enough walk in the clouded light of a half moon. The tide had just turned, and he would be able to save valuable time by cutting across the shallows of the intervening creeks. If their channels had changed since he used to come wildfowling here as a boy, he would just have to swim for it and hope for the best. Absurd if this was all quite unnecessary, if he had let Mercy fill him with groundless suspicion. By running away like this, he would merely have made an enemy of a friend, lost one supporter for the patriot cause.

"Hey!" Jackson's voice came soft yet urgent through the darkness. "Where the hell have you got to, Hart Purchis? Rum's out, grub's up, what's keeping you?"

The silence that followed was broken by the uneasy barking of the watchdog as his master presumably investigated the stable and found only the horse. "Hart!" he called again. "What are you playing at? Come on in—fire's lit, grog's hot. Don't play games with me, boy!" Now, surely, there was more than anxiety in his voice? Carefully masked, anger and fear were beginning to show.

Hart steadily put another hundred yards between himself and the farm, climbing a little as he crossed the arm of the creek. As he paused at the top to get his bearings from the dull gleam of more water ahead, a single shot from the direction of the farm sent birds scattering and squawking from their nests.

"Hart Purchis!" The voice was furious now. "Come back this instant or you're in bad trouble."

Trouble enough. Hart began to push his way quickly through the undergrowth towards the first creek. As a threat to him the shot was useless, but as a warning to an approaching posse? The tide was running out fast, but the first creek was still dangerously deep and he thought for a moment he might have to swim for it and wondered whether he would be able to breast that swift current one-handed. But he just managed to keep his footing and was climbing over the second spit of land when he heard a horse neigh somewhere to the west, where the track ran to Savannah. There was a posse, sure enough, and by the sound of them they were pushing forward hard along the soft, delaying sand of the track. If their officer should think to send a detachment out to search the shoreline, he was bound to be caught. But, surely, they would go first to find out the reason for the shot at the farm? And, equally, all logic would suggest that an escape would be made to the south. That was precisely why he was coming north.

And hurrying. The second creek, considerably shallower than the first, was a warning that his boat, if it came, would have to stay well out in the mouth of the appointed creek. If it came? He knew it would come. In a world that was indeed turned upside down he felt, now, that there were only two sure focusses of trust, William and his own ship's crew. Horrible to think that it might be Mercy who had sent those soldiers after him, so quietly through the darkness.

Horrible, and surely, not likely? Mercy knew nothing about the farmhouse and his doubtful friend there. Mercy could have had nothing to do with the significant firing of that gun. If she had not told him to trust no one, he would not be here now, plunging into the last intervening creek, but back at the farmhouse, drugged with rum, easy prey to the approaching soldiers.

Drugged. Mercy had drugged him. He was grinding his teeth again, but the shock of cold water caught at his breath and stopped him. He would not think of her. He could not bear to think of her. But how could he help it? Now he saw her in Francis' arms. Francis' hands, white like her own, were peeling back the bronze satin from a fruit worth the plucking. His foot slipped on a slimy stone and he went down under water, helpless for a moment, taking one salt, unexpected swallow before he staggered to his feet again and struggled on to the shore.

Between this creek and the next was swamp, and he had no time for thought, as he fought and jumped his way from tussock to tussock, praying that his old skill had not failed him. At least no one would follow him through this nightmarish, shivering quag, where simply to hesitate for a moment might mean a slow, horrible sucking to death. He was shaking with more than exhaustion when he pushed his way at last through tangling scrub to a view of the rendezvous creek, and, dauntingly far out, his boat, a darker shadow on the gleam of the water.

The agreed signals exchanged, he began the slow wade down the creek, slipping and staggering with fatigue, incredibly relieved when two of his men came to meet him and almost carried him the rest of the way. Dumped unceremoniously inboard, he could only lie there gasping and listen to the smooth splash of the oars as the boat moved steadily out to sea.

"You ran it fine," said one of his men. "Listen!"

The sound of horses, ridden hard, harness jingling, coming down the track to the head of the creek. A confusion of voices. Hart raised his head with an effort. "I could see you," he said. "Will they be able to see us?"

"Not a chance. The moon's gone in. And if they did, they wouldn't catch us."

"Good." Someone threw a jacket over him, where he lay, and he slid off into something between sleep and unconsciousness.

He slept for two days and was wakened with stirring news. Admiral d'Estaing had actually arrived off Tybee, fresh from his victory over the British in the West Indies. His fleet with its twenty-two ships of the line and attendant frigates and cutters, far outnumbered the British naval defences, and the element of surprise had been complete. He had captured several British vessels at the mouth of the Savannah River and taken the fort at Tybee, thus compelling the British to retire on Savannah.

"What's he doing now?" Hart pulled himself upright in his narrow bunk. "Why doesn't he attack at once?"

"Waiting for General Lincoln and General Lachlan McIntosh, I reckon. He sent the Frigate *Amazon* on ahead to Charleston, they say, to concert plans with General Lincoln. Well, I reckon it would be better if some of us Yankees were in on the attack."

"Yes, but—" Hart remembered the half-built abatis and

fascines of the Savannah defences. Still more he remembered what Mercy had said. If it must happen, let it happen quickly, as it had when the British had taken the town. "I must go to him," he said.

Finding the French fleet was easy enough. To see Admiral Count d'Estaing proved more difficult. Very sure of himself after his capture of St Vincent and Grenada and defeat of the British Admiral Byron, he thought Savannah his for the taking. Why should he trouble to see a shabby privateer captain, who doubtless had some axe of his own to grind? It was only when Joseph Habersham met a French party at Ossaba to concern arrangements for their landing that the possible importance of what Hart had to say was recognised.

And when he described the unfinished state of Savannah's defences and urged an immediate attack, Count d'Estaing merely smiled tolerantly and spoke of overall strategy and cooperation with the American forces now marching from north and west towards Savannah. "Trust me, monsieur, we will not give the British time to build up those tumbledown abatis you describe so vividly. In the meantime, your little ship will be most useful in keeping me in touch with our American allies."

On the eleventh of September, Hart's *Georgia* took its own small part in the unopposed French landing at Beaulieu, and he learned that General Lincoln was already crossing his troops over the Savannah River at Zubly's Ferry. Surely, now, the attack would not be long delayed. An anxiety he did not understand grew worse with every new delay. The night of the landing at Beaulieu, a storm scattered the French shipping, whose captains were inevitably unfamiliar with the shoals and sandbanks of this dangerous coastline. The solid little *Georgia* rode out the storm easily enough, but it was not until the fifteenth that news reached the reunited French fleet that General Lincoln had joined forces with Lachlan McIntosh and advanced as far as Cherokee Hill, only nine miles from Savannah.

The French too moved forward that day and camped about the same distance from Savannah as the Americans were to the west. Next day, d'Estaing sent a message to the town, formally summoning it to surrender. In reply, Colonel Prevost asked for a twenty-four-hour truce, and this the confident French admiral granted. Hart was grinding his teeth with anxiety, and was right to do so. During those vital twenty-four hours the British Lieutenant-Colonel Maitland, who had been cut off at Beaufort with a considerable body of men, managed the apparently impossible feat of crossing the marshes, dragging their empty boats when necessary, and so getting safe to Savannah in the teeth of the French fleet. Meanwhile, General Prevost had every available man at work on the abatis and fascines at which d'Estaing had sneered. A boom across the river to the west of the town made it impossible to approach or to send down fire rafts from there; houses and barns that might have helped the enemy's attack had been burned. On the seventeenth, Prevost formally refused to surrender.

Still d'Estaing moved leisurely. By the twenty-fourth he had a sap up to within three hundred yards of the abatis, and on the third of October he opened fire with nine mortars. Next day the cannonading continued with thirty-seven pieces of cannon firing from the land and sixteen from the water. General Lachlan McIntosh, whose own family were in Savannah, had asked General Prevost to let women and children leave the town, but Prevost had refused. Now, Prevost in his turn asked d'Estaing to let him evacuate women and children, the greatest sufferers, he said, from the random French firing. This time d'Estaing refused, and the bombardment continued, with an occasional pillar of smoke to bear witness to a burning house.

Hart's nails were bitten to the bone. The *Georgia* was in constant use between fleet and shore, and sometimes, venturing as far upriver towards the fortified bluffs as he dared, he could see a busy traffic of small boats between Savannah and Hutchinson Island across the channel. "They're shipping the women and children over to the barns there." One of his men confirmed his own guess. "Sensible. They won't be bombarded there, but they'll be uncomfortable enough, I'm afraid." All the crew knew that Hart's family were in Savannah.

"If discomfort's the worst of it," said Hart. "If only we'd attack and get it over with."

"We will soon, I reckon. There's sickness on the French ships, mortal bad, and food running short. And that admiral of theirs overdue back in the West Indies, so they say." He spat over the side. "If we'd attacked a month ago, when the frogs first came, I reckon it would have been a walkover.

Now, I'm not so sure. Did you see the British sailors man-handling those ships' guns ashore when we took that turn upriver? They'll be a nasty welcome, ask me, when we do attack."

That night a small boat came drifting silently downstream from Hutchinson Island with the tide and was picked up by a French patrol boat, whose commander fortunately spoke a little English. "He begged to be brought to you," the Frenchman told Hart a little later. "Said he'd tell us nothing otherwise. Not that I reckon he'll have much to tell. One of their slaves."

"Not a slave," said Hart. "William, what is it?"

"It's Miss Mercy, sir. They came for her this morning. They seemed know you'd been to the house, sir. Said she'd been harbouring a rebel. Searched. Mr Hart, you must believe me, I had no idea. I only made the secret cellar for her and the other ladies to hide in, if need came. I didn't know what she planned to do. How could I guess? Mind you, I reckon I'd have done it just the same!"

"What is all this?" broke in the Frenchman impatiently.

"Family trouble." Hart recognised the appeal in William's gaze. "I doubt the man has any real information, but if he has, be sure I'll report it."

"*Bien*. Then I'll get back to my duties."

Alone with William, Hart turned on him with all the accumulated force of the anxiety that had haunted him. "Quick, what happened?"

"They searched the house, sir. You never saw anything like it. Beds ripped open, panels broke, furniture every which way, and then Mr Francis, he said, what about the cellar?"

"Francis?"

William looked at him greyly. "He was in charge, sir. I never thought I'd see the day."

"At least he'd have seen the ladies weren't harmed. His own mother—"

"Bless you, they weren't there. I should have said. They moved to Hutchinson Island when the bombardment got so bad."

"Thank God for that."

"All but Miss Mercy. She wouldn't go. Well, I understand now. 'Course she wouldn't go. When they broke through my secret wall in the cellar and found the press, I saw it all. Too late."

273

"The press?"

"Her father's, sir. The one there was all the trouble about years back. You remember. The one he was killed over. It must have been hidden in Savannah all the time. She and Mr Miles must have smuggled it into the house when they did all that work for the club. Before I got back. It makes you want to laugh, if things wasn't so bad. Think of her dancing and singing with the British, and listening to every word they said, and going right down afterwards and writing it up for next day's broadsheet."

"Mercy?"

"She's the Reb Pamphleteer, sir. She and Mr Miles. She wrote it; he set it. Only . . . you mustn't feel too bad about this, Mr Hart, but seems like they'd been watching the house since the day you came. They caught Mr Miles sneaking out, very early, with the day's broadsheets. I don't know what he told them, but enough. They found the press, old broadsheets, everything."

"And Mercy?" He had led the enemy straight to her. Jackson would have known he would go to his own house, must have guessed that someone there had put him on his guard. Hence the watch. Hence the disaster. All his fault. "What have they done with her?"

"They ain't got her yet, sir. See, when they come knocking so angrily like, I opened to them, on account of all the other men are out working on the lines. When Mr Francis asked for the ladies, I told him they was all on Hutchinson Island. Surely he knew that, I said. His ma must have told him. I made kind of a noise about it and stood there, plumb stupid. You know Mr Francis, he thinks we're all trash, the lot of us. I don't reckon he even rightly knew which I was. So I kept telling him, louder and louder, that no one was home and no reason for them to come in. And Mr Francis, he lost his temper, like he does, and shouted right back, and I felt the draught you get when the back door of the office opens and knew she was safe out to the yard, so in the end, 'course, I had to let them in. But I surely didn't reckon on their finding that press, sir. I just didn't want Mr Francis bothering poor Miss Mercy as can't abide him, and no wonder. But lucky I did it."

"Where is she now? Did she get clear away?"

"Not off the place. Not then. They'd put men on the back entrance. She couldn't get out, but they gave her a bit of time, searching the house first. When they got out to our quarters, I hardly recognised her myself. I reckon she must have had it all planned. Black as me, she was, grizzle-haired, crouching by the fire, trying to light it and muttering to herself.

" 'Who's that?' asks Mr Francis, and 'My wife,' says I. 'Poor Amy, she ain't got her wits rightly since what happened to our Delilah.' You know Mr Francis, sir, he don't reckon much to what happens to us, but I thought he just might have heard about Delilah. It shook him a bit. 'Pity about that,' he said. 'Poor old thing.' And he gives Miss Mercy something between a pat and a shove, and she turns and curses him, low and bitter and so like one of us you wouldn't believe, and he kind of laughs it off and they go and search somewhere else. But you could see he didn't like it."

"Where is she now?"

"Hutchinson Island, thank God. They left a watch on the house, but they didn't care about a couple of stupid old blacks who'd got a fright and wanted to be with their ladies. I'm sorry about the house Mr Hart. I was in charge, but I reckoned Miss Mercy came first. Anyway, there's still men on guard there. I don't reckon they'll wreck it any worse than they have already. Mr Francis he'll see to that. I always thought he reckoned to end up with Winchelsea *and* the house in the square."

"There'll be time to deal with him," said Hart. "But what's to do now, William? You should have brought Miss Mercy with you."

"I wish I had, now. But she was tuckered out, time we got to the island, and honest, I didn't think I had a chance of getting through. And, true to God, she's safe enough among our people for a few days. She's with the servants," he explained. "The ladies know nothing about it. I reckon Mr Francis will have been over to the island asking, but he won't have found out more than that they left Miss Mercy behind when they moved there. And a lot of grumbles, if I know Madam Mayfield, about how awkward things are there. And he'll be angry when he finds he must have missed Miss Mercy at the house, and when Mr Francis is angry he does something stupid."

"Yes." Hart could not help being both amused and dis-

275

concerted by this sharp insight into his cousin's character. "But what do we do now?"

"I reckon it depends on what you think's going to happen. They're all pretty busy in town. Mr Francis won't have much time, not even to look for the Reb Pamphleteer, and by God they want her bad enough. I guess she'll be safe with our people on the island until after the attack, if it comes in the next few days. Well, there it is. You allies take Savannah, Miss Mercy's safe and a heroine. You fail, and I'd rather not think what will happen. She's stirred up a plenty trouble, has Miss Mercy, with those pamphlets of hers."

"I know." Hart could still hardly take it in. Mercy, the Reb Pamphleteer. It explained various things that had puzzled him when he had talked to her. It made his suspicions of her still more horrible, more ludicrous than somewhere deep down they had always seemed. And it put her, most terribly, in danger.

"I think we're bound to attack in a day or two," he said now, slowly. "Count d'Estaing's impatient to be gone; that I *do* know, everyone does. His sailors are dying like flies of the scurvy; he's overdue at the West Indies. Yes, I should say in the next three days at latest. You think she'll be safe that long?"

"I hope so. But, when you attack, Mr Hart, will you win?"

"I wish to God I was sure of it. What do you think, William?"

"I don't know, sir. If you'd attacked back in September, before Colonel Maitland and his men come in, it would have been another story. But, now—And, I tell you this, sir, those are desperate men in Savannah. There are rumours . . . Talk of things that's been said, by both French and Americans, about revenge for what happened when the British took the town. They've got their women there. Mrs Prevost and her children. And then there's Governor Wright, gingering them up. He says, 'Lose Savannah, you've lost America.' You wouldn't believe what they've done, 'less you saw it. They've turned that sandhill of a town into an armed fortress. There's an officer called Moncrieff . . . seems like he knows everything there is to know about fortifications. You're not going to find it easy, sir, and that's God's truth."

"We must get her out," said Hart. "But, for God's sake, how?"

"I got down here, " said William. "Bit of luck, bit of help,

276

I could get back, with a message. They've got blacks and Cherokees defending Hutchinson Island. And I don't like that much either. Not the Cherokees. Not if there was a sack."

"Dear God, no." Every moment things seemed worse. And it was all his fault. He had brought Mercy into this unspeakable danger. Cherokees . . . Francis . . . the British. It did not bear thinking of. "But what message would you take, William?"

"That's the question, isn't it?" They were staring at each other in a kind of mutual despair, when one of Hart's men knocked on the cabin door and handed him a sealed packet. "Looks like orders at last, Captain. The word's all over that we're attacking tomorrow or the next day. Want to bet they don't know in Savannah too?"

"No." Hart broke the seal and read through the orders quickly, watched by the other two men. Everybody knew that Americans with family in Savannah made a habit of crossing the lines at night and slipping into town to see them. How could anyone be sure they did not tell tales? But with the attack so imminent, the guard would surely be closer; any attempt to reach Mercy so much the more dangerous. "Thanks. That will do." He dismissed the man without satisfying his curiosity, then turned to William. "It's for tomorrow, thank God. And, best of all, I'm to weigh anchor right now and take his orders to Lieutenant Durumain on the *Truite*."

"But she's off the east end of Hutchinson Island!"

"Right. Bombarding the town, but without much success from all one hears. William, do you know the path across the island? The one the British used when they attacked the rice ships back in seventy-eight?"

William shook his grey head mournfully. "I used to, sir, but I don't reckon I could find it now. Or get through. I'm an old man, Mr Hart, I'm sorry."

"You've done more than anyone could already. That settles it." In his heart he was glad. "I'll have to go. So far as I can see, the *Georgia*'s to play an inglorious enough part tomorrow in what looks like at best a diversion. She'll do well enough without her captain, if I don't get back. You must tell me, as we go upstream, William, how I am to find Miss Mercy."

Presented with his orders, Lieutenant Durumain did not try to conceal his fury. "Seventy-five men!" he exclaimed. "I told d'Estaing that with five hundred I'd be over the bluff and

277

spiking the guns at the end of town before the rest of the attack was launched. But seventy-five, for a 'false attack.' What is a 'false attack,' Monsieur Purchis? I know only of the real thing."

"You'll have two American galleys in support," soothed Hart. "And my *Georgia*, for what she's worth."

"Which is a great deal," said the Frenchman warmly. "I have heard of your exploits, monsieur. But as for the use she'll be tomorrow, or the American galleys either, with only seventy-five men for the attack, we might just as well be amusing ourselves running races round the island."

Hart was inclined to agree with him, and it eased his conscience as he handed over command of the *Georgia* just after dark and slid quietly down into the boat that had rescued him from St John's. Once again, his picked crew had their orders; again, each one of them knew just what risk he was running. Hart had explained it all to them, behind locked doors in the big main cabin, just before they started. If surprise was the key to the plan for the Allied attack on Savannah tomorrow, it was still more vital for the rescue of Mercy. And so was his men's full cooperation in the face of the long, dangerous wait they would have for him. So he had told them just whom they were rescuing. They had been hard to convince at first. Most of them inhabitants of Charleston, they had all heard of the Reb Pamphleteer, had even seen some of the broadsheets that appeared mysteriously in Savannah. But to believe that this dangerous character, with a price on his head, was actually a woman! This was difficult, this was very nearly impossible. Luckily, William's story carried its own conviction, and two of the boat's crew were Savannahians and remembered the lynching of Mercy's father and the long, baffled search for his press.

In the end, they had voted on the project and agreed to go, with only one dissenting voice, though whether this was because they actually believed that Mercy was the Reb Pamphleteer or simply because they loved Hart and recognised how he felt about her, he would never be sure. Of one thing, though, he was certain. The man who had voted against could neither safely be left behind nor taken along. The man saw this at the same moment and looked suddenly terrified. "No need," said Hart. "William, you'll see he speaks to no one till we return. We'll draught another man as we go."

"Take my grandson," said William surprisingly. "He owes

the British something for Delilah."

"Your grandson?"

"He didn't tell you? Well, why should he? But proud to be serving under you, is Bill, and treated just like the others. You take him, Mr Hart, you won't regret it."

So here they were, rowing quietly through the darkness, oars silkily in and out of the water, heading towards the undefended north side of Hutchinson Island. This time, two men were to accompany Hart. Bill, who had begged to come, and one of the other Savannahians, who knew Mercy at least by sight.

No challenge halted them as they drew quietly into the cove Hart remembered from boyhood picnics. Why should it be guarded? To take Hutchinson Island would be no use to the Allies, since they would still have to cross the strongly held channel and climb the bluff into Savannah itself. It was not the general, but the particular enemy Hart feared. Francis undoubtedly knew by now that he was in command of the *Georgia*. Would he also know how much he would be prepared to risk for Mercy's sake? Was this, just possibly, a carefully baited trap into which he was walking?

But Francis did not know that it was among the blacks he would be searching. Or would he? Would he have finally realised that he had had Mercy actually under his hand, disguised as old Amy? If he had thought to check up and had discovered that Amy had been killed along with Delilah, it would be among the blacks that he began his search.

Hart quickened his pace, and the two men behind him followed suit, the current of anxiety running strong between them. They were through the worst of the swamp now, where they had had to follow Hart almost footstep for footstep, and were beginning to see and hear signs of life ahead. Most of the barns on the island had been built in Savannah's prosperous years, since Hart had played here as a child, but William's description had been clear enough. Once onto firm ground, he turned and led the way eastward, towards the exposed tip of the island, where the blacks had their quarters. Mercy had promised William she would stay in the hiding place he had found for her, a rat-infested shack well away from where the Purchis servants were quartered. Hart prayed, silently, that she had been able to do so.

24

Something was going on down in the shanty-town where the blacks were quartered. There was light there, too much light. Coming out from behind the last of the big barns that housed the white evacuees, Hart saw, with cold dread, that a huge fire had been lighted down on the flat ground where, as children, they used to have their picnics. By common consent, the three of them paused, straining their eyes to make out what was happening.

A group of Cherokees stood by the fire, unmistakable as its flames lit up their shorn heads and gaudy, painted faces. Among them stood one white officer. Francis? Impossible to tell, but horribly obvious what he was doing. One by one, the black women were being manhandled past him, each one held for a moment so that he could scrutinise her face by the light of the fire. The women who had already been inspected formed a larger group beyond the fire, and beyond them again was an uneasy crowd of men, kept in check by a couple of British soldiers.

It was entirely hopeless. Hart was grinding his teeth again. They were too late. Mercy must be in the smaller group of women yet to be examined. She would never pass close scrutiny. And what could they do, three of them, against that band of Cherokees?

"Captain," whispered Bill, "let me go down to the men. They don't like it. You can see they don't. Their women treated like that. And we hate the Cherokees. Some of them will know me. Bound to. I'll start something, you join in; it's a chance!"

"Yes." They all three knew how slim a one. "We two will spread out. When you start the fight, we'll come in, shouting and firing, as if we were a whole troop of men. But, Bill, if you can, wait till they spot her. That way, it will be easier to get her clear. If we manage to get to her. Good luck! And . . . thanks!"

Bill slid quietly away through the darkness, and the other two separated after a quick, whispered conference to wait in the shadows to east and west of the fire. Hart was praying that Mercy would wait till the last, or nearly the last, in that grim queue. If, as all logic suggested, the white officer was Francis, she would know he was bound to recognise her, and surely would put off the fatal confrontation as long as she could.

And now he noticed something else. The women were playing for time. They were slow in coming forward, though it meant rough handling by the Cherokee warriors who dragged them out. And when they were held for inspection, they wriggled this way and that, hiding their faces as best they could. One of them even twisted her head to bite the arm that held her and was knocked flat on her face for it, then picked up and dragged towards the fire, her struggling figure silhouetted back against its light.

They were going to throw her in. A low growl rose from the helpless audience, and at the last moment, a voice, Francis' voice, shouted, "Stop. Not her! That's for the one we want. Or the next one that struggles. You've had your warning." He turned to the small crowd of women who remained to be inspected. "Quick, now, and get it over with. I'll see no harm comes to the innocent."

He was answered by another low growl from the crowd, angrier this time. They believed him as little as Hart did. Even if he wanted to, would he be able to restrain his savage allies? There could be no good end to this night's work. If the Cherokees once got out of hand, it would not be only the blacks down at this end of the island who would suffer. Hart thought of his mother and aunt, of Abigail, and of all the other women and children up island in the barns, and cursed his right hand for its weakness. He could manage one shot with his specially adapted pistol, but reloading was impossible. Hand-to-hand fighting was his best hope, and at least, in the dark, it was a hope.

There were only a very few women left now, and suddenly one of them stepped forward, head up, faced Francis boldly, and pulled off her black wig to reveal a tumble of hair that glinted in the firelight. "I'm the Reb Pamphleteer!" She spoke not to Francis, but to the crowd. "And proud of it. Are any of you good enough Americans to stand by me? I warn you, there can only be one end to tonight's work if you don't!" The Cherokees had her now, dragging her

281

towards Francis and the fire, one with his hand over her mouth to silence her.

Hart was sweating with fear as he fired his one shot. Suppose he missed his aim and killed Mercy. No time to think of it. The Cherokee whose hand had covered Mercy's mouth crumpled sideways and fell into the fire. She seized the moment of surprise, slipped from the grasp of the other one, and vanished into the darkness as Hart and his men raised the agreed cry of "All along the line. Attack!"

It happened so suddenly that the Cherokees were taken unaware. One moment in command of what seemed a subdued and unarmed crowd, the next they were fighting for their lives against black men, some armed with knives they had concealed, others simply combining furious strength with surprise. Even the younger women had joined in, helping their men in a furious kicking, biting, scratching free-for-all by the chancy light of the fire.

Hart pushed his way through the seething crowd towards where he had seen Francis vanish in pursuit of Mercy. A Cherokee leapt at him, tomahawk raised, and he dodged sideways, caught him with an unexpected left-handed lock, and dragged him towards the fire, cursing his weak right hand that could not administer the coup de grace. "Here!" Bill was beside him in the dark. "He's mine. You go for Miss Mercy!"

"Thanks!" Now he was pushing his way through a group of older women who clung together, sobbing with fright. Beyond them was darkness where the curve of the shore blocked out the firelight. He paused, straining eyes and ears for any hint of the grim game of cat and mouse that must be playing itself out there. From behind came the din of the fight that still continued, but it too was muted by the rise of the ground. He made himself stand quite still for a moment, letting his eyes get used to the darkness, alert for a sound nearer than the oaths and screams from the fight by the fire. At last he heard it, Francis' voice, soft and persuasive. "Mercy, I can see you, thank God. You must know I mean to save you; asked for this unpleasant assignment so I could. You may be the Reb Pamphleteer, you'll always be my beloved."

Dead silence. Mercy would never, surely, let him trick her now? Hart moved very quietly, very carefully down towards the shore in the direction from which Francis' voice had come. If he could only surprise him as he searched for Mercy, the odds between them would be enormously lessened, and he knew he would need every possible advantage on his side.

"Ah!" Francis' voice was triumphant as the wind blew the clouds away from the moon. "Now I do see you, my girl. You'll be sorry you didn't throw yourself on my mercy when you had the chance."

He was answered by a shot, and laughed. "Missed, my dear! And no time to reload. Have you a knife too, I wonder? Proper virago you turned out to be. Pity really I need to take you back alive, but they want you badly in Savannah, and my credit depends on it. I wonder if they will allow you your shift as they ride you through town on a rail, before they hang you."

Now Hart could see him, a darker shadow against the faint phosphorescence of the river, moving along towards a black patch that must be a wharf. He could still see no sign of Mercy, who must have dived for the shadows when the moon betrayed her.

"Ha! Got you cornered!" Francis' tone sent a chill down Hart's spine. Did he really mean to take her back alive to Savannah, or was that just another of his lies? "Thought there was a boat tied up there, didn't you?" His feet sounded on the planking of the wharf. "Didn't know we found it when we landed. You won't get away that way, little Mercy, and little mercy is what I mean to have on you."

Hart was onto the soft sand of the shore now, able to move more quickly and yet without a sound. If only his pistol was loaded! But he had had to use his one vital shot to start the fight he could still hear raging back by the fire. No time to wonder how it was going. He reached the wharf and saw Francis half way down and something dark at the very end that must be Mercy.

"Francis!" he called. "I don't want to do it, but one step nearer to Mercy and I fire!" Would the bluff work? How much did Francis know about his injured right hand?

Too much. "It's too good to be true!" A laugh in Francis' voice now. "My little cousin as well! This is my day. No, Hart, you won't fire on me, because you can't, and Mercy won't because she's had no chance to reload, so which of you shall I have first? Mind you"—thoughtfully—"I might almost be tempted to come to an arrangement with the two of you. Mercy's life for yours, Hart? Come out in the open, hands up, where I can see you, and I promise to get her down river to your French friends."

"Don't, Hart!" As she spoke at last, Hart thought he could see Mercy bend as if to pick something up. Francis had his back turned to her, and Hart was only half way down the rickety wharf. If only he had a tomahawk he might have a chance, but try how he would he had not mastered the art of throwing a knife left-handed. He must get nearer, and fast.

"Stop!" Mercy was upright again. "Touch me, Francis Mayfield, and I'll drag you into the river with me and hold on. It flows fast here at the tip of the island. I've watched it all day and I know."

"Fool of a girl!" For the first time there was a note of uncertainty in Francis' voice. He knew Mercy well enough to know she meant every word. "Wait there, then, while I deal with my little one-handed cousin. You'll enjoy watching that, won't you? I do hope the moon stays out and the alligators are hungry." He half turned to see how close Hart had come, and Mercy threw whatever it was she had picked up. It caught him a glancing blow on the side of the head and he swore, staggered, and almost, for a breathless moment seemed to be going to fall into the river. And, as he recovered himself, Hart was on him.

It was a shocking fight, subhuman, bestial, and Francis, inevitably, unmistakably, the stronger. Horrible to remember how they used to wrestle as boys, as they swayed now, too close for knives, always aware of the hungry water below, and the din of the fight beyond the hill. And farther down the wharf, Mercy, who could do nothing.

Nothing? Suddenly, incredibly, Hart knew exactly what she was going to do. As they swayed and struggled, they had shifted positions so that Francis now had his back to the shore. In a moment, Hart knew, Mercy was going to distract him, shout something, do something. And that was his moment, the chance for the left-handed attack that Francis would not remember from those old, unbelievable, friendly bouts.

"Here they come!" screamed Mercy, and Hart, who had expected it, was ready when Francis' attention slackened for the one vital instant. He twisted, broke free, and brought his left hand up to get Francis squarely on the chin. Not hard enough to knock him out, the blow sent him back towards the edge of the wharf. He tripped, fought for balance, and then with one harsh cry was over, lost in the dark surge of the water.

"Oh, God!" said Mercy. "There *are* alligators!"

"Don't look." Hart had her in his arms, her face pressed against his shoulder. "There's nothing we can do."

She raised her head to look him full in the face. "And I wouldn't if I could. Oh, Hart!"

No time for this. "We must go and help the others," he said.

They climbed up the slope hand in hand. The sounds of fighting had died down. Someone had won. "Quietly," he whispered. "We may have to run for it."

"And leave them?"

"You're more important than anything. And not just to me. I've a boat the other side of the island, waiting. Your arrival, you Reb Pamphleteer, will be worth a thousand men in our attack tomorrow."

"But the others . . ." As she began to protest they reached the top of the slope and saw that the fight was indeed over. Triumphant black faces gleamed in the firelight, and Bill was just coming up the slope, obviously in search of them.

"Thank God," he said, "you found her." He did not ask what had happened to Francis.

"Yes. And the Indians?"

"Tied up. Those who survived. Captain, what are we going to do for the men who helped us. There'll be trouble here in the morning."

"Yes. There must be boats at the wharves?"

"Enough. But they'd never get past the guard posts."

"No, I'm a fool. But we're in control of the whole island?"

"For tonight. Unless anyone's noticed over in town, which I doubt."

"No, they've other things on their minds tonight. Very well. Talk to your friends, Bill. Thank them for me and tell them that anyone who wants to cross the island with us is sure of a welcome from the Allies. They've black troops of their own, as you know. Well treated."

"The French have." Bill's voice was dry.

"Yes." No use pretending not to understand. "But, Bill, don't you see, so long as some come with us the others can pretend they were fighting on the British side, and beaten. We'll tie a few of them up, alongside the Cherokees."

"Some of them are," said Bill as he turned away.

Mercy had stood close beside Hart, listening. "Are you going to visit your mother?" she asked.

Their minds had been running parallel. "I can't make up my mind." He turned to her with a kind of desperation. "It's a terrible risk . . . and such a chance. . . ."

"But she wouldn't come, you know. Still less Mrs Mayfield or Abigail."

"You're right, of course. Not across that swamp. Not anyway, I suppose. But, Mercy, will they be safe?"

"Oh, yes. No need to fret about them. You forget, Hart, what a Loyalist house we've been keeping. Just think of how angry it made you that day you came to see me." She was laughing at him. "Besides, where would the officers go for their entertainment if they closed it down. Everyone knows Abigail for the true blue Tory she is, and forgive me, Hart, no one takes your mother and aunt very seriously. No one's going to blame them for my carryings-on in the cellar." She smiled past him at Bill, who had returned with a considerable group of men. "And if we're going to get all these people across the island, we had better get started."

"You're right." It must be past midnight already, and all the time Hart was aware of the minutes ticking away towards the dawn hour set for the Allied attack on Savannah. Already French and American troops must be making their silent way towards the positions from which they were to launch their surprise assault. If it was a surprise. He looked across the river to where lights here and there must indicate Savannah, asleep on its bluff.

"Too many lights." Mercy had read his mind again.

"More than usual?"

"Many more than last night. And . . . listen!" Across the water came the muffled roll of a drum. "A surprise attack?" she asked.

"Yes. And not a chance of warning them that it's been blown."

Mercy put a warm hand on his. "I thought I'd never hear you grind your teeth again!"

Luckily, the *Georgia* had already moved upriver with the *Truite*, which made the task of getting the refugee blacks away much easier. The last, exhausted, mud-covered party were just being helped on board when a signal shot fired by the *Truite* announced the start of their diversionary action.

"You'll go below, to my cabin, and stay there." Anxiety made Hart's tone sharper than he had intended.

"Yes, sir, Captain Purchis." A hint of mockery underlay the exhaustion of her voice. "If I just knew the way."

"I'll show you, Miss Mercy." Bill had insisted on waiting to come off with the last escape party and had just climbed on board. "Captain's busy right now."

"So he is," she said.

Hart's sleeping cabin was little more than a cupboard with a berth in it, opening off the main cabin where two brass ten-pounders had already been run out for the attack. The men in charge of them grinned at sight of Mercy with her tousled hair and blackened face. "The Reb Pamphleteer," said one. "Huzza!"

"Thanks!" She swept them a curtsey with tattered skirts. "And good shooting."

"Thank you, ma'am. I hope we don't keep you awake."

"It would take more than gunfire to do that."

On deck, Hart was grinding his teeth again as he read his latest order from the captain of the *Truite*. The little *Georgia*, with her light draught, was to make the best speed she could down the Wilmington River to the Allied ammunition depot at Thunderbolt, where Hart must urge the need for more ammunition, more troops, everything for a stronger three-pronged attack from Thunderbolt, Causton Bluff, and the Savannah River itself. "Tell them their plans are blown," wrote Lieutenant Durumain. "The whole of Savannah is on the alert. Our only hope is in a last-minute change of strategy."

Feeling his way down the familiar channel of the Wilmington, Hart thought it a forlorn hope indeed. The moonlit night was ebbing towards morning now; the troops for the intended surprise attack must be fully committed; even a commander less obstinate than d'Estaing had proved himself would never change his whole strategy at such an eleventh hour. And, besides, his headquarters were at Beaulieu, far to the south, and he himself was doubtless already on his way across the treacherous marshes to lead the assault on the Spring Hill Redoubt to the west of the town.

The morning wind was light, and progress maddeningly slow. What had begun as a forlorn hope was merely ludicrous by the time the *Georgia* pulled into the familiar landing at Thunderbolt. They had heard spasmodic firing all the way, when the height of the bluff allowed it, but here was a scene of chaos.

"Ammunition!" The officer in command actually laughed as he read Durumain's letter. "More men! What we need is stretchers and men to carry them. How many can you spare? Our hospital here's full. We've taken over one down the creek; the British were using it. The wounded are coming in from the right wing already. It was only meant as a diversion, but, by God, it's been a bloody one. The British were expecting us, met us with music, mocking. 'Come to the Maypole, Merry Farmers All.' And musketfire. We Americans did our best, but if you ask me, the French marines hardly tried. And if the English expected us there, knew it for a diversion, what hope for d'Estaing at Spring Hill?"

"You've not heard?"

"Only rumour. Sounds bad. No time for that. How many men can you let me have?"

Hart left Bill to guard Mercy on the *Georgia* and took the rest of his small crew to help move the wounded. Extraordinary to come back to Winchelsea, at last, like this, leading a tired horse with a cartful of wounded, some French, some American, militia, some groaning, some swearing, some dying.

The house was changed beyond belief, beyond bearing. Not a stick of the old furniture remained, only, on the floors of the downstairs rooms, pallet beds put there by the British, now taken over by their defeated enemies. A grey-faced doctor came down the wide stair to greet him, his hands and coat stained with blood. "More? This way." He directed the bearers towards what had been the family dining room.

"Dr Flinn!"

"You know me?" And then, after a moment's gaze from eyes bleared with lack of sleep, "Good God! Hart." He looked about him. "Sorry about your house. The British did it. We just took over."

"No matter." It seemed extraordinarily unimportant. "How can I help? I'm afraid I can't carry— My hand."

"Of course. You speak French?"

"A little."

"Good. I can't get them to believe I'm a doctor. Can't say I blame them. Just a few words in their own language

288

would have made all the difference, would have in the battle. God, talk of muddle."

The rest of that morning was a nightmare of blood and stench, groans and screams, curses in French and American, and, through it all, Dr Flinn, white with fatigue, making decision after decision, until at last, towards noon, he was relieved by a French military surgeon. By now the full news of the disastrous attack on the Spring Hill Redoubt was in, but he hardly paid attention to it.

"There's something—" He mopped his forehead with a hand that left a smear of blood, and peered at Hart through red-rimmed eyes. "Something needs doing." And then, "My God, Saul Gordon!"

"Gordon?"

"He's off his head. Raving. The British thought him Mercy's accomplice." Flinn laughed shakily. "Saul Gorden and the Reb Pamphleteer. They confiscated everything he had—his house, the money he's made, the lot. Where is Mercy?" It had reminded him.

"Safe, thank God. On my boat. But what of Gordon?"

"He escaped in the confusion of the attack. Came here this morning, ranting, swearing vengeance. The wounded were just beginning to come in. I had no time. I locked him in the cellar." He felt in a pocket and produced the key. "Hart, go and see."

But Hart was looking past him at the door to the cellar stairs, and the thin trickle of smoke seeping out from under it.

"Don't open it," said the doctor. "There's no water nearer than the river. We've used it all up."

"We can't leave him," said Hart. "Besides, it's the only chance—to smother it down there." But when he opened the door a careful crack, a blast of smoke and flame swept up through the long hall. No hope for Gordon, down in that inferno, and not much for wood-built Winchelsea. Anyway, the wounded must come first. Mercifully, only the ground floor had been used, and half an hour of sweating, desperate labour had them all safely evacuated through outside doors and windows as the fire swept upwards through the house, making a great chimney of the hall and main stairway.

"I'm sorry, Hart." The last commandeered waggon had rolled away, and Dr Flinn turned to where Hart stood watching the great pillar of flame and smoke that had been his home.

"No need. Could you have lived there after what went on today? There would have been blood on it, always. Anyway, it hardly looks as if there will be a chance, after today's disaster." He managed a wry smile. "Francis had the promise of it, you know, from the British. I wonder if Gordon had too."

"I'll never forgive myself—"

"Don't mind it." He ought to tell Dr Flinn about Francis, but could not make himself. "It seems so trivial, compared with our defeat today. What will you do now, Doctor?"

"I'm an old man, Hart. I shall go back to Savannah. The British need doctors. They'll have me. They might even let me live in my own house. And you?"

"I've my ship still. I shall go on fighting. Will you tell my mother, Doctor? About the house? Break it gently? And give her my best love . . . to them all. And . . . good-bye."

It was daylight when Mercy woke, but which day? No gunfire now, but a rush of water to tell her that the *Georgia* was in motion. She sat up shakily, saw that someone had covered her with a blanket, and found bread and a mug of water securely placed in an ingeniously designed shelf by her head. Best of all, there was a bucket of water equally safe in a similar shelf at the foot of the berth and a sailor's shirt and trousers lying beside it.

The ship was too quiet. She wolfed the bread, trying to remember how long it was since she had eaten, washed off the worst of the black stain from her face, and was relieved to find that she could just get into the trousers. She smiled to herself, imagining Hart lining up his crew and deciding whose would fit her best. Hart! The ship *was* too quiet. She pulled on the shirt, grateful for its concealing size, ran her fingers through her hair, and opened the cabin door.

The sailor on duty outside came smartly to the salute. "Ma'am!"

"What day is it?" she asked. "What's happened?"

"We're beat," he said. "All along the line. They was waiting, see! For us, for the troops! D'Estaing's wounded, Pulaski's dying, Jasper's dead. They must be laughing their guts out in Savannah today. I'm glad you got away, ma'am, that's for sure." His expression, as he studied the trousers and called her "ma'am," was comic. "You'd be dead as mutton else."

"But Captain Purchis?" she asked. "Is he—"

"In a rage, ma'am. In a flat, boiling, bloody—ahem—rage."

"But he's not hurt?"

"Hurt? Captain Purchis? No, he don't get hurt. We see to that. But he sure is mad as hell today, and no mistake." He straightened suddenly as Hart came storming down the companionway from the deck. "Sir!"

"You're awake!" Hart nodded dismissal to the man. "Has he told you?"

"We're beaten."

"Horribly. Absurdly. God almighty! Allies who don't understand each other's language. Muddle. Disaster. And he won't try again."

"He?"

"D'Estaing. He's off to the West Indies and plague take the lot of us. The *Georgia*'s to help cover the retreat. Retreat! It's a shambles. Oh, God, what's going to happen to Georgia now! The British and Loyalists are going to take cruel toll for yesterday's disaster. Thank God, at least we got you clear, Mercy." He seemed really to be seeing her for the first time. "But what in God's name am I to do with you?"

She considered saying, "Marry me," but decided against it. Looking down at her trousers. "You wouldn't consider taking me on as ship's boy?" she suggested.

"I would not. It's no time for joking. I've told d'Estaing I'll cover his paltry retreat and then I'm taking you to Charleston. It's the only thing."

"Oh, no, it's not." She regretted the sharp answer the moment it was spoken.

"No?" His face had been white with rage and fatigue under the tan, but now angry colour flooded it. "The Rebel Pamphleteer has orders for me, has she? And what are they, pray?"

"Oh, Hart, I'm sorry! I didn't mean— Only, there are things I know."

"Such as?"

"That the British are planning an attack on Charleston. It's part of the whole strategy, don't you see? They've given up in the North, at least for the time being. They think they'll get more help here in the South."

"And they're right," he interjected bitterly.

"I'm afraid they are. And holding Savannah will settle it

for them. They're bound to attack Charleston now, sooner or later."

"You could be right," he said slowly, and this time she managed to swallow a quick rejoinder. "Well, in that case," he went on, "I'm taking you north. You'll stay with the Pastons, of course. Things are quiet in New England now, just as you say. You'll be safe there. And popular. The Reb Pamphleteer!"

"Hart?" What had happened to that instinctive understanding that had flowed between them when they were in danger?

"Yes?" His face was still rigid with anger. Not at her, she realised. At everything. This was no time. . . .

"Nothing," she said. "Just—I'm sorry."

25

The inevitable outcome of that betrayed, disastrous dawn attack was mutual recrimination between the French and American allies. The bitter tension between them was not eased by the light-hearted way French officers went to and fro across the lines to Savannah on one pretext of business or another. "Anyone would think the British and French were allies," said Hart bitterly, "not French and Americans."

"I've noticed it before," Mercy agreed. "They have the same habits and convictions. And in their hearts, they all look on us as barbarians. But at least, Hart, they have brought us the good news that your house and family are safe, and poor Mrs Mayfield rather better than one might have expected. That was a clever story you invented for her, of Francis trying to save me. I'm glad she believes it. And"—she looked down at grey homespun skirts and changed the subject—"I'm glad they've brought me some clothes."

She was the old Mercy again, the one whose image he had carried so long in his heart. Her hair, neatly braided once more round her head, still had the faintest hint of red about it, to remind him of the scarlet woman she had seemed that day in Savannah, but otherwise it was hard to believe that any of it had happened. Only from time to time, she would shake him with a casual remark that showed just how much she had learned from her guests when she was running that strange establishment in his house. He did not like to think about it and could not stop.

When the list of the few British officers who had been killed or wounded came through, his first feeling was rage at the disproportion between the tiny British losses and the huge Allied ones. Mercy too was looking grave, and he assumed she felt the same, only to be disabused by her remark. "Poor things," she said, "in a way they were my friends."

He turned on her, white with fury. "You'd better not let the men hear you say that!"

"They would understand," she said. And then, with an effort, "Hart, I've received a most courteous letter from Captain Bougainville. He writes on behalf of Admiral d'Estaing to offer me safe-conduct with their fleet to the West Indies. I think I'd better accept."

"You will do, of course, what you think best. Naturally, you'd find life much more luxurious—much more what you're used to—on a French line of battle ship. No doubt you'll make many new 'friends' during the voyage. French or English, as you say yourself, what is the difference?"

"Hart!" But, as happened so often in the close quarters of the little *Georgia*, they were interrupted. This time it was by Bill, who had established himself in Jem's place as personal servant to Hart and now brought a message from Bougainville himself, inviting Hart and Mercy to dine with him on his *Guerrier*.

"They want to fete the Reb Pamphleteer, I have no doubt," said Hart. "Do you wish to go?"

"I suppose it would be a courtesy. Particularly if I am to sail with them?" Her tone made it a question, but he ignored it.

"It's for today," he said. "I suppose you're right. We should go. Things are bad enough between the Allies as it is."

"Yes." It was what she had thought, but managed not to say.

"They'll be in full dress," he said gloomily. "And laugh behind their hands at our plainness."

But when Mercy joined him on deck, there was nothing plain about her. She was wearing the low-cut bronze satin that had so scandalised him that time in Savannah, and her hair, loose in ringlets about her shoulders, seemed to take back some of its colour from the satin. She smiled at his look of shock and swept him a low curtsey which let him see she had done something to the neckline of the dress so that it was considerably less revealing than before. "I may be the Reb Pamphleteer"—she smiled up at him and rose gracefully—"but I thought I would show our French friends that we are not all bluestockings in America."

"You're showing them a great deal," he said angrily.

She laughed and twisted a light gauze scarf round her shoulders. "Is that better? I'm sorry I left my emeralds behind. I feel undressed without them."

"Who bought them for you?" He had longed to ask the question.

"Mr Gordon." And then, laughing, "Oh, Hart, your face! But it's not fair to tease you. He bought them with my money. The way things were in Savannah, jewels were the best thing to buy, if one could only come at them. I am afraid I shall regret them when I start earning my keep in the West Indies."

"Earning?" How could he not have thought of this?

"Well." She smiled up at him. "It was careless of me, I know, but I left my savings behind along with the emeralds. Anyway, I have no doubt there will be some rich French planter who just needs a Reb Pamphleteer as governess for his daughter."

"You'd do better to come to Charleston with me."

"Are you telling me or inviting me? But here is Bill to tell us the boat is ready. I do hope the French have something better to give us than the year-old provisions they've been starving on. I'm hungry!"

She was the only woman on the *Guerrier*. She was the Reb Pamphleteer. In that dress she would have been the centre of attention anyway. No, thought Hart, angry with himself all over again, it was not the dress, it was that sparkling, intelligent look of hers, the breathless interest with which she was listening as Captain Bougainville talked of his passion for natural history.

But another of the guests, Count Dillon, had crossed the big cabin to join Hart. "Captain Purchis, I had the pleasure of meeting your mother when I was in town today. I have

294

a message for you from her. She asked me to tell you she is anxious about Miss Phillips."

"Anxious?" Impossible to keep the hostility out of his tone.

"Yes. I told her that we hoped for the pleasure of mademoiselle's company on the voyage to the West Indies, and she asked what I thought would become of her when we got there. Well, she had reason, had she not? Besides"—an elegant uplifted hand stopped Hart's attempted interruption —"she told me, forgive me, that they had been living on Miss Phillips' savings since the British took Savannah. I was to say she was infinitely regretful, but now things are so bad in the town she has had even to pawn the emeralds mademoiselle left behind. I know it is painful for you to hear this from me, and I apologise, but it is something, your mother said, that you need to know."

"It is indeed." Hart made a supreme effort. "And I thank you."

Dillon bowed and went on remorselessly. "It was a fine gesture on d'Estaing's part, that invitation, but I think he did not quite consider what kind of a reception mademoiselle might get in the West Indies. Loyalties are divided there as they are here, monsieur, and her reputation goes before her. Would you hire a lady, a young and beautiful lady who had run such a house as she did and—as man to man—acted the spy to boot? Would you hire such a one to teach your daughter? And there seems only one other profession open to her."

Luckily for Hart, the company rose just then to toast the King of France, and his point made, Dillon tactfully moved away before it was possible to speak again. Hart got through the rest of the occasion as best he might, watching Mercy, who was penniless and, so far as he could see, without either reputation or future, flirting light-heartedly with one French officer after another. At last it was time to go. "I must talk to you." His grip on her arm was one of iron, but she did not flinch.

"Not on the *Georgia*!" She turned back for a last, smiling farewell to Bougainville. "In fact, I have a favour to ask of you. Could we possibly go to Winchelsea before we return to the ship?"

"Winchelsea!" It was a whole new chapter of suffering. Though it was still well within the Allied lines, he had refused to visit the house since he and Dr Flinn had left it burning.

"Yes. Dear Hart, I know, and I'm sorry. But perhaps you forget. My father's grave is there. The way things are going, I may never come back to Savannah. I would like to say good-bye to him. To tell him I did what I could."

It seemed to him to sum up the whole disaster. But if she could face it, so would he. He gave the orders to his men, ignoring their surprised looks, and settled himself beside her in the stern. "A successful party." His tone was drier than he intended.

"Very." She smiled at him blandly and lapsed into the French they both spoke. "I'll say one thing for the French: they have manners. They may have been convinced, to a man, that I'm a harlot and a spy, but they treated me like the lady they don't think me."

"Mercy!"

She smiled again, provokingly, and put up her parasol to keep the sun off those too-white shoulders. "Father always said facts were best faced." She lapsed into English, twirling the parasol in her hands. "I wonder how the McCartney girls have fared."

"What made you think of them?"

"Parasols—and spying. This unspeakable war has made informers of us all. Come now, Hart, what were you when you came to see me in Savannah back in August?"

"A spy!"

"Thank you. But at least you and I have only changed sides once, Hart. Unlike Francis." A shiver ran through her despite the heat of the October sun. "Hart, do you think it was quick?"

"I'm sure of it."

"And we couldn't have saved him?"

"Not possibly. Besides, if we had, he would have turned on us."

"I'm glad you see that. I was afraid, perhaps you were minding. . . ."

"Of course I mind!" Explosively, "He was my cousin. My aunt's son. And the blackest kind of traitor. Why did he do it, Mercy?"

"For Winchelsea. William saw that. I was afraid you never would. He didn't care which side won, so long as he ended up as Mayfield of Winchelsea. I don't wonder you couldn't see it, so fond of him as you were, but Lord, I was afraid

296

for you, back when we were all young." She sighed. "How long ago it seems."

"A lifetime."

"Do you know you have touches of white in your hair? It suits you. I wonder if I shall find I have too, if I can ever get all this dye out."

"I hate it."

She smiled at him lazily. "You're the only one. Do you not think it might win me a rich husband down in the West Indies?"

"Mercy, don't!" Presently, he must tell her that his mother had pawned the emeralds on which she doubtless counted for security in her new life, but not now, with the rowers so close. It must wait for their arrival at Winchelsea, one more misery added to the general wretchedness of this "homecoming."

They landed at last at the new landing stage. "Where first?" he asked as he helped Mercy ashore.

"Oh, the house, don't you think, and get it over with? Hart, I've wanted to say I am·so sorry."

"Sorry?"

"It's my fault. I know it. So do you. If I hadn't made a fool of Gordon, taken his wine, let him imagine things— The British would never have suspected him. It would none of it have happened."

"Nonsense!" Why did this enrage him so? "He was mad. That was all. It was bound to happen and, in a way, I'm not sorry. I could never have lived there again. Won't get the chance now. It's all just part of the general horror."

"Our part. I loved it too, Hart. You made me very happy there. All of you. You were so kind. Made me an American."

"All of us? Mercy, there's something I have to tell you. That Frenchman, Dillon, gave me a message from my mother."

"Oh?"

"Yes. I suppose she had no time to write." He had minded, horribly, the casual publicness of that message by a stranger, betraying, as it did, Mercy's penniless state and his mother's responsibility for it. "Mercy, did you really support them all on your savings? On what I'd paid you?"

"At first I did. Why else do you think I took that salary from you? I trusted Saul Gordon as little as I did Francis. It was merely taking your money in order to use it for your best interests. And by the time it was used up, the place was self-supporting." She laughed. "Lord, they were poor card-players, those British officers. But generous. Well, it's easy to be generous with looted goods. They said we made them feel at home. I think they specially liked being beaten at whist by your mother and aunt."

"You don't mean to say they played too? Mother and Aunt Anne?"

"Of course they did. I've never seen them enjoy themselves so much. And their health's better, too. Your mother's not needed her drops this age, and Mrs Mayfield hardly speaks of her nerves. At least, not before Francis—I don't know now. I even begin to think that Mrs Purchis has forgiven me."

"Forgiven you?"

"For being right about Saul Gordon. I think she must have, don't you, or she would not have troubled to send you that message by Dillon. Oh, dear, I hope they manage to get things going again without me. I told Abigail, before the three of them left for the island, that if anything should happen to me she would just have to come out of her decline and take over. I hope she does."

"Decline? What do you mean?"

"Poor Abigail. The only Loyalist among us, and she couldn't face the British officers. Not after she sent Giles Habersham away. I wonder if he will ever come back. Oh, Hart, look! At least the ilex avenue is still there."

"A miracle they didn't cut it down for firewood."

"Lucky the siege didn't last longer or they would have."

They both knew that when they reached the avenue they would be able to see the place where the house had been. She reached out and took his hand. "Don't mind it too much. Do you know, I have the strangest feeling that this isn't the end. That you'll be back, to rebuild."

"As a British slave?"

"Never! As a free American. Just because things seem so bad right now, we mustn't forget what we've accomplished. Think! Four years ago, there was no such thing as the United States of America. Now, we've a government, an army, allies. And more sympathisers even in England than you would imagine. I used to get messages, secretly, to the Reb Pamphleteer: encouragement, even money. We won't despair, Hart. We mustn't. Oh!" They had reached the avenue and could see the blackened ruin of the house. "Oh, Hart!"

It was worse even than he had expected. The blazing ruin he had left had still had the outline of a house. But, built mainly of wood, it had burned almost to ground level. Only here and there a blackened tabby wall stood crazily among the rubbish. And, somehow worst of all, in its burning the house had scorched its surrounding trees so that they too shared the general look of desolation.

"Please, Mr Hart, don't go any nearer!" The small black boy had run up so quietly that they had neither of them seen him come. "Grandpa says it ain't safe!"

"And who are you?" Hart looked kindly down at the eager young face.

"You don't remember me?" He was disappointed, but not surprised. "I'm Bill Junior. Grandpa sent Mother and me and a couple of others to keep an eye to the place till things is better. It's sure good to see you, Mr Hart, and Miss Mercy. But don't you go no nearer, please. It's my job to see no one does."

"And very well you are doing it. Thank you, Bill Junior." Hart reached into his pocket and brought out a coin. "And thank your mother and the others, too."

"I will, sir. And we'll be ready to start right in building when you come back." He grinned equally at them both and turned to run off as fast as he had come in the direction of the servants' huts, which still stood beyond the wreck of the house.

"You see," said Mercy. "They know we'll win."

"Yes. Maybe they're right. I don't know. Mercy, there's something I've got to tell you. Now." He turned his back on the ruined house and set his jaw as he gazed down at her.

"Yes?"

"Your emeralds. That was the other thing Dillon told me. That my mother had pawned them."

"Well, of course," said Mercy, "that's what they were for. We all knew that. They were our emergency reserve. Oh!" She saw it. "You thought they were mine. Well, in a way I suppose they were. But once I'd left them behind. . . . Sensible of her, I think. Don't mind it, Hart. I'm much more capable of earning a living than they are."

"You'll have to marry me," he said.

"I'll have to do nothing of the kind, Hart Purchis!" She turned on him, eyes flashing, and he knew how fatally he had blundered. "I'd rather run the brothel you thought I did. 'Have to marry you,' indeed! You, who never fail to believe the worst of me! If you'd seen your face, that day in Savannah, you'd know why I would rather accept a *carte blanche* from one of the Frenchmen who have been so good as to offer it."

"Mercy, no!"

"No? Well, you may be right about that. I'd make an awkward enough mistress, would I not? And still worse a wife, particularly for a privateer captain. As you say yourself, I've grown used to a life of luxury. Do you think I am going to pig it on board your *Georgia*!" She turned with an angry swish of satin skirts and started to walk rapidly towards the trees that marked the family graveyard.

"Mercy!" One last, long look at what had been the house, and he hurried after her. "I've done it all wrong; I know I have. But you must know I've always loved you. That's why I minded so much."

"Always? And, pray, what of Bridget McCartney?"

"Poor Bridget." His tone dismissed her as totally without importance. But then, "Yes, it's true; I did try to make myself care for her. After Francis had told me of your engagement to him. I was"—he sounded surprised—"I think I was angry. I had always, somehow, deep down, felt you belonged to me. So I used to visit the McCartneys, make myself pay her court. No use. When I talked to her, tried to woo her if you like, your face always came between us. Try how I would, I could not stop loving you."

"Oh, poor Hart, and trying so hard!"

"What else could I do? There you were, secretly engaged to Francis . . . letting Saul Gordon dangle after you. And then, just sometimes, so kind, so good. And then again . . ." He caught her hand and pulled her round to face him. "Your father will wait. Answer me this, Mercy Phillips. Do you, by any chance, remember my asking you to marry me, before, when I was ill? Or is it such a trifle that it has slipped your memory? 'If we survive tomorrow,' I said, 'marry me next day.' And you said, 'Yes,' smiling that smile of yours, handed me a drugged potion, and had me smuggled out of town."

"And so you are alive," she said. "It's a strange thing, but I prefer you that way. Your Cousin Francis arrived, bright and early next morning, to arrest you. As ill as you were, how long do you think you would have survived that? I rather think you would have been killed 'trying to escape' on the way to British headquarters. There would have been no wedding for us that day, or any other."

"But you said yes," he persisted. "You've deceived me often, Mercy, but, it's a strange thing, I don't believe you have ever actually lied to me. So, what did you mean when you said yes? Just to keep me quiet, as you pacify a sick child with sweetmeats? Or, Mercy, that you would have if you could?"

"Think what you like." She pulled away her hand. "As you did when you came to Savannah and thought I was running your house as a brothel. I must go and say good-bye to my father."

He let her go, turning for a long, last look at the ruin of Winchelsea, then slowly followed. He found her leaning against the broken stump of the Judas tree, her eyes aswim with tears, gazing down. The grave that had been a shallow depression in the ground now had its stone. "James Phillips," he read over her shoulder. "The truth shall make you free."

"You did it," she turned to him, ignoring the tears that ran down her face.

"I ordered it," he said. "Years ago, before I went to Harvard. To tell truth, Mercy, I had forgotten all about it. Jem must have just gone on working on it, through everything."

"Jem?"

"Yes. My man Jem. Jem that's dead. He was our stonemason."

"And I'll never be able to thank him. Oh, Hart"—she looked up at him blindly through the rising tide of her tears —"I do thank you. How did you know that was what he always said?"

"You told me. Don't you remember? Mercy, I remember everything. That first day, when you were so angry because you thought I had failed him. The way you played the great lady for my mother and aunt. The shirts you made for me. Twice. When I went away. You sent them after me, the second time. With no message. I'm wearing one of them."

"I'd noticed."

"I was a boy and loved you. Didn't even know it until I saw Francis kissing you that night of the birthday illuminations."

"You saw?"

"I saw. Do you wonder I believed Francis' letter when it came? Believed Saul Gordon's lying story. Tried to make myself love Bridget McCartney. Went away. And, coming back, believed the worst." He was getting it clear as much with himself as with her. "And all the time, try how I would, I couldn't help loving you. You broke my heart when I was a boy. I'm a man now: I love you still. I've nothing to offer you, but danger and the fear of death—the chance to pig it, as you say, on my *Georgia*. But, mind you, Mercy Phillips. I've noticed some changes on her since you came aboard, and all for the better. The men love you, and they know I do. You'd be dearly welcome."

"And a terrible handicap to you."

"True. This is the time for speaking truth. I'm the *Georgia's* captain, and I have a duty to her and to my men. I'd not keep you on board a moment longer than was necessary to get you safe to the Pastons'. It would be a sad strange marriage for us, but what is not sad these days?" He put a gentle hand on her shoulders to make her look down on the gravestone. " 'The truth shall make you free.' Mercy, for your father's sake, for mine, forget all the foolish things I've said and done, and tell me the truth. If you have ever loved me, if you could, if you can, for the love of God say so. Life is too short, life is too precious, and happiness too rare to let it go on a question of pride. I misjudged you; I'm ashamed. What will you think, Mercy, if you wake one morning on that fine French ship of yours and hear that the *Georgia* has sunk with all hands?"

She stood there, silent for a moment, looking down at the gravestone with its message from her father. Then she looked up at Hart. "I think my heart would break," she said.

"Mercy!" She turned so easily and naturally into his arms that it seemed as if she had always nested there. Her head just fitted into the hollow of his shoulder, and he found himself gazing with amazement at his weak right hand as it gently stroked her hair.

"But, Hart." As he bent to kiss her, she pulled away just a little, to meet his eyes. "Before . . . I must tell you . . . I *have* lied to you. Often. Well, I had to." She looked down again at the stone. "I never will again."

"Never?"

"Never. Oh, Hart, the luxury of it. Just think of having one person in the world to whom one always tells the truth."

"Perhaps that's what marriage is." His right hand was busy among the ringlets he had resented only that morning. "That —and other things. Mercy, my once and always darling, you are going to marry me? I asked you all wrong before, but you must know in your heart how much I love you. Remember, back in the dark, on the island, how we each knew what the other was thinking. Surely, you knew then?"

She smiled a smile he had never seen before, quite without the sparkle that had charmed her admiring circle of French officers. "Yes, I knew. But then, I had loved you for so long and so hopelessly."

"Hopelessly?" He took her up on it.

"Of course. Purchis of Winchelsea." She turned away from the grave and back towards the scorched trees that showed where the house had been. "Hart, you must think more of this. It's still not too late. You've made me very happy. I'll always love you, but there's more to this than happiness. Think of your mother, think of Winchelsea. I've no reputation left, Hart. I felt it today, on the *Guerrier*, as you did. Do you think they are betting on which of them will have me first, those gallant Frenchmen? I do. So whatever happens, I'm not for the West Indies. If you'll just take me north to the Pastons, I'll thank you kindly, and we'll start learning to forget."

"Oh, no, we won't," said Hart Purchis. "I may have put it badly, but when I said you'd have to marry me, I spoke the truth. Do you think, now you've admitted you love me, I'll ever let you go?" He turned beside her, his arm round her waist, to gaze towards where the house had been. "Purchis of Winchelsea is dead. But Hart Purchis, privateer captain, is very much alive, and his heart is yours. Dear Mercy, let's have no more of this foolishness. Because a parcel of Frenchmen jump to idiotic conclusions, you choose to forget that you are an American heroine. I shall have a hard time of it, I reckon, living up to my part as husband of the Reb Pamphleteer."

Still she pulled away from him. "You jumped to those conclusions too!"

"Because you drove me insane in that dress of yours. If I find you beautiful beyond resisting, must not other men? Mercy, if you do not wish to be raped, here on your father's grave, better say now, 'Hart Purchis, I forgive you, and will marry you.'"

"Oh, Hart." Now she turned to him, hands held out. "Of course I'll marry you." And then, gleaming up at him, "You can rape me too, if you like."

"I do *not* like." But the embrace into which they plunged left them both shaken. "We must find a minister," he said at last.

"Or my name's quite gone," she agreed with him. "And Mistress Purchis of Winchelsea must be mistress only in the best sense of the word."

"Oh, Winchelsea." He turned for a last look. "I think we must say good-bye to that, my love. It's a poor man you're marrying, and a hard life."

"And all I want. But, Hart, look." She took his warm right hand from her breast and held it to show him where, low down, the broken Judas tree had thrown out a new shoot with just a few small green leaves. "Don't say good-bye to Winchelsea," she told him. "We'll be back, Hart, you and I."